Judith Rossner stunned [...] MR. GOODBAR, the viv[...] singles bar murder on Manhattan's Upper West Side.

Now, in AUGUST, you will enter into the most private reaches of the psychoanalyst's office. Here, behind closed doors, in the unsparing intimacy that must exist between patient and analyst, Dr. Lulu Shinefeld will begin the analysis of Dawn Henley, a lovely Barnard freshman whose bizarre childhood and tenuous future have twice brought her to the edge of suicide.

Parallel to the drama of Dawn's story is the revelation of Lulu Shinefeld's own private life. Divorced and the mother of three, her insights as an analyst will force her to confront the truth of her relationships with her peers, her lover, and her children.

Harrowing, fascinating, totally absorbing, AUGUST is the story of two women's journeys toward self-discovery. It is very much a story of our time—a novel of love and loss and the healing strength of self-knowledge that critics across America have hailed as Judith Rossner's finest book.

"As tense as a thriller, as suspenseful as a mystery and as satisfying as a good romance . . . a searing story of the search for identity and love."

—*Book-of-the-Month Club News*

AUGUST is . . .

"An extraordinary novel . . . a spellbinding trip."
—*West Coast Review of Books*

"A moving exploration . . . a compelling, dramatic tale."
—*Newsweek*

And in the final analysis, AUGUST is...

"A tour de force."   —*Richmond Times-Dispatch*

"An exquisite piece of work."
                            —*The Charlotte, N.C. Observer*

"Reads like a detective story, is entertaining."
                            —*The Quincy, Mass., Patriot Ledger*

"Inherently satisfying...wholesome, filling, and sticks to your ribs."   —*Harper's* magazine

"Totally fascinating, even compelling."
                            —*Cincinnati Enquirer*

"Engrossing and even suspenseful."   —*Detroit Free Press*

"Rossner's best."   —*Review* magazine

Books by
JUDITH ROSSNER

*To the Precipice
Nine Months in the Life of an Old Maid
Any Minute I Can Split
Looking for Mr. Goodbar
Attachments
Emmeline
*August

*Published by
WARNER BOOKS

AUGUST

A NOVEL BY

JUDITH ROSSNER

WARNER BOOKS

A Warner Communications Company

WARNER BOOKS EDITION

This Warner Books Edition is published by arrangement with
Houghton Mifflin Company

Cover design by Gene Light
Cover art by Fred Marcellino

Warner Books, Inc.
666 Fifth Avenue
New York, N.Y. 10103

 A Warner Communications Company

Printed in the United States of America

First Warner Books Printing: August, 1984

10 9 8 7 6

AUTHOR'S NOTE

It would be useful to remember that the psychoanalysis that takes place within this novel bears
approximately the resemblance to a real analysis
that the novel bears to life.

AUGUST

1

Dr. Lulu Shinefeld opened the door to her waiting room and said hello to the girl who was scheduled for a consultation. The girl, whose name was Dawn Henley, nodded coolly.

"Would you like to come into the office?" Dr. Shinefeld asked.

Dawn Henley stood. She was tall, even taller than Dr. Shinefeld, and quite beautiful, with dark brown, almond-shaped eyes, a startling, almost olive complexion, and honey blond hair cropped to shoulder length along a straight and severe line. It was July. Dawn wore white cotton pants, a white T-shirt, and sandals, but she might have had on a ball gown for the grace with which she preceded the doctor into the office, sank into the chair facing the doctor's, and inspected her surroundings.

The waiting room was nondescript, but the fur-

1

nishings in the office were attractive, if spare. The walls were white; the couch, brown; the two chairs were covered in a splendid cherry red wool. A kilim rug with predominating colors of brown, teal blue, and red covered a portion of the wood floor. Aside from the rug, the artwork in the room consisted of a semi-abstract painting, in which shapes suggestive of humans seemed to be posing for what could have been an old-fashioned family photograph, and a small sculpture resting on the table at the foot of the couch that was reminiscent of one of Henry Moore's primordial shapes, an egg embraced by some delicious, unidentifiable object. On the doctor's desk stood a slender blue vase that held three purple irises. Through an open door near the windows, it was possible to see another, smaller room with a thick brown carpet. Visible in this room were a bookcase containing various primary toys, a large dollhouse and a couple of yellow plastic beanbag chairs.

Dawn's eyes came to rest on the doctor.

No adolescent unease here. No suspicious glances or shifting in the seat. The girl's expression was neutral.

"So," Dr. Shinefeld said with a smile, "let me think of what you've told me. I know that you're eighteen years old, that your home is in Vermont but you've been going to boarding school in Westchester, and that you're entering Barnard College in September."

Dawn nodded.

From her canvas shoulder bag, which she'd placed on the floor, she extracted a small cassette recorder, which she placed on her lap.

"Do you want to tape our conversation?" the doctor asked.

"It seems like a good idea, don't you think?"

"Why's that?"

"Well," Dawn said coolly, "then one can be clear later about what was said...and anyway, if something should happen to one of us..."

"Yes?"

"Well, then, everything wouldn't be lost."

When the doctor didn't reply, Dawn turned on the recorder.

"What is it?" she asked in response to a flicker of expression on the doctor's face. "You don't mind this, do you?"

"I don't know," Dr. Shinefeld said. "I'm certainly not accustomed to it."

"Well," Dawn said calmly, "if it really bothers you, I'll turn it off. But see if you can't get used to it."

Dr. Shinefeld was disconcerted. While many patients attempted to control sessions from the moment they entered the room, the recorder added a new dimension. Anyway, control in that sense might not even be what Dawn was after.

"All right," the doctor said. "Well, then... perhaps you'd like to tell me why you're here."

"I have no reason," Dawn said without animosity. "That is, while I don't mind being here, I wouldn't have chosen to see another analyst if Vera... my mother... hadn't asked me to."

"Why do you think she asked?"

"It's actually quite clear why she asked. I had an automobile accident in which I nearly killed myself. That had happened to me once before. I mean, it was a bicycle that time. I was thirteen, but I went into a car in such a way that I really had to take full responsibility for what happened. My neck was broken, and one arm and leg. As soon as I could move around again Vera sent me to an analyst. Dr. Leif Seaver. I know you must know him, since he gave me your name. As I told you on the phone."

For the first time a hint of feeling showed through Dawn's extraordinary façade.

The doctor nodded.

"I saw Dr. Seaver for four years," Dawn said. "Until the beginning of June, when I also graduated from high school. He was... extremely helpful to me."

This last had an almost rote quality. The doctor waited.

"Then, a couple of weeks ago...I had another accident. I was driving the car this time. I was in Vermont, near Marbury. Where Vera is. Where I grew up. Anyway, I fell asleep at the wheel. It would've been the end except the boy who was with me grabbed the wheel, so we went into some bushes instead of a tree." She smiled. "He thinks he's in love with me. You'd think if someone nearly killed you, you'd never want to see her again..." Her tone had grown abstract. "A few people think they're in love with me."

"Both times you said *think* they're in love," Dr. Shinefeld pointed out. "Is that different from *being* in love?"

"No," Dawn said. "Not really. I guess. I mean, if you think you're in love, then you're in love. Anyway, who can say you're not?"

4

"Have you ever thought you were in love?" the doctor asked.

"Oh, yes," the girl said without hesitation. "I was in love with Dr. Seaver."

"What was the difference in the way you felt about Dr. Seaver and the way these boys feel about you?"

"That's easy," Dawn said. "They're in love with the way I look. I have the kind of looks you're supposed to have in this country. Blond hair, long legs, all that junk. None of it has anything to do with *me*, with who I *am*. If I showed any of them what's inside my head they wouldn't want to have anything to do with me. Dr. Seaver—Dr. Seaver didn't care what I looked like. He barely looked at me when I talked to him. I remember that right from the start. Nothing I said ever surprised him because he didn't even *see* the Outside Me. And I didn't care what he looked like. I knew some people would think he was ugly, sort of knotty looking, and with that funny little hunch to his back so at first when you see him you think he's just sort of scrunched over on purpose. I didn't care about any of that."

There were tears in Dawn's eyes. She didn't bother to wipe them.

"Why do you think you had the accident?"

"Because he left me."

"You finished the analysis?"

"He thought I was finished. I was sort of okay. He didn't understand I could only do all the things I was doing because I had him."

"Did you tell him that?"

"I tried to, but I must've not said it right because I can't believe he would have done it if I had. I was in

5

a trance a lot of the time. Maybe that sounds crazy, but it's true. From the day he started to talk about ending, I was in a sort of trance... The same thing happened after the first accident. For a few minutes I was so numb, I didn't even know anything was broken. They said I was in shock. Well, this was the same sort of thing, where I didn't exactly feel what was happening, only it lasted for months and months instead of for minutes."

Dr. Shinefeld was silent. She was already deciding to find the time to see Dawn if the girl wished. Her history even before Seaver was fascinating, from what Vera Henley had told her on the phone. Seaver himself was an interesting man; his reputation, most particularly as a diagnostician, was superb.

"Why do you think you had the first accident?" the doctor asked.

"Because my parents got divorced. I imagine you know about my parents."

"My conversation with your mother wasn't very long. I'd prefer that you tell me whatever you think I should know."

Dawn smiled. "Well, there's a lot, and it's pretty crazy. At least most people would think so. I grew up taking it for granted."

Vera Henley wasn't Dawn's natural mother, but her aunt. Her mother had committed suicide when Dawn was six months old and her father had drowned the following year when his sailboat capsized in a storm off the northern Massachusetts coast. Dawn had no memory of either of her two unfortunate parents. When she spoke of her parents she meant Vera and—well, Vera was actually a lifelong lesbian who had lived, since before Dawn's birth, in what was essentially a marriage with another woman, Tony (Antonia) Lubovitz. Vera and Tony were who Dawn meant when she talked about her parents, and it was their "divorce" that had been the precipitating factor in her first accident.

This was where life became confusing, because while Dawn had just referred to Vera as her mother, she had actually called Vera Daddy during their first years together. Tony was the feminine of the two women, wore makeup, jewelry and skirts, although it was also Tony who left each morning to work as chairman of the mathematics department in a Vermont high school three towns away. Vera didn't work and had never made any pretense at being other than who she was. Although (Dawn smiled shyly) this was New England they were talking about, and her aunt obviously hadn't gone around town proclaiming that she wasn't just a rather athletic old maid. Not that anyone would ask. One of the reasons Dawn loved Marbury was that really, whoever you were was all right as long as you followed the rules for public behavior. Upon coming to live with Vera, Tony had taken the name Henley, and the two women were assumed to be relatives. Dawn herself had never thought about the matter of their sexuality until she was in analysis with Dr. Seaver. Like a lot of other kids she knew, she'd rather taken it for granted that her parents, who shared a bedroom, had no sex life to speak of.

None of the children had ever questioned Dawn about her household, although at the beginning of school there had been nomenclature problems with the teacher. In the previous year, Vera, anticipating some such problems, had tried to train Dawn away from Daddy and toward Aunt Vera. What had remained with Dawn was that she was to call Daddy Aunt Vera when she was talking to other people. In first grade (Vera hadn't sent her to the optional kindergarten) Dawn had begun to read, learning from the primer that Daddy went to work and Mommy stayed home and took care of the children. The book was quite clear on this. Daddy might leave for a variety of places—bank, office, store, etc., but Mommy's work was done at home. It would not have occurred to Dawn's friends to support her claim that the opposite was true in her home because that would have involved arguing with the teacher, but as it turned out their support would have been useless. Dawn explained to the teacher that it was her daddy who stayed home and her mommy, Tony, who went to work. The teacher's task became clear. The child had suffered some elementary confusion and would have to be straightened out with drills. The drills were not done in a punitive manner, and by the time Parents' Day arrived, Dawn was calling Vera Mommy and Tony Daddy—in school. By the time she had acquired the conceptual vocabulary that would have enabled her to explain to her teacher that both her mommy and daddy were women, the class was absorbed in Vasco da Gama and the multiplication tables and no explanations were called for.

Dawn seldom invited other children to her home. The few who lived nearby remained her friends throughout eighth grade, but she rarely sought them out. After a full day at school she wanted only to return to the bosom of her family. The long New England winters that horrified so many people represented love and warmth to Dawn Henley.

The walk from school was about half a mile, and Dawn would make it with the other children unless they dawdled, in which case she would break away from them in her eagerness. Sometimes she and Tony, who would be driving from three towns away, reached home at the same time and raced, giggling, for the door. Dawn still recalled with pleasure arriving once before Tony's car was in sight, hiding behind a bush, then dashing to the front door just in time to beat Tony up the steps.

Afternoons were occupied with homework, sewing, baking. Tony gave Dawn piano lessons. In the evening they read, knitted and played cards, chess, and checkers. The television was in a little room of its own. No one watched it very much.

Dawn supposed the most important thing to say about Vera and Tony was that for all she'd learned of their problems, she adored them both and felt they'd given her much more than average parents gave their children, in time alone. In her analysis with Dr. Seaver, she had come to see that there were periods in her life when, like any child, she'd wished for one of her parents to "disappear" so that she could have the other to herself. That was, as Dr. Shinefeld must already know, why she'd had the accident when they separated; it was guilt over getting that old wish, for she still had them both but they didn't have each other anymore. With Dr. Seaver she'd understood that loving them both so much hadn't balanced out her jealous, hostile feelings but had tended to make them more intense, harder to bear.

They had been an extraordinary couple. What one lacked, the other possessed in abundance. Vera was your prototypical New England WASP patriarch— large and strong, with features almost identical to those of her brother and their father. What she lacked in warmth (the cuddling of little Dawn was left to Tony) Vera made up in strength, bravery and a broad range of talents. Aside from being a superb skier and horsewoman, she knew more about animals than most veterinarians, and she could fix, or build, for that matter, almost anything in the house. She was an excellent cook and a nearly miraculous gardener.

Tony was dark, pretty and plump. Her grandparents had emigrated from Russia, but she'd grown up in a Brooklyn ghetto that mirrored to a considerable extent the conditions of the old country. It was only when, over her parents' objections, Tony accepted a scholarship at a college outside New York that she finally lost the accent foreign to her English. Tony's clothing was marvelous, exotic even by New York standards in those days just before the sixties. Embroidered Roumanian blouses with drawstring necks and full sleeves. Full skirts of trimmed velvet in the winter, cotton when it grew warmer. Huge earrings and pendants set with turquoise and other stones; delicately wrought rings and bangle bracelets that rattled and clanked on her wrists as she gestured. Her shiny black hair, which came down to her waist, she braided, knotted, and swept up with an array of golden barrettes, tortoiseshell combs, and special hairpins with enameled heads that Dawn had never seen anywhere else, even in Europe, where she'd been sent on a graduation trip just this past June. Tony didn't like to cook, although she could do it if the occasion arose. She was a dressmaker and made most of her own clothes and Dawn's; Vera's attire consisted of men's shirts with jeans in the summer and slacks in the winter. All of them had sweaters knitted by Tony. Her mathematical abilities went beyond mere proficiency, and Tony had told Dawn a few years earlier, after the divorce, that she had sacrificed a fellowship to leave Boston because she'd promised Vera (they had met in Vermont the previous summer and fallen in love; Vera was twenty-one years her senior) that when she finished college she would get a job that would enable them to live together. It was inconceivable to Vera that they could be comfortable under the scrutiny of a university town.

Dawn smiled.

So Tony had given up a more interesting career for love. Just like a lot of other women.

The doctor returned Dawn's smile. They had gone past the full hour she allowed for consultations. The buzzer had sounded and a patient was waiting.

"How old were you when the women actually separated?" she asked Dawn.

"Fourteen," Dawn said. "It was my first year in boarding school."

Dr. Shinefeld hesitated. "I'm reluctant to end now because I have other questions I'd like to ask. But there's someone waiting. Would you like to come back later this week?"

Dawn shrugged. "Sure. If you want me to." She switched off the tape recorder and returned it to her satchel.

For a moment Dr. Shinefeld considered asking her to come without it the next time. Then she decided the moment wasn't opportune. The truth was that she would have liked to ask Dawn for a copy of the transcript.

☙

As it turned out, the request was unnecessary. Dawn began the next session, at two o'clock on Friday afternoon, by offering the doctor a copy. "In case you should find it useful."

"Thank you," the doctor said. "That was very thoughtful."

Dawn had an overnight bag with her as well as her satchel. She was going from the doctor's office to Penn Station, where she would board an Amtrak Metroliner to Boston. She was going to visit Tony and her husband.

"A man?" Dr. Shinefeld asked.

Dawn nodded.

"Was he the reason for the divorce?"

Well, Dawn thought, yes and no. Vera claimed that Tony had left her for Leonard Silverstein, but Tony said it wasn't true and that *Vera* had really left *her*, in spirit if not in body, years before. Where once Vera had met her eagerly at the door, Tony claimed, now her "housewife" barely seemed to notice her arrival. Where once Vera had listened with reasonable interest and unwavering support to Tony's stories of her

12

day among students and faculty, now Vera seemed uninterested in Tony's life and increasingly turned in on herself. Restless. Vera had started talking about going to Europe at the very beginning of that school year—just as it became impossible for Tony to do so.

And Vera was drinking. Liquor had been a problem in the Henley family, and for a long time Vera had refused anything stronger than beer. But gradually she'd begun to drink whiskey, and by the time Dawn was preparing to leave for boarding school Vera was drinking quite heavily.

Dawn herself, by the way, had never really accepted the boarding school decision, although she didn't argue because she took it to mean that Vera and Tony didn't want her with them anymore. She'd been over all that a good deal with Dr. Seaver . . . Strangely enough, she'd felt the same way about her graduation trip to Europe. That she was being sent away. Some sort of collusion between Vera and Dr. Seaver. So she wouldn't notice that her sessions had ended.

For a while Dawn had believed that Vera's decision to send her to boarding school had nothing to do with her—Dawn's— developing sexuality, with the fact that she was growing breasts, had begun to masturbate, and so on. Lately she'd become uncertain again. It was the punishment aspect. While she was with Dr. Seaver she'd lost the sense of having been sent away as a punishment, but now it was back . . . as though she'd never really believed his version. It was only that his ideas had been more powerful than hers in her own mind while she continued to see him.

Dawn was quiet. For the first time in the hour she

seemed uncertain of what she wanted to say next. Perhaps she was waiting for a response.

"How did you find boarding school?" the doctor asked.

"Oh, it was all right. At first I was miserable, but then I got used to it. Like the others. But when I went home for... I couldn't wait to go home for Christmas, and when I got there, it was awful. Tense and unpleasant. Different from ever before. I should've known something was up. Then, when I went home again at Easter... Tony was gone." Dawn paused where perhaps her voice had once broken as she remembered. "The whole house was quiet. Tony was the one who made noise, who talked, who played music. I still... when I remember..." She shuddered. "The only important thing that happened to me at Sidley was the art classes. I learned to make lithographs. Art class was the only reason I wanted to go back after the accident. What I didn't want... Vera rented our house and moved down to Westchester to be near me at Sidley. That hurt me almost as much as the divorce. It was the only house I'd ever lived in."

"The only house?"

"Mmm." Dawn seemed barely to notice the question. "But once Vera made up her mind... She took an apartment near school, and I had home study until I could walk again. I still lost half a year. I couldn't concentrate on my work and I was having terrible dreams. It was worse after the casts came off. And even worse when I was finished with the crutches and the neck brace. They were so awful, they gave me some kind of focus. Once they were off I became aimless. I didn't want to do anything. That was when Vera started bringing me to New York to see Dr. Seaver. Later she went back to Marbury and I came in on the railroad."

"Do you think Vera chose a male analyst on purpose?"

"I think she got a few names from the guidance people at school and talked to them all. He sounded the smartest to her. Actually, I think they were all men. She just took it for granted that I should ... He *was* terribly smart, as you probably know. I should say, he *is*."

Dawn laughed, a little embarrassed.

"Anyway, it **was** that year that I started making prints. Someday I'll show you ..." She laughed again, embarrassed again. "I forgot. This is a consultation. If you think I should continue, you're going to send me to someone else."

"Not necessarily," Dr. Shinefeld said. "I know we began on the phone on that basis, and I'll be happy to refer you elsewhere if you want me to. But if you'd rather work with me, as long as you have a certain flexibility in your hours, I can see you when I return from vacation. After Labor Day."

Dawn smiled sadly. "Labor Day. When all the analysts come back to New York and give birth to their patients."

But her manner had altered radically in that moment after Dr Shinefeld's offer to continue seeing her. She had become almost childlike, and there were tears in her eyes.

A few moments passed.

"When are you leaving?" she asked after a moment.

"The end of July. Two weeks," the doctor told her.

"Will I see you until then?"

"It can be arranged."

Dawn nodded.

"You remind me of Tony...except that you're bigger. And not so fluffy."

Dr. Shinefeld smiled, and they paused together in that restrained mutual good feeling that was so essential to satisfactory treatment while raising such difficult issues for those involved in it.

"What I was going to tell you before," Dawn said after a while, "was that I did a series of lithographs, in my last year at Sidley. My last year with Dr. Seaver. I was making the best one to give to Dr. Seaver on my birthday." She smiled. "I wanted to give it to him on *his* birthday, but he wouldn't tell me when it was." Amusement didn't keep her from falling into sadness, now. "Anyway, he didn't want me to give him anything on my birthday *or* his. He'd already begun talking about the end of treatment. That was why I made that series in the first place...That whole year was a nightmare. Not exactly a nightmare; I just didn't feel anything most of the time. I don't understand what happened to me. He thought I was all right, but I wasn't."

"Have you considered seeing Dr. Seaver again—rather than another analyst? Or at least talking to him before you see someone else?"

"Oh, yes," Dawn said. "Of course. It was the first thing I thought of when I woke up. I was knocked unconscious and I bruised my head on the steering wheel, but I wasn't hurt, just shaken up. There was something else that happened, actually. Before the accident. But I don't know if I can talk about that yet. It may have to wait until September."

The doctor nodded.

"When I came back from Europe three weeks ago and I knew... something was wrong... I called and said I needed to talk to him. He said it was too soon and I guess I pleaded with him but... Anyway, I called again last week, after the accident, and when I told him he said he'd see me... Vera didn't think it was a good idea. I think she knew that I loved him too much. She thought I should see a woman and I liked that idea, in a way, but first I needed him to know what had happened to me... I'd brought the print. Not to give him. I just needed him to see the message. The words were very important. I showed it to him, thinking of all the times we'd argued about it, and I kept waiting for the light to go on. He was finally going to understand this terribly important thing and explain it to me, and then I'd feel better. Instead he said, *Nice work, Dawn. You're doing some really nice work. Keep it up.* He didn't even remember the arguments! I felt as though I had no importance to him at all, and never had. I was less than a patient, I wasn't even a person!"

"Was that when you decided to see a woman?" the doctor asked after a moment.

"You'd think so," Dawn said with a wry smile, "but not quite. I was still... You have to understand something. Vera was my father until I met Dr. Seaver. Then he became my father. He didn't stop being my father just because he wouldn't see me anymore."

Dr. Shinefeld glanced at the clock.

"Is it time for me to go?"

"We have another minute or two."

"I don't remember what I was saying."

"We were talking about when you decided to see a woman."

"Oh. Yes. Well, I told him I was thinking of doing that. And he said I had to make the decision myself. He could refer me to some good women analysts if that was what I wanted. Or, he said, perhaps it would be just as well to work it out with him. I was about to thank him. Or to cry. And then he added . . ." She paused, trying to get over the words. ". . . that since he knew me already, if I came to him the work would go much faster." Her voice trembled, and her lips twisted so she wouldn't cry.

"And that was the end for you."

"Of course. I could see that the same thing would happen all over again."

Dawn stood and stretched, then put the cassette player in the satchel.

The doctor picked up her appointment book and they arranged times for the following Tuesday and Friday. At Dawn's request, regular appointments were scheduled for the additional week in July. Dawn was staying in Westchester with a friend from Sidley. She would spend August with Vera in Vermont.

The hour was at an end. They walked together to the door, which the doctor opened.

"Dawn?" the doctor asked on impulse as the girl passed over the threshold, "what were the words at the bottom of the lithograph?"

"Dylan Thomas," Dawn said. *"After the first death there is no other."*

ᵔ

At the outset of her third visit, Dawn offered Dr. Shinefeld a transcript of the second, then seated herself, as she had previously, in the chair facing the doctor's. Dr. Shinefeld hadn't spoken again with Vera Henley. The matter of Dawn's continued visits had been arranged between the girl and her aunt.

"In your analysis with Dr. Seaver," Dr. Shinefeld asked as Dawn reached for the tape recorder, "did you lie on the couch?"

"Yes, sure," Dawn said, momentarily distracted from the machine.

"Would you like to do that now?"

Dawn glanced at the couch uneasily.

"I feel as though I hardly know you," she said, then laughed. "I know that's not the only reason, because Dr. Seaver asked me the second time and I did it right away. I guess I feel as though...if I lie down, I'll get attached to you. And I don't want to get attached when you're just going away for the longest time."

"Tell me about the longest time."

"No," Dawn said after a moment. "I don't want to talk about that now. I'll do it when I come back."

She had been looking toward the couch, avoiding the doctor's eyes, which she now met. "You know that I'm not a lesbian, don't you?"

"Actually," the doctor said, "I don't know anything about your sexual preferences."

"Well then, we're even," Dawn said. "Because neither do I." She giggled. "I mean, I don't actually have any at the moment. Yes, that's what I mean. I prefer at the moment not to have any sexual preferences."

Dr. Shinefeld smiled. There was a lengthy silence.

"I had an abortion when I came back from Europe."

"Oh?"

"I never slept with my boyfriend until April. My *then* boyfriend. Alan Gartner was his name. Not that it matters. I never even worried about getting pregnant, that was the weird part. Before that, I didn't sleep with him just because I didn't feel like it. I never slept with anyone before him, either. He thought I was on the pill but I wasn't on anything. I'm chattering like this because the whole business made me crazy and still does."

"When did you have the abortion?"

Her eyes filled with tears. "Three weeks ago. A week before the accident."

"Don't you think you might feel a little less crazy if you talked about it?"

Dawn studied the doctor's face. "You know what I'm thinking? That I still haven't turned on the tape recorder and you don't want me to turn it on."

The doctor was silent.

"I wish I could understand why you don't like it."

"It might be more useful to understand why you *do* like it."

"Are you going to make me put it away?" Terribly anxious and childlike.

"No, but I'd like to keep talking about it."

Dawn laughed. "Okay. Go ahead. Talk." There was

a nervous, slightly hostile edge the doctor hadn't heard in her voice before. Dawn switched on the recorder.

"You could die," Dawn said after a moment. "Or get sick. Or go away on vacation and never come back. Or maybe get sick of seeing me. The first year or two I was seeing Dr. Seaver he never went away for more than a week at a time. Then suddenly... everything changed. August! Easter! Christmas! I don't know what else. The first time he went away for August I really thought I was going to die before he got back. I went up to be with Vera, but then I couldn't stand being there. She was so unhappy. But that wasn't it. Dr. Seaver ruined me for people like Vera. It wasn't just that she didn't understand anything that had happened to me. She doesn't *want* to understand things like that. She's all closed off. It was worse than being alone... It wasn't just because Tony was gone. Tony was right, Vera was the same only more so. Before Dr. Seaver, I thought that was just the way men were... Anyway, Vera couldn't even stand it when I played the radio. I think music reminded her of Tony, so she just decided to shut that out of her life, too."

Dawn shuddered. "I left after four days. I felt guilty but... I told Vera I'd taken a couple of incompletes and I had to work in the school library. I was really going to Boston. To Tony. But I didn't want to tell her that. She'd have felt worse. Not that she ever let me know how she felt... Anything I know about what happened between them I know from Tony. I figured I'd be able to talk to Tony about how I felt, but even she didn't really understand. Not the way

Dr. Seaver did. Sometimes I didn't even have to explain things to him...He spoiled me for other people, you see..." A long pause, and then, her voice breaking: "That was the worst of it. He spoiled me for everyone else in the world and then said I had to get along without him."

Dawn had picked Alan Gartner because he was older than the boys from school and looked a little like Dr. Seaver. He had black hair and he was very tall and skinny, with tortoiseshell glasses. And he was reasonably intelligent. Boys, as Dr. Shinefeld had probably noticed, were terribly *boring*, and Alan was somewhere in between Dr. Seaver and the boys of the world. He had a doctorate in literature but was acting with an improvisational group at a café in the Village. During the last year she'd tried to explain to Dr. Seaver about the difference between going out with a Young Man and a Man. Dr. Seaver had told her a lovely story, as a matter of fact, about his daughter. (She hadn't known until then that he had a daughter and she'd been horribly jealous; she had a dream in which his real daughter died and he adopted her to take the real daughter's place.) Anyway, when Dr. Seaver's daughter was in nursery school, she'd asked one day who she could marry who wasn't already taken. He had explained that by the time she was ready to marry, there would be many boys who were ready too, and he'd mentioned two or three from her nursery school whose names he knew.

"Oh, no!" the little girl had protested vehemently, "I don't want a boy! I want a man!"

Dawn had understood very well the point of that

lovely anecdote. But she was quite old enough to understand that people grew up and changed. Boys, on the other hand, didn't change fast enough. There might have been a time when it made sense for girls to wait for them. But in this world, why would you wait for someone to grow up when the chances were he'd leave you for someone else when he did? Of her three best friends at school, the parents of two had been divorced during the last three years because the man left for a younger woman. The third—that was Bevvy Gartner, actually, Alan's younger sister—her parents' marriage had been what you might call open at one end from the beginning. Bevvy's father had always done pretty much what he wanted without having to pay for two households. Probably he'd leave, too, once Mrs. Gartner got old and pathetic enough so she really needed him. Alan still lived at home when he wasn't traveling or living with some girl who had her own apartment. It seemed to Dawn that more and more kids weren't exactly leaving home, and maybe it was because they didn't have real homes to leave.

The office was quiet. The sounds from Central Park West were muffled by the air conditioner's hum. Briefly Dr. Shinefeld had a sensation familiar to her from other moments of intense absorption in patients' lives—that the office wasn't in a large building but was floating around freely somewhere in space with the two of them inside. It was at times like this that she most missed cigarettes. For a while after she'd stopped smoking, she had kept a saucer of rock candy on her little table and sucked on a piece when she felt in danger of being sucked too thoroughly into a patient's psyche. Occasionally, though, forgetting herself, she'd crunched on the candy, and once a patient had leaped off the couch, at once frightened and angry, demanding to know what she was doing. It was all very well to analyze the patient's fear of being devoured, but of course one wasn't allowed to be the active catalyst for such associations. Pencils weren't bad to chew, but pens were better for taking notes, which she found herself doing now. She had the wry thought that she was going to miss the transcriptions once she'd persuaded Dawn to leave the recorder at home.

"So," Dr. Shinefeld said, "if I die while I'm on vacation, you will have a piece of me in the transcriptions."

"You're not sick, are you?" Dawn asked, clutching the arms of the chair.

"Not that I know of."

"I don't suppose you'll tell me how old you are."

"No."

"You're not that old. You look about Tony's age and she's ... forty. Much younger than Vera ... Vera's healthy as anything ... You can't even promise me"— but she seemed almost to be trying to find a way to bear to do what the doctor wanted her to do— "that you won't get sick."

"No," the doctor said. "Although I'm also a rather healthy person."

Dawn didn't speak or move.

"There is one promise I can make to you," Dr. Shinefeld said after a while. "That I won't ask you to leave here until you're ready. In other words, you can be the one to decide when you're finished."

"Finished." Dawn's eyes filled with tears and her voice quivered. "That has such a funny sound. People don't get finished. They're not jobs. Or books." But she relaxed in the chair.

"It's the analytic work that gets more or less finished."

"But what if I finish and I leave and then a week or a month or a day later something terrible happens to me? Something I have to talk to you about?"

"Well, in that case you'd call me up and come back and we'd talk about it."

"Why wouldn't Dr. Seaver let me? What was such a big deal?" Dawn cried. "He said I was going out into the world, that I had to really be finished. Then, when I found out I was pregnant and came home to have the abortion, I called him up and...He was still...In my mind...I don't really want to tell you this...If Alan's sister wasn't my best friend, if I hadn't needed her help, I never would've told him. In my mind Alan had nothing to do with the baby. I mean, he was barely in my mind at all. It was Dr. Seaver who was there. I kept thinking, now he'd *have* to understand. I really don't know what I thought he'd understand. Except...This is awful. I don't know if I can say it...I delayed. The abortion. This is very hard for me to talk about. In my house...I didn't know about menstruation until I got to boarding school. Which was before I got my period, fortunately. Even Tony didn't like to talk about those things. Anyway, I didn't want to have the abortion right away. The truth was, I'd been feeling sort of nice while I was in Europe, and I'd thought to myself, Dr. Seaver was right, it was really hard for a while but I'm getting over him. It never occurred to me that ... It was as though Dr. Seaver had left a big hole right in my center and somehow it had gotten filled up. I didn't know—at least I didn't know I knew—it was only that I had his ... the baby ... It was his baby in my mind, not stupid Alan Gartner's, and that was why I was all right." Dawn was crying. "I didn't want to give it up. At least not until I was ready. I didn't want to lose the baby just because I wasn't supposed to have it in the first place!"

Now she was crying in earnest, the only sign that she wasn't oblivious to the world outside herself, Dr. Seaver, and her aborted baby being that at some point she clicked off the recorder.

"No sense recording seventeen hours of me crying my eyes out," she said when the tears had finally abated. "I hardly ever cried until I got to Dr. Seaver's. Vera and Tony used to tell me how when I was little, if I fell and hurt myself, I never cried."

"Why do you think that was?"

The question surprised Dawn. "I don't know. They thought I was brave. I might've talked about that a little with Dr. Seaver. I remember telling him I just didn't mind if I hurt myself a little. What's the big deal if you fall off a bike and scrape your knees." There was no bravado in her voice. She was puzzled at how easily girls cried. "Crying is worse than most of the reasons people cry."

"Why?" Dr. Shinefeld asked.

Dawn turned on the tape recorder. "It can make you choke, for one thing. Especially if you're lying down. Dr. Seaver said I choked to cut off the bad feelings ... as though I were afraid of getting them

26

out of my system . . . but I don't think that was right. It's more that I can't help it. I choke if I cry a lot."

"Why did you turn on the tape recorder just now?"

"Because I could tell I was going to cry."

"But after you cried, you didn't turn it right back on."

"What were we talking about?"

"You said that crying was more unpleasant than most of the reasons people cried, and I asked you why.

"And that's when I turned it back on." Dawn laughed. "Well, I can believe it. Just thinking about the question . . . It makes me uncomfortable. It makes me wish I had a friend here."

"I guess that's why I don't like the tape recorder," Dr. Shinefeld said.

"Cassette player," Dawn corrected.

"I feel as though it's your friend and it comes between us."

Dawn laughed but then quickly became serious. "It's not that I don't like you. I don't even *want* anything to be between us. I want to feel better. If I didn't like you . . Dr. Seaver gave me three names. I picked yours first. But if I didn't like you I would have tried the others."

"Was my name the first on the list?"

"No, the last. But he said there was no order of preference."

"Why do you think you picked mine?"

"I don't know. I liked the sound of it. It sounds like water gurgling. Lulululu." Dawn giggled. "And Shinefeld. A shining field. It sounds so wonderful. I thought you must be beautiful. I had to see what you looked like. You are beautiful, you know. I can't tell if you're one of those people who can tell she's beautiful, because it's not in the conventional way. Not where I come from, anyway." A long pause. "I remember when I was looking at the piece of paper he gave me." Slow and thoughtful, now—Dawn was trying to remember the details. "The other two were on the East Side, so they were less convenient to school. On the other hand, with the Number Five bus, that's no big deal. And they were both in Dr. Seaver's neighborhood, so I'd maybe see—Oh, my God! I know what it was. It was your initials. They're the same as Dr. Seaver's! I remember how they struck me when I was looking at the piece of paper, because he makes his capital letters five times as big as the small ones." Dawn turned off the cassette player. "You see," she said, "I really couldn't bear not to see him anymore. But I couldn't see him, either. It was too frightening. So I picked someone safer. A woman with his initials. I was hoping from the beginning you'd say I could keep seeing you. I didn't know what I would do if I had to try the others."

Lulu Shinefeld turned the corner of Seventieth Street onto Central Park West. It was ten to two and she'd just finished lunch. The day was crisp and sunny, and she was minding that she had to go back indoors. As she walked toward her building, Lulu became simultaneously aware of the doorman grinning at her and the girl with her face hidden behind

AUGUST

a camera—of course it was Dawn—snapping pictures of her.

Dr. Shinefeld smiled grimly and proceeded into the building. Dawn ran after her.

"Are you angry with me?"

"Let's talk upstairs," the doctor said.

Dawn's mood in the office was contrite and extremely anxious. She was willing to apologize, to analyze, to do anything, in fact, that might appease the doctor short of offering to give up the film, which the doctor did not suggest she do.

"I'm going to make a series of prints," Dawn said. "Of you, sort of. While you're on vacation. But I need a photo to look at. Even if the print doesn't end up having anything to do with the photo... I didn't bring the cassette... I didn't even transcribe the last tape... You're angry with me."

"I was a little annoyed," the doctor said. "Not because you wanted to take a picture of me. I'm willing to talk about that. It's more about your not asking. And with the fact that we weren't in the office."

"But I couldn't do it indoors. I don't have the right equipment. My flash is in Vermont. And if we'd talked about it, you would only have wanted to analyze me out of it. And if you had, then I wouldn't have the photo!"

It was an unproductive session. Dawn was defensive and angry with the doctor for being angry when it was clear to her that the need to take the picture had been an absolute if she was going to give up the cassette recorder. It had seemed pointless to the

29

doctor to deny an irritation that had been palpable to all concerned, but there were moments when she wished she had tried. Dawn spoke less freely than she had during previous visits, as though she were all too aware of the power of free association and was afraid that in the unraveling of the meaning of her act she would find herself giving up the film without really wanting to. On the other hand, it was surely self-defeating to deal with a girl who thought that crying was more painful than pain by pretending not to be annoyed at her acting out. In any event, Dr. Shinefeld was certain that the bond already established between them was strong enough to withstand this early storm and that Dawn would return as scheduled.

∽

At their next meeting it turned out that Dawn had believed Dr. Shinefeld might refuse to see her again. Her own anger during the previous session had been a conscious preparation for being cast out in disgrace. She and the doctor discussed on a rather elementary level the various degrees of anger, ending with that rage so powerful as to make one abandon another. Dawn said that neither Tony nor Vera had ever really gotten angry with her. Vera was very firm and had no problem giving orders or forbidding various activities. But there was little visible change of emotion if Dawn did occasionally, very occasionally, disobey. Tony was light and gay, tending to respond to both good and bad with little jokes and laughs and wasn't Dawn a wonderful girl? Dawn had never experienced the feeling she knew was common among her friends, that a benevolent parent had turned into a raging beast. Bevvy Gartner said that when she was younger she'd called her mother the Hulk, after the comic strip man who, when he was angry or in pain, metamorphosed into a great green monster.

"Did I turn into a great green monster?" Dr. Shinefeld asked.

"Well, no," Dawn said, "but I thought that if you let even that much show, there must be much worse somewhere. Analysts don't usually show anything at all."

"You generally see us in the office. Away from our offices we're just like other people."

"I wonder," Dawn said. "I wonder if that's possible."

The snapshots of Dr. Shinefeld had been overexposed and came back from the drugstore with the doctor's face blurred. Dawn was in a panic.

"Are you thinking it's just as well?" she asked, sitting on the edge of the couch. She didn't want to lie down. "Maybe I did it on purpose. Set the meter for the wrong exposure. I had to fail because I knew you wouldn't want me to do it. But I needed them. I still do. I'd be afraid to go through that whole routine again and make you angry again, but that doesn't mean I need them less than I did before."

"Tell me."

"I *have* told you." The girl was wild-eyed. "I'm sick of saying the same thing over and over again."

"Why?"

Judith Rossner

"It's like a kind of whining. I don't like to whine. I get sick of myself. And it doesn't *help*."

"Sometimes," the doctor pointed out, "as you repeat yourself, new elements are added."

"I can't."

"Can't what?"

"I don't know. I can't go past a certain point. It's as though there's a wall. Once or twice I tried to find out what was behind the wall, but...It's solid...Oh, my God, every time I think of the photos I want to run out of here screaming."

"Talk about that."

"I can't. I'm at the wall."

"I know that it might be difficult for you to lie down just now," the doctor said, "but if you could do it anyway, and say what comes to mind, something useful might come up."

Dawn lay down, but her body didn't relax at all.

"My mind is a blank. I mean it. I'm not saying it just to...Even the normal things aren't there...Usually when my mind wanders, I make up stories about the rug. About the people who wove it, say, or the dyes they used for the colors. Now when I say *dyes*, I think about *dying* without the *e* and then I'm right back at the wall."

"Is the wall about dying?"

"No. It's just a wall that keeps me from getting anyplace."

"A place you want to go?"

"No. There's no place I want to go."

"So the wall is sort of protective. It serves as—"

"Don't you see?" Dawn burst out. "We're sitting

32

here talking about walls and all I can think of is that I don't have a picture of you!"

"Then maybe you'd better talk about what you'd planned to do with it."

"First I was going to make copies and put them in different places so I couldn't lose all of them. Then I was going to enlarge the best ones, maybe one up to poster size if the image held. Then I was—What's the sense of all this? I don't have it! I don't have anything of you!"

"Don't you have me, in a sense, even when I'm not here?"

"No! I don't! Certainly if I can't be sure you'll ever be here again! I was going to do a lithograph...not just one, another whole set...something with the rug. You and the rug." She rambled on about various projects she'd considered in connection with the photographs, but when she stopped talking, she was as rigid and upset as she'd been all along.

"Tell me," the doctor said after a long pause, "about *After the first death there is no other*."

There was a moment when the tension in the room was as powerful as an electric charge. Then Dawn's body went through a remarkable series of motions, beginning with a violent shaking of her head, back and forth on the pillow, the movement then extending to her hands, her torso, and finally her legs, all thrashing around in a series of violent, rigid motions that resembled nothing so much as the convulsions of severe colic. Finally she relaxed, quite thoroughly. Her body took on the air of a beatified saint. Several minutes passed.

"Uh..." Dawn said, "...What were we talking about?"

The doctor debated whether to answer the question. Finally she said that they'd been talking about the lithographs Dawn had done.

"Oh, yes," Dawn said easily. "You mean, the *First Death* series? What about it?"

When the doctor failed to respond, Dawn sat up and turned around. "If you don't answer I can't tell for sure that you're there."

The doctor smiled. "I'm here."

"I *know*. But when I can't see you I don't always feel as though you are...You know, when I was a little kid I could never stand to play hide-and-seek. I couldn't stand to be It. And if I was hiding I was too worried about how It would feel, so I'd let her see me or make some noise so she'd find me...Something happened to me just now but I don't know what it was."

The doctor waited.

"Did you know something happened to me?"

"Yes."

"Good. Because I don't know what it was, but it was pretty weird. And it would be weirder if you thought everything was normal."

"Mmm. I can understand that."

"But what happened?"

"Maybe you can tell me what you remember."

"I don't remember anything," Dawn said. "That's the funny part. I was in a *white space*. Once or twice with Dr. Seaver I was in a white space, but it wasn't complete because the words *white space* were printed in it. This was total." She shuddered. "What's that about?" But she was fairly calm. "I'm not scared now," she said after a moment. "But if I don't know what happened I'm going to be scared later."

"In fact," the doctor said, "I think that's what happened. You got scared."

"Of what?"

"Well...of something I said. It's possible that I was too abrupt with you."

"Too abrupt? How? What did you say?"

"I referred to the caption on the lithographs."

"After the first death?" Dawn was incredulous. "But how could that bother me? I've been trying to find out...For most of the last year I was with Dr. Seaver I was trying to get him to...I *need* someone to tell me what it's about."

"Sometimes," the doctor said, "a patient wants to know what something's about in order to gain mastery over it with words... without actually living through the painful feelings that meaning involves ...She may be terribly eager to learn some *why* but also quite frightened to know. It makes sense if you realize that virtually every aspect of life that's been buried has been buried for what the self considered to be an excellent reason. In other words, she's trying very hard to find out something she already knows but wishes she didn't."

Dawn giggled. "I like that."

The doctor was silent.

"But if I didn't want to know, why did I keep trying to find out?"

"Did you?"

"You know that I kept asking."

"Asking what?"

"To bring him the lithograph."

"Why?"

"I needed him to see it. Part of it was showing off, but also I needed him to see what was written on the bottom."

"Why?"

"So he could tell me what it meant."

"Did you ever just say the words to him?"

A long silence. "I'm trying to remember. I must have. I'm not sure. I think...The truth is, sometimes I tried and I couldn't. I got all choked up. That's why I wanted to show it to him. I couldn't say the words."

"Why do you think that was?"

"I don't know," Dawn said. "I remember I was very excited about the whole series. I went around high all the time. Kids at school asked me if I was *on* something, but I was just naturally high. Of *course* I talked to him about it. I talked to him about everything. He was a part of everything I did...First I was doing this series of prints, then...I remember I felt mischievous when I said it was going to be for my birthday...Anyway, by then nothing I said got to him. You probably think I knew *that*, too. But I don't think so. I think it was that I was desperate by that time. Nothing else worked. I don't know what I mean by that. Yes I do. The part of what you're saying that's true...It wasn't that I was afraid to know. It was more that I was afraid to unlock the last secret. I mean, I didn't *feel* afraid. I hardly felt anything. But it kept passing through my mind that if I knew what that line meant, I'd know all I had to know, and then we'd *really* be finished." She began to cry.

At their final session she had explained to Dr.

Seaver that there was something terribly important they hadn't figured out, a great secret of her life. He had said that many patients had that feeling at the end of an analysis, that if they'd only unlocked one more door, everything would be all right. In reality, life was difficult, and there was seldom a time when everything was all right. There were many secrets and many doors, and one didn't stop opening them because one ceased having analytic sessions. She had learned a new system of thought, Dr. Seaver had told her, and she would continue to think that way, and to learn.

And Dawn had lain quiet on the couch, thinking, *Don't argue. It will feel worse if you argue. Don't cry. You'll get hysterical. You'll choke.*

Anyway, he'd been wrong. Because she hadn't been able to think that way at all since he'd left her. That way of thinking was about him and therefore too painful. She hadn't been vaguely analytic about any-thing she'd said or done since the first week of June. She still found herself reluctant to think analytically unless she was right here in the office.

◠

Dawn had forgotten the catalyst for her brief "fit" of amnesia. Indeed, she appeared to have forgotten the fit itself, although she was eager to discuss the issue of whether she'd been unfair to be angry with Dr. Seaver. She was looking for a way to return to her former state of untempered adoration.

The issue was a complex one for Dr. Shinefeld. A misstep might send the girl back to Seaver, apologetic at having "blamed" him for not understanding what he hadn't been told and eager to resume the transference romance. Not only was the doctor reluctant to lose her patient, but she suspected that Seaver had been somewhat blinder than the circumstances dictated. She was coming around to the belief that like a number of other analysts, he had a deep resistance to exploring that period of life before the relatively comfortable and specific Oedipal attachment began. This was the most difficult and frightening period of life for the obvious reason that words did not exist that were adequate to describe the over-powering feelings engendered in an infant who did not yet have words to describe and sort out those feelings. If that were the case, then, Dr. Shinefeld thought, she might be more helpful to Dawn than Dr. Seaver could be at this stage.

Dawn spent considerable time evaluating the merits of female as opposed to male psychiatrists and eventually held fast in her determination to return to regular treatment with Dr. Shinefeld. The matter of the first death seemed to have vanished and would not reappear until August had come and gone and the bond between Dawn and the doctor had been reestablished.

2

LULU SHINEFELD, who remembered her childhood as having been spent in dark, quiet places, entered her element as soon as there were more than three people in a room and got high on crowds. Now, at the beginning of August's first big party, she walked briskly across the great lawn from the East Hampton cottage she shared with her two sons (and until recently with her husband) to the larger home of her landlords and best friends, Bonnie and Duke Mayer.

Lulu always arrived early and stayed late at parties, but the boys, who were seven and eight years old, had gone over even earlier to swim in the big pool that Duke Mayer's father, the original owner of the estate, had installed when his beloved wife became too feeble, at the age of seventy-three, to negotiate the ocean's fierce waves—not to speak of the several hundred yards that sloped down to the beach.

The pool was sixty feet long, and a number of children, including Lulu's boys, were diving and playing water volleyball—kids never seemed to just swim anymore. A few adults, all familiar to Lulu from East Hampton or from social and professional groups in New York, lounged around the pool or watched Duke set up the barbecue. Bonnie brought out a tray to the barbecue pit and stood talking to Duke and their guests for a moment. Lulu halted her approach to watch them standing there, in front of the great white house with its green shutters and seven brick chimneys.

They were a perfectly matched set, Duke and Bonnie Mayer, tall and lean with dark eyes, curly black-gray hair and complementary tennis serves. For all the years she'd known them (it was only seven, actually), Lulu still marveled when she came upon them together, looking like a world-class brother and sister team in some utopian sport where people improved as they edged past forty. If Lulu's ties to Bonnie were deeper, together the Mayers were her best friends, not to say the parents of her children's best friends. Both were analysts: Duke, a psychiatrist; Bonnie, like Lulu, a clinical psychologist. They all lived in the same building on Central Park West—the Mayers in a duplex penthouse, Lulu and her family in a three-bedroom apartment two stories below—and had met when Bonnie and Lulu were wheeling their infant sons to the playground every day. If it was unfair to say that Bonnie and Duke had been instrumental in the break-up of Lulu's marriage, it was reasonable to say that the *idea* of them, of people who liked each other so much and understood one another so well, had put additional stress on a troubled marriage.

Cars slammed in back of Lulu.

Bonnie moved.

The moment passed.

Three people overtook Lulu as she moved toward the patio, a man and two women, glancing, as they passed, to see if she was someone they knew. Lulu nodded pleasantly; they commented on the perfect day. Lulu found herself pretending to have forgotten something and fell behind. She wasn't quite ready to join the party.

There had been recent traumatic events in her life. This was the first distinct sign from the interior that she was not prepared to absorb them and move on.

Lulu walked over to the section of the lawn that rolled away from the pool and patio, around to the back of the big house, then down to the beach, where the sounds from what was still a small party were drowned by the steady crash of waves against the shore. The sky was light; the sunset was reflected on the water. Lulu wore a full-sleeved white cotton blouse and white pants, sashed with a bright blue and orange scarf, and sandals. Now she took off the sandals, rolled up her pants, and walked slowly along the water's edge, holding a sandal in each hand, occasionally clunking the sole of one against the other as though she might, by this simple act, bring together her past and her present and proceed in some reasonable way.

She was forty years old and had left her second

husband, Nathan Shinefeld, several months earlier for reasons that she sometimes thought he understood better than she did; certainly he had a better rhetoric to cover them. That Nathan had been dipping his toes into adulterous waters provided an excuse as much as a reason, although it was certainly true that she had always assumed that if one of them were going to screw around, it would be she; and indeed, in a world run according to the simple law of supply and demand, that would have been the case.

Perhaps she had been harboring through the years a need to avenge herself for the fact of her adored first husband's having left her within months of their marriage, and when she was already pregnant—with her daughter, Sascha, now twenty-two years old and lost to her mother.

Perhaps. But when Lulu posed this possibility to herself, no emotional bells clamored back from the recesses of her brain.

What did ring a bell was a misquote, the only remembered part of a dream she'd had one morning that dispersed in the daylight as her eyes opened: No life at the end of the tunnel.

Her long marriage to Nathan Shinefeld had been mostly of the peaceful sort. Nathan was a well-meaning person who had married her when she was the mother of a three-year-old girl; who had, however reluctantly, aided and abetted her in bringing into the world two more children; who had encouraged her to use her energy and her underdeveloped intellect by returning to school for a Ph.D. and who then supported her training analysis as well as her efforts to set up a practice. He was also a man whose excellent brain had become ossified from inadequate exposure to the air outside the New York Psychoanalytic Institute; who had learned little or nothing from being a father, from being a husband, from being a person in a lousy world; a man for whom the Freudian prism had been a comfortable prison, a refuge from the very truths it revealed as well as from those it didn't encompass; a man who, by remaining exactly the same for eighteen years, had deteriorated steadily in her eyes. Respect was so much more important than love, so much less ephemeral.

Then, too: Sascha had put the final exclamation point on her adolescent revolt by running away from home two months before high-school graduation; and Lulu's mother had committed suicide a couple of years later, the final salvo in a long war between herself and her husband to establish for once and for all just who was supposed to take care of whom. Lulu's mother had taken an overdose of sleeping pills (a tautology, in Lulu's opinion), and Lulu's father had survived her death as he had survived his life, by putting away half a bottle of gin every night before dinner and an equal amount of Scotch during and after (he never let beer or wine interfere with his drinking).

If Lulu and Nathan Shinefeld had forged a stronger bond, they might have been able to hold fast through the strains of suicide, boredom and an adolescence of which Lulu's sharpest memory was a scene in which she'd entered a marijuana-smoke-filled room pounding with music so loud as to bring tears to her eyes, faced half a dozen stoned adolescents (in this period Sascha seldom entered the house in other than wedge formation), shouted at Sascha to be heard above the music, shouted more frantically when Sascha ignored her, and had then become aware of her two infant sons, one a year and a half old, the other two years and three months, who had walked and crawled to a spot outside the door and were staring into the room as though their mother and Sascha were part of some exotic animal act.

What strong feelings were there that might hold Lulu and Nathan through these difficult times or, even more, through the *blah* times? Nathan's feelings for Sascha were actually stronger than his feelings for his own sons, but Sascha was gone now, and in truth, Lulu's sons seemed unaffected by either the storms or the lulls in the family. Almost from the beginning of their lives they seemed to have had that blessed sense that they were in this mess together, and the less they had to do with any of the grown-ups, the better off they'd be.

It wasn't sexual feeling that had brought Lulu and Nathan together nor did sexual jealousy drive them apart, although it seemed to Lulu that Nathan's adultery was of the meaner sort, not spurred by an oversupply of high spirit but by a desire for revenge against an imperfect wife and a recalcitrant daughter. Then again, it did appear that during this past decade, from 1965 to 1975, a decade just now beginning to go by the name of the sixties, a certain number of those rather *blah* families, not unhappy or happy but just suffering from an excess of real life, who in previous eras would have remained intact, instead came apart like the outer layers of some great package delivered to the world along with a warning note that a bomb was ticking under the surface of the nuclear family.

Besides, Nathan's girl had the clap.

And when all that was taken care of, when the penicillin was absorbed and the apologies more or less swallowed, what was left? They had no real life together except on Saturday nights with a few old friends. She couldn't even talk about her cases with him anymore; his responses were too predictable to be useful and his sense of humor—had he ever actually had one?—had been buried in an unmarked grave.

Lulu began picking theoretical arguments with him on subjects removed from her true concerns. She lost them the way she'd once lost chess games: After a classy start, she would become confused to realize that she'd provoked him out of a combination of sexual restlessness and aesthetic discontent, and then, impaled by her own insight, she would be unable to marshal her forces toward a triumphant end.

He didn't bother to get angry with her.

In the end they came apart because there wasn't even anger or nonsense between them.

The problem now was to believe that the separation had made some kind of sense, that she hadn't disrupted everyone's life (and finances) without getting closer to achieving a pleasant equilibrium for herself. It was difficult to accept that the end of a marriage that had given her so little, that had appeared to be so disconnected from her deeper self, had left her feeling depressed, disoriented, and devoid of sexual feeling.

In the past couple of months Bonnie had introduced her to three men with each of whom she'd gone through a similar experience: However well they originally concealed depression, at some point in the evening each would become aware of being in the company of another soul as needy yet as incapable of arousal or satisfaction as his or her self and then swiftly retreat, mentally if not physically, two masses of negative particles that might end up attached to anything but each other.

Lulu dried her feet on the grass, brushed off the sand, put on her sandals and walked slowly up the hill to the Mayers'.

By now there were close to a hundred people scattered around the grounds and clustered on the patio. More or less the usual. Duke's pals from the Institute, a couple of whom had also hung on to their first wives. Duke was scrupulous in his analytic connections but generous in his acceptance of casual friends, which was just as well, for Bonnie tended to attract a wide range of humans whom she was incapable of rejecting if it happened to turn out that they were dumb or crazy, though as a concession to Duke, she would save them for the big parties where they couldn't do much harm. There were Florence Klein and Hildegarde Rizzo of the No-Such-Thing-as-a-Vaginal-Orgasm Mafia. The man in plaid pants had an organic vegetable stand on Route 27 and played the cello with a middling good quartet during the winter.

Lulu's older son, Teddy, came over to announce that he and his brother were sleeping at the Mayers' after the party. She kissed the top of his head and he disappeared.

Nodding and smiling at the familiars, she moved swiftly toward the makeshift outdoor bar, where a lovely looking young man, who doubtless deplored what alcohol did to the temple of the body, was presiding over a large array of wine and beer and a small collection of hard liquor. Tossing a mental coin between prudence and the scant possibility of pleasure, Lulu asked for a dry gin martini on the rocks. An attractive gray-haired man came to the table, eyed Lulu for long enough to determine that she wasn't nineteen or gentile and could be safely assumed to be an enemy of his new life, poured a glass of wine for himself, and left quickly.

She asked for a few onions in her martini.

"You know," the bartender said earnestly, "it's not really called a martini if it has onions in it."

"No," she said just as earnestly, "that's not true. I know there are people who make that claim, but the real, honest-to-God truth is that if it has gin and vermouth in it, it's a martini."

They smiled at each other and Lulu moved away, first to the barbecue, where she picked up one of Duke's House Specials, a Monumental Charcoal-broiled Burger with Barbecue-soy Sauce in a Pita Pocket, and got into a conversation with Karen Turner, a friend of hers and Bonnie's, a lawyer who'd been left after fifteen years of a terrific marriage for a woman who looked so much like her as to have been her daughter—and indeed their ages were the only apparent difference between them. The new Mrs. Turner, with her husband's encouragement, had entered law school within six months of the birth of her first child, and Karen Turner had made a vow not to deal ever again with a man she could take half seriously. Though she'd been assured by her friends that she could date most of the available men of her own age without violating this policy, Karen had preferred to play it safe. Her current friend was the tennis pro at a local club during the summer and wintered in Acapulco. Karen, in turn, introduced Lulu to two couples, Charles and Anna Herman being the ones whose names she remembered, for she had seen him occasionally at professional meetings and knew that Karen and his wife were with the same law firm.

Anna Herman was a small, thin woman with a pretty face, long, dark hair, a tense, rather childlike voice, and the kind of no-nonsense manner that very small women assumed when they were determined to be taken seriously rather than to get by on a certain natural benevolence that accrued to them from men. She divided her time between the Civil Liberties Union and various private cases of social interest.

Charles Herman, M.D., a psychiatrist, was a large, red-haired, freckled and balding leprechaun with a belly that protruded over his wrinkled white ducks to what appeared to be the point of hazard and the air of trying constantly to control chaos by chopping it, karate style, with his hands. He undercut his wife's reasonable arguments on the subject of the insanity plea with a profusion of gestures and a series of sly jokes that Lulu might have found humorous had she not already decided that he was repulsive. Once or twice Lulu sensed that Charles Herman was mugging for her approval, but she wouldn't meet his eyes. His energy was threatening, his disorder suspect. If she wasn't interested in a gray merger with another depressed person, she was far from prepared to deal, even casually, with this large, sloppy gnome whose desires flapped in her face like red longjohns from a clothesline. She finished her martini and the House Special and moved back toward the bar. The drink had already begun to do its work.

"May I have another one of those?" she asked gravely.

"One martini with onions coming up," said the bartender, grinning.

She smiled. How sweet. He was flirting with her. Was he twenty-five years old? No. Closer to twenty. Well, what difference did that make? She had a kind of pleasant feeling that she hadn't had in a long time. Of course, she hadn't had a martini in a long time, either.

"But if I come back for another one," she said, "give me a glass of water and send me away."

"Oh, I couldn't do that," the young man said.

"Promise to try," Lulu said winsomely as he handed her the drink.

"Are you here with anyone?" he asked.

Lulu shook her head. "My kids. Or at least my kids are here and I'm here."

"You want to go to a party after this thing?"

Lulu grinned. "This thing is actually a party."

"Yeah." He grinned back. "You know what I mean. A real party. With music."

"Mmm," said Lulu, who loved to dance. "Maybe."

"My name is Brad," said the young man.

Lulu laughed. "Not really . . . Brad. Brad Gibson?"

"You know," Brad said, "you're actually a very attractive woman."

"Thank you," said Lulu, who was getting better looking as she aged, or so she liked to think. Not so much better looking. It was that her features had been too strong for a young girl, her energy threatening until she developed a poise that promised the world that she could control herself without help from the outside.

Lulu drained the glass and held it out to him.

He whistled softly. "Water?" he asked. "Or maybe a white-wine spritzer?"

"A white-wine spritzer," Lulu agreed readily. "That seems like a reasonable compromise."

"You haven't told me your name," Brad said.

"I know," Lulu replied, giggling. "That's because I feel silly."

She took the glass from him and, promising to find him later, moved away, down onto the grass, where a few people were having what appeared to be a spirited argument. Florence Klein was in the group, speaking angrily, gesticulating. And there in the middle, on a chaise longue, was Leif Seaver, whom Lulu hadn't seen since some time before Dawn Henley had become her patient. She had better be careful to listen and not speak; already she had that lovely, drink-induced sense that nothing that happened here could matter very much. Quietly she sat down at the fringes of the group, examining Seaver, but not really listening yet.

Leif Seaver had done pioneering work on middle-aged men and the fear of death that led them to abandon their families and begin younger, duplicate families that would allow them, as they looked around each day, to pretend that they were fifteen or twenty years younger than the mark at which reality placed them. He had written movingly of the misery of many of these men, cut off from their own histories and suffering terribly: finding themselves at social gatherings with twenty-year-olds for whom they represented, at best, a paterfamilias; jogging frantically to rid themselves of middle-aged flab; feeling embarrassed upon bumping into old friends; living, often, with a continuing sense of unreality. One such patient of Dr. Seaver's, a man highly esteemed in his profession and who had led an exemplary life, public and private, had, on the day he turned fifty, packed a suitcase, kissed his wife goodbye and moved to a hotel. Shortly after divorcing his wife, he had married a beautiful eighteen-year-old model and not long after that had suffered multiple fractures during a brawl at a discotheque when he tried to beat up a nineteen-year-old boy who made a pass at his new wife.

Another patient had been compared by Seaver to the hero of that brilliant movie, *Seconds,* in which the tired, middle-aged hero gives every cent he has to lose his suburban-husband identity. A flabby, white-haired man has plastic surgery, loses weight and does body-building exercises. His hair is dyed, his vocal cords are cut, and his fingerprints erased. He comes out of it all looking and sounding like Rock Hudson and finds that his inner self was anchored to his outer being more securely than he'd ever realized, and that he has lost his very self in the rejuvenation process. A woman to whom he is drawn turns out to be, like himself, a "second." A particularly haunting scene in the movie was one in which the hero returns to his suburban home, hoping against hope that his wife will recognize him, and of course being disappointed.

In fact, Lulu had noticed, this was a problem men didn't face with their first wives, who actually became one point of a triangle that duplicated the early years of their first marriages, when there was a young bride waiting at home and a "mother" left behind, missing them terribly. There was also some evidence, also not discussed by Seaver, to suggest that in finding a young girl, these men were trying to retrieve the lovely young mother remembered from the years of their most intense Oedipal attachment.

In any event, Leif Seaver, having completed his work on the subject, had ditched his wife and four children for a hot-eyed, thirty-year-old graduate student who was charming, intelligent and able to move with assurance in academic circles. Nothing to laugh at in the obvious sense. Not one of those pathetic cases that made you wonder if the guy was interested in sex or just in breaking and entering. Nothing, really, to laugh at, at all. They had a two-year-old daughter and Mrs. Seaver was pregnant again. That was Mrs. Seaver sitting on the grass next to her husband's chaise longue, her little girl asleep in what remained of her mother's lap.

AUGUST

Lulu sighed. There were times when she could wax analytic-philosophical about it all, others when she couldn't help but take it personally. Sometimes she knew it ill became her, a woman who'd left her husband when her boys were seven and eight years old, to condemn the male sex for parallel behavior. But after all, she'd left Nathan Shinefeld because she thought he was an awful schmuck; it wasn't possible, unless it was essential, to live with someone you thought that of. These men were leaving women who were often, by the men's own admission, more than satisfactory wives. For women, this epidemic lent to the aging process a sense of doom beyond its normal difficulties and humiliations. Women looked at a gray-haired man and saw father; men looked at a gray-haired woman and ran from death.

Lulu found one of her hands fussing with her hair and smiled sadly to herself. She had just seen the first gray hairs at her temples. She would look distinguished—like the vice-president of a bank. Small comfort for the loss of color that was more painful than wrinkles or the rear-end spread that she could no longer get rid of just by eating lightly for a week. Along about this age some women with dark hair like hers began to dye it, others began to grow blond; even if it was impossible to blame them, the results were often bizarre. Nor was it easy to know when you ceased to look as though it might be natural and began to look as though you might be insane.

Florence Klein was making a case for the inability of male analysts to treat female patients properly. It was Seaver, clearly, with whom Florence was angry;

53

Lulu wondered if the other woman managed not to know that Seaver was an attractive man, for all his lumps and bumps, as Dawn had called them.

"Even when they think they want to understand, they can't afford to," Florence was saying. "They're too afraid of losing their balls!"

Of course, it was possible to express this thought in a way that suggested it was a legitimate aspiration of men to hold on to their balls. With this acknowledged, you might enter upon a reasonable discussion of the difficulties.

Who was it who had said that a normal person need not recognize his or her own madness because it had been deeded to the surround?

Unless Lulu was mistaken it was a male. Joel Kovel. Writing on the parallels between the subjugation of blacks and of women for overlapping if not identical reasons.

Seaver was bored. If they'd been standing, he would have drifted away by now, but he was comfortable on the chaise, with his young wife and his sleeping daughter close by.

The corollary, Kovel said, was that reality held deposits of crystallized madness that it imposed upon the developing individual.

A fairly high proportion of Lulu's patients consisted of developing individuals. Developing female individuals of whom it was clear that the insanities of the Now culture had combined with the insanities of the Then cultures to eat like acid at their unevolved souls.

Seaver was saying, with what degree of earnestness or good will it was difficult to judge, that it seemed to him that a lot of women wanted it both ways. They'd greeted with pleasure the discoveries that everyone had been a woman to begin with, that boys began life in full identification with their mothers. Yet they weren't willing to grant that if that were the case, men might contain within themselves the knowledge of what it was to be one.

Surely this was a piece of sophistry when he knew (he had to know, didn't he?) that the boy's first sense of full identification was based on non-knowing, and that the early forms of learning, of making order out of the chaos of infancy, were intimately bound up with the process of sorting himself out from the woman who'd once seemed to be him. Would Seaver laugh knowingly if she said something like this, or did it only seem elementary because she was drunk?

"Anyway," Lulu heard herself saying, "that might not be the main issue."

The group, not having heard her voice until now, waited.

"The main issue may have more to do with the nature of the transference." She was speaking to Seaver although she was trying to avoid doing just that. "You know. In what happens to the patient simply by virtue of being in a room with a male analyst, who becomes father, or a female, who becomes mother."

"It's my experience," Seaver said, "that the analyst becomes both the mother and father."

"It's not my experience," Lulu said.

"Is that true?" Seaver asked with interest.

Lulu nodded, sipped at her spritzer, which was nearly finished.

"It's my experience," she said, "and I know it's true of at least some other women analysts, that as soon as a patient feels herself—I assume we're dealing only with females at the moment—in the grip of the transference, she often begins searching frantically for a male in her life, or toys with the idea of a male analyst, or holds on to a husband she went into analysis to get the courage to shed. Not because she likes him more but to keep some sort of balance of power."

"So you're suggesting that she's willing to cede to a man but not to a woman the power to be all things to her."

"At least sometimes. There may be others where the same struggle is experienced with a man."

"But you think that generally speaking, to be in helpless thrall to a woman is more dangerous. Comes too close to the earliest stages of helplessness."

Lulu nodded.

"And if I argue that a great many women seem eager to do just that, to place themselves in thrall, so to speak, you'll argue that they're more eager to do it with a man."

Lulu nodded.

Seaver was silent. That he would even listen to the argument was a sign of self-assurance; most of everyone's patients were female, after all, and few male analysts were eager to consider the possibility that their sex made them less than the optimal doctors for those patients.

Lulu stood up a bit rockily. It was quite dark. The new Mrs. Seaver's head rested on her husband's thigh very much as her daughter's head rested on her own. She was probably asleep. She was much too happy now, with her lovely daughter and the baby inside her, to become absorbed in such issues. In any issues. Give her some time. (It was impossible to separate the philosophical from the vengeful in this thought.) Leif Seaver had seldom been seen at parties when he was married to his first wife, an attractive and intelligent woman. Once he'd written a humorous piece for *The New Yorker,* published under another name, about the incestuous world of the New York analyst and how it affected his pleasure in parties, ending with a charming admission that he'd always hated parties, anyway.

Lulu looked over to the bar, where business had slowed and Brad Gibson was looking restless. He caught her watching him and came over to take her glass and get her another spritzer, whispering that he thought he'd be able to leave pretty soon.

Why, for Christ's sake, should she be embarrassed? Were her kids watching? Why should she care if anyone else noticed? The new Mrs. Seaver was probably more intelligent than this handsome young man, but really, was that what the whole affair had been about? The night was getting chilly and the word *patriarchy* was floating around in the group, but beside Lulu, Brad the handsome young bartender stood shedding heat. She herself felt considerably warmer, more alive, than she'd felt in some time. Was it only two martinis and some wine that she'd required in all these months?

Lulu giggled. "Are you going to be a patriarch when you grow up?" she whispered to Brad, at once marveling at her own seductiveness and feeling pleased with the growing darkness that gave it some cover.

"Actually," Brad said, "I'm going to be a chemical engineer. But I'm going to do it without growing up."

There was the crystallized madness, or one of the crystals, of Sascha's generation. Since it was no longer possible to foresee any advantage in growing up, most of them had decided not to do it. The madness was only in thinking that if you escaped life, you escaped death.

"How old are you, Brad?" she asked, then realized she'd only asked him because she was thinking of Sascha. "Never mind. Don't answer that. Let's just go to your party."

3

AUGUST HAD BEEN okay, Dawn told the doctor. She'd spent a lot of time moving around, visiting people. Keeping busy. She hadn't had time to make prints, as she'd planned. At the beginning of September, Vera had driven Dawn and her belongings down to the Barnard dormitory, where she was now settled. In her first sessions she spoke of matters connected to her move to Manhattan, to school, and to her social life. She was willing to lie down but had little to talk about when she did, the exception being Dr. Seaver and the abortion she had forced herself to endure in July. It was not until the approach of the winter holiday season that signs of anxiety became clearer.

Dawn was trying to decide which of the boys she was dating she liked best so she could go through the season with him. What she really wanted, she said, was to find someone with a vacation plan so compelling as to prevent her from visiting either Vera or Tony. If Tony's home was the less depressing, Dawn didn't feel like spending the entire holiday with Len Silverstein, who was sweet but terribly quiet, or with his two daughters, one of whom was really obnoxious. Dawn wanted a boyfriend with a warm, jolly family that filled up the house.

Vera was the only living member of her generation of the Henleys. When they had all been together, this hadn't mattered. It was only after the divorce—no, it must have been when she was describing holidays to Dr. Seaver—that it had suddenly seemed strange to Dawn that for most of her life she'd had perfectly lovely holiday dinners with three people at the table.

Last year she'd gone to Chanukah at the Gartners', and that had been fun. Alan and Bevvy had warned her that it would be horrendous—too many cousins and aunts and uncles, too much noise, too much food. But none of it had bothered her. It was going to the deadness of Vera's afterward that had bothered her. Vera wasn't even interested in skiing anymore. Dawn couldn't say that she was looking forward to winter the way she usually did. Maybe it was because she herself didn't feel like skiing. Nothing to do with Vera. The second accident had undermined her faith in herself. She'd had a dream in which she skied off the edge of a mountain and the mountain suddenly wasn't there anymore.

Dr. Shinefeld wanted to talk about the dream but Dawn wanted to talk about the doctor's holiday plans. Or at least if Dr. Shinefeld took a vacation or kept on working. The doctor said she took ten days at Christmas, a week in February, then Easter vacation.

"Like the school holidays or the Jewish holidays?"

"They tend to overlap considerably. Especially in New York."

"You do have children. I knew it."

The doctor was silent.

"I don't mind, really. At least, I don't think I do. Not the way I minded with Dr. Seaver ... I'd mind if I was expecting you and you couldn't come because of them. At the end of summer that might be too much. The first time Dr. Seaver went away ... I don't think it'll be as bad with you ... In July, before you, I had Alan. And Bevvy. I wanted them to go away except I needed them. The abortion. I don't like that word, there's something ... I can't stand to think of it as a baby. A fetus is different. Don't you think? I need to believe it's not the same. I can feel that it's not. I couldn't stand to think of killing a baby but this didn't feel like a baby. Someone you'd never seen. Not that it felt wonderful, but it wasn't as bad as it would've been ... Except, then, why did I need to have an accident and see someone again? It wasn't just Vera. The accident was Vera's reason for me to see someone but I didn't mind the accident that much. I kept having dreams about kittens. Kittens in swimming pools. Kittens in baskets. The one in the pool—there was a mother cat, too. Sort of holding up the kitten. Keeping it from drowning ... I'm terrified of the water but I'm such a good swimmer that no one ever knows it. The kitten had all different colors in its fur. Brown and white and a few red hairs here and there. Like Dr. Seaver. Maybe you don't know that he has red hairs in his beard. I don't know if you ever... You told me you knew him but you didn't say how well... I need to know."

"Why?"

"I don't know. Because I want to know if you talk to him about me."

"No, I don't," the doctor said. "It's not my practice to talk with other analysts about my patients unless I arrange to consult with one for that purpose."

"Oh, but it would be all right with me," Dawn assured her. "As a matter of fact, I'd like it. I like to think of the two of you... sitting around in the evening, talking about me." She giggled. "That's what I was seeing. The two of you sitting in front of the fireplace in Vermont... I can't believe it, it's too perfect! My mommy shrink and my daddy shrink, sitting there together in our house."

"Tell me more about it."

"Well, I'm not sure I want to do that. I'd rather just fix it where it is."

"Why's that?"

"Because it's too good. And because... I don't know what you might do next. It's all very well for the two of you to sit around and talk about me. But next thing you know... I wouldn't want the two of you to go off together someplace."

"Like where?"

"Oh, you know. Not just the bedroom. Anyplace... If I thought you saw Dr. Seaver regularly I'd be horribly jealous."

"Because of what might happen between us?"

"Because of what *was* happening between you."

"Which would be?"

"That you were *seeing* him. And *hearing* him. That you could *talk* to him and he could hear *you*. I can't stand to think that anyone's doing that. Except maybe at his regular sessions."

"That would be all right?"

"It would be a little bit all right. Because then I would know that they didn't exist, either. I would feel sorry for them because someday he's going to do the same thing to them."

The doctor was silent.

"If I thought you were really going away with him on vacation," Dawn said, "I wouldn't be able to talk about it at all. I'd just lie here and cry until I choked to death."

~

This remark heralded a period in which Dawn did virtually no analytic work but became thoroughly absorbed in her social life. She spent the Christmas vacation with a boy named Rob Grace, whom she'd been dating for a while and whose father had a lodge near Sugarbush. On New Year's Day, she and Rob drove to Marbury and spent the night with Vera. Dawn returned from Vermont with a sketch of the doctor that she'd done while she was there.

"Don't ask me why I put glasses on you," she said. "My hand did it without me."

Dawn hesitated. She'd been sitting on the edge of the couch but now she lay down.

Silence.

Dawn burst into tears.

"I feel as though you're angry with me!" she sobbed.

"I feel as though *you're* angry with *me*," the doctor replied.

"That's not true," Dawn cried. "I'm not angry. If you think I'm angry, then you don't know how I really feel."

"All right. How do you really feel?"

"I don't know. Until I got here, I thought I was fine, and now I know I haven't been fine the whole time, I was just holding my breath until I could get here. And that makes me—" She cut off her words. "I know what you're thinking. You're thinking I was going to say it makes me angry, but . . . I was going to say it makes me scared . . . Rob has this terrific father. I might as well tell you that right away and get it over with. Tom Grace. He's divorced. Well, I don't know if he's legally divorced, but he hasn't lived with his wife since Rob was little. He has a girlfriend but I don't think he likes her much. He flirted with me. I felt guilty in front of Rob. He asked me for my phone number and I gave it to him, but I kept wondering what you would think. He's not that old. Maybe your age. Whatever that is. No, I guess he's older. He must be more than forty if Rob's twenty-one. Anyway, the most important thing is, he's lots of fun. Jolly. He calls himself a plain old businessman but he isn't. He's an international art dealer. Always hopping off to Rome, or Paris, or Amsterdam . . . Compared to him, Rob is—well, he's a boy, of course. Sweet. You know I like him. But he's dull. Kind of quiet. Morose, even."

"I'll bet he's morose," Dr. Shinefeld said. "With a jolly father who makes time with his girlfriends."

"No," Dawn said. "He wasn't that way because of the weekend. He's that way all the time. And he hasn't lived with his father since ...Maybe we'd better not talk about them. Him. I don't want to hear anything bad. I'll probably never hear from him, anyway, so it won't matter."

"Wishes matter."

"You mean the wish to hear from him? Well, I want to hear from him, all right. And I hardly ever care one way or the other if I'm going to hear from someone."

Her voice had a defiant tone. Dr. Shinefeld was assumed to disapprove. Already the doctor regretted her impulsive comment the moment before.

"Do you think I shouldn't have anything to do with Tom?"

"I have no idea."

"You've already said something bad about him."

"My remark had to do with Rob's feelings."

"I thought you were saying more than that."

"If I was, then I shouldn't have been. I know nothing about him."

"He's the most interesting man I've met," said Dawn. "Except for my English professor, who's married. Tom isn't married," she repeated uncertainly. "At least he hasn't lived with his wife in years... He's going to South America in a couple of weeks. He said he'd call when he got back. In April, he's going to Paris. I kept thinking, wouldn't it be nice if I had something special to do the next time Dr. Shinefeld goes away. He reminds me of you, a little. I'm not sure why. His glasses." She laughed. "I don't know why I said that. I know perfectly well you don't wear glasses." She twisted around on the couch to look at the doctor's face. "Do you?"

"No."

"Then what's that about?... Tony and Vera both wear glasses now, but they never used to. Vera didn't until a few years ago. When I see Vera in my mind, I don't see her with glasses. No. Wait a minute. There she is and she does have them. Tortoiseshell." Dawn shook her head as though to get rid of a fly. "I feel funny. This has never happened to me before."

"What's never happened?"

"I'm confused. But over something I've never even thought about before. Dr. Seaver wears tortoiseshell glasses. Alan and Bevvy wear glasses. Sally Fleury, in Marbury... I don't know what I'm doing. I feel like a real nut. Professor Thornbush wears glasses. D'you think more people get glasses when they're older or stop wearing them?"

"What do you think?"

"I don't know. I guess, well, Tony and Vera both did when they got older. It's funny, when I said that about Vera, I felt as if it wasn't true. But I know it is. After Sugarbush I got interested in the whole question of glasses. I told you Tom wears glasses and Rob doesn't, didn't I? But they really look quite a bit alike, except Tom's better looking because he's older, you know, his face has some character. Aside from that, the one with glasses and the one without them, there was something weird about it. When we got to Vera's, almost right away I went up to the attic to look at photos. No. Not the attic. I don't know why I

66

said that. When I was little Vera used to store a lot of stuff in the attic, but then after Tony left Vera made Tony's workroom into a storage room, and that's where everything is now. I spent a lot of time looking at photos. I've never done it before. I've got pictures of Vera pretty far back and she wasn't wearing glasses in any of them."

"How far back?"

"What do you mean?"

"How far back do the pictures go?"

"I don't know. All the way, I guess."

"Are there any from when you were a baby?"

"No," Dawn said. "Of course not. I wasn't with her when I was a baby. I mean, I was almost two years old when I went to live with Vera. Why did you ask me that?"

"I just wondered."

"The pictures of me when I was a baby are up in the attic . . . with my birth parents' things." Dawn laughed. "Birth parents. I picked that up from a girl at Sidley who was adopted. She had her adopted parents and her birth parents. Or adopting. How did we get started on this, anyway?"

"We were talking about photos."

"Oh, yes. Well, they're in different places. Vera's photographs are in one place, with Tony's, except that Tony took most of them when she left. And Gordon and Miranda's pictures are in another—Do you know who I mean when I say Gordon and Miranda?"

"Your birth parents?"

"Right."

Dawn was visibly relieved that the doctor was willing

to adopt her locution device. Or her circumlocution device.

"All their belongings, Gordon's and Miranda's, all their small things—photographs, letters, books—are in trunks in the attic. I mean, they're not hidden away, exactly. You can get to them if you want to. But they're not convenient, like the stuff in Tony's room."

The doctor waited to see whether Dawn would find it necessary to specify whether she ever bothered to go to the attic to look at the pictures.

"I can imagine going to bed with Tom but not with Rob," Dawn said suddenly, then laughed.

"Oh?"

"Don't ask me why."

"Why not?"

"I meant to be funny. I know it's your job to ask . . . It's because I can imagine being comfortable with him. I'm not talking about sex. I'm talking about lying down with someone, having them just cuddle you. Rob's so eager. All over me. Or he would be, if I let him. Awkward. I can't imagine . . . He wouldn't even know what he was doing. Well, maybe he would, but I don't feel . . . This is a stupid conversation."

Silence.

"Do you know what I think I'm going to do? I think I'm going to use that sketch to make a pastel. Then, if that works out, maybe I'll go on to an oil."

JANUARY WAS LOST to analysis. She was, Dawn informed the doctor, a nervous wreck. She'd just let her schoolwork go. She didn't know why except she suspected it had something to do with Dr. Shinefeld. Where once her week had been organized around going to school, now it revolved around her sessions and she couldn't concentrate in school. She was going to fail at least two courses. She'd never gotten anything worse than a B before, even when she was doing home study! Maybe she would have to drop the analysis. Or school. She missed two or three sessions in a last-ditch (successful) attempt to get in a paper for the third course she'd been worried about failing. But after turning in the paper, she was edgier than before. It might get her through but it wasn't good work. Dr. Shinefeld was interested in what it was about analysis that made concentration difficult, but Dawn only wanted to discuss this from a procedural, or behavioral, point of view. A friend at school was seeing a shrink who was modifying his behavior. Making him stop smoking, and so on. Maybe that was what she needed right now. Or maybe Dr. Shinefeld did that sort of thing in addition to regular psychoanalysis? Analysis was all very well and good if only the doctor could make her behave and do her schoolwork at the same time everything else was going on.

It was the last week of January.

"Speaking of behavior," Dawn said, "Dawn's father—I mean, Rob's father—is coming home from Brazil next week. I just got a postcard. He mailed it when he got there, but it was just delivered. I'm not seeing Rob anymore. I told him there was someone else. And there is. He saw me going to the movies with someone this Saturday. Rob'll never even need to know, unless..."

"Unless?"

"No. Nothing." She swiveled around and sat up. "I can't get over the feeling that you're mad at me."

"Talk about it."

"I just did. I feel as if you disapprove of me and Tom Grace."

"First of all," the doctor pointed out, "there is not yet such a thing as you and Tom Grace. While you anticipate a—"

She stopped speaking because Dawn looked as though her face had been slapped. Or—closer—as though the ground she had been standing on had shifted.

70

"I don't mean to suggest that you are not at the beginning of a friendship with Tom Grace. I am simply trying to get you to consider some of the fantasies attached to it. If we can look at your expectations together, we might find, for example, that they are so high as to endanger a reasonable friendship. That's not something you've generally done with boyfriends. On the other hand, you don't talk about Tom Grace the way you—"

"You're right," Dawn said suddenly. "You're absolutely right. That's just what I was about to do. Oh God, I'm so glad you said that!"

Dr. Shinefeld wasn't sure that *she* was glad. She had fallen into that perennial trap, trying to save a patient from getting hurt, and only time would tell where the balance of usefulness lay.

"Now you don't sound as if you dislike him," Dawn said. "You wouldn't if you met him, you know. I wish I could bring him here. I mean, if we get to be— Whoops! I'm doing it again. I've got to psych myself to feel as independent with him as I do with the others."

"Why do you think you don't?"

Dawn thought about it. "Because he's older. He makes me feel young."

"How young?"

"Oh, you know, like a little kid."

"And that feels nice."

"Well, sure. I mean, if I felt like some awful, whiny little kid, I wouldn't like that. But this is a happy little kid. Like when Tony and Vera took me to the Common in Boston and to the Ritz-Carlton for blueberry muffins. Do you know the park with the swan boats? When I was little, I had a book about a duck family that used to swim around in that lake. When I went there, it was a dream come true . . . The last day we were at Sugarbush I slept late and Rob went out on the slopes with Roz. When I woke up Tom was having coffee and reading some magazine articles. About Indian art. For his trip to South America. We had coffee together and sat there talking for I don't know how long. I was *happy*, d'you know?" Her voice had grown wistful. "I was happy in a way that I haven't been for a long time. I was happy that way when I was with Dr. Seaver."

"When else?"

Dawn considered. "Never, really. Well, an occasional holiday with Vera and Tony. But even at home . . . There were moments, but not long periods of . . . I was all right. But I wasn't happy. Do you know what I mean?"

"Yes."

"Thank goodness. I need you to understand . . . I wouldn't really stop coming here, you know. I need you. But I just . . . That's the problem, you see. I can't need you that much. I can't have this office be the only place in the world, the way it was with Dr. Seaver. Before you went away, I was afraid I was going crazy. I really don't know what would have happened to me if I came back and you weren't here. I would—"

'Yes?"

"I don't know. That's what I can't stand to think about. It's too awful to—" Dawn's words were interrupted by a cough that gradually became more severe, racking her body. She stood up, grabbed some tissues from a box on the doctor's table, and began walking rapidly around the office, as though she could escape the spasms. Finally she stopped moving, but the cough continued. Her body was bent over, close to convulsion. When she looked up, her eyes were frightened. The doctor went to Dawn and put an arm around her, holding her firmly. Dawn looked at her wildly, then began coughing up phlegm into the tissues clenched in her hand. Suddenly she threw off the doctor's arms as though they were restraining rather than supporting her. The doctor stood back. Dawn began to heave and finally to throw up. She kneeled on the floor. When her stomach was empty, her body continued to heave. Then she was still. She remained in a kneeling position, staring down at the vomit on the rug as though it were tea leaves that told the future. Or the past.

She looked up at the doctor with dull eyes. She looked back at the rug. After quite a long time, she signaled to the doctor that she wanted the box of tissues. Then the wastebasket, with its plastic-bag liner. Slowly, meticulously, she cleaned up the vomit, dropping the tissues in the basket as she finished with them. She was beyond embarrassment. When she had cleaned up as well as she could she took the plastic bag from the basket, knotted it, and held it out to the doctor.

"That's all right," the doctor said. "Just leave it in the basket."

Dawn replaced the bag, went to the couch, lay down, and instantly, or so it appeared, fell asleep.

The doctor allowed her to sleep for the remainder of the hour. When the next patient buzzed, the doctor said Dawn's name in a low voice, then went to the couch and gently shook her shoulder. There was no response.

"Dawn," Dr. Shinefeld said gently, although the girl still appeared to be in a deep sleep, "I have to ask you to wake up now."

Gradually, Dawn came to life. Her eyelids moved, then her mouth quivered, then the rest of her body made an effort at motion. She sat up, but she was still groggy.

"I'm sorry to awaken you," the doctor said, "but the next patient is here. I think it would be good for you to rest awhile in the waiting room."

From her satchel Dawn took a pencil and a notebook. Once she'd opened the book, she stared at the blank page for a moment. Then she wrote on it, tore out the page, and handed it to the doctor. It read: "I'm all right but I can't talk. I'm afraid I'll choke again."

While the doctor was looking at the note, Dawn collected her belongings and stood up.

"I really think you should stay for a few minutes," the doctor said.

At the door, Dawn turned as though she were going to speak, changed her mind, reached for her notebook, again changed her mind. Then she turned and went out to the powder room. A few minutes later, when Dr. Shinefeld opened the door to greet her next patient, Dawn was sitting in another chair in the waiting room. Her eyes were closed, and she appeared to be asleep.

◠

Soon after his return from Brazil, Dawn entered into an affair with Tom Grace. She was high a great deal of the time. In her analysis, she was willing to touch on and even associate freely to important issues that had been held at bay by her anxiety over being dependent on Dr. Shinefeld. For the first time in many weeks she spoke of the disastrous ending to her first analysis.

"I don't know," said Dawn, who often began her most telling monologues in that fashion. "Sometimes I think the trouble began when Dr. Seaver moved. A year, maybe two, before we finished. You know, he lived in this beautiful brownstone, with his office on the ground floor and the kids and dogs—everybody— upstairs. Then suddenly they moved to this bachelor apartment. No, I don't know how big it was, but it was different in a bad way. It was way over on the East Side, and all modern. It didn't have a family feeling anymore. Maybe the family was in a separate place. Vera and Tony were the only ones who knew I saw Dr. Seaver. He was a secret. I looked the same as ever, but something was happening to me. I loved to go to the first house. There were two gardens. A little one in front and a big one in the back. I could see it when I was lying on the couch. It reminded me of... There was a little greenhouse bay window in his office, looking out on the back garden. Sometimes I wanted to be one of his flowers and stay on a shelf in that window. It wasn't an office, it was a home. The new place, the room with the couch, had all the same stuff. Almost as though he was trying to *prove* it was the same. When it wasn't. Everything but that room was different. Modern, cold, sterile. Like a real doctor's office. And First Avenue! First Avenue's a whole different place! It's no place to—" She broke off with a laugh. "I was going to say it's no place to raise kids. That sounds weird but I'll tell you . . . I think I felt as though we were making a baby togeth-er and the baby was *me*. The real me. The real Dawn Henley was going to come out of it all. Not exactly come out. Stay in. Because the problem was never on the outside, it was inside . . . Sometimes I think I have no insides at all. Or the pieces are there but they're . . . that's what they are, bits and pieces. May-be that's why I got pregnant. I was making a baby to take the place of the one we were going to make that wasn't finished. The Dawn baby. Who wasn't ever going to get finished. When I didn't have the baby inside me anymore, I felt as if I had nothing inside. Or it was shattered. And I wanted to shatter my outsides so he could see the real me again. Dr. Seaver was the first one who saw that there were pieces that had to be put together. But then he stopped seeing and they began to come apart again." She was crying. "They began to come apart as soon as he said we'd finish someday, but then when it was really the end . . . I'll never understand how he could have done that to me. There's something . . . I think it reminded me of the divorce. Except that I didn't come home to a new place. Tony had moved but Vera was still in the house. It was more empty and quiet than ever. She brought down some new furni-ture from the attic so the rooms wouldn't look empty

Richard Ferry

where Tony had taken her things. But it wasn't modern furniture, it was from the attic. For all I know it could've been. No. But—"

"Could've been what?"

"Oh, I was going to say it could've been from my birth parents. I mean, it was up there, along with the trunks full of pictures and stuff. But I don't think so. Anyway, what difference does it make?"

"What difference did Dr. Seaver's furniture make?"

"But that was a whole other matter! Every piece of furniture he had was full of *him!* I knew where everything was in the old room and the new room. I knew how he sat in his chair. When you talk about the old furniture . . . you're talking about two people I didn't even know!"

"Ever?"

"Not that I can remember. I mean, I tried once or twice with Dr. Seaver. I tried to see if I had any old memories. Past Tony and Vera. But I just didn't."

Her manner suggested that since she had no memories of it, there had been no such time.

"Tell me about Dr. Seaver's furniture," the doctor said.

"His chair," Dawn said slowly. "That's the most important thing. The chair. The couch was mine but the chair was his. It looked . . . lonely . . . when he wasn't sitting in it. *The Lonely Chair.* That's what I called one of the lithographs. It was a beautiful chair. Very deep and comfortable. Brown leather. Very glossy. Sometimes I thought it got polished. It swiveled, but it also rocked. It was sort of the chair in the lithograph, except it wasn't. The one in the print was old-fashioned. Wood. And the corner of the couch was in it, too. Then there's another one of Venetian blinds. It's funny. Hard to describe. You'd have to see it."

"I'd like to see the lithographs sometime."

Dawn's head turned.

"You mean that?"

"Yes."

"You want me to bring them in?"

"If you want to."

Dawn laughed. "That's really funny. Because of the whole business with Dr. Seaver...I assumed you'd have the same...Would you ever tell me if you thought he did something wrong?"

"Probably. But it's difficult to judge."

"I believe you, but it's hard to imagine...I guess I see you as sort of a matched set. And one of you's not about to tell me..." She laughed. "Unless you got divorced. I mean, that's when I heard Tony's complaints about Vera. When she left. What does that mean? I feel as if you'll tell me about Dr. Seaver if you get divorced." Another laugh. "You know, I don't even know if you're *married*. I asked about your children, but I never asked...You have so many rings on your finger that I can't tell if one of them's a wedding ring."

It was impossible for Dr. Shinefeld not to recall at that moment that Nathan Shinefeld had once made the same comment.

"Of course," Dawn said, "you could really be married to him. You could have kept your own name. There's no law that says that wasn't you sometimes over my head in that brownstone. Running after the little kids. Baking bread. I don't know if she baked

78

bread. My picture is . . . I don't think Dr. Seaver's wife works. I think she stays home and takes care of the kids. . . . Sometimes I think I'll go crazy if I can't find out about your life. Other times it doesn't seem to matter at all."

"Actually," the doctor said, "it appears that you don't mind the idea of my being married to Dr. Seaver as long as we stay with you. Or, let's say, as long as I'm in the kitchen and you're downstairs talking to him."

*

Dawn seemed to forget about the lithographs. Indeed, in the ensuing weeks any issue that wasn't visibly about Tom Grace seemed to get lost. Dr. Shinefeld encouraged her to talk about her lover, or at any rate did nothing to divert her attention, though sporadically Dawn would exclaim that the doctor should be making her do her schoolwork instead of encouraging her to fool around with Tom.

"Encouraging you?" the doctor asked. "How am I doing that?"

"Well, you sure aren't *discouraging* me."

"No," the doctor said. "I don't conceive of it as my place to do either."

"Your place. That sounds funny. Now what is your place, exactly? Somewhere between the desk and the flowerpots. Or between me and Tom. I don't have the vaguest idea of what I mean by that."

"Why don't you talk about it for a while?"

"Don't feel like it. I'd rather show you . . ." She rummaged around in her satchel and brought out a

79

large envelope with a photograph of the view from Tom Grace's apartment overlooking Central Park. Lovely, almost Japanese in quality, it showed the lake surrounded by trees in that state where their leaves were about to open and every branch had a fuzzy green aura.

"Isn't it beautiful?" she asked dreamily. "Sometimes I just sit and look out of the window until he comes home. Sometimes I think I could spend the rest of my life just looking out of that window. If he were with me, of course."

To talk about making love with Tom as though it were the same act as it was with Alan would be ludicrous. Until now, Dawn said, she hadn't really known what sex was about. She described her erotic experiences with a kind of tense gaiety, occasionally pausing to ask, "Is that usual?" or "Have you ever heard of that before?" Sometimes it seemed that her life was, so to speak, a whirl of Jacuzzis.

$\curvearrowright$

As Easter approached, Dawn was spared any separation anxieties regarding the doctor because Tom was taking her to Paris. She was nearly feverish with excitement and, upon her return, described their ten days together as the great fairy tale of her life. Tom was talking about going to Japan this summer, and while it would be very exciting if he could take her, she didn't believe she could ever again have so magical a time as her ten days in Paris.

School was, well, school was going to be a disaster. She was going to end up with almost no credits from her first year unless she pulled herself together quickly. The truth was that she learned more from one of Tom's impromptu lectures on art than she'd gotten from her first two semesters at Barnard.

She was considering going up to Vermont to explain to Vera, as well as she could, what had happened to her this year. She would say that she'd needed to have her fling in the city before settling down. She did feel guilty about Vera's spending all that money for nothing and didn't know how Vera would react when she heard that the money had virtually been thrown away. Dawn would have gone to Vermont already except that Tom had no desire to meet Vera, and the thought of a weekend without Tom...The truth was, she didn't care about school right now. If Tom asked her to marry him, or even to live with him, she'd pick up her belongings and move down to his place and stay home and cook and clean and for that matter have babies...Rob, by the way, seemed to have known for a while.

She was staying around New York this summer, of course. Tom shared a house in Southampton with two other successful men, a TV producer and, would you believe, a straight male model, and she looked forward to spending some time out there. If he went to Japan and China, she could only pray that he'd take her. At first she'd sort of assumed he would, but lately, well, he'd had some business problems and he wasn't sure.

The quality of Dawn's euphoria began to change after that April vacation, but it wasn't until May that her happiness turned into a visible, pervasive anxiety. At first she spoke of that anxiety as being about school, about how she would tell Vera, about the conference with her school adviser at which she would have to persuade him to give her another chance. Maybe she should go to summer school and try to make up some of the credits she hadn't earned during the year.

The truth finally emerged toward the end of May because Dawn was too frightened to contain it any longer.

"I'm turning him off. I can't stand to say it. I can't stand that I'm *doing* it. But I am and I can't help myself. I'm clinging to him like a baby and he can't stand it and I can't stand it and I can't stop. He's told me straight out. I love him. He's so absolutely honest about everything. He said when he met me I was so extraordinarily independent he couldn't get over it. He said beautiful women are worse than others because we're not used to doing things for ourselves, someone always wants to do them for us. But every time he called me 'babes' he used to think of what a baby I *wasn't*, and now I've turned into one right in front of his eyes. When he's out of my sight I can't think of anything except when he'll come back. It began when he mentioned Japan the first time. I couldn't tell if he was planning to take me, and I asked him and he said sure, if it worked out that way. But just knowing he planned the trip without me, that is, it isn't crucial whether I go or not...six weeks...He could be away for six weeks and I couldn't be away from him on purpose for six hours...That was when I started looking at the front door every time he went through it. Having trouble breathing if he was late coming home. Of course I turned him off. It's all my own fault. I'm a horrible drag on his life. It's a miracle he hasn't kicked me out already. I think he's waiting for the vacation. He has to let me see him sometimes or I'll...I'll wait on the park bench if I have to and...I don't know what I'm talking about. I think I'll probably kill myself if he leaves me. Why not? He's the center of my life. If he leaves me I'll have nothing in the center. Why should I live? For school? To come here? Continue to live so you can come to a shrink who persuades you that you have a reason to live? Who would know the difference if I died? Vera's got her bottle and Tony's got her husband. I don't have any real friends. You'd never know the difference if I disappeared from the face of the earth. You'd just get someone else to fill my space. That girl who was waiting the day I came out, the day I choked..." This was her first reference to the event. "She looked as though she was in a big hurry. She'd probably love to come an hour earlier. She's busy. Not like me. I have nothing to do but come here."

Dawn continued in this vein for most of the hour, venting her hatred of herself and her rage at everyone else in the world—except Tom Grace. Finally, she lay spent.

"You knew this was going to happen. You warned me."

"No," the doctor said, "I didn't know. It was just one of the possibilities."

"One of the possibilities." Her voice had become bitter. "Why was it the one you mentioned?"

The doctor was silent.

"You should have warned me. I mean *again*. Maybe

you could've saved me. Aren't you supposed to be taking care of me? You should have told me what could happen. I've never been in love before. I had no idea...With Dr. Seaver it was different from the beginning. I knew he was married and had children and there were only certain times I could see him. He was my doctor, not my boyfriend. With Tom I never knew. He was my first real lover. *Is.* Tom *owns* me. Do you know what that means? If Tom throws me away...I'll be like a rag doll someone threw into the garbage. You've got to help me to keep him."

She was becoming frantic again, which was unfortunate, because what Dr. Shinefeld might have said at the beginning of their time, when it could be discussed, she could not say now, when it would contribute to the girl's panic.

"Obviously," the doctor said, "we have a great deal to talk about."

"Oh my God, it's not the end of the hour, is it? Don't make me go. I really can't go now." She sat up.

"We can take a few more minutes."

"When am I coming back? What's today? Tuesday? You mean I'm not coming back until Friday? Two times a week isn't nearly enough."

More than once Dr. Shinefeld had suggested that it would be useful for Dawn to have at least one additional session, but Dawn had resisted, each time with a different reason. Now those hours were filled.

"Do you have any extra time this week? I'll come any time. I have to talk about how to deal with Tom I can't wait three days. I really can't."

The doctor looked at her book. She had no free

hour on Wednesday but could give up her lunch hour on Thursday.

"Could you come at one on Thursday?"

"Yes," Dawn said. "Yes, of course. But how about tomorrow?"

"I'm sorry," the doctor said. "I don't have one free hour."

"Then tell me what to do about Tom. Tell me how to be with him!"

"I think you know I can't do that," the doctor said levelly. "But perhaps ... it might not be a bad thing for you simply to stay at school for a couple of days. Avoid Tom. Take a break, so to speak."

Dawn stared at the doctor, wide-eyed, as though an extraordinary proposal had been made.

"Oh, no," she finally said, "I couldn't do that." But the thought of the possibility had calmed her down just slightly. She smiled. "It's a funny idea, but I can't do it." She stood up. "Thank you. I'll see you tomorrow. I mean Thursday."

And she walked quickly out of the office as though the doctor had, after all, given her some useful idea.

◌

On Thursday Dawn was calmer. She'd had a lengthy discussion with her adviser in which she'd explained that a personal crisis had prevented her concentration on her studies this year. He was a pleasant, sympathetic man. She'd even explained—stretching the truth slightly—that she was seeing a therapist because she'd become so worried about not being able to focus on school. The adviser had suggested that she make up some of the credits she'd lost in summer school. She had told him that her mother wouldn't allow her to do that, that she'd have to go home for the summer and help on the farm.

"New Yorkers always think everything outside of New York is a farm... Actually, I don't know why I lied. I never used to lie. I'd tell the truth or keep quiet. Now I lie when I don't need to."

"Tell me."

"Oh, I don't know. I feel on the defensive a lot of the time. As though I've got some dirty little secret. It began even before Tom, it just got worse when I started with him. You know, when I didn't tell people about Dr. Seaver, it was because that made the visits more precious. If I don't tell about you, it's... a deeper secret... I think it embarrasses me that I come here. Maybe it's just that I've done it before and it didn't work. I don't know. Wherever I go I'm trying to get something no one wants to give me. I want too much, that's the problem. I never thought of myself that way before. People, boys, especially men... were always trying to give me more than I wanted. When I first met Tom he was always giving me presents. There was a very valuable Japanese print. I told him to hold on to it for me, I'd be afraid to keep it at the dorm. Then there was a pre-Columbian statue. I left that in his apartment, too. Now I'd be afraid even to ask if I could take them home... Oh God, he's the best person in the world and I've made him sick of me. Please don't let me talk about anything else because nothing else matters. The school year is ending and Tom is ending and— No! I didn't mean to say that. If it's true, I

don't know it. I can't stand to know it. I just
need...Things were better, the past couple of days.
I couldn't stay away but I left him alone. I sort of
pretended...If it happens, it'll happen, but I'm certainly not going to make it happen.

"What I have to do is to pretend to be independent until I can get that way. Do you see what I mean?
We can talk here about being a baby, and I can find
out why I'm that way, and meanwhile, I can sort of
pretend with Tom. That's what I've been doing since
Tuesday. Stop telling him how I miss him when he's
not there. Stop being so *greedy* for him. I've been
eating too much when I'm with him, much more
than I'm hungry for. Now I've stopped. I'll tell you
something. All my life I've been a secretly greedy
person. You know those enormously fat people you
see on the street? I think about food just as much as
they do. It's just that I have better self-control.
Usually. That's been slipping away but now I have it
back. Self-control is the key to this whole thing. For
now, anyway. It's like...I've been trying to store up
nuts for the winter. If Tom goes to Japan, I'll have
something left. But he knows that's what it's about
and it turns him off further. He hasn't mentioned
Japan since last weekend. I'm not going to bring it
up. I got the summer school catalogue just in case. I
can always tell the adviser my mother changed her
mind. If Tom says he's not going to take me, I'm
going to be very cool. I'll stay in the city and go to
classes and come here and not do anything else. I
don't want to talk about that yet, though. I want to
talk about why I'm a baby with him...Okay?"

"Sure," the doctor said.

Silence.

"I need you to say something. You always say, *Tell me*. Now I'm saying it. I know I have to talk more, to associate, but I'm scared and I...I want you to tell me something I need to know."

"Well," the doctor said, "most of what you need to know will come from you, not from me. That's important. When you come to realize it in a deep way, you'll feel less dependent on doctors, oracles, anyone. But for now...It's occurred to me to point out one truth to you. And that is that love, almost by definition, creates a need where none existed before."

"Yes, Dawn said after a while, "that's good. I like that. It's true." Pause. "But I need him *too much*."

"How much is that?"

"You're not understanding and I need you to!"

"Then why don't you assume, at least in this instance, that I do," the doctor said, "and see where you can get with my question?"

"Which question? How much is too much? How can I answer that? Too much is more than he wants to give me."

"All right. Then how much it's all right to need depends on how much the loved person wants to give. And that varies. Some people, men *and* women, love to be needed and can never give too much."

There was a long pause. Then—

"Are you saying that he's not a wonderful, giving person?"

"Am I?"

"Because he is. Extremely. Nobody likes to be clutched at. Nobody wants to have someone tracking him so he can't breathe. Following him to the bathroom, for God's sake. Nobody wants a baby in the body of a grown woman!"

"A grown woman? Is that what you are?"

"That's what he thought I was!" Dawn was angry at herself and at the doctor but perfectly understanding of Tom Grace. "A grown woman in the body of an eighteen-year-old. Instead I turned out to be an eighteen-*month*-old in the body of an eighteen-year-old!"

"An eighteen-month-old?" the doctor asked with interest. "Is that what he said?"

"No. Yes. I don't know who said it. Me, I guess. He's too nice to put it that way."

"Why do you think you picked that age?"

"I don't know." Dawn was exasperated. "What difference does it make? You're getting me sidetracked. I don't have time for analysis right now. I'm in a race against time. To save myself with him. I put on a good show for a couple of days . . . I pretended to be a reasonable human being. But it was a strain. I could feel the baby in me pushing to get out. I don't know how long I can keep it up. I want to be a grownup *fast*."

"Is it conceivable to you," the doctor asked, "that you might behave maturely with Tom and this friendship might still end?"

"No," Dawn said flatly. "If I were a grownup, then everything would be all right . . . Maybe I should talk to Dr. Seaver." Sullen. "Maybe I need another man's advice on how to deal with Tom . . . Actually, I'm doing the same thing with Tom as I did with Dr.

Seaver. They both turned me off because I wanted too much from them."

"What did you want from Dr. Seaver?"

"To keep seeing him."

"Was that too much?"

"What I really wanted was to be with him all the time. There was only one period—it was just before he said I'd have to stop—and I was so busy that once or twice I wished I could put off going there. But once I knew it would end, I never...All I really wanted was to see him until I felt the same way when he wasn't around as when he was."

"And you don't think it was all right to want that?"

"Well, when you ask me that way, I hear it as though it was. But that's not the way I felt."

There was a long pause and then Dawn asked, in a voice so low that it was obvious she didn't dare to hope for an answer, "Do you think Dr. Seaver made a mistake with me?"

"Yes," the doctor said after a considerable length of time. "I don't know the circumstances that led to the mistake, and I'm uneasy about saying it for that reason. But it seems fairly clear, at least in retrospect, that it was a mistake to terminate your analysis when he did. As he did."

After a moment of silence Dawn burst into tears.

"Oh, God, I can't believe you said that. I never thought ...Doctors never say when another one's made a mistake. Vera talked about that when Tony was ill. She said they always cover for each other...I really love you, you know. I feel as if...." The tears stopped. "I never thought of him as someone who could make a mistake."

"Why do you think that is?"

"I guess because I needed him not to be. I need *you* not to be, also. With a shrink, a little mistake goes a long way."

The doctor smiled.

Silence.

"I can remember when I began to think he might not take me. Tom I mean. It was right after Paris. He was talking about a printmaker he was going to see in Kyoto. The phone rang. He went over to talk, and instead of waiting for him to come back to the sofa, I went over and sat next to him, and when he was finished, he went to the bathroom. I started to follow him and he turned around and laughed and asked what I thought I was doing. I was startled. It was as though I'd been in a trance. I would've followed him right into the bathroom if he hadn't..." She trailed off. "Until then," she said after a while, "it was different. I was in love with him. I was happy all the time. He hates depressed women. Rob's mother was depressed, that was why he couldn't stand living with her. If I'd only been able to stay happy..."

"Can you remember what he said about Kyoto that frightened you?"

"All I remember...I think it was that he said *I*. Instead of *we*. When he talked about Paris, it was always the things *we* were going to do. This wonderful mom-and-pop place near Notre-Dame with the best fish soup in the world. And then Lyon, we'd drive to this three-star restaurant, he'd already made the reservations for two...When he talked about Japan, it was that *he* was going to Kyoto to see the printmaker. Or there was such and such a restaurant that *he* wanted to try."

The doctor was silent.

"I know what you're thinking," Dawn said suddenly. "You're thinking he was sending me a message."

"What kind of message?"

"That I'd better shape up or else."

"No," the doctor said, "that's not the message I hear."

"What do you hear?"

"I hear," the doctor said carefully, "that he wants to be free to go to Japan by himself."

"Well, of course!" Dawn jumped to the defense of her lover. "Of course he wants to be free. No one wants to feel as if he's responsible for some pathetic kid hanging on him, clutching at him, following him to the bathroom."

"You said that began after the ph——"

"Ohhh..." Dawn swung up to a sitting position. She was angry again. "I don't know why you're pretending...Don't you see that all he was doing was uncovering the real me? The little baby who needed him so badly she'd drive him crazy?"

She stared at the doctor angrily as though waiting for some response to her impossible question. The doctor looked back at her with a trained calm.

"When I try to talk about Tom, you do something funny, and then I get mad at you."

"I don't mind your being mad at me."

"But I don't want to be mad. I don't want to use up my time that way. I need to focus on Tom. I know about getting out your anger. I did it with Dr. Seaver. So what? Look at what came out of that!"

"What?"

"NOTHING! That's what came of it! Here I am, in treatment again with another analyst!"

"Is that because you got angry at him?"

"I don't know what it's because of, and I don't care, at least not right now. I want to know about *Tom*."

"You said you felt as though you'd done the same thing with Tom as with Dr. Seaver."

"This is no good," Dawn said decisively. "What time is it, anyway? I think we'd better talk about something else. Let's talk about when I was a baby...I didn't forget about the lithographs, you know. I remember that I told you I was going to bring them in. But they're at the bottom of my trunk in the storage room and I haven't had a chance to get to them yet. If I don't go to Japan...If I stay in the city and just go to summer school and come here..." Apparently Dawn was blocking the knowledge that Dr. Shinefeld would be away for a good part of the summer. "But I don't want to stay here, I want to go to Japan! I want to be with Tom! And you're not helping me!" She burst into tears.

"If I wanted to help you," the doctor asked, "how would I do it?"

"By helping me get rid of the baby in me," Dawn said promptly.

"But isn't that, in one sense, what all of our work is about?"

"I don't know," Dawn moaned. "I never really thought about it that way. I always thought it was about putting my insides together. Making me into a whole person again. Not again. I never thought of myself as a whole person, except maybe for a while with Dr. Seaver. But all that must've happened is, the shell must have grown thicker! The center is still...What's that poem? *The center cannot hold.* It can't hold because there's nothing there. I need you to put something there. I don't care what that sounds like. I know all about penis envy. I went through all that with Dr. Seaver. I remember the first time I saw one, and I *know* I wanted it. I went crying to Vera and told her I wanted one. I was in school already. I was six years old. Dr. Seaver got a big kick out of that. He said most women had to be convinced of it, they get angry at the idea, and here I was . . . Anyway, that's not what I'm talking about. Do you believe me?"

"Yes."

"Then do you know what I'm talking about?"

"I think so."

"What?"

"Your sense of yourself."

"My sense of my *non*self, you mean."

"We're talking about feelings," the doctor reminded her.

"But I don't feel as though that's all we're talking about."

"I understand that. But you should know that it's the case."

"Sometimes," Dawn said after a few moments of silence, "when you say something . . . When I asked you if you thought Dr. Seaver made a mistake and you said yes . . . It makes me feel for a minute as if I'm real. I need you to be certain of things. Not everything, but some things. I have a friend in school who has a shrink that doesn't talk. That would drive me crazy. You ask a question and they don't say *anything*? *Ever*? It must be like being a baby in a dark room and . . . What time is it? Am I coming tomor-

row? Friday. Good. I feel all right. I just...Keep
your fingers crossed for me...I don't suppose that
shrinks actually believe in crossed fingers."

"Tomorrow at two," the doctor said.

❧

When Dr. Shinefeld opened the waiting room door
on Friday she found Dawn in a state of extreme
agitation, her arms and legs moving almost spas-
modically. When she became aware of the doctor's
presence, she looked up. There were tears in her
eyes. She didn't move.

"Hi," the doctor said. "Why don't you come in?"

Slowly Dawn rose and followed her into the office.
At the couch the girl paused, looked around, then
moved to the consulting chair. She looked exhausted
and unkempt. The shirt she was wearing with her
jeans was the one she'd been wearing on Thursday;
it was rumpled and dirty. Her hair was greasy and
uncombed.

"I tried a trick and it didn't work. It serves me
right. I decided one of the problems was, he felt as if
he had no choice but to take me. He needed to feel
that I wasn't going to slit my wrists if he didn't. Even
if I am." She began to cry but continued speaking. "I
told him I thought I should go to summer school
and I waited for him to say, *Don't be silly, kiddo, we're
going to Japan for six weeks,* and instead he said he
could see my point but how would I feel about being
in Manhattan all summer, and I said I'd be fine, I
had plenty of friends here and I could get away on
weekends...I was getting more and more numb but

I had to go on. I said if I didn't like it I could talk to my shrink about it. And as I was saying that—that I'd be all right because I had you—*I remembered about August!*"

The tears became a flood which took a considerable time to abate. When she had calmed down enough to speak, Dawn continued.

"I can't tell you what that moment was like. It was as though I were being punished for every bad thing I ever did. I was using a trick to get what I wanted, and it not only didn't work but suddenly . . . I realized . . . I didn't even have it to use . . . I stared at him. My mouth must have been hanging open. I don't know what I looked like. I was stunned, and then I was terrified that he'd see what I'd been doing and it would really be over. I had to get out of there before I got hysterical. He's never even seen me cry. If I have to cry I go into the bathroom so he won't see me. I ran out of the apartment and I haven't been back since. I called him at the office a couple of hours ago. We're supposed to go to Southampton. I pretended nothing had happened. I asked him when he wanted to leave the city and said I'd meet him at the apartment. I have to go to the dorm, get a little sleep before he sees me, or he'll know something's terribly wrong. We're leaving late. After the traffic. I haven't slept. I spent the first part of the night on the subway. Hoping someone would murder me. But I was too miserable for anyone to bother me. Then I slept, half-slept, in some bushes in Riverside Park. Some people right on the other side of the bushes were making love. Fucking, I should say. That's what everyone calls it, now. Tom says fucking. Or once in a while he says, *Let's make like, babe*. Anyway, they were...fucking...and they were making a lot of noise, and I lay there thinking how happy they were, and that I'd never feel that way again. My head was on a rock. I did that on purpose. I didn't want to be too comfortable. I was afraid if I fell into a deep sleep I'd sort of..."

"Yes?"

"I don't know. Never wake up. Melt into a puddle of misery."

"Is that why you don't want to lie down here?"

Dawn looked surprised. "I really didn't think about it...Anything can happen more easily when you're lying down. If he goes without me...and you go away..." Tears spilled down her cheeks. "I really don't think I can make it. Maybe I should just go home. What's the sense of bothering now if I'm not going to make it through the summer? And I'm not going to make it if he's leaving me."

"What do you mean?"

"I mean, what's the sense of talking and talking and costing Vera more and more money if I'm just going to kill myself in a couple of months?"

"Why are you going to kill yourself?" the doctor asked.

"I can't imagine...All those hang-ups on your answering machine yesterday were me. I went *crazy* trying to figure out which were your between times. Finally I tried twice in a row, fast, thinking maybe you'd know from the two fast calls that something was up. But the second time the line was busy. By evening, when I knew I could get you at the other number, I was too angry to talk to you. Not at you.

At the machine. Keeping me from getting to you all day. I had this picture of myself: trying to talk to you and throwing up into the receiver instead . . . Summer school begins next week. I'm not registered yet but my adviser said if I could get my mother to change her mind, he could still get me in next Tuesday. I imagine we'll talk about Japan over the weekend. He's going in the middle of July and staying through August. Did you hear what I said? I said *he's* going. I must be beginning to believe it myself. Memorial Day weekend . . . Memorial Day." She shuddered. "Sounds like a good time to die."

On Tuesday Dawn was calm. And depressed. "Numb," as she put it. It had happened. It was over. Her speech was slower, more careful than usual, her grammar impeccable. He had done it in the kindest possible way and Dr. Shinefeld was not to say a word against him. He had told her that she was free to use the house in Southampton while he was away. She could have her own bedroom most of the time, except perhaps when all his kids and the other men's kids were there. He did not wish to be tied down. He did not wish to be totally responsible for another human being's welfare. He wanted her to continue with school, get her degree, become a mature, independent young woman. He wanted her to become who she had seemed to be when they met.

She had forced herself to spend time on the beach, to play volleyball, to help in the kitchen and talk to the others, although she'd really wanted only to lie in bed, to sleep. From the moment he'd told her—in the car late Friday night, driving out on the Long Island Expressway. Funny, she wasn't afraid to sleep anymore. That was actually all she seemed to want to do.

Tom had made love to her with greater frequency and apparent enthusiasm than he had since their return from Paris, but she had been numb through that too. He could have been Alan Gartner, for all the feeling she'd had. He hadn't seemed to mind. Nor had he tried to make her come.

The doctor was startled. For all her talk of waterbeds and Jacuzzis, Dawn had never mentioned anything so specific as an orgasm.

In her first weeks with Tom, Dawn now said, she'd never come. She didn't even know what it was about. He had wanted to make her do it, and finally she had, at first because he gave her grass, but then later without it. That was over now. Not that she minded. Not that she ever wanted to sleep with anyone again. She was certain that she would never have such pleasure because there had been an abandon that she wouldn't be able to summon in the future.

❧

Dawn's mood lightened somewhat when summer school began. She had been sleeping virtually all the time except when she came to the doctor. Now she slept less and did her assignments, although she never participated in class or socialized with other students. As usual, she'd been approached by some of the boys. As usual, the girls thought she was a snob. She wasn't going to take the second summer session; she would go to Vermont at the end of the first one, in the middle of July. Vera wouldn't bother her much, now that she was already totally depressed. She'd just sleep. Was there someplace she should call Dr. Shinefeld if she felt that she was about to kill herself? Or should she just do it?

"By all means, call me," the doctor said, smiling slightly.

But Dawn had twisted on the couch to see the reaction and caught the smile. "Are you laughing at me?"

"No. I think it was what you might call a fond smile. It has to do with my conviction that there's no chance you'll kill yourself."

"Well," Dawn said petulantly. "I wish I were as sure as you are."

"I do believe," the doctor replied, "that it's me you want to kill. And possibly Tom Grace."

"No, not Tom!" Dawn said quickly, then heard herself and was flustered. "It's just not true. I don't want to kill you. I only want to stop you from going away."

"Tell me."

"No. There's nothing to tell. It's a good thing I'm numb, that's all. Have you noticed how numb I am? I guess I'm protecting myself, the way I did . . . If you think I can handle Tom's leaving me now, you're wrong. If I don't talk about it all the time it's because I can't stand to. I don't even know what I have been talking about. I come here every day just because . . . See how out of it I am? I don't even come here every day. It's wishful thinking. Actually, I wish I could be here to begin with and not have to come ... Do you have a daughter?"

"It wouldn't be useful for me to answer that," the doctor said. "It would be more useful for you to talk about wanting to be my daughter."

"If I were your daughter I wouldn't have to be embarrassed that I need you so much. It's humiliating to need someone who just ... I couldn't stand it if I thought at the end of a session you forgot me until the next time we were together. I don't mind the girl who comes after me so much. Once I had a fantasy that she was my twin sister, and when you went away we spent the time together. But I can't stand to think of being in a string of ... like one show after another on the television set and it doesn't even matter which one is on ... One of the differences between Tony and Vera was, anything Vera ever did for you, she was doing because she needed it. I hated to be sick because I'd be home with Vera all day and she took care of me, but she didn't notice I was company. Tony used to say if I hadn't come along she'd have had to have a baby just to have someone to take care of. To cuddle ... I wish you would cuddle me."

She began to cry, the first time since the separation from Tom Grace. "I didn't mean to say that. It just came out."

"Let it keep coming."

But the reserves Dawn was willing to draw on just now were very shallow, and the tears ended quickly.

"I don't mind about sex," she said, her voice dispassionate again. "It's the other ... being touched ... talking ... Do you have extra time now? Are people on vacation? I'd love to come every day while you're still here. Store up. I guess that's dumb, but I'd like to do it. Where are you going on vacation? No. You're not going to tell me. Is there a place where I can call you?"

"Yes."

"Where?"

"I'll give you the number before I go."

"Will I be able to call you any time? Like before?"

"Yes," the doctor said. "But some times will be better than others. I'll tell you the times when you're most likely to catch me."

"I haven't thought a lot about your being away. I suppose I couldn't handle it. I almost took out the cassette player yesterday. Then, I don't know, it felt silly. Also, I think . . . I wanted to hear your voice but not mine. I hate myself too much right now to listen to my own voice."

"What would happen if you heard it?"

"I'd feel nauseated. I'm a whiner. I couldn't stand to hear me moaning and groaning and sniveling."

"I don't think you'd hear much of that. I think you would hear a young woman who goes to great lengths to avoid whining. Who'd rather beat up on herself than complain about the abuse of her love and trust. About not being allowed to be someone's baby, even though that's part of what love is about. At least for a while."

There was a long silence. Then Dawn repeated her earlier question about whether the doctor had additional time.

"I have it," the doctor said, "but I'm not sure that it's a good idea for you to take it. Let's both think about that. Even if you come through the end of

July—that is, if you don't go ahead with your plan to leave two weeks before I do—our separation might prove more difficult for you if you've gotten accustomed to coming every day. Think about it."

Dawn decided that she would come for the full three weeks, and that she would do five days the following week; four the one after that, and three, now her usual number, the last. Dr. Shinefeld accepted this arrangement.

The following Monday, Dawn arrived with a large portfolio. Her expression as she walked into the office was apprehensive.

"It's the lithographs," she said. "The whole series."

"Thank you."

"This is an act of faith, but it's also being sneaky."

"Oh?"

"I want you to keep them here. Not just today. All summer. I was trying to figure out how to pretend to forget them when I leave, but I know I can't do that. Even if I could do it for one night I couldn't keep it up. I don't want you to analyze me out of wanting to leave them here."

"Once," the doctor said, "I had a friend who had a daughter who was about two and a half but extremely precocious. In order to go to a therapist, she had to leave the little girl with a sitter twice a week. The little girl was unaccustomed to sitters and complained, and the mother, who was in the habit of talking things out with her in great detail, explained that she was going to appointments with a doctor who helped her work out things that she thought about. It was beneficial for her daughter, she said, that this be done. 'For example,' she told the little girl, 'last week I was complaining to the doctor about your bringing your toys into my bedroom and then never taking them out when you go. And the doctor told me that this was your way of saying, *Mommy, I'm going now, but I'm leaving a piece of myself with you.*' The woman's daughter listened, wide-eyed, and after a moment said, *Mommy, the next time you see that doctor, please ask what the world is made of.*"

The doctor still got goosepimples whenever she told that story, which was about Sascha.

"That's it," Dawn said. "Oh my God, that's it." She wept. "I thought you'd be angry. I didn't think you'd tell me a story like that." It was a pleasurable crying, the enormous relief of being understood.

"I wasn't going to show you the prints today," Dawn finally said, "but I will if you want me to."

"What do *you* want?"

"I guess what I'd really like is for you to look at them when I'm not here."

"Why is that?"

"It's because I know there are secrets in them. And you'll understand the secrets and not tell me what's in them until you're sure it's okay for me to hear."

"Well, that's a wonderful explanation of the way you feel, but if you want to look at them with me, I don't think you'll see more than you can tolerate seeing."

"All right. But let's do it tomorrow."

"Fine."

"Are you really going to let me leave them here all summer?"

"Yes."

"And then I'll take them back in September?"

"If you like."

"I don't have to if I don't want to?"

"You may be ready, by then."

"You know what I'm doing now? I'm testing you. Whenever you do something wonderful, I have to find out the step beyond. I don't think I've done that with anyone before. It's as though there's no way everything I want is possible. So as soon as I find out something I thought was extreme is okay, then I have to know what isn't. I have to make sure I don't just take that step that's too much and then, *blam!* It turns out that one step beyond what was all right is this little landing labeled OUTRAGEOUS and that's where I went and you never want to speak to me again. No, that's not it. It's that I'm lying here thinking all's well, then I don't get a response to what I say and I turn around and you're gone. Forever. I've just said the one thing in the world that would make you disappear. And I had no idea!"

Frightened by her fantasy, Dawn sat up and swung her legs over the edge of the couch.

"It would be good if you could lie down and talk about what scared you."

"No," Dawn said. "I don't think so. Let's look at the pictures."

"All right."

But instead of moving to get the portfolio, she lay down.

"You know the phrase *well defended*?" she asked. "Of course you know it. The way I first heard it was, a psych major I was going out with at the beginning of the school year said to me—when I wouldn't let him, whatever, in the movies—he told me I was well defended. But I'm not. I mean, I'm well defended against being felt up in the movies by someone I hardly know, but the other way, which he also meant...I am but I'm not. I am until someone gets past that top layer—Tom Grace, Dr. Seaver, you— and then I haven't got any of the layers in between. I'm either this terribly cool, mature person or an absolute infant. There's nothing in between. Do you know what I mean?"

"Yes."

"Is it true or is it something I'm imagining?"

"I think that in some sense it's true."

"How?"

"That's what we have to find out. Together."

∼

"The lithographs," Dawn said the next day. "When I left I forgot them. Just the way I was supposed to in the lie. Where are they?"

The doctor had placed the portfolio between her desk and the wall. "Right over here."

"You know something weird? At this moment I can't even remember them. I mean, I remember *After the First Death*, but I've said that so many times it has no meaning anymore. Or the meaning's remote.

Maybe I want it to be remote. I can see now that I'm frightened of something in those pictures but... Anyway, it's only Tuesday, and I'm coming every day this week. Being depressed isn't actually as bad as I thought it would be. I can stand the way I feel. I'm doing all right in my classes, you know. I guess it's easier to concentrate when you're depressed than when you're high. Or anxious. I guess there should be something in between being horribly anxious and horribly depressed, but anyway..." She began to talk about her courses. She was taking her second required English course, English being the only course she'd gotten a halfway decent grade in the previous year. Also an ancient history course in which she particularly liked the professor. Then, suddenly, she interrupted herself. "This is ridiculous." She stood up determinedly, brought the portfolio to the couch, unzipped it and sat down beside it. "Here goes."

Dr. Shinefeld stood near the couch and looked down at the first of the lithographs. There was no doubt that it was the Lonely Chair.

It seemed to the doctor an extraordinary piece of work, although she knew she was no more capable of being critical of Dawn's work than of disliking something by one of her own children. Still, it seemed that the Lonely Chair might make a stranger weep. Done in sepia tones, so that it had something of the quality of an old photograph, the print was a portrait of a large, slat-backed, wooden rocking chair so intimate, so detailed, and so permeated by a sense of sorrowful isolation that it might have been the face of an aged, abandoned human.

The next print, of a garden, was also primarily in

sepia. It was called Dead Marigolds, and the blackened orange heads of the marigolds gave the print its only additional color. This was followed by a somewhat crumpled and twisted patchwork quilt, done entirely in sepia, and then by the print that Dawn had described as being of Venetian blinds.

"Whoops," Dawn said, "it's sideways."

She turned it around, appeared puzzled, turned it to the way it had been, with the slats in a vertical position, then once more turned it back so they were horizontal. The slats were sepia, as was the window frame, which also served as the frame for the picture. The slats were dark and between them poured the light, a yellow so cold that it was almost silver. What was apparent to Dr. Shinefeld was that Dawn's unconscious had been in command at the moment she turned the picture so that the slats were vertical; they didn't resemble window blinds, but the broader and more widely spaced slats of a child's crib.

Dawn turned to the last print in the portfolio. "This isn't really part of the series, but...in my mind, it is."

It was a large bowl of fruit—pears, an orange, some grapes—in their true colors, except that the most prominent piece was a large apple out of which a chunk had been bitten and the pulp turned to sepia, the only sepia in the picture, shading around the edges to an ugly blackness that gave the apple the appearance of having been wounded rather than partially eaten. On the table that held the bowl of fruit there were several other small objects—a jade elephant, a china bowl, and what appeared to be the replica of a tightly wrapped Egyptian mummy, which stood facing the artist.

"That's it," Dawn said. "That's the bunch of them."

The doctor returned to her chair.

"They're quite wonderful," the doctor said to Dawn, her voice shaking slightly as she sat down again. "I was very moved by them."

"Moved? Really?... You're all right, though, aren't you?"

"Quite all right. Art is supposed to do that, you know."

Dawn appeared to be pleased, if baffled, by Dr. Shinefeld's reaction. She herself was quite remote from the emotions that had inspired the prints.

"Why did you say," the doctor asked, "that the apple wasn't part of the series?"

"Because I did it after the others. When Tony was in the hospital the second time."

"When was Tony in the hospital?"

"Last year."

"What was wrong with her?"

"Oh, you know, it's when she had the mastectomy. I know that's what the picture is about. The apple. I know it's about Tony's breast being..." She trailed off. "It's not possible that I haven't mentioned it before."

The doctor was silent.

"Are you saying I never told you that Tony had a mastectomy a few weeks before I finished with Dr. Seaver? I can't see how that's possible...I had to tell you. In that first session. Maybe you forgot." A pause. "I just realized, we have the transcripts. We could check it out...I never told you?"

"No."

"That's incredible. Well, maybe it's not. I wasn't all that upset at the time. I mean, it was in that numb period. There was no sense in getting upset because what was I going to do with myself then? Someone has to be there with you, before...Dr. Seaver thought I didn't get more upset because I was okay. You know, he understood me a thousand times better than anyone before him, but it wasn't like you. Men just don't understand the way women do. I'll tell you something funny. Vera doesn't understand. Just like a man. It isn't men she hates, anyway, it's women. Well, not hates, but...She can't stand any sign of weakness...Womanliness. I know it's not all the same but...You know, Tony told me that when she started to get sick...have trouble with, you know, her uterus, and she thought she might need to have a hysterectomy...Maybe I didn't tell you that, either. Tony told me that was when Vera started being cold to her. As if she'd committed some kind of sin...Dr. Seaver said taking any part of the body is a castration, and Vera...I don't know if she's ever been sick in her life. If she had a cold, she refused to admit she had it. Worked as hard as ever. Went out. It wasn't as though she was just unsympathetic to other people. It was herself, too. Can you imagine if they'd been together after Tony's breast was...? Len was wonderful through the whole thing. Kind. Made her talk about it with him."

"Is Tony still under treatment?"

"What for?"

"That's what I'm asking," the doctor said carefully. "About any postoperative therapy."

"Oh, I don't know. I doubt it. I never asked." She

giggled uneasily. "Maybe I'm like Vera that way. I'm not exactly unsympathetic, but I'm not all that fond of hearing the gory details. Do you think I should have asked more?"

Only if you wanted to know, was what the doctor might have answered at a time when less caution was required. "Not necessarily," she said now.

"Good." Dawn was more than willing to drop the subject. "How did we get started on this? Oh, of course, the apple. I think when I painted the apple, that was when I really tried to get Dr. Seaver to look at the series."

"Oh?"

"I had a dream after I did it. When I just think about it now, I . . . It was hideous. The bite in the apple turned into a mouth. A hideous mouth. Gaping black lips, just a couple of teeth in the front but they were really fangs. Oh, God, do I have to talk about this now?"

"You tell *me*."

"No. Yes. I'd better. If I don't it's going to stick in my mind . . . I think it feels worse now than it did the first time. The picture is definitely worse." She put her hands over her ears and shut her eyes as though to block out all avenues. "Ohhhhhhhhhhh!"

"What are you seeing?"

"I can't tell, that's the worst part of it. It's the apple and the mouth that's biting it, but I can't even tell which is which, they're all running into each other and—No!" She sat up. "That's it. I really don't want to do this anymore."

"Okay."

"Is it really?"

"Of course."

"What I really want is a cigarette."

"I didn't know you smoked."

"I don't. Not usually. Grass with Tom. I just... There's something reassuring about holding a cigarette... You don't smoke, do you? There isn't even an ashtray in the room. Would you be angry with me if I smoked?"

"What do you think?"

"I think I'm being a pain. I *know* I'm being a pain. Maybe I should leave now. I have nothing else to talk about and I really... that is, what I should talk about I can't talk about, so maybe I ought to go." She looked at the doctor inquiringly.

"Of course," the doctor said. "You're free to go if you wish."

⟡

Dawn spent most of the next session talking about Tom Grace. She said she was afraid that if she refused to talk at all about how much she missed him, she would be overwhelmed by bad feelings when the doctor left. This was her first reference to August.

Dawn remembered the wonderful times she'd had with Tom and cried, remembered more and cried more. She said she knew Dr. Shinefeld wanted her to see Tom's bad points so she wouldn't care so much about losing him. She did not appear to hear the doctor's demurral.

By Thursday she was quite anxious but not yet willing to do more than acknowledge the source of her anxiety. She had done well in summer school—an A in English and an A– in Ancient History. She was worried. So much had happened, she didn't know if she could stand to be around someone like Vera with whom she couldn't share any of it. In the past she'd been a self-contained person. That was one of the things Tom had said about her at the beginning, that she didn't spill out of herself like other teenagers. But of course she'd turned out to be worse than a teenager once she'd fallen in love.

"I don't really know why I'm feeling worse instead of better . . . I keep thinking of, There is nothing to fear but fear itself. It's true. Mostly I'm frightened of feeling worse than I already feel."

On Friday she began by referring to the one day of the following week when she wouldn't be seeing the doctor. Then she admitted that the week after, with "two dark days," would be worse. She wished she'd arranged to come five times right through. "You know," she said. "The old storing-up-nuts principle." This led to the notion that summer was her winter. Dr. Shinefeld thought this was an interesting notion, but Dawn wasn't inclined to expand upon it. Maybe, she said, in the fall.

❧

On Monday Dawn sat in the consulting chair and told the doctor that the previous weekend had been the worst one of her life.

"Worse than after Tom left me," she said, "because then the worst had happened. I wasn't frightened, just depressed. Now I'm depressed about Tom and frightened about you. I almost went to Southampton to throw myself at his feet. Then I realized that he'd already gone, and I really touched rock bottom. Maybe I never believed until then he was going without me. Every time the phone rang I'd think to myself, He's in Japan and he's miserable without me and he wants me to join him.

ℂ

All that week Dawn wrestled with the issue of her separations from Tom Grace and Dr. Shinefeld, those two powerful figures who'd been supposed to balance each other's weight in her life and were, instead, abandoning her at close points in time. But the following week, her last, she arrived at the office in a poised condition.

"I'm all right," she announced almost diffidently. "I'm not sure why, but I am."

She had gone back to the dorm on Friday afternoon, feeling as bad as it was possible to feel. She had stayed in bed through the evening, the night and the following morning. She'd had a succession of nightmares that had diminished in intensity, each one upsetting her less. They had begun with the apple and the mouth and ended with Tony sitting on the edge of her bed in Marbury, reading her stories.

"I don't know what went on in my head. I don't *want* to know. Maybe if I know it'll stop being all right. I want to be in Marbury. To do some lithographs...Remember you said you'd give me your phone number? Are you still going to do that?"

On a slip of paper, the doctor wrote down the

number of the phone in East Hampton. She said that would be for what felt like a real emergency; a message left on her machine in New York would reach her within a couple of days. Dawn folded the paper and put it in her pocket without looking at it. She had to stand up to do it, and when she had finished, she didn't sit down again.

"If you don't mind," she said, "I think I'm going to leave now."

"Are you certain that's what you want to do?"

"Yes," Dawn said. "Quite certain."

"Would you like to set up our appointments for the fall?" the doctor asked. "That was part of what I assumed we would do during this week."

"Oh," Dawn said, "yes. Of course."

"Shall I assume that we're continuing on our three-day-a-week schedule?"

"I guess," Dawn said. "Although that might turn out to be more than I can handle and do my schoolwork."

"Well," the doctor said, "you can always reduce the number of sessions if you need to, but sometimes it's difficult to add hours."

"Will it be this year?" Very polite, very remote.

"It looks as though it might be."

"Well then, by all means, let's say three. Maybe we should say five."

"I won't have those hours regularly. But if you think you might want to come that often..."

"No," Dawn said, "I won't want to come that often."

"All right then, three."

"Okay. May I go now?"

The doctor stood up. "If you should change your mind and come this week, I'll be here."

"Thank you. You're very kind."

The doctor held out her hand to shake Dawn's, but Dawn didn't respond to the gesture and the doctor let her hand fall. "If I don't see you again, have a pleasant summer. I hope you get a lot of work done."

"Work?"

"The lithographs."

"Oh, yes, of course. Thank you."

Dawn began to walk out of the office, returned, shook the doctor's hand, then quickly left.

5

Lulu kagan shinefeld had grown up on West End Avenue in Manhattan in one of those crust-stable middle-class households that make it possible to argue for or against the notion that the sum of one's neuroses is equal to the square of the neuroses of the previous generation.

A middle-class childhood is actually not to be sneezed at, except by those who have had one. No premature deaths or ultimate economic disasters marred the surface of Lulu's early years. If her mother's expectations of life had been early disappointed, there was neither the money nor the leisure to indulge her sporadic depressions. And if George Kagan was the first Jewish alcoholic on the block, he did his heaviest drinking at home and cushioned the booze with enough food so that his vital organs were not destroyed early on.

Anita Kagan had grown up under the domination of a brother ten years older whom she adored. Brother Josh was a writer and Anita had some talent as a painter; it had been the sustaining fantasy of Anita's childhood that someday they would be a happy team, Josh writing books of an unspecified nature that she would make beautiful with her drawings. It didn't occur to Anita that she should paint and not just illustrate. To do that, she would have had to admit that the wellspring lay within herself, and any such admission would have caused the end of her supremely egotistical brother's attentions to her. Anita had grown up in a fatherless household, had settled those affections usually reserved for a father upon Josh, and was incapable of seriously considering any path that might alienate him. It was a given of Josh's love for her that he cleared any place she had in the sun. It was because Josh lived there that Anita had insisted upon moving to West End Avenue when she married George Kagan, a second cousin, during the Depression. Josh left New York soon after, but George and Anita remained until the end of Anita's life in that apartment that Josh had found for them.

In 1942, when Lulu was seven years old, her father had left his family's business to join the navy, and while Anita had been pained by this defection, she had, in fact, flourished in her husband's absence. In an employees' market, she rapidly found a job in the art department of an advertising agency and was soon paid enough to employ the live-in housekeeper her husband had claimed they didn't need and couldn't afford. The ailments that had plagued her with stunning ingenuity and unremitting force ceased so abruptly after George's departure as to make one wonder if his very presence had not been their cause. They didn't reappear when he did, yet the good spirits and sense of expectancy with which Anita had gone through the war were replaced by a depression that pervaded their lives like a shroud that had worked its way under the collective skin.

The shape of the world had changed.

While George was away at war his elderly parents had died, but his two older brothers had survived and prospered. After the war, they were less than eager to welcome back the kid who had left them "for adventure" during their difficult years, and George had to content himself with a subordinate position and a salary barely higher than the one he had earned before. Though he could never muster quite enough rage—or courage—to leave the business, he and his family were deeply alienated from the families of his brothers.

Unfortunately, the family constellation had been important to Anita, who had loved at least one of George's brothers, the one who'd been married when they met, at least as much as she did George. She had relished the family Sundays and holidays with the brothers and cousins scattered around her mother-in-law's apartment much more than she enjoyed evenings alone with her husband.

Lulu always fought sleep and perhaps that was just as well, for her mother seemed to need her at night. While the housekeeper provided crucial support through dinnertime, Anita was in need of more companionship and entertainment than George was willing or able to provide. She would listen to any conversation that wasn't about George's business, which was dull, not to say unprofitable, but his business was what interested George and was all he had to talk about. Furthermore, he was drinking, and it was clear to his wife and child that he took more comfort from the bottle than from either of them.

When George Kagan returned from the navy, Lulu was an active, strong-willed eleven-year-old, raised by a housekeeper during the war and disinclined to accept him as the authority in the house. Then the housekeeper who had been with them throughout the war gave notice when her boyfriend returned from the army.

Not only was the loss of Hestia a serious one to Lulu, but after she left, the housekeepers kept changing. A soft, comical, and endearing black girl of seventeen, just up from Georgia, when she had come to them, Hestia had been a companion, confidante, older sister, and instructor in various arts useful and not so useful but unrelated, in either event, to what Lulu might have learned from her parents, or her friends, or her parents' friends on West End Avenue. Indeed, it was from Hestia that Lulu acquired that sense possessed by so many southern white children from a much earlier age, that there were certain qualities of warmth and vitality for which one might most realistically look to black people, certain truths and consequences one would never learn from whites—an impression that would have important ramifications in Lulu's adolescence.

Her best friends were the few middle-class black kids at the Little Red Schoolhouse. She had moved through her early school years with relative ease by virtue of a sound intelligence and a strong sense of the distance between the territories of Have To and Should. Now, at war with both the martinet who replaced Hestia and a father who thought that if his brothers couldn't forgive him for fighting for their mother country, at least his wife and daughter should, Lulu was unable to shed the tension of family battle when she went off to school each day. All pretense of interest in her studies collapsed. The Little Red became Elizabeth Irwin High School, but Lulu never found in either a subject compelling enough to divert her from the family drama or from her unfolding adolescent sexuality. In her fourth year of high school she had an overall average of sixty-eight. Her college boards marked a new gap between I.Q. and achievement. She managed, against all odds, to be refused admission to a decent Ivy League college.

She was accepted at the College of the City of New York on the basis of her entrance examination, but she couldn't really say what she wanted to learn there, and her father was of the opinion that it would be no great crime for Lulu to go out into the world and find out what it was like to have to earn a living and get along with white people.

"Isn't there anything you really want to do?" asked the counselor her despairing mother consulted.

Well, what she really would have liked to do was to join the Peace Corps and go to Africa, but the Peace Corps wasn't going to be invented for another seven or eight years, and in the absence of someone to take care of, Lulu wanted, she guessed, to be taken care of herself.

She took a summer job at the Five-and-Ten an
began to look forward to attending City College.

Lulu met Woody Samuelson at a Gershwin concer
in Lewisohn Stadium that she attended with her bes
friend, Laura, who lived on Convent Avenue an
whose father was a judge. In the hot, sticky dusk, th
two girls faced each other on the tightly packe
bench, pulling their T-shirts away from their mid
riffs, fanning each other. And becoming aware, a
some point, that a man sitting in back of them wa
regarding them with interest. They giggled. Almos
imperceptibly, what had begun as an attempt t
relieve discomfort evolved into a performance.

"You make a lovely picture," a deep, soothing voic
said.

They turned.

He appeared to be somewhere between a boy an
a man. (He confessed to twenty-six years later tha
night and thirty-two later that month.) He was ver
tall, with curly black hair and a complexion so swar
thy that her father would pretend not to believe tha
Lulu had bridged the gap to white men, thoug
Woody was not only white but Jewish. He had large
dark, mournful eyes and sunken cheeks, and a gui
tar rested upright between his legs.

He smiled dolefully. One of his front teeth wa
missing. Later he would tell Lulu a very interestin
story about how he'd lost the tooth and still later h
would tell her an entirely different story.

After the concert, Woody and the two girls walke
to Laura's home on Convent Avenue and Laur
invited them in for a glass of juice and Woody too

out his guitar and sang "Sometimes I Feel like a Motherless Child" and Laura cried and Lulu fell in love with him. Later that night, as Lulu and Woody walked down Broadway to Eighty-sixth Street and then down West End Avenue to Seventy-fourth, Woody put his arm around Lulu's shoulder and she looked down at his long, slender hand and noticed that he wore a wedding ring, but it didn't matter, it was too late, what difference did it make? Married or not he was a motherless child!

It turned out that it didn't matter even more than that because Woody was already separated from his wife, even though he hadn't "bothered" to get rid of the ring.

Woody grinned his charming, missing-tooth grin.

"I'll pawn it if you say you'll have dinner with me tomorrow."

Lulu made it clear that she would have anything with him.

Woody Samuelson had knocked around a great deal before returning to CCNY two years earlier to get his B.A. with a major in filmmaking, an exotic occupation on the nature of which no one was too clear in those days except that it had nothing to do with American movies. In his last year, he had been a sort of special assistant to the Film Department. He had made a documentary about the Plains Indians. He wanted to use his camera for the social good. He was a Stalinist who believed that if anything were to happen to Stalin, all hope of world peace would die. (It was 1952, and Lulu was not to talk about Woody's views with other people.) Now he had just gotten his

degree and would soon be off to establish a film
department at a place called Rakoon Junior College
outside Atlanta, Georgia.

He had to do something about his divorce, Woody
said, looking around the six-room apartment on
West End Avenue that Lulu later realized must have
seemed princely to him. He had been, he said,
unfortunate in his choice of wives. Yes, there had
been one before this one. The first marriage had
been of a reasonable duration; this last was a brief,
unmitigated disaster, too painful to talk about. Laura
had reminded him of his first wife. Woody took full
responsibility, he assured Lulu, for both failures; he
had picked women who were not prepared to be
wives and mothers.

Lulu's parents were in Europe. The full-time housekeepers were a thing of the past. Anita's talents were
less in demand now as young, aggressive artists elbowed
their way past her to the choice assignments. The
trip to Europe had been the dream of Anita's life
and finally, that year, Anita had quit her job and
they had taken off, Anita chattering about destina-
tions of which George only wanted to know that
there was a restaurant, and a bar.

It was the only blissfully happy summer of Lulu's
remembered life.

They slept in her parents' bed, ate her parents' food,
listened to her mother's classical records, and were
cleaned up after once a week by her parents' maid.

He was a lover whose energy and skill would be
rendered more rather than less extraordinary in her

mind by the passage of time. She'd been in bed only with black boys having the same kind of stamina and sometimes a talent as well, but too young and too intent upon their own satisfaction to pay that so-exciting concern to hers, and too concerned with bolstering their own self-esteem to pay tribute to her sexuality—less remarkable to them, anyway, who were unaware that not all white girls fucked like this.

Nobody was going to try to stop her from marrying Woody. They would like to point out, though, that a man who was getting set to take a third wife by the age of thirty-five (they'd found out from a friend of a friend, someone in the Film Department) was likely to run through a few more by the time he was done. She would be the letter C in a veritable alphabet of women.

"Come here, C," Woody said when she told him. "I want to kiss the back of your neck before I get rid of you."

Lulu giggled. It was understood that the image was ludicrous because Woody had never felt about either of his first two wives the way he felt about her.

Her parents wanted her to See Someone.

"I do See Someone," Lulu said. "I see Woody all the time."

Also, she suspected that she was pregnant, although she hadn't told Woody yet because she was afraid of disappointing him if she were wrong.

He'd had the plane tickets since before he met her in June: Mr. and Mrs. Luther Samuelson. They both thought that was pretty funny.

* * *

Can it be called paranoia when it fits reality as though it were the pattern and reality the cloth?

It was, in any event, a matter of record that paranoia of the Jew-in-a-Hostile-World variety had never visited Lulu (partly, no doubt, because she'd seldom left Manhattan except to go to summer camp in August) until the day she and her new husband took the plane to Atlanta.

Woody was abstracted. He announced his intention to plan the entire term's work on the plane and get it over with.

On her way to the bathroom, Lulu, who was unaccustomed to thinking of her long, wavy, dark brown hair as remarkable, couldn't find another female head that wasn't covered with silky, blond hair. On the way back she double-checked. The few exceptions were irrelevant and they weren't the ones Woody was staring at, anyway.

Lulu tried making jokes but the fact that Woody also had dark wavy hair and was Jewish didn't appear to give him the feeling that they stood on common ground.

"It's all right for cornstalks to look like that, Woody, but people should have expressions!"

He ignored her. She had already begun to be boring.

The miracle was that they were all that way at Rakoon—even when apparently descended from short, hairy Jews, viz. Francesca Kantrowitz, to whose charms Woody so rapidly capitulated. As though one or two generations of sunshine and tax incentives had been enough to alter the genetic structure of an ancient and honorable race.

By the time the Welcoming Committee—Francesca and four other virgins—made itself known at the terminal, fear had ripened into a terror that kept Lulu awake through the night, as it did for most of every night, from that first one, when Woody couldn't make love to her because he'd injured his back carrying luggage, through the one just a month later when she finally told him that she was pregnant and he told her that he was in love with Francesca Kantrowitz.

Lulu fled Atlanta so she wouldn't be in their way.

Her parents were actually very good about it. None of that special Jewish Water Torture, an endless drip of I-Told-You-So's.

She didn't tell her parents that she was pregnant until it was too late to have an abortion because she was afraid they'd talk her into it.

The days and nights ran into each other, equally unreal, although it was easy to tell the difference between the two because in the daytime you didn't need electric lights.

"I hope you're at least going to get some child support from the son-of-a-bitch," her father said when he'd reached the point where he could talk.

"I can't do that," Lulu said.

It would make Woody angry, and if he were angry, not only would he despise her but he would hate their child, who was going to have a Russian name, which would please him. In the back of Lulu's mind lingered the hope that Woody would come to realize he was a stranger in a strange land and return to her. She took heart from his not having made any move toward a legal separation. When her father realized that, he let her know that the papers had come and he'd returned them with a threat. The least the lousy bastard could do was give his child a legal father.

Lulu hoped Woody would understand that it was her father, not she, who was threatening him. Still, it didn't affect her as strongly as it would have if she had been awake. She continued sleeping little and never fully awakening. In fact, she didn't even half-wake up until she'd had Sascha, and gradually the exhaustion of childbirth wore off, and the pleasure of having an infant took hold of her.

And her parents said, when they saw that the surface of the depression had passed, and that she was content to drift on with them, an unwed teenaged mother with an I.Q. of 165 and no desire to do anything in the world but take care of her beautiful little girl baby, that they would have to insist upon psychiatric treatment as a condition of continuing to live with them.

Then, in her rage at being forced out of the cocoon, Lulu woke up, and, once awake, knew that she was in pain.

For the next two and a half years, there were two people in her life, Sascha and Dr. Winkler.

It would occur to Lulu after some years of practice that the fantasizer's mind is best compared to a sack of mercury, or even a less elusive substance. Pressure on one part of the container, the brain in this case, caused the mercury to slip away to another, a process that in therapy could easily be misperceived as a cure.

"Our work," says the doctor, "has left you sadder but wiser. You are now deeply mired in reality."

But reality can easily become the current fantasy, sweetened considerably by being a gift of the doctor's. Embraced as though it were a child he had given her, and just as likely to have its problems accurately perceived.

Going straight was the issue of Lulu's alliance with Dr. Winkler. If he didn't talk a lot, it was nevertheless clear that he didn't want her to act crazy anymore. That was his business, after all. And Lulu had always been looking for a nice sober man to please.

She not only entered City College after six months of therapy, she devoted herself to her studies and earned good grades. Once in a while a boy invited her to a movie. If he asked a second time, she would greet him at the door to her parents' apartment with Sascha in her arms and ask if he'd known she was an unwed mother. If they didn't dig unwed mothers, that was the end. If they dug unwed mothers, Dr. Winkler wouldn't approve of them, so it was also the end.

During Lulu's third year of college Dr. Winkler started missing appointments because of an unspecified illness.

Woody came back to New York that summer. Wifeless. He said he'd done a lot of thinking after Francesca and realized that what he was doing didn't make sense. (Later he let slip that he was paying heavy alimony.) Woody wanted to see his daughter. He wanted Lulu and Sascha to go with him to Los Angeles, where he would begin teaching in the fall. Lulu crept out to see him, to make love with him on a mattress on the floor of a friend's apartment on 110th Street. She was terrified that her parents would find out and evict her. Or that Sascha would see Woody and somehow *know*.

Dr. Winkler got well enough to see Lulu a few times. (Her mother had found out and called him.) Lulu told Dr. Winkler that Woody was around, begging her to bring Sascha to California. She said she was tempted. Dr. Winkler said that her temptation must have to do with her instinct to create a hell that made reality pale by comparison. He assumed, Dr. Winkler said, that even if Lulu hadn't gotten any smarter on her own behalf, she would not take such a terrible risk with Sascha's life.

That son-of-a-bitch Winkler, what did he know about masochism? He'd chain-smoked Pall Malls at every session she had with him and soon he was dead of lung cancer at the age of thirty-four. (They hadn't actually proved anything yet.)

Dr. Winkler had been dead for a month.

Lulu was okay, she kept telling her parents. She didn't want to See Someone Else. (They died, like real people.) She was finishing college, wasn't she? No, she hadn't figured out what else she wanted to do, but maybe she just needed more time.

They met Nathan Shinefeld in the ophthalmologist's office.

Lulu had been having occasional bouts of blurred vision since Dr. Winkler's death and everyone thought it best to check out the physical possibilities. There was nothing wrong with her eyes; the blurring refused to put on even a passing show during the examination. In Lulu's journal that night, she wrote that the only result of the visit was that Sascha had made them a friend in the waiting room.

Sascha made a lot of friends. She was three years old and speaking lucidly in complex sentences. She was small for her age, with Woody's huge dark eyes and olive skin and Lulu's silky brown hair that waved without curling unless it was damp. Sascha talked to people on the streets—men, mostly—and in that unexceptional Eisenhower year of 1956, New York was not yet so overstocked with single women and young children that eligible men had gotten into the habit of lowering their eyes at the approach of such a duo—Help! There's a naked need walking down the street!

Nathan was looking at *National Geographic* through horrendously thick eyeglasses. Sascha climbed onto the empty seat adjoining his, stood up so that she could look down over his shoulder, and said in her distinct speech, her voice small but penetrating, "That looks more like a kangaroo than a horse."

Nathan looked at her and smiled. "That's because it is a kangaroo."

"Oh. No wonder."

Nathan smiled at Lulu. "That's a very articulate little girl you have there."

Lulu smiled back.

"Or is she a midget?" Nathan jested.

"I'm not a midget," Sascha said. "I'm just a little small for my age."

Nathan was impressed. "How old are you?"

"Three," Sascha said. "I have my own checkers."

"You're kidding me."

Sascha shook her head. "On the table in my room. If you visit me you'll see them."

"That's very nice of you."

Why did people so value the approval of children, the most easily purchased in the world?

"Can he visit us, Mommy?"

Lulu laughed uncomfortably. "How do you know he wants to?"

"Oh, I'm sure it would be a pleasure," Nathan said. "If your husband doesn't mind."

"We don't have a husband," Sascha said.

Eleven months later, they had one.

Nathan was a (precocious) graduate of the New York Psychoanalytic Institute who was already established in an office with an older analyst, one of his teachers. He had grown up in a comfortable suburban home, an only son among four daughters. His father was an engineer who spent about ten months of every year traveling, and Nathan claimed to have grown up unhappily surrounded by women, always the outsider until he reached New York Psychoanalytic. Then he met Lulu and Sascha and found his domestic role.

Later, Lulu would say that Nathan had adopted Sascha before marrying Sascha's mother, and while this was a jest, it had been clear that Sascha was an important part of the package. What pleasure Nathan's love of Sascha gave Lulu, who had previously gone to absurd lengths to compensate for the fact that Sascha's father was permanently out to lunch! How happy she was to share this kind man with Sascha during his available hours! How natural, in retrospect, that Sascha had always thought of herself as an equal member of the partnership Nathan had joined!

It did seem to work.

No agony and no ecstasy. It was a bargain Lulu thought she was ready to strike. If she had doubts and would have liked to consult Dr. Winkler, it was also true that if Dr. Winkler had been alive, she wouldn't have had to get married in the first place.

Sexually, Nathan was inexperienced for his age and tended to resist Lulu's subtle, embarrassed attempts to show him what would please. On the other hand, Woody had been a woman-pleaser, and look what had come of that!

Nathan was impressively informed and interesting on psychological issues, yet there was a tension in his conversation with people that seemed remarkable in someone who'd begun to earn a living by conversation. (Only later would Lulu understand how much easier it was for Nathan to relate to people from the pedestal of analytic neutrality.)

Anyway, Nathan's tension didn't threaten Lulu as would (now) Woody's easy charm.

Nathan's cynicism about people and the world did not extend to Lulu and Sascha, for whom his regard was high.

And it was most assuredly to no one but Nathan that Dr. Lulu Shinefeld owed her career. For it was Nathan who said that she had a talent along psychological lines; Nathan who wanted her to become independent so she could support Sascha if something were to happen to him; Nathan who reluctantly consented to her having a child if she would first get her Ph.D.; Nathan who negotiated with Lulu's father the loan of money to pay for school and housekeepers and then for her training analysis.

How surprising it was that Nathan, who claimed to have grown up unhappily surrounded by women, never displayed toward either of his sons the affection and interest he'd shown toward Sascha from the day they all met. Teddy and Walden (both names chosen by Nathan) always needed scholastic and athletic achievements to crack the shell of their father's preoccupation with his patients and the affairs of the Institute. Sascha needed only to be herself.

The conception of Lulu's second son was a happy accident that occurred when Lulu was weaning Teddy and didn't realize that she was ovulating again.

"We know," Nathan said angrily, "that there is no such thing as an accident."

"Actually," Lulu replied calmly, "what we know is that many incidents that are described as accidental aren't. If you argue that my getting pregnant is too much in line with my desire for another child to be a true accident, I will have to agree with you. On the other hand, it never occurred to me that I was about to get pregnant. It failed to enter my conscious mind."

"And to what do you attribute this failure?" inquired Nathan frostily.

"To a deep-seated desire to have another child," replied Lulu, smiling sweetly, as indeed she might, for this was an argument in which both sides perfectly suited her purpose. She couldn't lose.

She couldn't lose the baby, anyway.

6

Dr. Shinefeld walked toward her office on the day after Labor Day. It had been a more than reasonable vacation. Nathan had taken the boys for the last two weeks in August and they seemed to have enjoyed themselves. Nathan was not yet with a woman and the boys had apparently sensed that for the first time in their lives, their father had some positive interest in them beyond their homework. They'd come home for the last few vacation days in East Hampton rested and rather happy, willing to overlook the fact that their mother had been contented in their absence.

Lulu had had dates with some dull men and been pleased to find herself unresponsive to their second calls. She'd spent time with Karen Turner and a few other women she liked but hadn't had time for when she had a husband as well as a full-time career. She felt calm and competent and was looking forward to the work year.

In the office, the doctor looked at her book; there were only three appointments that day. Some of her patients hadn't returned from vacation, and that was fine. She liked to keep her first week light while her brain returned to a working mode. She took out her notes on each of the three patients, made a pot of coffee, and settled down to read.

At two o'clock Dr. Shinefeld opened the waiting room door and experienced a moment of difficulty in retaining her professional composure. The girl sitting in the waiting room was virtually unrecognizable; the doctor might have passed her on the street without realizing that she was Dawn. Her hair had been dyed to a dark brown approximating the color of Dr. Shinefeld's and was plaited into a single braid. The jeans that had once appeared to be part of a trim schoolgirl's uniform were now sloppy pants in a larger size—Dawn had gained at least twenty pounds—and she wore a man's shirt that was a few sizes too large.

"Hi."

As she walked past the doctor into the office, Dawn didn't appear to have any sense that an explanation for her appearance was required. She sat down in the consulting chair. Dr. Shinefeld sat down facing her and smiled.

"So," the doctor said. "Here we are."

"Yes," Dawn said in an abstracted fashion, "but I've lost my place."

She looked at a spot over the doctor's shoulder.

"I don't know what I mean by that. For the past

138

five weeks, all I've been thinking about is getting back here but now I just feel strange. I don't know where you were or if you thought about me...Maybe if I just start talking about Vera, you won't even know who I'm talking about." Dawn burst into tears. "I know it's not true. I know you remember." She looked directly at the doctor for the first time since she'd entered the office. "Don't you?"

"I certainly remember everything and everyone important."

"Am I still Dawn?" the girl asked abruptly. "That's the real question, but I don't want you to answer because what if it's no?"

"Can I persuade you to lie down on the couch?"

"Sure. I didn't even think about it." She lay down. "Ooooohhhhh." She sounded contented. "I'm tired...I guess I must exist. Can you be tired if you don't?"

"Could you talk about that feeling?"

Dawn sat up and swiveled around on the couch so her feet touched the rug.

"No. Too scary. It's like asking me to jump off a cliff...or over a wall...when I don't know what's on the other side."

"Do you want to know?"

Dawn considered. "Yes, but not right now." She lay down again. "I'm so sleepy I can hardly keep my eyes open. Funny, I've been wide awake for most of three days and two nights. Since I came back to New York. Now all of a sudden I can't keep my eyes open." Her speech was growing slurred.

"Not that I wasn't...all right...I never even cried. I was just...off someplace...in purgatory...Not purgatory...someplace...between being alive...and ...being...dead."

She was asleep and remained so until Dr. Shinefeld gently shook her awake at the end of the hour.

☙

"I didn't do any of the things I meant to do," Dawn announced at her second session. "I just spent most of the time keeping my shell intact...Humpty Dawnty sat on a wall. *You* can fall off a wall or jump over it or sink into the ground and accidentally find yourself on the other side...I had a friend at Sidley who took acid and looked in the mirror and couldn't see her own reflection. That's the most terrifying thing that ever happened to anyone. That's why I never took acid or anything like that. I never even did grass until...you know...

"It was a weird summer. I just hung out the whole time, with Vera, with a couple of kids from town who're still there. I didn't feel like seeing anyone I'd have to make an effort with. I was depressed but not needy, so it was okay with Vera. I helped her in the garden a lot. I was happier there than anyplace else. Digging in the dirt. We put up a lot of vegetables. And preserves. Vera hasn't done that in a while, it's too much work, but with me...It's hard to believe Vera's sixty-two years old. God, just saying it gives me the chills. I never think of her as old but I guess she is...I didn't feel like going to Boston. I should've. There were some questions I wanted to ask Tony..."

"What kind of questions?"

"Oh, I don't know. Stuff about my early life that I

never asked, that I didn't think Vera would want to talk about. I was curious to know if Tony knew my birth parents or if she just heard about them. I don't know what gave me the idea of ... Yes, I do. What a ridiculous thing to say. It was the photographs. I haven't told you about the photographs yet. It's funny, they seemed like such a big deal and then ... I feel weird. My face and the tips of my fingers are tingling. Like pins and needles. And my ears ... feel as though they were listening to seashells. It's important, actually, but I didn't feel the importance then. I only feel it now. I was turned off. Maybe not off, but way down ... One day it was raining. I was alone in the house. I decided I wanted to do something about my room. I wanted it to be more cheerful. I was wondering how Vera would react if I told her I wanted to paint my walls red, but then I figured even if she didn't mind, red walls would be a little overwhelming. Suddenly I thought about the furniture in the attic. Don't ask me why. Tony used to say I was the only little girl in the world who didn't want to rummage in the attic. Anyway, I went upstairs and there it was, the first thing I saw. The chair. The Lonely Chair. You know what I'm talking about, don't you?"

"Yes."

"It made me feel so sad ... Strange ... I don't remember seeing it before but I must've. I must've been up there at least once when I was a kid, and it stuck in my mind ... There was a crib. I guess it was mine. An old sofa. Some faded green upholstered kind of stuff. Then some dining room chairs. And the trunks. All lined up against one of the low walls.

Maybe eight or ten of them. A few big steamers and then some of the old wooden kind. Full of books, clothes, junk—I don't know why Vera saved them. She's not sentimental. Maybe she thought I'd want them. I kept looking until I got to some photo albums. Maybe I wouldn't have even opened the first album if I weren't coming here. Of course, that's probably why I was up there in the first place. In the whole time with Dr. Seaver I never... Once or twice things came up, he asked if I had memories, but then, you know..." Dawn took a deep breath and exhaled. "Cut out the bullshit, Dawn," she muttered. But she was having difficulty breathing. Finally she sat up.

"I don't know what's going on. I can't get a deep breath. Do you mind if I stand up and sort of walk around the room while I tell you?"

"If you have to," the doctor said. "But it would be better if you could let your anxiety come out in words instead of discharging it in physical action."

Dawn considered. "I can't. Maybe sitting down in your chair. I mean, in the other chair, facing you. But not lying down."

"Okay. Why don't you do that, then?"

Dawn moved to the chair, faced the doctor nervously. She licked her lips, made another attempt to catch her breath.

"I can't stand this. It was pictures of my parents that's all. Oh my God! Did you hear what I said? I called them my parents... I just called my parents my parents, that's all I'm really saying, isn't it... Vera was in a lot of them but that's not who I meant. I just have to stand up. I can't breathe." She remained in the chair but her body was so tense it appeared she might rocket out of it at any moment.

"It's Vera and my father. They look like the same person except my father wore glasses. They could've been twins in the pictures. Twins of the same sex. Vera's older, but that doesn't show once they're grown up. Lots of the two of them in tennis clothes. White shirts, shorts. You can hardly tell which is which when he's not wearing his glasses." She stood and began pacing around the room. "No, it's worse than that. In some of them you'd have assumed Vera was the man. They were about the same size but somehow, their whole manner, *she's* the macho one... He looks *delicate* compared to her. He just looks very... There are pictures where they're both on horses—same outfits, you know, jodhpurs, jackets—only she looks like a general of the cavalry and he's sort of draped over it sidesaddle!"

Dawn's agitation had increased as she spoke.

"It made me feel crazy! Maybe it shouldn't have. What's the big deal, after all. If she's a lesbian, why shouldn't he have been a... Of course, he had a wife. They had me... I guess you noticed I dyed my hair. Blond felt wishy-washy, bland. Bland blond... It was after I saw the photos. I didn't know who I was... or what... It was partly about wanting to look like you, but it was more that I needed to look... specific... like a real person." She stopped, looked around, seemed surprised to find herself standing. She returned to the chair and sat down.

"I thought I had all that stuff worked out with Dr. Seaver. Who's a woman and who's a man and what makes who what. Now... If I'd felt then the way I feel now I'd have taken the jeep and driven to New York. Right into the elevator. Your office. Forced you to talk to me. Not on the telephone. I needed to *see* you. To see who you were. To see if..."

She paused, appeared to be bewildered.

"Why aren't you wearing your glasses?"

The doctor waited. In fact, she had gotten her first reading glasses that week and wore them suspended from a braided ribbon around her neck. She restrained herself from fingering them. Dawn was staring at her face.

"You do wear glasses, don't you? Or am I going crazy?"

"I've been using these reading glasses," the doctor said, placing the gold-rimmed half-spectacles on her nose.

"No. Those aren't the right ones." Dawn was on the verge of tears. "You used to have different ones, didn't you?"

The doctor shook her head.

Dawn stared at her wildly for a moment. "No. Of course not. It's Tony who had different ones ... No, I don't mean Tony, I mean ... not Vera, it's my father. My real father. Vera never wore glasses until a few years ago. My father wore them and then he didn't wear them. No ... Oh my God! When he didn't wear them he was Vera! I can't believe it," she said, sobbing. "That's why I always called her Daddy. I probably never even knew she wasn't! Why didn't I see it this summer, when I looked at the photos. My brain doesn't work when you're not around. That's scary, actually ... But I suppose it would be scarier to see something like that when you weren't around and I couldn't talk about it...I'm so tired. I feel as if I just walked here from Marbury." She lay down on the couch. "Do you mind when I fall asleep here?"

"No."

"I haven't told you everything." Drowsily. "I haven't told you about Miranda...You know who Miranda is, don't you? My birth mother? I'll tell you something you don't know yet. You know why I was always aware that Miranda committed suicide? It was practically the only thing Vera ever told me about them. She didn't want me to think Miranda was sickly. In Vera's book, killing yourself is a much smaller crime than being sick. It's voluntary. Not this disgusting thing you just let happen...It doesn't sound that unreasonable when I say it, actually. When Vera says it...Vera's lip curls when she tells you someone's sick. Your mother killed herself, my dear, because she did not wish to live. Sounds so reasonable...I was surprised when Vera was ready to let me see a shrink as soon as the psychologist at Sidley said I should. And this time it was *her* idea. She's not the kind of person who believes in shrinks...Maybe shrinks are okay because they get the mind to be in better control of the body. I talked about that a lot with Dr. Seaver, how Vera felt about her body. She was very angry with me when I ran home from school in first grade and told her I wanted to get a penis. She didn't even answer me, she just stomped around the house. I had to wait till Tony came home to hear how someday I was going to have breasts— you know, all that junk, little boys have this but little girls—"

"Junk?"

"I mean it's junk to tell a little kid to wait five or ten years for what she wants. What kid can stand to wait five *days*? Tony ... I mean, it was better after I talked to her, but still ... I went up to my room and put a pair of socks in my underpants. I think I tried different things, and the socks were best. They felt good. I did it every day for quite a while. I forgot about it after I stopped, but then later ... I don't remember when I stopped thinking about things like that, but I did. There were a few years when I never thought about sex or anything connected to sex." She laughed. "Connected to sex. Pretty funny. A penis is connected to sex, all right."

A lengthy silence followed this remark.

"I don't know how I got started on sex. I was going to tell you about Miranda. But now I don't feel like it. I'll tell you what I was going to say, but I don't feel like talking about it a lot. It's that Tony looks like her. Not the way Vera and my father look alike, the features, but there's a sameness. Miranda had long, dark hair; she wore gypsy blouses, big full skirts, like Tony. Very sixties. Very New York. Jewish, I guess I mean."

"Was your mother Jewish?"

"No. At least if she was, I don't know it."

"You know," Dr. Shinefeld said, "one of the things that has struck me is that when you talk about Vera in general, you draw a pleasant picture. Her abilities and so on. But when Vera comes up in some specific connections—your mother's suicide, your wanting a penis, and so on—she sounds like a rather cold, forbidding woman. If those specific times are an example of how it was to live with her, it must have been difficult."

"Not really. You just had to ... You weren't supposed to behave like a child."

"Oh?"

"There were rules. I knew what they were. That was very good for me. Dawn was measuring her words. "A lot of kids these days have no one to tell them what to do. That doesn't work for anyone. I followed the rules, and life was comfortable most of the time ... Are you waiting for me to discover that my whole childhood was a nightmare? Because it's not true, and I don't want it to be. I can't stand to even ... How did we start on this? What were we talking about?"

"The resemblance between Tony and your mother."

"Yes." Dawn's agitation had subsided but was still there, seeking its reason. "It was as though Vera saw my father had gotten himself a lovely gypsy from New York and she had to—Oh, but now you've got me doing it again. Now you're going to tell me I'm saying something awful about Vera and how can I pretend—" The last words were lost in a storm of tears.

Dr. Shinefeld waited.

"It makes me hungry when you do that."

"Do what?"

"I don't know. Something. You're making me very nervous. And being nervous makes me hungry."

"Oh?"

"Not that I was nervous all summer. I guess you noticed that I gained a lot of weight. I don't gain weight very easily, you know ... Most of the time I eat

147

too much. I eat whenever I'm not doing something else, even if I'm not hungry, but no one realizes how much I eat because of my metabolism and because with my height, I can stand it. I used to eat proper amounts in front of Vera, but as soon as she wasn't around... This summer I just ate all the time, and purposely ate stuff that was fattening. Potato chips instead of pop-corn. Coke instead of diet soda. I think I wanted to look this way. Different... Maybe you didn't notice. Or maybe you don't care. I don't care, either. It's a relief to be able to walk around the campus without having girls stare at me because they hate me and boys because they..." She had become more and more agitated as she spoke. "It's a relief not to get twenty phone calls a day. Can you understand that? Can you understand any of this?... Why aren't you answering me? What are you thinking?"

"I'm thinking that you're very angry with me."

"Why? Or are you just playing games?"

"I never do that," the doctor said.

"I *feel* as though you are. I feel as though there's always a secret answer and you know it but you won't tell. You're toying with me. You're the almighty god goddess, and I'm just this poor mortal baby, stumbling around, not knowing where I'm going. You come and go when you please but I have to be here when you tell me to be. *So what if I go away for five weeks at a time and forget about you, Dawn? I'm still going to come back and tell you what your childhood was really like, and if you don't like it, you can...*" She sat up and turned around. "Who do I have besides you and them? *Who?*"

The session was over, but it was clear to the doctor that she couldn't let Dawn leave.

"No one?" she asked. "Is that the way you feel?"

"The way I feel? It's the way it *is!* I really only have you and Vera, and Vera never disappears for five weeks at a time!"

"And that is why I think you're angry with me."

Dawn stared at the doctor for a moment. A terrible struggle was going on within her. Finally her whole body responded to a command to quiet itself.

"No," she said calmly, "you're wrong. I would be angry with you if I didn't have Vera. But I have her, so it's all right."

Then she stood up, picked up her satchel and walked out of the office.

*   ᕙ   *

Dawn didn't appear for her next session and came in the following week mildly apologetic, pointing out that while she had, of course, the right of non-attendance, she should have called so the doctor could use the time instead of just sitting around, waiting.

"I know that it must be very difficult," Dawn said blithely. "Planning your life, making a budget, and so on, if people do a lot of that kind of thing."

The doctor was mildly amused in spite of herself. "It's general analytic practice that patients pay for time they don't use unless the doctor has been able to fill the hour."

"*What?*" Dawn nearly leaped off the couch in an ecstasy of righteous wrath. She could understand if, say, the doctor insisted upon "our paying" for a session like the previous one, when Dawn just hadn't shown up, and the doctor must be very angry with her. But was she really hearing that if she'd given notice, Vera would have had to pay anyway, just because the doctor didn't have enough patients to keep her busy? Furthermore, was it possible that such cruel and unusual punishment had always been the doctor's practice and the doctor had kept it a secret from her? This called into question the doctor's entire ethical system. She was upset...shocked ...stunned. She didn't know how she was going to pass on this news to Vera.

"Was this not Dr. Seaver's practice?" the doctor asked calmly.

"I'm sure it wasn't," Dawn said after a moment. "It didn't come up because I never missed a session."

"It never came up here, either. I rather assumed you knew already."

"I didn't know and I don't believe it's his practice. I'm going to call him up and ask him."

"Fair enough."

"Fair! How can you talk about fair?"

Dr. Shinefeld offered the standard pragmatic and analytic explanations for charging patients for hours reserved for them.

"We are not, you know," Dawn said after a long pause, "made of money."

"We?"

"Vera and I."

"Oh."

"You don't like it when I call us we?" Dawn asked

with self-conscious cunning. "Is that what all this is about? Are you trying to separate Vera and me?"

"No," the doctor said. "Are *you* trying to separate Vera and *me*?"

"What do you mean? You *are* separated. You have nothing to do with each other."

"How do you feel about that?"

"I think it's just fine! Well, not fine, exactly, but... when you look at it, there're certain advantages... All right, I *do* like it. I do *not* want all my eggs in one basket." Dawn burst into tears. "You two are all I have in the world, you know! Tony is sick, and I've given up men, and I didn't make any girlfriends last year because I was so occupied with Tom Grace, and now I don't like the girls who talk to me. The same girls wouldn't talk to me if I looked like myself!"

"Oh?"

"You think it's not true?"

"I'd like you to explain it to me."

"The girls who just need a sidekick, someone who's no competition. Or the other fat, hopeless cases. If I lost weight... Not that I'm planning to, but... My hair's washing out and I most likely won't bother to dye it again, it's too stupid... But that's not the point. The point is that if I look like Dawn... instead of like the little orphan child of Dr. Lulu Shinefeld..." A significant pause to see if this would pass. "Those same girls would drop me. This girl was in my English class last year. One day I was standing outside the classroom with someone, I don't even remember who he was, and I must've been blocking the door, not really blocking it, but she had to walk around me, and out of the blue she began shouting at me that I didn't know there was anyone else in the world. This year she's decided to be my friend. I don't even think she knows it's the same person. It's not, in a way. Do you see what I mean?"

"I think so," the doctor said slowly, "but there's so much going on here at once. If you don't mind, I'd like to try to get the various things you're saying clarified in my mind. This isn't in order of importance—but you mentioned that Tony was ill. Have you had some word that her illness has recurred?"

"Recurred? It doesn't have to *recur*. It's *cancer*. Cancer doesn't just disappear."

"That is not a fact. It's a feeling you have."

"I don't understand what you mean by a *feeling*," Dawn said angrily. "First she had a thisectomy, then she had a thatectomy. They're hollowing out her insides and chopping off her outsides and soon there'll be nothing left. I wish she was dead alread so I wouldn't have to worry about it!" As her tirad ended, Dawn burst into great hacking sobs that took a long time to subside. Then she grew calm. "What else do you need to have clarified?" she asked in a sardonic tone.

"Well, I was interested in hearing you refer to the girl you usually look like as the real Dawn Henley. The golden girl, so to speak. It seems to me that until recently that golden girl was the mask and the real Dawn Henley was the less than beautiful person behind the mask."

"Mmm, that's true... It's as though there are always two of me, a beautiful one and an ugly one. Only sometimes the ugly one's on the outside and sometimes she's on the inside. Well..." She laughed. "I can understand that. I'd rather have two of me than one of me. There are two of you, after all."

"Two of whom?"

"Mmm. I don't know why I said that... You and Vera, I guess. Tony and Vera. There are two of the people I need so there should be two of me to need them. As a matter of fact, if there are two of me, I don't need either of you half as much!" She was enormously pleased with this construction and twisted on the couch to see if the doctor was enjoying it.

The doctor smiled.

"Now, Dr. Shinefeld," Dawn said playfully, "are there any other questions you'd like to ask either of us?"

"Are you interested in telling me about the little orphan child of Dr. Shinefeld?"

"Well... The bad Dawn Henley probably wants to say that *you're* supposed to be telling her."

"Not really."

"I didn't say *really*. I said that's what she would say."

"But *she* is *you*."

"Anyway," Dawn said, "why does one of them have to be good and one bad? Why can't they both be all right?"

"Why, indeed?"

"No," Dawn said after a moment, "it doesn't work that way. You have to have some contrast. You can't just have a couple of Goody Two-shoes... Goody Four-shoes, I guess it would be... all sweet and dull like the Bobbsey twins. The Dawnsey twins. Yiich. They'd just get fucked over all the time. By the Tom

Grace twins." Pause. "I never used words like that much—like fucked over—here. Did I?"

"I'm not sure. It would be fair to say that your language isn't sprinkled with them."

"Well, I'm working on it. I decided I like those words. The kids at Sidley teased me about not cursing, but now...Fuck. Shit. Prick. They make me sound tough. I like that. I started this summer, except I had to be careful because of Vera. I guess I think she'd kick me out of the house if she ever heard me say *fuck*."

"And what will *I* do?"

"You? Nothing. Analyze me."

"What is there to analyze?"

"Nothing, I guess. We wouldn't have to analyze why I was breaking the rules because there aren't any rules here. At least they're different." She laughed. "Different rules for different fools...That sounds angry but I don't have any reason to be angry now. I feel fine...I remember I was angry at the beginning of the session but I don't even remember why, so it couldn't have been very important."

"Perhaps. But usually analysis is the opposite of real life in that respect."

"Now what," Dawn asked irritably, "is *that* supposed to mean?"

"That the more important a subject is, the more likely one is to forget it—or repress it, as we say."

"I'm not repressing anything!" Dawn exploded. She sat up. "Do you see what you're doing? You decided I must be angry with you so you're forcing me to be angry to prove you're right! But you're wrong. If I'm angry now, it's nothing, and it's going to go away. It's gone already." She lay down. "Now, what were we talking about?"

"About your being angry at the beginning of the session."

"At what?"

"First there was Vera and having to pay for sessions you don't attend."

"I don't even know if she can afford *this*. I'll have to talk about it with her sometime. I've never asked for more than she could give me, but she doesn't live as though she has a lot to spare. I don't know how she'd feel about paying for something she isn't getting. Of course, she's not getting this, either, but I am, and she does love me, in her own way. As far as my own reactions go, I can see where you might make a case for getting the payment no matter what. You have to live, too. Maybe a certain number of people come to sessions they wouldn't bother coming to, but then they remember they're paying anyway. Anyhow, it's not a point I'd care to argue with you . . . What else?"

"What else?"

"What else do you think I'm angry about?"

"You say you're not angry about anything."

"But you don't believe me . . . That makes me feel as though you're calling me a liar. And *then* I get angry."

"All right."

"You mean you really think I'm lying?"

"I think the idea of being angry with me is frightening to you, so you convince yourself that you're not."

"Why is it frightening? It feels *good* to be angry. I'd rather be angry than scared."

"I suppose we're talking about being angry and then getting scared."

"I'd rather stay angry." Dawn heard her own words. "I mean, if I have to get angry in the first place. But I don't see why I have to."

"Well, one reason would be that you feel dependent on someone who abandons you for five weeks at a time. Who turns you into the little orphan daughter of Dr. Shinefeld."

"I know I wasn't really an orphan." Dawn's voice was small and meek. It was apparent that she did not consciously apply the word to herself.

"But you felt like one."

"Yes and no. Having Vera there, with all her habits and her rules and her...is very reassuring, you know? Vera's going to live forever, and she's forever going to be doing things the same way and assuming that you should, too. But there's also...She can be very...I don't know if I...It was awful! That's the truth! She's awful to live with! I don't know how I could've stood her when I was little, how I could've gone on year after year just...Vera has more rules than the rule book, and when you're with her, you just do what she wants. It's the only way to live with her. Not that she'd punish you. Or yell at you to pick up your clothes, or do the dishes the minute you finish eating. She doesn't *have* to. You do it because she wants you to do it and what she wants is stronger than what you want because she's stronger than you...me...than anyone. She's like John Wayne. I used to have dreams about John Wayne and that's who it was. Vera! Only she used to be more like him because he was okay if you didn't cross him and he could be kind. Not that Vera is *un*kind, but since Tony, there's no feeling of... Tony must've been the one who softened her. Tony never exactly argued, but she'd joke around, or wink at me. It was like a promise that it would all pass. Or she'd talk to Vera when they were alone... Thank God I don't live there anymore! If I'd had to stay there alone with Vera after Tony d——"

This time there was a very long pause. Finally, she went on in a quieter tone. "You know what I almost said, don't you? I don't care. I wanted to say it. Maybe that makes me some kind of a monster, but it would be better if she was dead, in a way. I know I'm really sick. How could I do that to her? She was the light of my life, Tony. She was the sunshine. Vera was the house, but Tony brought the light into the house. I think that right from the very beginning I loved her more than I loved Vera." Dawn wept.

"And she looked like your mother, too," the doctor said softly.

Dawn wept more fully.

When she spoke again there was a considerable change in her voice. It was calm, almost remote. "Why did you say that? About Miranda?"

"I was making a connection."

"You wanted me to cry."

"You *were* crying."

"You wanted me to cry harder."

"I wanted you to see that your anguish, and your rage at Tony—at the possibility that she'll abandon you by dying—are connected to your feelings about your first mother."

"Just because they look alike, you mean?"

"No. Not just because they look alike."

"Then why?"

The doctor paused, debating with herself, then finally said what had come to her mind.

"Because after the first death, there is no other."

"Oh God," Dawn said. "Oh my God!"

This time, the tears ended with the session.

~

On Wednesday afternoon Dawn glided glacially into the office. Nor was she about to melt—not even into a chair. She stood in the middle of the room, waited for Dr. Shinefeld to settle down, then began speaking.

"I don't like what you did the other day. Making me feel ways I don't want to feel. You were treating me . . . Sometimes I feel like a marionette. Or a hand puppet. This isn't what I meant to say, but . . . I go through all these crazy fits here, and when I leave, I don't even know if the feelings I left with were mine. How can they be if I go home and they're gone and I collapse because there's no one pulling the strings anymore? I don't have the feelings because you're not there, pulling them out of me—or putting them into me—I don't even know which it is. No wonder I have to put you and Vera in separate places. The two of you together would crush me in a minute . . . You see? There we go again. I love and admire Vera. I told you that and it's true. What came out the other day . . . I was with Dr. Seaver for four years and none of it ever came out, not like that, and he's the world's greatest shrink, and so maybe the reason they never came out is, they weren't there! Maybe they're your

158

ideas, not mine. Of course, if I were to lie down and you were to say *Tell me*, in that voice you have that wrings things out of people that maybe were never there in the first place..." Dawn paused to see if she would be challenged.

Dr. Shinefeld nodded.

"Why are you nodding?'

"I'm acknowledging that I hear what you say."

Dawn shifted. She was still wearing over one shoulder the heavy book satchel the doctor hadn't seen in a while.

"Maybe you noticed that I brought my satchel today. I wanted you to see the number of books I have to carry around this year because I wanted you to understand when I tell you... I'm thinking of not coming here anymore, and it seems to me that if I'm going to stop, this is the right time to do it. Before I get all involved again. I'm doing very well in school so far. Except I couldn't do schoolwork or anything else after the last time I was here. I was saner when I began with you than I am now. Aside from the car accident I was all right. I understand that all you do is bring out the craziness deep inside me, but what difference does that make? It keeps me from functioning. I have to get an education and do something with myself so I'm not always dependent on the Tom Graces of the world. I never even thought about earning a living until recently. I'm going to be twenty years old next year, and I assume Vera will stop supporting me when I finish school. My needs have been pretty modest until now, except for all this psychoanalysis. Perhaps at some point Vera will be unwilling or unable to spend a hundred and fifty dollars a week, or whatever it is...Do you charge fifty dollars per session?"

Dawn's speech, for a while sprinkled with *I means*, and *Oh Gods* and various New Yorkisms, had reverted to its original New England Waspishness.

"Sixty."

"Good grief! Do you know that's higher than Dr. Seaver?"

"Possibly. It's also possible that fifty was his rate when you saw him and he's raised it since."

"Well, I suppose I can find out if I really want to. But at the moment, money isn't of paramount importance." She shifted again, obviously becoming more uncomfortable under the weight of the satchel. Finally she took it off her shoulder and rested it against the door, which she also leaned against. "Although...To be candid, I have to say that I cannot conceive of paying you sixty dollars an hour if I could have Dr. Seaver for fifty. I'm sorry if that offends you. You've always encouraged me to be frank. In any event, I obviously have to make some decisions. Decide whether to continue in analysis, and if so, in which kind. Then I have to find out what Vera's resources are and whether it's reasonable to ask her to continue spending this kind of money." Dawn looked around the room as though to find some alternative to the couch or chair that would be comfortable without compromising her.

"Te——I'm curious," Dr. Shinefeld said. "You've raised many issues..."

"Not because I expect to solve them here."

"Yes, I understand that. But the phrase *which kind*

of analysis intrigues me. Are you contemplating another form of therapy?"

"I meant you or Dr. Seaver."

"Is it our personalities that you'd call different? Or
our methods?"

"Everything," Dawn assured her. "It was an entirely different experience going to him."

"Could you tell me how?"

"What difference does it make?"

"Well, after all, you're talking about leaving treatment with me. You should know, if you don't already,
that I care about you and don't want you to do
that—although it's certainly your privilege to leave
when you choose. In any event, I'd like to examine,
for my own sake, the possibility that I've made some
mistakes with you."

"You mean you think it's possible? You don't just
think I'm being crazy?" Dawn looked around the
office, eyed the chair, looked back to the doctor. "I
have to think. It's hard to explain." She watched the
doctor suspiciously for a moment, then eased herself
toward the chair. "I never felt as though he was
pushing me ... or pulling things out of me ... I don't
know which is worse, having something rammed
down my throat or pulled out of it ... but I never felt
that way. When he told me something I didn't know,
I felt as though he was *teaching* me. Not *pushing* me."

For a while Dawn was lost in thought. When she
looked at the doctor again, she spoke with a mild
reluctance.

"I'm thinking that maybe I haven't been fair. I
mean, maybe the reason I feel so different is just that
you're a woman and he's a man ... What made me

think that is ... I was trying to remember what Dr. Seaver said to me when he wanted me to associate. And I realized ... Suddenly I heard him say *Tell me* ... I don't know if he said it all the time or just ... Anyway, even when I hear him say it now, it doesn't sound the same as when you say it. It doesn't bother me. Not that it always bothered me when you said it. That just began ... when I came back." She slumped down in the chair. "I guess the truth is, I loved to explain things to him. He was teaching me but *I* was teaching *him*, too, because there were things only I could explain ... about what it was like to be me. With you I don't have the advantage, of being different. There's nothing about me you don't know—or couldn't know—because it's the same as yourself or because ... Maybe he was a little smarter than you are, but you have, whatever, a different kind of power over me. I remember the day you told me that story about the little girl, you know, *I'm leaving a part of myself with you* ... It was magical. It changed the whole world. All the colors got brighter. *Literally*." A dark cloud passed over Dawn's face. "Don't you see it's scary for someone to have that much power over you? Especially a woman? And a woman can have it more easily ... in the way I'm talking about."

Dawn had become more agitated as she spoke; now she collected herself and grew calm.

"The more I think of it, the more it seems like a male-female issue. I may simply be more comfortable with a man. When I was uncomfortable with Dr. Seaver it was different. I wanted more from him than I could have." Dawn laughed shyly. "I wanted more from him, and I want less from you... I suppose that sounds foolish, but why should I care when I'm talking about leaving?... That's part of the problem. I'm still worried about what you think. It still seems more important than what I think. Not just that. The truth is that I value... I don't just value you... I love you." Her voice trembled. "I used to get angry at Dr. Seaver. I'd yell at him—well, not yell, exactly, but raise my voice. Argue. It was fun. I felt as if he *encouraged* me to express my ..."

She was silent for a long time.

"I hear what I'm telling you. That when he encouraged me to talk I liked it, and when you encourage me I don't. So it's not anything that's your fault that I'm talking about. I shouldn't have been so... Then the problem is, to decide. After all, if that's the way I am... maybe there's nothing for me to do but go back to Dr. Seaver.... But that's frightening, too. And I don't want to never see you again. Is it possible I could see him and just come here once in a while?"

"No."

"Why not?"

"Because that would be acting out a conflict in your mind instead of trying to understand it."

"I can't bear the thought of never seeing him. I've never been able to. I still think I see him on the street sometimes, and the person I'm seeing doesn't even look like him. It's only that I want it so badly that I keep making him up."

"Was that true during the summer?"

"Not really. I was too much involved in... I was

163

thinking about coming back here. It was you I was missing."

"Why do you think your eagerness to see Dr. Seaver has surfaced now?"

"Because I've been upset about what's going on here, I guess." She began to cry. "All summer long, I couldn't wait to come back here. I kept thinking ... Bliss. I'd come back and sink down on the couch and ... I'd be your baby again."

"But in fact, when you came in that first day, you sat in the chair."

"No," Dawn said. "Are you sure?"

"Yes."

"And then what happened?"

"I suggested that you lie down and you went quite willingly, as though it hadn't occurred to you before."

"Which would make sense if I hadn't been thinking about the couch all summer. So why did I do it, then?"

"I think you were conflicted about lying down when you came in. Being swamped by the feelings that were aroused by our long separation, and by the events of the summer. Your discovery of the photographs, and the lonely chair. Your difficulties with Vera." *Your inability to face Tony*, the doctor had been about to add, but then decided it was too much at once.

"I wasn't ready to face it all. I just wanted to enjoy being back here. I wanted to feel *good*."

"And did you?"

"Yes, but not in the way I expected. I relaxed, but then something told me not to relax, to watch out. I felt . . . It had more to do with what went on here the second day."

"Yes. Well, when I said that I might have made a mistake, what I had in mind was that I might have pushed you a little too fast into dealing with terribly difficult matters. But it seems to me that the material that came up, about your very early life, came of its own accord. It was on your mind anyway. And it was related to your feelings about being abandoned by me."

"So you thought we would be able to work it out together."

The doctor nodded.

"Together," Dawn repeated. "You did it for a good reason."

"Or for what I *thought* was a good reason. I might have been wrong."

There was a long pause. Dawn looked at Dr. Shinefeld, looked away, came back.

"All summer long I felt pushed by Vera and then I came back here and got pushed by you. Tony's the only one who never pushed me. Tony's the one who . . . *After the first death there is no other.* That's what you said that freaked me." She wept briefly, but cut off the tears. "I didn't want to hear it. It makes me feel like some creepy, pathetic little baby, always getting abandoned, over and over. As though there's nothing I can do to make my own life. There's a chain of circumstance. It began with my sick—with sick Miranda—and then it went on to sick Tony, and then . . ."

"Yes?"

"No . . . I was going to say it went on to you, but

you're not sick. You don't remind me of either of them. Well, maybe a little physically, but...How could you remind me of Miranda? I never even knew her. That's what I mean about making these connections."

"You're not really making them. You're finding them."

"But it's like finding the bars on a cage. It makes me feel worse."

"If I thought that was more than a temporary condition," Dr. Shinefeld told her, "I wouldn't be doing this work."

ᕤ

"I dreamed about the Lonely Chair," Dawn said at her next session. "Except it was a lot of them. I don't remember most of it. In another part of the dream there was someone moving around, tiptoeing. No, not tiptoeing. Sort of sailing. Not quite touching the ground when they walked. Maybe they were just shadows. It was the quietest dream I ever had. All my dreams are very quiet or very noisy. Nothing in between. I used to have a different kind of dream. Until last year. Last year I hardly had any dreams, actually. My old dreams were very noisy, lots of people, lots of action. Whole family *sagas*. I had my own village and all my dreams automatically took place there. Dr. Seaver got a kick out of them. It was a beautiful little village, like in a Breughel painting, only it was called Patterson. It has—had—a wall around it and a big house in the middle, a kind of town hall, with a barbecue, where everyone collected for parties and meetings. Always something going on. Lots of animals. Dogs, cats, mice, turtles, gerbils, rabbits. My recent dreams are just about things. No animals, even. The chair, with its shiny wooden slats that you can see between. The crib...I don't know why I said that about a crib. I never had a dream about a crib...although...the way the chairs were lined up in this dream, they were almost more like a crib than a chair...Very still. Not rocking." She shuddered. "Empty. It's the Empty Chair, that's what I should've called it. I wonder why I called it lonely...I made the chair lonely instead of the person who was looking at it. Empty." Her voice quivered. "That sounds much worse, doesn't it...I feel as though if I start crying now, I'll never stop. Does that happen to anyone? To start crying and then...it just goes on forever and ever? I guess you'd have to be taken away to some special home. A place for people who aren't exactly crazy but they started crying in therapy and never stopped...I guess I could find a place for it in Patterson. The Home for Eternal Weepers. I don't know, it's pretty crowded already. That's the whole idea of Patterson, actually, that it's crowded. You know, it's funny, I never talked to Dr. Seaver about the village as a whole. I mean, he knew it had a name. We analyzed that some. *Marbury, Patterson*— you know. But we sort of took it for granted that they were where I had dreams...I don't know what I'm getting at exactly, except the stuff about noisy and quiet, for instance. Full dreams, empty dreams ...Before Dr. Seaver I hardly ever remembered my dreams. When he asked me about dreams, I really started having them. But I had to make up this whole town before I could stand to dream. I'm not sure I ever thought of it that way before. You see, there really is something to be frightened of, isn't there. I used to have a whole village and now all I have is a chair...or a crib...or both."

There was a momentous stillness in the room so that suddenly the hum of the air conditioner was audible in a way that one didn't normally notice.

"A crib and a chair," the doctor said.

"I can't stand it. I can't stand for the chair to be empty. I keep wanting to put someone in it."

"Oh?"

"Mmm. But all I can see is a shadow. I can't seem to...Oh God. Now I see...after all that...it's Tony." The dam burst and Dawn wept. "Tony's been preying on my mind. I feel guilty, and I keep pushing her away, and now here I am right back where I was. I don't think I can stand this."

"Try to keep talking about it," the doctor suggested.

"I just don't want to love anybody who's sick. I know I sound just like Vera. I *am* just like her, in that way. There are things I want to change, but that's not one of them...I always thought I hung out with boys because they were who sought me out, and that's part of the reason, but also, boys...Women groove on sickness much more than men do. On taking care of sick people. Tony used to love it when I was sick. She'd make me tea and toast and tell me stories, use it as an excuse not to go to school that day...Oh my God! What am I doing? I can't believe I'm attacking her because she took care of me. She was the only one who loved me even when I was sick! She didn't *need* me to be sick—she was just warm and good and..."

Dawn dissolved into tears but soon began speaking again. "I'm making excuses. Turning everything against her so I don't have to visit her ... She's ... mutilated. There's a place on her arm where she had the surgery ... It's like a deep cut. A fold. You can see the scar ... She wears these dresses in the summer that don't hide it enough. She isn't even self-conscious. It's all I can think about when I'm with her. At least in the winter she's more covered up. The last time I was there she was wearing this African batik print kind of dress. Black and white and brown. I hated it. The print is beautiful, but the brown ... the sepia ... that's what it is. I hear it as soon as I call it sepia. It's about the prints ... What about the prints? ... They're about death ... I've always known that, even when I didn't know it. Even if I still don't know what I mean when I say it. The mood is death ... There are two prints in the series that have the same colors as the dress ... The marigolds and the apple. Sepia, black, and white ..."

"Yes?" the doctor prompted gently.

"There was something else that happened at Tony's the last time I was there. I forgot until now. It's weird, because it's the main reason I was miserable while I was there." Dawn paused, as though sensing her own eagerness to move away from that most painful of topics and wondering if the doctor would challenge her. The doctor did not.

"Len has a daughter. Two, actually. I met the other one once, but she's not important. They're both older than me. I. Did you hear the way I corrected myself? Have I been doing that a lot? That's not me, that's Vera in me ... Where was I? Len's daughter.

Susan. This absolutely ordinary human being who got married and had a baby and thinks she *owns* it. Sheri. With an *i*. Can you believe it? All her mother could think about was the toilet. Every time the baby took a deep breath, Susan wanted to know if she had to make a pee-pee...or a poo-poo..." Dawn shuddered. "I don't know why but it struck a real nerve in me. It's funny I never mentioned it."

"Well," the doctor said, "you've been concerned with being coerced...pushed, pulled, and so on. Some feelings about Vera's and my controlling you have come up since then."

"Controlling. When you say that, it makes me want to jump off the couch and scream at you to leave me alone."

"You can, you know."

"What?"

"Scream at me."

A moment of silence. Then Dawn laughed. "Oh no. I couldn't do that. Not here, certainly. It's not even you I'm mad at. It's Vera...or Tony."

"I'm a stand-in."

"For who?"

"Either one."

"Oh yes. Transference. I talked about that with Dr. Seaver. He explained how my feelings for him weren't just my feelings for him, they were really mostly for my Vera father. I don't see what difference it makes. Maybe it makes him feel better to send me away if he can tell himself it's not him I care about, but what difference does it make to me? If it's the wrong kind of love, or you can't have him, it's transference and you have to analyze it. If it's some Dartmouth preppie,

170

you don't have to analyze it because it's okay. Kosher. Tom Grace taught me that word. He learned it from the people he did business with. I'll tell you something—anyone who ever thought he was in love with me... I think transference is what I meant when I said they only thought it was love. They saw something they liked, so they took my outsides and put someone else's insides into me. Maybe I did the same things with Tom Grace and Dr. Seaver. Only I don't think so. I think I fell in love with who they *were*. At least, with who I *thought* they were. That's the important question, actually. Whether I thought they were who they really were. If I was wrong, maybe I could fall out of love with them. If I was right, well then, I'm stuck with it, aren't I. It's not possible to fall out of love with someone that good."

"Would you care," Dr. Shinefeld asked, "to discuss love and transference as they apply to you and me?"

"Hmm, let's see, love and transference." Dawn was consciously cute. "I love you, all right, at least when you're not being like Vera. Or maybe I love you all the time but I *like* you when you don't remind me of Vera. I liked you as soon as we met, but it wasn't that I had a choice. I thought a woman would be good for me. Maybe I was a little resentful, too, that I needed a woman even if it wasn't what I wanted."

"So," the doctor said slowly, "there was a kind of safety in dealing with me that stemmed from my not really being who you wanted."

"That doesn't hurt your feelings, does it?"

"No. I'm trying to understand what it means in the analysis."

"I came in with this attitude. But when I saw you

171

looked a little like Tony, talked like her, dressed a little like her, I felt safe."

"I'm afraid our time is up," the doctor said. "But I think we should explore the possibility that my being safe because I was like Tony is only part of the story . . . and that being like her makes me unsafe, as well."

$\backsim$

Dawn began the next session by repeating those last words of the doctor's, which she had interpreted as a warning that the doctor, too, could fall ill at any moment.

"No," Dr. Shinefeld said, "I wasn't warning you at all. Certainly not about any illness of mine. What I was bringing up was the various meanings for you in the fact that you find Tony and me to be similar in some ways."

"The first time there was anything wrong with Tony . . . Not the whatever you call it. I don't know when it was. Before I went to boarding school . . . There was no warning . . . She came home late from school because she had an appointment. Vera didn't even say doctor appointment. The next day she went to the hospital in Burlington instead of going to school. They told me she had to stay over because the trip was too far for one day. But it was for tests . . . Tony told me after, she lied because Vera insisted . . . You know when I just said *after*? I meant after the divorce, but I can't say that anymore. It sounds phony, as though I made it up that they were married in the first place . . . I guess I wanted it all to be real. They never told me to call them Mommy and Daddy, you know. I remember I asked them once, when I was with Dr. Seaver, and Tony said I just did it all along. First it was Daddy and Tony, then, when I heard other kids, Daddy and Mommy ... When you're a kid, you want everything to have names. I still like to know what things are called."

"Why do you suppose you don't want to know what Tony's surgery was called?"

"What do you mean? First she had the womb one, the hysterectomy, then she had ... Well, if I could think of it last year and not this year, it's because everything connected to Tony has gotten worse in my mind. When I feel guilty toward a person it doesn't make me nicer to them, it makes me worse. You should see me with Rob Grace. I don't know if I told you, he's in my English class ..." Dawn proceeded to discuss at length Rob Grace's friendliness toward her and his apparently unquenched thirst for her affections, and how it made her treat him badly even though she had to say there was something nice about his liking her with twenty-five extra pounds. "... Where were we?"

"Someplace you didn't want to be."

"Tony's surgery." (a small giggle) "You're right. I didn't. I didn't even want to know ... Mastectomy. Maaaaahhhhhs-tectomy," she repeated, drawing the first syllable out to a bleat. "It's a stupid name. It sounds like surgery to remove your mother ... I know why you're not talking. It isn't funny. I hardly ever make jokes. Only when it's something so awful I can't stand it ... I don't want to feel this way about Tony. I want to love her again. No, that's not true, I don't want to love her again because if I love her and she dies I won't be able to stand it. But I don't want to act like such an absolute...ASSHOLE!" She brought forth the word with great difficulty and then began to sob. "I really can't stand the way I'm acting. She was everything in the world to me, and I've thrown her in the garbage can along with her breast and her—I know what it is but I don't want to say it. I don't want to think they threw her womb in the garbage can because I feel as though I came out of her womb and they threw me away with it." Dawn sobbed uncontrollably for some time. "I always knew that I felt as if she was my mother, but I didn't know...It's as though I came out of her womb. Tony. My mommy. Oh my God, I don't know what I'll do if she dies!"

"I think," Dr. Shinefeld said, "that your assumption that her death is imminent is very much related to what happened to your real mother."

∽

It wasn't until more time had passed—until, in fact, the Christmas vacation with its attendant separation from Dr. Shinefeld was upon her—that Dawn felt enough internal pressure to confront the meaning of those words.

Dawn was exploring and venting her hitherto unavailable feelings about being controlled by Vera, whom she now didn't want to see. She was also trying, against her own strong resistance, to work out her feelings about Tony and her illness. Fear, of course, was at the heart of the matter, and Dawn touched on the various meanings of Tony's illness, and their possible connection to the unremembered loss of her "birth mother," like a half-frozen kitten exploring, inch by inch, the stovetop where she might be saved...comforted...burned. When some question touched upon the nature of Dawn's life as an infant, the answer was always the same: Dawn had never thought to ask. She didn't even know the name of the town where her parents had lived, though she thought it was a small town like Marbury, except in Massachusetts. As far as she was concerned—and apparently as far as Leif Seaver had seen—the crucial facts of Dawn's life had been forged in the Marbury triangle.

Now Dawn was planning to spend Christmas with Tony. She had gone so far as to call, apologize for her delinquency, and say that a lot had happened. She didn't have to give much notice, Tony had told her, but if Len's entire family should happen to come, Dawn might not have a room to herself.

Once committed to the visit, Dawn became anxious about how she was going to feel all week in that household.

"I can't believe that I'm letting myself in for the same thing all over again," she moaned. "I can't believe I'm going to sit there for a week and watch fucking Susan push her kid to the john."

Dr. Shinefeld didn't interrupt this potentially useful monologue to point out that almost a year had passed and the situation had likely altered.

"I have a picture of myself trying to talk to Tony and Susan is being...There's a moment when I'm absolutely frozen, and then I stand up and I begin to scream at her for everything she ever did to her baby and everything Vera ever did to me. But then something cuts me off. It's not like when I don't scream at you. It's more that I feel . . . I don't know . . . that if I do it I'll break something . . ."

"Break something?"

"If I close my eyes I can . . . Uh-oh, I don't think I want to see it . . . All right. Closed. There I am. I'm standing in the middle of Tony's living room screaming and—Ahh!" She broke off with a short, frightened shout. "Oh my God! Everything started to break up. I mean in the room. It was awful. The people, the furniture, the whole place crumbling." She began to shiver, grabbed the bright red afghan that had appeared at the foot of the couch when the cold weather began, wrapped it around herself, and sat hunched over on the edge of the couch. "You got me to this place. What if I get into it again when you're not around?" Dawn heard her own angry voice and began the rationalizing process. "I know this is what we have to do. And I know you can't follow me around like a baby . . . *But at least you can tell me what's going on. It's too scary to be in this place by myself!*"

"Well," the doctor said slowly, "as far as I can see, you're on the horns of a terrible dilemma. To have a mommy— at least a Vera mommy, or a Susan mommy, or a Dr. Shinefeld mommy—is to be ordered around, pushed, controlled, have things pulled out of you, put into you, and so on. But if, in your rage, you should succeed in destroying the whole world of mommies, then perhaps you'd have nothing. You'd be alone. And that would be even worse."

Dawn began to cry. After a while she lay down on her side, still swaddled in the red afghan, in an almost fetal position, and continued to cry, then whimper, for some time.

"That's it," she whispered. "That's really it... I'm so tired..."

⌒

"You're nothing like Vera, you know," was the way she began her next session. "Only in that you have power over me. It's more Tony you make me think of. I suppose everyone you love has power over you. But they ought to be careful. It can be too much ... You're both of them, actually. That's the main problem. Sometimes you're Tony and sometimes you're Vera, but sometimes you're both. No wonder I can't stand to be away for long."

"But also, it's a wonder that you can stand to come."

"It's true," Dawn said after a while. "But I don't really feel that way. At least not most of the time." She twisted on the couch. "Another dilemma, huh?"

The doctor smiled.

"I really love you, you know."

The doctor waited.

"You're supposed to say something. You're supposed to say, *I love you, too, Dawn, and I can't stand to be away from you, either.*"

"I will think about you and be concerned for you. Not being able to stand to be away from someone you care about—that's something else. That's analyzable."

7

In 1971 Sascha Shinefeld had capped an adolescence that was like a black comedy of the sixties by running away from home shortly before she was due to graduate from the only private school in Manhattan that could have imagined giving her a diploma.

It was Nathan's dictum that no one had an unconscious except one's patients, and for a long time Lulu had been too distressed by the philosophical immorality of this idea to notice that it was the only reasonable basis for raising children. How could a young woman earning her Ph.D. in clinical psychology have been expected to close her eyes and ears when she returned to that most fascinating laboratory of all, her own home? There was so much to observe in the behavior of any child, and one's own child was by definition the most interesting.

There had been a great deal to learn, for example

from the dynamic of the Trusty Trio, as Sascha had dubbed the members of their household when she began reading comics. This phrase was more than felicitous and was a logical product of Sascha's conviction that there was parity among them. If, for reasons of size and convenience, Nathan happened to share a bedroom with Lulu, that didn't mean that anything occurred between Nathan and Lulu that couldn't happen between any other two members of the Trusty Trio.

Nathan and Lulu had never attempted to correct their daughter's misperception of her place in the world. Nathan had adored Sascha as though she were his own and accepted with ease her childish fantasies. Lulu, in her desire to make up to Sascha for the loss of her real father (a loss Sascha might not actually have experienced, certainly not in the manner Lulu did) and in her inability to bear the thought of seeing Sascha hurt again, had helped her daughter to perpetuate the myth of the Trusty Trio.

Life had conspired with them as well. Lulu's classes were arranged around Sascha's school schedule and Nathan's hours at home. Gladly did Nathan allow his wife to bounce off to school the moment he got home from work. Often Lulu would prepare dinner for the three of them, hastily eat by herself in the kitchen, then run off to class, leaving Nathan's and Sascha's places set and their food warm in the oven. In this period Sascha wrote a school composition about family roles, explaining that she and her mother both went to school, but her mother was also the housekeeper.

By the time Lulu was in her second analysis and

able to find the reflection of her own childish desires in Sascha's, it was too late to do anything except anger Sascha by appearing to alter the foundation of their lives. Still, they might have been able to muddle through if Lulu, faced with the possibility of beginning her professional life without the additional children she desired, hadn't cashed in her chips with her husband. Or, more specifically, thrown away her diaphragm.

It began, as do so many family disasters, at the dinner table.

Sascha had greeted with alternating disbelief and disgust the news that Lulu was pregnant. Sascha's behavior had already become identifiably Early Adolescence (she was a few months short of fourteen), and because of the coincidence of timing, it had been difficult to determine how much of her behavior was due to socioglandular forces and the extent to which it had been aggravated by the recognition that the Trusty Trio was about to turn into a quartet.

"How come you never told me," Sascha asked casually as she helped herself to salad on this particular night, "that my Real Father wanted us to go to California with him?"

Lulu put down her fork. Her heart was beating wildly, as though she hadn't spent hundreds of hours in her recent analysis discussing what she would do if the subject of Woody—or if Woody himself, for that matter; he was still, after all, a recurring figure in her best dreams—should ever appear in their lives. Lulu looked at Nathan and was startled in spite of herself. He was staring at his adopted daughter in an agony of disbelief. There were tears in his eyes. His lower lip was trembling.

"I thought," Nathan said, "that you loved me."

So much for twenty years at New York Psychoanalytic and fifteen years of practice.

"Of course I love you, Nathan," said Sascha sweetly. "I *adore* you." She went to his chair, hugged him from behind, kissed his bald spot. "That doesn't mean I can't love my Real Father."

Lulu had a wild impulse to leave the apartment, the city, the planet. She marshaled her forces and remained immobile.

"Am I to infer that you've been in touch with Woody?" she asked quietly, although her heart, which didn't know about being marshaled, continued to knock at her chest.

Sascha leaned past Nathan to hammer the table with her fist. "DON'T TALK ABOUT HIM THAT WAY!"

"Which way is that?"

"As though he were some kind of an insect! As though he had nothing to do with me!"

A premature response can often serve to cut off the patient's own response to what she is saying. Leave time for the patient to hear her own words.

"WELL?"

"In point of fact," Lulu said reluctantly, "he hasn't had—"

"THAT WASN'T HIS FAULT!"

"Oh?"

"YOU KNOW PERFECTLY WELL THAT IT

WASN'T HIS FAULT! YOU KNOW YOU WOULDN'T LET HIM SEE ME WHEN HE CAME BACK TO NEW YORK!"

"Sascha," Lulu said slowly, "I understand that we need to talk about this. We *should* talk. But this isn't the time or place for our first conversation about your father."

Your father. Oh, God, she'd called him that so naturally. She didn't have to look at Nathan to see the betrayal and reproach that would be in his eyes. After twelve years of having been folded away neatly in a box, the truth had sprung up out of the box and punched them all in the nose.

That was, of course, only the beginning. The adolescent anger that had begun to manifest itself, and that had often appeared to be set off by some dialectical error of Lulu's, had now found its true source—and gained enormous strength in the process. Sascha, whom Lulu thought very beautiful, with her parents' dark hair and coloring as well as the best of each of their features, and who by fourteen had almost reached her mother's height in addition to having gained a considerable force of personality, was now angry all the time.

Nathan had retreated into himself (nor would he emerge for the birth of his sons), but Lulu tried desperately to get their daughter to See Someone. (Please See Someone, Sascha! Please let someone else take some of the heat!) The very suggestion, however, that Sascha was in a difficult period brought her daughter's boiling rage over the edge of the pot. As did the idea that there was anything in the world that bothered Sascha that hadn't been caused by her mother.

Clearly, Lulu's insistence upon starting another family at the absurdly advanced age of thirty-two provided perfect fuel for this rage, though Sascha claimed total indifference to "how many little brats" would be "cluttering up the apartment." Sascha said she was hardly around anymore, so she wouldn't notice who was there and who wasn't.

Then reality, in one of its common failures of decency, decreed another blow to the established order of Sascha's life.

Five years earlier the colleague with whom Nathan had shared rooms had died. Nathan had moved his office to the two virtually unused rooms, the first tiny but the second a reasonable size, at one end of their large apartment, and created a separate entrance for his patients. Nathan's accessibility in emergencies had been important to Sascha. Now, with Lulu pregnant, that space was needed. Nathan found an office on West End Avenue, only ten blocks away.

Sascha laughed off the idea that she cared where Nathan was during the day. "Don't be stupid, it's not as though I don't have someone else out there to rely on... By the way, I think I'm going to go out to Berkeley and stay with Woody this summer."

The lights in the apartment appeared to dim. Lulu's eyes fluttered. Something expanded in her head. Her hands went to her large belly and rested there as though it were the ballast that would keep her from being thrown back to the day fourteen years earlier when she'd lain in the hospital, cradling her newborn daughter and pretending that Woody stood beside her, admiring Sascha.

"Stay? With Woody?"

"And his family. *For the summer, I said.*"

Sascha was scornful of her mother, who didn't know, as any human of good will would have, that Luther Samuelson, a.k.a. Woody, was now in the first stable marriage of his life (the first "to a reasonable woman," as Sascha put it), to a woman several years older than he, a professor of anthropology at Berkeley with grown children of her own.

"Will you take your hands off that fucking thing?" Sascha screeched. "You put your hands on your stomach and you go into some kind of trance! It's disgusting."

"I'm sorry," said the guilty mother, who was actually somewhat less absorbed in this pregnancy than she'd been in her first one, but who had been wondering which wife this was—F? K? W?—and whether, at the age of forty-nine, Woody was really in a solid marriage, or if he was still, with his remarkable combination of stamina, tenderness and skill, screwing an endless procession of upwardly nubile young girls while Lulu's own center of gravity moved ever closer to the ground.

Lulu licked her lips. "I'm not in a trance. I—"

"The only reason I'm telling you is, they say I have to have your consent."

"Consent?"

"Oh God, I can't believe this. Consent to stay with them!"

Pause.

"I don't know, Sascha. I'll have to talk to them."

"Talk to them! Why do you have to talk to them? This has nothing to do with you!"

"Then why do they need my consent?"

"They don't need it, they just—Maybe they think you'll sue them or something. They know what a beast you are because I told them already. If I can't go there, I'll run away altogether!"

After a lengthy conversation with the cool and obviously responsible Mrs. Fifth or Eighth Samuelson, Lulu permitted her daughter to go to Berkeley to hear, in greater detail than correspondence and phone calls had allowed, her father's account of his life and trials.

Sascha had apparently been trying to contact Woody for some time—perhaps since the day she'd learned to write a letter and find a stamp—but her efforts had been desultory until Lulu's pregnancy, and her mail hadn't reached him. He'd moved around a lot. Perhaps the addresses had been out of date. And then there were those years when he was submerged in that part of the Berkeley underground where there wasn't any reading light. (He had explained to Sascha in one of his letters that he'd had his sixties, dope and all, during the fifties, and by the time everyone else was into all that stuff, he was ready to settle down. Sascha left his letters around where Lulu could find them and become provoked to murderous rage at his version of events or aroused and nostalgic at his flair for bullshit and his patriarchal tone.)

That June, only a few days after Sascha's departure, Teddy was born, an easy baby, or at least Lulu didn't mind if he wasn't, since she'd finished training but wasn't practicing yet and there was nothing else she had to do and the relief of Sascha's being away had balanced out her anxiety about Woody.

By the time Sascha returned, the baby was three months old.

Sascha came home—how else?—angry.

She was mad at all the terrible things she'd found out about Lulu, none of which she was willing to specify except for Lulu's unforgiving attitude toward Woody as evidenced by her refusal to reunite with him "before it was too late."

She was mad at having to spend another interminable year in filthy, scummy New York instead of in beautiful, clean Berkeley.

What she was most angry about, although it was awhile before Lulu learned this from a conversation with Woody's wife, was that she'd wanted to finish high school in California, and the sixth and undoubtedly sanest Mrs. Samuelson had been quite firm in her opinion that this would not work.

If Sascha couldn't communicate with her mother without shouting, she couldn't talk to Nathan at all. She said she felt him being hurt and angry all the time, and it was difficult for Lulu to deny that this was true, although it was she, not Sascha, who was the lightning rod for Nathan's anger. If Nathan didn't strike like lightning, he made it clear in a variety of ways that he considered Lulu responsible for her daughter's defection. This was not, of course, without its own perverse justice—that justice under which mothers are held responsible for everything from life's random-negative quality to the genesis of every neurosis developed by those passing through it.

Hadn't Lulu encouraged Nathan to believe that he could truly become Sascha's father—a vacant position? Hadn't she given him the impression that Woody was lost to them all—and vice versa? How could she have failed to take into account the horrible possibilities? And how was it possible to blame the young girl Sascha for those events whose most innocent victim she had been? Yet *someone* had to be blamed. *Someone* had made Nathan this angry, and being an analyzed person and a practicing psychoanalyst, he was not about to delve into the possibility that he was still laboring under some shitload of his own.

Sascha claimed that she herself was never angry except at home with Lulu, and eventually both the truth of her claim and its explanation became clear: When she wasn't home, she was stoned. Unfortunately, it became clear only because Sascha ceased to draw a line between home and outside and began to be stoned all the time.

What was saddest about that whole dreadful period was that Lulu and Nathan had endured it so separately. As though the house of cards they'd constructed on the foundation of Nathan as Sascha's father having toppled, there was little point in holding hands in the wreckage.

They couldn't even talk about how it wasn't safe to be middle class anymore. When Lulu made this wry observation to Nathan, he pointed out that half a dozen families they knew had managed to keep their kids straight by avoiding such idiocies as starting a whole new family at an inappropriate time.

~

Several years later Lulu's best friend, Bonnie Mayer, had two little boys and Lulu had two little boys (Bonnie also had two girls, but they were seven and eight). Nathan talked about nothing but money although Lulu had begun to practice and it was reasonable to hope the most difficult years were behind them as far as money was concerned . . . As far as everything else was concerned . . . Well, Lulu's friendship with Nathan had been a casualty of their lives.

When he complained that she wasn't holding up her end (she wouldn't work full time until the boys were in school all day), Lulu told Nathan that maybe they'd be better off if he taught less, they were a little more broke—and his sons got an occasional look at his face. When Lulu asked Nathan to talk to Sascha about dope, Nathan suggested Lulu might call Sascha's Real Father and ask him to do that and Lulu said she couldn't help it if the little ingrate had wanted to know the guy whose sperm had brought her into being.

Bonnie was the only one Lulu could talk to now.

It was Bonnie to whom Lulu ran when she realized that Sascha was no longer sticking to grass but was playing around with acid.

It was Bonnie on whose shoulder Lulu cried when Sascha ran away from home and Nathan said with apparent calm that Sascha was no doubt on her way to California but would likely disappear for a while just to put a fright into her easily manipulated mother.

It was Bonnie to whom Lulu ran to talk about Woody after a conversation in which he told her, in that beautiful, deep voice that was three thousand miles away but might as well have come from under the bed, that he understood what Lulu was going through, they both did, and would do everything possible to help.

For months there was no word from Sascha.

Lulu told Nathan that she couldn't stand it anymore, that if he didn't communicate with her, help with their life, she was going to leave him. That if she didn't have four- and five-year-old boys at home, she would have left him already. She was sick of having him take out his anger on her.

Nathan admitted to Lulu that he had been angry and in fact had "acted out" his anger in an immature way by having a little affair. Well, a sort of affair.

The girl, who was sixteen years old, had picked him up in the delicatessen on Seventy-second Street that was Sascha's favorite restaurant. Nathan had accompanied her to the home of her working mother, gotten into bed with her, and had then "remained faithful" to Lulu by failing to sustain an erection long enough to make love to her. He had, in fact, ended up delivering a lecture on middle-class morality to the disappointed young thing. Nathan felt that these last facts should "obviate the need" for Lulu to be angry.

Indeed, Lulu did not feel shaken by anger but, rather, soggy with disgust. She made some remark about the ultimate example of those who couldn't do and therefore taught, a remark that finally enabled Nathan to achieve both direct anger and a sustained erection the next time he ran into the little girl on Seventy-second Street.

Nobody heard from Sascha for six months. Then she began to call Nathan at his office with some regularity, but the condition of her calling was that he was allowed to tell her mother only that she was in good health. Nathan accepted this condition with equanimity, primly advising Lulu that he was trained to keep confidences and that even if this had not been the case, there was no way that he could violate his daughter's confidence without doing both her and himself a grave injustice.

Somewhere along the line Sascha had become his daughter again.

Eventually, Lulu was able to ascertain by calling Woody that Sascha was living in California, not with him but at a radical commune near the Berkeley campus.

"Lulu?" said the kind sixth Mrs. Samuelson, "may I take the liberty of speaking to you honestly for a moment? I know what you've been through, and I hope you don't think I'm presumptuous."

"Not at all," Lulu assured her.

"She's a very powerful girl," Mrs. Samuelson said. "I think she's going to be all right, but it won't do any good to come after her now. She needs to find her own way... You know, she tends to exaggerate the far-out things she does, drugs and so on. She confessed to Woody that she only did acid once and hated it.

Judith Rossner

She needs us all to worry about her. But she's strong.
I think she actually takes quite good care of herself."

Thus spake the anthropologist who was not Sascha's
mother to the psychologist who was.

"Thank you," Lulu said. "I'm very grateful to you.
You've really helped me a lot."

192

8

"I CAN'T TELL YOU what a wonderful Christmas it was," Dawn said. She had worn a blue and white stocking cap Tony had knitted her for Christmas because she wanted the doctor to see what Tony had done on six days' notice. Now Dawn took off the cap. Her hair had reverted to its true color over the past few months and she looked like herself, if still a somewhat overweight version. She was bubbling with news.

If Susan was as big a pain as ever, the baby was even more adorable, and almost fully toilet-trained. The work Dawn had done with the doctor had enabled her to keep Susie at a certain remove, even through the altered but continuing toilet drama, and Susie's younger sister had turned out to be a real peach. Tony was in terrific shape. The doctor had been right. It was purely neurotic to have been sitting around worrying that she was about to die.

"And now," Dawn announced dramatically, "for the important stuff. Some of it you're not going to believe. Are you ready?"

The first staggering item was that her infancy had been spent right in the middle of Boston. This had astounded her; it seemed almost to stand in contradiction to some memory. Did Dr. Shinefeld remember the wall Dawn hadn't been able to get over? Once or twice Dawn had pictured a stone wall around a big old house. It was spooky.

What was spookier still was that apparently Vera hadn't wanted to adopt her. It was Tony who'd insisted. That Tony was biased in the manner of a divorced partner had not occurred to Dawn, nor was she inclined to consider it now. There were more important matters on her mind, most particularly the matter of her father's death. Clearly this was what Dawn had been building toward.

Gordon Henley had died by drowning when his sailboat capsized off the northern Massachusetts shore, where he was vacationing with a friend and with his daughter, Dawn, then more than a year and a half old. The friend—Tony didn't remember his name, if she'd ever known it—had been out on the boat with Gordon. Both men were strong swimmers, but there had been a sudden squall for which they were unprepared; the friend had been washed up on the shore, half alive. An autopsy had revealed a considerable amount of alcohol in Gordon's system.

It was August. The Henleys were a small family, none of whose members could be easily located.

Gordon's parents lived in California and were traveling in the Far East. When the people at the hospital had found Vera, she had wanted to make the necessary arrangements by phone. Then she had been told that there was no one to take care of the baby, who was ready to be discharged. Tony was in New York. Vera couldn't reach her and finally got in the car and drove alone to the hospital, then to Boston.

Gordon's will was simple: He'd left everything he owned, including his daughter, to his sister. Vera told Tony that this didn't mean they had to take the baby, but Tony convinced Vera that a baby was the only thing in life she wanted and didn't have. A couple of days later, the new family was assembled in Marbury.

Dawn paused, waiting for some response from the doctor.

"I was wondering if it was possible," the doctor said, "that the house is the house you remember. Was it owned by your family?"

"I think so," Dawn said. "I'll check. Anyway ... Tony said I was a good baby from the beginning. If I was unhappy, I just whimpered a little. If I didn't get what I wanted, I stopped ... When I say that now, I hear, I still don't like to cry, even if I do it a lot. It has nothing to do with being good. Only with being scared." She was saddened by her own discovery. She twisted to see the doctor's face. "I suppose that means I was never a particularly good person."

The doctor smiled. "It's just as likely to mean that a lot of what passes for being good has more to do with being scared."

Dawn grinned. "Oh, I love that. Thank you ... Tony

said they got me a crib, but I whimpered as soon as they put me down in it, so she took a mattress from the daybed in the room and put it on the floor and that was my crib from then on. If they told me to stay in it, I stayed. If I didn't, all Vera would have to say was that I'd go in the crib if I didn't listen. Tony imitated the whimper a little. Weird."

"Can you do it for me?"

"No...I mean, I could, but...some other time. I don't feel like it now. I hate whimpering, you know that."

Silence.

"But I'll tell you what came into my mind when I was talking about the crib...I thought of the Lonely Chair. I mean the dream of the lonely chair that was really the crib. The empty crib...The Lonely Crib and the empty chair." A long pause. "That's what I really mean, isn't it?" An uncomfortable laugh. "Funny, I never thought of it that way before. It seems sort of obvious, all of a sudden...How come you're so quiet? What are you thinking about?"

"I was wondering whether Tony happened to mention where you were when the accident took place."

"Accident?"

"Your father's drowning."

"In the house," Dawn said promptly. "With the housekeeper. I mean, she didn't mention it, but that's where I would've been."

"Mmm."

"Why'd you ask?"

"Because it would be interesting to know the answer."

"I gave you the answer."

"Perhaps."

"I don't like the way you said that."

Silence.

"You're making me nervous."

"Oh?"

"I feel as though you know something, and you think I know it, too, but I'm keeping it from you. You don't trust me. Like Susan trying to pry some shit out of that poor kid when the kid doesn't have any in her! And then Susan acts as if the poor kid's holding out on her. She gets mad. It's really crazy. It's the kid who should get mad, not Susan. I mean, a year later she's still mad that the kid doesn't do it on *her* schedule."

Dawn burst into tears. "You know how I feel? I came in here all excited because I was giving you a present, and now it turns out not to be what you wanted...I feel stupid."

"Would you say you feel somewhat the way, uh; Sheri might feel if her mother kept urging her to make a poo-poo and she urinated instead, and in the wrong place?"

Dawn stopped sobbing and giggled.

"I love the way you said 'Uh, Sheri,' as though for a minute you were refusing to believe anyone would give a kid that name...Yes, that's it. I gave you the wrong stuff at the wrong time...I guess it's pretty dumb to think of it as giving you something. I know it's for me, what goes on here, not for you."

"It's hard work," Dr. Shinefeld said. "It has to have rewards for both of us."

Dawn twisted on the couch. "You know something? Whenever you say something wonderful, I want to turn around and look at you. I did it this time because . . . it's almost the end of the session. But whenever you touch home base . . . I feel a *lust* to see you. To drink in your face." She looked away. "Oh, God, I don't think I can stand what I just said. Is it time for the session to end?"

⌒

Dawn's father took on a reality in her mind that he hadn't previously had. He had become a source of speculation, a romantic figure she regretted not having known long enough to remember. She rejected the idea that she might need to grieve for him but was extremely curious about the details of his life. If she felt like crying sometimes when she thought of him, Dawn said, it was for the sheer loss of knowledge that should have been hers. She wanted to know what he'd done for a living and who had been sailing with him when he drowned. She had a dream in which she met the companion, who turned out to be a now-famous opera singer named Benuto Barzini. Benuto had once been in love with her mother and had been heartbroken when she married Gordon. But upon hearing of Miranda's death, he came to comfort Gordon and the two became fast friends— "on the boat of her memory," Dawn said.

Frequently Dawn phoned Tony in search of answers to questions that came up. Tony was only able to help occasionally. Yes, she was fairly certain that the house had belonged to the Henley family. Her memory of Gordon's friend's name was that it was closer to Gerald Smith than to Benuto Barzini. Dawn would have to go to Vera for definitive answers. Tony knew that Gordon had been a graphic designer of some talent, a fact that Dawn felt brought her closer to her father. Tony wasn't sure if Gordon had actually had a job. There had never been any need for Vera or Gordon to earn a living; the family was wealthy and there were trusts from grandparents that could support them independently of their parents.

"Tony told me at Christmas, but I forgot to tell you. She thought it was funny I still didn't know. There's a lot of money. I come into a trust fund when I'm twenty-one. I think I forgot because I felt silly about telling you. After all that fuss I was making over whether Vera could afford you."

The money didn't appear to have any emotional importance to Dawn beyond being a source of embarrassment in relation to the doctor.

As the February vacation approached, Dawn found herself thinking about going up to Vermont to do some skiing and talk to Vera. She had vented so much bad feeling about her aunt that she was now able to retrieve some of her old affection. Dawn was going to take a girl she'd met in school who was also a skier and with whom she'd become "a little friendly." Lillian was from northern California and wasn't going home for this vacation.

"For a minute," Dawn said of her first phone call to Vera in months, "I was half-hoping she'd bawl me out for not calling. But that was a fantasy about somebody else. Vera could never admit to missing anybody."

ᘒ

With the vacation only a week away, Dawn grew anxious about how she would "be" with Vera. Having Lillian there—at some point Dawn casually acknowledged that her choice of a friend with a first name similar to the doctor's was probably no coincidence—would be helpful in some ways, though maybe not in others.

"Lillian's a nice girl but she's got what they call a California head. She's got a brain but it's kind of light, all at the top of her head. I like her because she's cheerful. Not cheerful like me. She isn't all full of...shitstorms and monsters...The trouble with Lillian—with anyone—is that they don't really understand what's going on. They don't know about here, and what goes on here is truer than anything else. More important. To me. That's why I don't have a lot of girlfriends. Although I guess I never really have...

"I'm just glad it's not summer. A lot of people hate New Year's...and January...Tony used to hate January." She laughed. "August is my January...You're going to say, *Tell me.* I heard it myself. August is when my father died. Maybe I have some kind of... not a memory, exactly...Every year around Memorial Day, I feel the way some people do before the Christmas holidays...Since I began with Dr. Seaver, anyway. Or when he began leaving in August..."

For her remaining sessions, Dawn was able to draw

on her feelings of abandonment when Dr. Shinefeld went on vacation to talk about what the loss of her father might have meant to her.

What did not arise was Dr. Shinefeld's sense that unless there was some error in the dates she had been given, Gordon Henley had died right around the first anniversary of the death of his wife.

രാ

"I feel as though I got to know Vera a little for the first time. I felt very loving toward her, except...Maybe I should tell that part first and get it over with."

It hadn't been easy to get Vera to open up and talk, but she had been taken with Lillian, and that had helped. They had done a lot of skiing for the first time since Tony left, although you'd never have known it, seeing her on the slopes, a woman of almost sixty-three; even now the long hair braided into the single pigtail was only half-gray. Afterward they'd sat around drinking hot toddies. Maybe Vera liked having drinking company...The bad part was that Vera had no use at all for her brother Gordon. Dawn wasn't sure that she did, herself, if Vera's description was true.

Dawn took a deep breath. "They were lovers. Gordon and the other guy on the boat. Vera claims my father was always a homosexual. He denied his true nature when he married my mother." She began to cry. "Oh, God, there it goes. I thought maybe I could just get past it. I don't even have bad feelings about homosexuals, the way some of my friends do. Some girls talk about them as though they're withholding something out of spite." A long pause. "It's all so pathetic. It's a pathetic accident that I ever got born. The fucked-up daughter of a fucked-up suicide and a fucked-up faggot... I don't want to be some kind of a freak accident.

"Vera wasn't even putting him down. Only when I asked some specific question she had to answer. It was more what she didn't say. She'd look at me with those incredible eyes of hers... Did I ever tell you about Vera's eyes? They're gray. Clear and shiny. When I was young I never lied because I was sure Vera would see. They look as though she understands everything. That's why it's always a shock when she turns out to be who she is... Lillian's very agreeable until she starts to talk about her kid brother. I think that may be what loosened Vera up a little. Lillian was talking about how her mother spoils her brother. The only person Vera's harder on than herself is Gordon. I'll tell you what she said that made me cry. I don't know how I got the courage... We were drunk. Well, Lillian and I were drunk, Vera was relaxed. I asked Vera how she felt about taking me when she got that phone call. Vera looked at me for a long time. Then she said, 'My dear child, can you imagine for one moment that I believed that we were satisfactory people to bring up a young girl?'

"I never changed my mind so fast about anything. Suddenly I could see how she must've felt, what must've gone through her mind when they asked her to take me. She was a *lesbian*. She never lied to herself about it the way Gordon did. That was one reason she had no use for him. She felt that his marriage was a lie, that his wife suffered for it, and then his...me...I suffered for it. She'd always known that marriage and kids weren't for her. She liked to do men's things. I think she was suggesting that before Tony she wasn't sexual. She just knew she didn't like men. Anyway, nobody in Marbury had ever bothered them, but she thought maybe having me there would blow the whole thing. Make it look as though they were pretending to be married... Lesbians have a much worse time than homosexual men...You know, I had a dream that night but I can't remember what it was. Something about Tony and Vera. Maybe they were making love..."

"Yes?"

"No. That's all I can remember. I can't even remember that. I just have this vague idea that that's what it was about."

                      *

In the ensuing weeks, Dawn spent a lot of time recalling and trying to deal with the information she had gotten from Vera.

Her father's lover had been a man named Gregory Barnes who taught at Harvard. Vera wasn't sure of his field. Maybe Fine Arts. Unlike Gordon, Barnes had appeared to be very masculine. Vera had seen him only once after agreeing to take Dawn. When she was cleaning out the house on Beacon Street, he had called to ask for one of Gordon's paintings. Gordon was "a dabbler." Painting as well as other things.

"Vera said it was their mother's fault that he was weak and irresponsible. Their mother favored him. I remember when she told me that, she said, *Thank God*, as if being favored was a curse she'd been spared. Grandpa Henley was in the navy. I knew that before. From the photographs. They had no friends because they were always moving around, but Grandma Henley kept Gordon with her all the time, wouldn't let his father discipline him, confided in him as though he were a girlfriend... Vera adored Grandpa Henley. He was everything she thought a man should be." Dawn giggled. "Maybe a woman, too. Vera said their mother was ugly, but when I looked at the pictures, I thought she had a sweet face. Vera kept telling me how there was nothing Grandpa Henley couldn't do. Some famous millionaire made a remark about how anyone who had to ask how much a yacht cost couldn't afford one. Grandpa Henley went out and built one as cheaply as he could. He already had one. It just made him mad to have anyone say that people were helpless if they had no money... He sounds like a pretty extreme character, but Vera doesn't talk about him that way. She said he taught them both to be self-reliant, but only one of them learned." Dawn burst into tears. "My poor father! Can you imagine growing up with a father like that and Vera for a sister? Twelve years older? He was supposed to be the boy! It's all so sad. Everyone getting all fucked up and turned around. They were probably wonderful people before they... Vera's still wonderful. Did I ever tell you how beautiful she is?"

"You said she has wonderful eyes."

"Not just her eyes. She's beautiful. When I said that to Tony last time, Tony said *handsome* would be more accurate, but handsome's just some dumb word.

It has no real purpose except to keep you from saying a man's beautiful so you don't make him sound like a woman.

"Vera and Gordon were both beautiful. When Vera was young...not really young...She was in her forties already when she took me. But her hair was still blond and she never cut it. She wore it in one long braid down to her waist. And she's very big, you know. Not fat, just tall and big-boned. And I would look up at her and..."

"And?"

"Did I ever talk to you about the Winged Victory? It had the most overpowering effect on me. Tom...I think it was one of the first things I did that bothered him. Every day I wanted to go back and visit her before I did anything else. I remember the first time I saw her, coming into that hall, not expecting anything, then looking up that staircase and there she was. My face started tingling. I had goosepimples. I forgot about Tom. I went up the steps. And when I reached the landing, and I could really see how beautiful she was, how *alive*, even without her head, I started to cry." She cried now. "I guess it's like being a baby again. Lying in your crib. Looking up. Because she's on this pedestal. And there's this beautiful...I don't know why I said that...I was never in a crib at Vera's...I asked her, you know." Dawn sat up. "I just remembered something. Vera told me when I was there, and I forgot. Vera drank so much even she finally got drunk. She told us that Tony seduced her. She'd always thought of herself as someone with no interest in sex, but Tony...Can you believe I managed to forget that entirely? Maybe it's not such a big deal. But . . . I suppose it's about things not being what they seem."

"Which things are those?"

"Well, I don't mean things, of course," Dawn said a trifle irritably. "I mean people."

"Which people?"

"Are you being dumb on purpose?"

"Yes."

Dawn laughed. "Sometimes I really love you, you know that? Whoops. Too close to Easter to start loving you again. Not when I have to go away."

"Have to?"

"You know what I mean. You knew before, too."

"Sometimes I can guess what's on your mind. Often I can't."

"I feel as though you always can."

"But it's important to know it isn't so."

"Why?"

"Because you cede me more power than I have, and then you're frightened by that power. Also, because your assumption that I know is sometimes a way for you to avoid knowing."

"I don't remember what we were talking about."

"About people who aren't what they seem."

"Mmm. Vera and Tony . . . I accepted them the way they seemed to be. Tony was the female. The object. Oh my God, if any of the girls in school heard me say that . . . But I mean, face it. The girls the guys go after are the objects; the ones they don't want go after them. Isn't that your experience?"

"I've actually seen considerable variations in the pattern."

Silence.

"What about Vera? Does it bother you that she was the passive one?"

"Oh no. With Vera it's more..." Dawn thrashed around on the couch, finally came out with it. "She was forty-two years old when she found out she was a lesbian, and it wasn't even anything inside her that pushed! It was only that Tony came along. I'm not even twenty, yet. How do I know who I am or what kind of animal I'm going to turn out to be?"

Upon inquiring of the head operator on the Harvard switchboard, Dawn found that Gregory Barnes was still at Harvard, but in the Chemistry Department rather than Fine Arts. She hadn't tried to reach him. She was planning to visit Tony at Easter and try to find him then. Maybe she would watch him from a distance and get a feeling for who he might be, then talk to him if he looked like the sort of person who could help her to learn about her father.

Dawn's regrets at having missed her mother were abstract to the point of loftiness; she once said she only wished she'd known "that poor lady" well enough to mourn her.

Lillian wouldn't mind going with her to Boston and they could both stay with Tony, but Dawn definitely wanted to be alone when she met Gregory.

"Gregory?"

"Dr. Barnes."

Flustered, Dawn confessed to an elaborate fantasy about Gregory Barnes. Following her father's death, Gregory had been psychoanalyzed and gone straight. Actually, she pointed out, there was only Vera's word that he hadn't been straight all along. Gregory was now divorced. He would be somewhere around forty. (Vera had said he was much younger than her father.) Gregory and Dawn were attracted to each other. Dawn refused to sleep with him because she had to return to New York, but she promised to come back to Boston that summer.

She had gone on a diet so she would look good when she met Gregory. Whether he was homosexual or straight, she wanted him to like her, and homosexuals who liked women at all were, as the doctor probably knew, at least as particular as straight men about how they looked. Anyway, Dawn said, the truth was that while it would be nice to have Lillian around, she was also jealous of the other girl as a potential rival. Lillian was pretty if not beautiful, intelligent if not sharp, and would probably know better than to do that stuff about her brother when a man was around. Dawn was afraid that she wasn't being nice to Lillian because she'd begun to feel pressured about taking her along.

∽

"You're not going to believe this," Dawn said grimly as she settled down for her last session. "Just as I was getting used to the idea of having Lillian, she called me. Some old boyfriend came to town and she wants to spend the vacation with him."

"How do you feel about that?"

"I'm furious. I can't believe I went through all that analysis of being jealous just so she could back out at the last minute and leave me..."

"How?

"Just leave me! Leave me alone for ten days, to drive to Boston alone, to handle Tony, leave me...And please don't tell me I wanted to be alone. That was with Gregory Barnes."

"Who is it who's actually leaving you alone for ten days?"

"Nobody," Dawn said. "Please. You think I don't know that I'm not really going to be alone."

"You feel as though you're going to be."

"Yes." Sullen.

"Why do you think that is?"

"Because I don't have a choice, I guess. About when I go, or with whom..."

"If you could take anyone you wanted, who would it be?"

"That's a dumb question. I don't know. I guess Lillian's as good as anyone."

"At least she's got the right name."

"Oh, God. For one thing, it's not even the same name. I know what I said. But that was just something that crossed my mind once. It doesn't mean she's only my friend because— You act as if everything in the whole world's about you!"

"Tell me."

"I can't believe I'm back in the same old rut. Do you do that with everyone or just with me?" Dawn continued in this angry vein for some time, asking the doctor, among other things, whether she did the same kind of thing with her own children, and, if so, whether it might not be best for Dawn to take the children with her to Boston to get them away from a mother who must drive them crazy.

"You really are being coerced, aren't you," the

doctor finally said. "You can stay here with me, and be asked stupid questions over and over, or be abandoned by me, and go it alone."

"It makes me want to kill you when you say that."

Dawn sat up abruptly and swiveled around. She looked terrified. "You know I didn't mean that, don't you?"

"What if you did?"

"But I didn't! I love you too much to mean it! I don't understand why you won't let me take it back!"

"Because you need to know that the wish didn't kill me. That your anger doesn't have the effect on other people that you fear."

"Why?" Dawn's agitation increased. She stood up, ran her fingers through her hair, looked around the office as though it were a cage. "I'd much rather you knew I didn't mean it. You can't love anyone and want them to die at the same moment."

"That's not true. Desperate love and need can trail enormous rage in their wake."

Dawn picked up her bag and headed for the door.

"Dawn? Please don't go just yet."

"Why not?"

The doctor hesitated before she spoke. "Because I'm concerned about you. I wouldn't be concerned if you were just going back to your dorm. But I gather you're picking up the car now and driving to Boston."

"I thought it was you I wanted to kill," Dawn said bitterly, "not myself."

"People who kill themselves are usually angry at someone else."

"You think I'm going to kill myself?"

"I don't think anyone as angry as you are should ever get behind the wheel of a car."

"Then why did you make me so angry?"

"You were angry when you came in here."

"But that was at the *other* Lulu." Dawn heard her words, stared at the doctor with a combination of amazement, amusement, and chagrin, then dropped her satchel and flopped into the chair facing the doctor's, her body slack. Finally she cried.

"I guess I can never have another friend named Lulu, Lillian—anything like that. She'll always be you. It's too depressing. Although I can see another side to it. Because that means I can always find a substitute when I need one. Maybe not a good one, but better than nothing...I do need to have more than one Lulu in case something happens to the first one."

The doctor was silent.

"I was so frightened!" Dawn wailed. "That was one of the worst moments of my life!"

"When you said you wanted to kill me?"

"Oh, God, you don't know what it does to me, just hearing you say that! *What if something happens to you now?*"

"Listen to me, Dawn," the doctor said, because they didn't have much time. "I have some things to tell you."

Dawn became quiet again.

"The first thing I should say is that there is no likelihood anything's going to happen to me while you're on vacation. But if it should, it wouldn't have anything to do with your saying you wanted to kill me."

"I would feel as though it did."

"I understand that."

"Anyway, I'm not angry anymore."

"That's fine. But if you were, it would be all right. Your wishes can't kill me. Infants, who have no real sense of their own limitations, believe that their angry wishes hurt people. If an infant is angry at someone who disappears, she believes she caused the disappearance."

Dawn nodded slowly. "But she didn't make it happen. It happened because of something else."

"Right. If it happened at all. There's something else for you to remember. A large portion of that rage, or whatever else you feel, which appears to be directed toward me, isn't for *me*. I'm a stand-in for someone else."

"When Dr. Seaver used to tell me I was really in love with someone else, it made me angry. Now . . . Maybe because it feels better to think I'm not really angry at you. But it's not just about being angry. If you tell me that when I say I love you, I'm really talking to someone else, I don't mind that, either." She smiled and stood up, yawning. "This isn't the time to get into that, is it. I guess I have to go. I'll be all right. No accidents. I promise."

"Have a good vacation."

"Thank you. You too." Impulsively, Dawn took the few steps to the doctor's chair, leaned over, and kissed the top of her head. Then she loped out of

the office, opening the door before the doctor had
risen from her chair.

$\mathcal{C}$

A disappointed Dawn returned from vacation to tell
the doctor that Gregory Barnes was on sabbatical.
She had gone to Vera's after two days and one useful
thing had come out of the Vermont visit. Vera thought
she remembered the name of a girl who had been
the housekeeper in the first year of Dawn's life:
Caitlin MacLeod. An older woman had followed her,
and Vera thought this one had been a relative of
Caitlin's. In general, Vera had been helpful about
Dawn's past, though once again reticent about her
own. She had suggested that Dawn might want to go
through the trunks in the attic that held her parents'
possessions, and Dawn said she was certainly going
to do that sooner or later.

Dawn and the doctor spent considerable time ana-
lyzing Dawn's Gregory Barnes fantasies. In May,
Dawn said that now that she finally understood all
the neurotic bullshit behind her drop-in-on-Gregory
daydream, she saw that the way to approach him was
through a letter. Promptly she wrote one, dispatching
a copy to the Chemistry Department and the original
to the home address listed in the Harvard directory.
She did not care to contemplate what she would do
if she hadn't received a reply by the summer.

Dawn had done well in the first half of the school
year, but then she'd let herself slip again, and now
she would have to be content with passing grades, at
best, in everything but Art History. She planned to

go to summer school but rent a car and get away
weekends, taking turns between Vera and Tony
and ... who knew what else?

Lillian was absorbed in her boyfriend who had
come east. She appeared to be jealous of Dawn and
they were spending little time together. Dawn said
that if she had one or two girlfriends who were
available, she wouldn't be so scared about being left
alone when Dr. Shinefeld went on vacation in August. Dr. Shinefeld would have liked Dawn to talk
about being alone in August, but Dawn said that
everyone needed someone she could trust to talk to.
She didn't want to discuss it as though it were a
symptom.

Furthermore, she was struggling with her increas-
ing anxiety about a reply from Professor Barnes.
"Even if I'm not having Gregory fantasies anymore
I'm still an orphan, and he's still my sole link to my
parents ... Did you hear what I just said?"

"Yes."

"I called myself an orphan."

"I know."

Dawn burst into tears.

"You won't believe this, but I never knew I was an
orphan before. I mean, I knew my real parents were
dead, but I ... The truth is, I barely knew that. I
knew but I didn't know. Tony and Vera were a way of
not knowing. I called them my parents so I wouldn't
have to think about not having any. About being an
orphan. Oh my God! An orphan!"

Gradually the tears stopped.

"I'm like this little kid that was adopted and didn't
know she had other parents. And then she finds

out...and she needs to know more. I need to know more. Nothing else seems important compared to that. Not school. Not coming here. Nothing."

$\backsim$

At the following session, Dawn told the doctor that she'd decided not to go to summer school. She needed to do something more structured that would force her to pay attention, take her mind off...this stuff she was getting into here. A few days later she announced that she'd gotten a summer job at NBC television, where one of her friends suggested she try. She was slim and lovely, with her hair swept up and a white cotton suit and blue blouse that she'd bought for job interviews. It did not occur to Dawn, until there'd been considerable discussion of matters like a working woman's wardrobe, that if she were going to work in Midtown from 10 A.M. until 6 P.M., some change in her analytic schedule would be required. Then she was stricken—or believed herself to be.

"I can't believe I did it without thinking twice. Are you angry with me? You don't think I did it on purpose, do you?"

"I think it may have suited a purpose."

"What purpose?"

"*You* tell *me*."

"Well, I'm not trying to get out of coming here, if that's what you think. But I need to feel that I have something *to do*. I've been feeling very blah...sort of...I came out of nothing and I feel like nothing and I'm going noplace...I guess it's about this orphan business. I don't know why just a word means so much. Well, it's not the word. It's what the word means."

"What does it mean to you?"

"It means—I'll tell you what it means. You're pathetic. Once you lost everything. And everyone knows. You were nothing... are nothing. I don't know what I'm talking about... Remember the story about the little girl who said I'm leaving a piece of me with you? Well, you didn't even have someone to leave it with! Or not the right person, anyway! You couldn't even tell... Oh my God I just realized something. I just realized, when that happened to me, I probably couldn't even really talk!"

Dawn began to cry—and then to choke. She sat up and, without apparent effort, stopped crying and dried her eyes. When she spoke again her voice was calm, with only the slightest quiver to betray suppression.

She looked at the doctor. "I'm not going to throw up on your rug again."

The doctor waited.

"Maybe you think I don't remember when it happened just because I never talked about it. That's because I couldn't talk about it. There's nothing worse to me than throwing up."

"Really?"

Dawn nodded. "It's disgusting. I don't even want to talk about it. Not now, anyway. I'll tell you one thing. When I think about staying in New York all summer, even last summer, the first picture I have is walking down Broadway in the heat, and there's a Burger King somewhere along the way, and half the time I pass it someone has ... on the sidewalk right in front ... and when I think about it, if I see a picture of it in my mind, or ... That's enough to make me want to leave New York altogether. The smells all over New York are bad in the summer, to begin with."

"Do you pass that Burger King often?"

"Mostly when I'm coming here. But sometimes I'm thinking about other things and I forget ... or I'm going to a store on that side. There's a linen place near there where I buy a lot of stuff. I'm very fussy about sheets. I don't know if I ever mentioned that. In general I'm the cleanest person I know— towels, sheets, clothes. But the worst is sheets. I change them every day. I was always that way. I guess it's the same old thing, being cleaner than Vera could make me be. Anyway, how'd I get into this? I still haven't figured out what to do about ... My God, there isn't one of my regular sessions I can make! God, I'm upset. What time do you start in the morning?"

"Nine o'clock."

"No good. When do you finish?"

"My last appointments are at five-thirty, but those are taken. During the summer, people will leave the city and my schedule will loosen up, but the next couple of weeks are tight."

"What about an emergency?"

"An emergency is an emergency. It's different from regular sessions."

"Well," Dawn said after a while, "here's what I think I should do. Next week I won't come. I understand that I—we—have to pay for the sessions. That's fair ... I have to see what it's like. My boss ... he reminded me of Tom Grace, only younger ... If he likes me, maybe I can get some flexibility in my hours ... I know he likes me. They wouldn't have hired me if he didn't."

She stood up. She was smiling, but her manner was strained. There were about ten minutes left in the hour.

"Well, I guess I should get along. I have a lot of shopping to do. I'll see you, uh, a week from Monday, unless I call."

She sailed across the room, opened the office door and started through the opening, then tripped on the saddle so that she fell forward on her face and stomach into the waiting room. Quickly she pushed herself to a sitting position. She was crying.

"Why don't you come back in for a moment?" the doctor asked.

"What for?"

The doctor was silent.

"I don't know why that happened," Dawn said, walking back to the chair facing the doctor, sitting down, wiping her skirt, rubbing her knees.

"Maybe you were telling me," the doctor said, "that I was letting you go too easily."

"But I'm the one who wants to go! Although ... it's true ... You were just ... You didn't even argue with me."

"I didn't see any point. And I think it's important to you to feel that you can come and go."

"Oh, God," Dawn moaned, "I love you too much. I don't know if I can stand to do this." But she'd stopped crying. "I have to, though. I have to try it. School just isn't ... I need something more regulated than school. Where they'll know the difference if I'm not there."

"Can you talk about that?"

"What's the point? Isn't it almost time to go?"

"Almost."

Pause.

"I'm being stupid. You're fucking up August so I'm fucking up June and July. But that's not all it's about . . . Oh, God, can I call you next week? I could call during the time I'm usually here." She brightened. "Maybe I could do my sessions on the telephone!"

"You can call," the doctor said, "but I'm afraid it isn't the same on the phone."

"Why not?"

"It's hard to say. For one thing, I can't think well on the phone."

"Well, that's okay." Dawn giggled. "You couldn't see me and I couldn't see you. We'd be even, for once."

ᐒ

By Thursday Dawn had permission from her boss to take two long lunch hours a week if she would make up the time at the end of those days. She also had an invitation from a man at work, the head of a neighboring department, to come out for the weekend to a house in Southampton that he shared with a group of single people. She could have her own room.

What Dawn really wanted was to drive up to Vera's and begin going through the stuff in the attic, but she was afraid that if she did this she would "start obsessing about Gregory Barnes," whom she avoided thinking about by working hard. He was her "missing link." In her free time she thought of little that wasn't related to finding out what she could about her family. It was obvious that the family she wanted to find was her father's; as far as the doctor was aware, Dawn didn't know her mother's maiden name and hadn't thought to ask Vera what it was.

ᘒ

A week from the following Monday, Dawn came in at her usual time, happy but breathless, full of gossip about her job, her boss, and the weekend in Southampton.

"I called you a few times during the week, but I just hung up when I got the machine. I didn't want the machine, I wanted—" she laughed—"a fix."

The doctor smiled. "So. Here you are."

"Here I am."

"Sitting up."

Dawn looked surprised. "I didn't even think about it." But she didn't move.

The doctor waited.

"I know I'm doing something, but I don't know what it is. Do you?"

"Well, you've suggested that you're erecting a structure that'll prevent you from missing me during vacation."

"Mmm. Well, that sounds good. Doesn't it?"

"Yes and no."

"After all," Dawn said, "if I keep thrashing around in the dark pit...the orphan pit...how do I know I'll be able to get out of it on time?"

"We have several weeks before vacation," the doctor pointed out. "It might be more useful to talk about the dark pit now."

"No. If I talk about it, I'll fall into it."

The doctor was silent.

"Did I ever tell you," Dawn asked almost nonchalantly, "that there's a sort of river around Patterson? Not a river, exactly. More of a moat. Full of slime and alligators."

"Oh?"

"That's all. It's never exactly *in* the dreams. It's just sort of there. I don't even remember when I realized it was there. Just the past couple of years, maybe."

"You didn't know it was there when you were in analysis with Dr. Seaver?"

"I don't think so."

"Why do you think that is?"

"I was just happier then." Dawn was still in the cheerfully nonanalytic mode. "When I was with Dr. Seaver, the dark pit was the outside world. Now the pit's right here in the office and the outside world is what saves me. I know that isn't exactly right because of how I feel when you go away . . . The office is the symbol of my mind, I guess. But at least if I fall into a black hole in your office, you can drag me out. What if I get to the edge and then you go on vacation?"

"Well," the doctor said, "I suppose the first thing for me to tell you is that this year you would be able to reach me if you had such an emergency. And feeling that you were in the bottomless pit certainly sounds like an emergency. On the other hand, try to remember that what we're talking about *is* a feeling. Not a reality. There's no real pit, mental or physical. Furthermore, you're not likely to make a discovery your mind can't handle even when I am around unless you're ready for it."

"Suddenly I see something and it hurts like crazy and I didn't really want to see it?"

"It hurts, yes. But it doesn't affect you the way the incident itself did when you were a little girl. Your self, and the ego that is sort of the captain of the self, weren't as well developed then. When you were an infant they barely existed. Now they exist and have considerable strength. You have an existence aside from the existence you might relive here with me. Or on vacation. There's a grown-up Dawn to keep you company when you let yourself venture back into infancy. Dawn has a rather strong ego, even if she doubts it sometimes. And Dawn—"

"What is an ego?" Dawn interrupted. "I mean, really. If my ego is the captain, what's it the captain of? What is my self?"

⌒

Dear Miss Henley:

I have been abroad and recently returned to find your letter(s) awaiting me.

I am willing to speak with you when you are in Boston, though I am leaving shortly for my home in Provincetown. If you are going to be in that area, perhaps you would care to call me and come by.

Yours truly,
Gregory Barnes

In a postscript, Professor Barnes had written the dates and phone number for each house and said that he was sorry he couldn't answer questions about housekeepers.

"He isn't exactly dying to see me," Dawn said. "On the other hand, why should he be? He doesn't know if I'm friendly. He may not even know that I know they were homosexuals. Maybe I *don't*. The truth is, I have no way in the world of being sure until he tells me ... Isn't that true?"

What was true was that with Barnes almost in sight, Dawn's Gregory fantasies were recurring.

It was the end of June. She was beginning to express boredom with her job. She was seeing Mark Randel, the fellow with the Southampton house, and had begun to sleep with him, though she couldn't say that she cared for him. She'd decided it was time to sleep with someone again. She was actually more interested in her own boss, Jack Robbins, who had informed her in "his own Tom Gracey way" that he was going to come after her sometime when she wasn't working for him. While she was more attracted to Jack, she didn't really think either of them had any depth. It was a thin-ice kind of world they moved around on, and she could manage on it because she had the right skates—looks—to get around. All that did was make her feel as though she wanted to be in a place where she didn't need skates to keep from falling through the ice and drowning. That Gregory Barnes might be affected by her looks was a different matter; another set of rules governed any contact she might have with her father's friend. With some qualms, she allowed Mark Randel to drive her to Provincetown for the Fourth of July weekend. They had no hotel reservations; she was willing to sleep in down bags on the beach if need be. The day before the trip, Dawn left work early and had a haircut, a facial, a leg-waxing, a manicure, and a pedicure, all but the first being new to her.

❧

The following Wednesday Dawn entered the office in a way that reminded the doctor of the girl she had met at their first consultation two years earlier—poised somewhere beyond the brink of credibility. Something had happened in Provincetown that had sent her burrowing back into the old shell, which was no longer a perfect fit.

Dawn sat in the consulting chair and looked around the office as though she hadn't seen it in some time. Her eyes met the doctor's. No smiles today.

"Well, he's wonderful, all right. He's a homosexual, but it doesn't matter. He also happens to be the handsomest man I've ever seen in my life. Like Robert Redford only better. His manners are exquisite, he's incredibly urbane. Not at all...effete. I've never used the word *urbane* before in my life. He lives with another man. They've lived together for several years. They've been together more than sixteen, but until a few years ago they didn't dare to be in the same apartment...I have to admit that I wasn't crazy about his friend. Guido. He's Italian and Hungarian. Very little. Ugly. Gregory met him in Europe a couple of years after my father died and brought him back here, and ever since . . . He hovers over Gregory. Horribly possessive. Fusses and hovers . . . He does all the cooking and housework . . . I had the feeling Gregory outgrew him a long time ago but he's too kind to send him away."

For some time Dawn was absorbed in a description of the Barnes home, which was right on Commercial Street, elegant and terribly private, yet facing the water; of Provincetown, which she thought might just become her favorite place in the world; and of the people she'd met, every one of whom was fascinating. All these judgments were delivered as though they were about people and places she'd learned of secondhand.

"If I sound strange, it's because I haven't digested what I heard. I want to tell you and I don't. I wish you could've been there with me and have a sense of him. Very English. Terribly sharp. You hope you'll be very good and he'll never direct any of that sharpness at you. He invited me to come back and it felt like a great honor, even if it wasn't exactly an invitation to stay with him. Maybe I'll spend August in Provincetown. I'm getting bored with work. The Cape's much more beautiful than Long Island, anyway, don't you think?"

"Tell me."

"He said that my father adored me and took better care of me than any mother he'd ever seen. He said that if Vera . . . He detested Vera more than she detested my father . . . He never even knew Vera existed until after . . . My father never mentioned her. He just had that one awful experience, when he went to Boston to get the picture. Gregory said he got an excellent picture of Vera from that meeting. He said that if Vera had given me the impression that my father was some foolish, flighty faggot—those were his words—I should forget it. He said my father was a wonderful, talented man who was absolutely devoted to me, better than any...But I said that already." Dawn had begun to cry but she didn't stop talking. "Gregory said that I was a real pain in the ass, just like most babies, but that my father had infinite patience with me. They'd have plans and Gregory would want to leave me with someone, but my father would put me in the car-bed and take me along...Gregory said there was nothing my father couldn't have done if he'd had the will to do it. Gordon was a good painter and a superb draftsman. He was also very good at math. Gregory was astounded at his grasp of chemistry when he talked about it to him. Gregory said that he was thinking of just asking for one painting of Gordon's, but then after he talked to Vera, and he got the picture of this—his words—man-hating bulldyke..." Dawn shuddered. "After he talked to her, he decided to ask for all Gordon's work. He wanted it to be seen and he could tell she wasn't going to show it. But she'd only part with one piece. I saw it. It's still hanging in the house in Provincetown. It's the coastline. It's lovely. He's right about Vera. She never hung any of the paintings. If there'd been a painting of my father's in the house where I grew up, I wouldn't have been able to pretend that he didn't exist all those years...Would I..."

It wasn't a question. Now that she was back with

the doctor, Dawn knew how strongly she felt about what she'd heard. She wept.

"I want to go to Marbury and look for his other work. But I'm not ready to see Vera. It's about my father. She must have hated him. She should have let Gregory have the paintings. I just hope everything's still in the attic. Maybe it sounds stupid, but now that I know more about him, I really miss him for the first time . . . Oh, God, this is awful . . ."

The remainder of the session continued with Dawn's anguished tears over her father punctuated by spurts of memory: Gregory describing how they'd rigged up a double-umbrella system so Dawn could crawl around on the beach blanket without getting burned (The doctor asked if it had sounded as though she was not yet walking during this period; Dawn wanted to know why she would have felt like walking when her father was right there with her all the time); Gregory telling her that they had a favorite restaurant where they would set Dawn's car-bed in front of the jukebox, and she'd become absorbed in the lights and colors until finally she fell asleep; Gregory explaining that he had learned to cook that summer because Gordon had no interest in either eating or preparing food.

The doctor waited; a momentous issue was at hand and she couldn't tell whether Dawn was remotely in touch with it.

"Was there no household help?" she finally asked.

"No," Dawn said—rather proudly. "They didn't want a housekeeper around in the country. They wanted the privacy. And my father just wanted to take care of me himself."

She sat up on the couch. "I'm starved. What time is it? I didn't have lunch. It feels as if I've been here forever."

"Forty-one minutes, actually."

"I think I'm too hungry to talk anymore."

"Did the hunger just come over you? Or did you have it before and not want to stop for food?"

"I don't know," Dawn said. "Hunger is hunger, isn't it? Even to a shrink? I have to be careful with Gregory Barnes. I can't push him to get things out of him. He'll just tell me to go away. I guess I like him for that. I know what I can't do and can do. If I do something he doesn't like, he's not going to just suffer in silence until . . ."

"Until what?"

"Poof! He disappears . . . Or I do . . . He disappears me. Just can't stand looking at me anymore . . ."

ᔔ

Dawn had had a dream in which she was walking past Burger King. She'd awakened frantic, unable to breathe, the smell of vomit permeating her senses. She was choking and felt as though she would throw up or suffocate if she stayed in the dorm. So at eleven o'clock at night she'd walked-run down Broadway to the first air-conditioned movie theater she could find. She didn't even remember the movie that had been playing, except that there were a couple of policemen in it. She sat in the back row, gulping down cold air, her heart beating like crazy, her head aching. She could still smell the vomit. She tried various food remedies—popcorn, chocolate mints, and so on—but they only worked while they were in her mouth and she couldn't eat much because she was nauseated.

"If I think about it, the smell comes back." She sat up. "What's that about? It makes me crazy. Today, on the way here, I had to cross Broadway and walk past Burger King—as if I had to see if it was really there. The vomit, I mean. It wasn't, but I felt almost as if someone was cheating. Do you know what that's about?"

"Maybe if you keep talking we'll find out."

"And maybe if I keep spilling my guts out I'll...Oh, God...that was just like talking about vomiting. Spewing out this foul stuff..."

"Which foul stuff?"

"The contents of my head."

"What would you say are really the contents of your head?"

"A lot of garbage, that's what. Garbage and vomit." Dawn was angry now. "Is that what you want to get out of me? Maybe you'd like it if I threw up right in the office!"

"I'm willing," the doctor said evenly.

"What? You want me to throw up in here?"

"I can't say I want you to. But if it were to happen that you did, it wouldn't bother me particularly. We'd just clean it up."

"Are you saying that to remind me that it happened once? You've brought it up before."

"I don't believe it was I who brought it up. In any event, I'm saying it because it's true."

"I think you're still angry with me about the other time."

"Oh?"

"I didn't even help clean it up. I just lay there while you did it. Maybe that's why you . . . I was going to say, why you went away, but you didn't go away . . . I don't know why I said that."

"As a matter of fact, I didn't clean up, either. You did it yourself, while I watched."

"I'm sure that's wrong . . . I feel crazy, anyway, when you say you wouldn't care. If you think that, one of us has to be."

"The issue isn't really whether vomit is pleasant or unpleasant but the degree of feeling you have about it. We have a lot to learn from anything that causes feelings that strong."

"All right," Dawn said, her manner almost crafty, "then tell me what you learned from the last time I threw up."

"Well," the doctor said slowly, "I suppose the first thing I learned was why you try to avoid crying."

"What do you mean?"

"Well, if I remember correctly, we've never talked about vomiting except in connection with passing that Burger King. But you've told me more than once how you hate to cry. Once you described how you would feel if you needed me and you couldn't find me. You began to cough, and then to choke, and then—"

"Stop!"

The doctor stopped.

"You scared me. I thought I was going to start choking again . . . I still can't get a deep breath. I don't think I can stand this. Any of it. Right now I just want to be in Provincetown."

"The problem is that you're rather close to something that's troubling you. It might be better to bring it out here where we can look at it together."

"Together." She seemed terribly young at that moment, and of course she was very frightened. "You mean," Dawn asked, "I'm too close to bury it?"

"It's possible that you could ... if that was what you were determined to do."

"And then maybe have another accident," Dawn said after a while. She licked her lips, which looked almost parched. "Wrestling with it at the wheel ... When I talk about it that way, I sound as if I know what it is. But I don't. Or at least I sound as if I'm sure there's something there. And I'm not even sure of that." Her voice had taken on a dream quality, although she was still sitting up on the couch.

"When I said that about Provincetown ... even before you said anything, I thought to myself ... but it could happen there, too. Sometimes I remember what you said about keeping these things from myself for a good reason ... When I talk about Gregory Barnes I always sound as if I simply like him, but actually ... I had a dream, I don't remember it but he was terribly powerful ... I certainly don't think he *wants* to have any power over me. But sometimes I felt as though he was sort of measuring out bits and pieces of my life to give it back to me ... or not ... whatever he happened to decide ... Something like what you do, except when you don't answer me it's for a reason. Sometimes you don't even know the answer yourself ... He really ... I don't know if I told you, Gregory didn't have the same opinion of the baby me as Vera did. He said I was difficult. Of course he never wanted to take care of a baby in the first place. A lot of homosexuals marry just because they want children . . . He said this to me . . . But children would be enough reason for him not to get married. He said I was very lively, even if I couldn't walk. I know you asked me if I could walk but I didn't remember . . . I also didn't talk except for some sounds of my own, but he said I understood almost everything even if I ignored a lot. I crawled around very fast. Mostly in circles, around my father. I would do it over and over until he—Gregory—had to leave the room. And he said I cried if I didn't get what I wanted. Or if . . . My father wasn't allowed to leave the room for a minute. He didn't mind, but it got to Gregory. The only thing he ever argued about with my father was he wanted to get babysitters and go out without me once in a while. But my father wouldn't leave me with anyone . . . My mother hadn't even been dead for a year, and the housekeeper from Boston didn't come to the beach. I know you asked me about a housekeeper, but I didn't . . . I must have forgotten this whole part of the conversation . . . Gregory didn't hide his resentment that my father wanted to be with me all the time." Dawn began to cry. "They were both paranoid to begin with about being discovered. It was much worse then for homosexuals, you know . . . With Gregory it was a career at stake, and with my father's family . . . Gregory said the admiral would've disowned my father. They couldn't afford to have some housekeeper they didn't know . . . snooping around . . . watching them . . . God! I just had the weirdest . . . Wait a minute!"

Dawn stopped crying. For a moment it seemed that she had stopped breathing as well. The clock on the wall became audible; someone ran across the floor of the apartment above them; the air conditioner cycled heavily.

"No," Dawn said, "it's not possible."

But she was staring at the doctor, and the expression on her face said that she was already feeling it was true.

"No."

There was panic in her eyes now.

"He wouldn't have left me alone to go sailing and drown." Her voice cracked. "It's not possible!"

She began to sob—great racking sobs—punctuated at first by repeated denials that the man who had been described to her as a doting father would have left her to go sailing with his lover.

"I don't know what I'm doing!" she cried out when the sobs had died down some. "How can I be crying this way when I don't even know what happened?"

But her feelings weren't going to wait to find out what had happened. With that disclaimer, she began to sob again, more violently than before, and eventually she choked, staring at the doctor as though she were in desperate need of help and the doctor was oblivious to her need.

The doctor pushed her own chair forward and took Dawn's hand as the girl's body shook and heaved. Gradually Dawn stopped gasping and choking and calmed to a point where she was weeping again. Then she slumped back in the chair. Dr. Shinefeld remained close for another moment, then pushed her chair back to its normal position.

That night Dawn called Gregory Barnes to ask where she'd been when he and her father went sailing. She told Gregory that she was writing an autobiographical essay for which she needed to fill in some gaps in her life. He was not someone she would want to tell that she was in analysis; she was sure he despised that sort of thing. Apparently, she had called Gregory in the hope that he would dismiss the version of events she had constructed in the analysis, and he had confirmed the essentials, instead.

She reported this to Dr. Shinefeld in a voice without affect.

It wasn't that her father hadn't been concerned about her; as things had worked out, his concern hadn't mattered. It was five o'clock on a beautiful day, one or two clouds in a bright blue sky, no way in the world to predict the squall that had overtaken them and capsized the boat. Even so, Gordon had asked the neighbor's boy, a youth of about ten, to check on Dawn, asleep in her crib, if he hadn't returned in an hour. And then again in an hour and a half. If the baby awakened and the men weren't back yet, the boy was to notify his parents, who were playing tennis at that moment and with whom Gordon maintained good, neighborly relations.

The boy checked at the first hour but then went into town for dinner with his parents and simply forgot.

The first anniversary of his wife's death was upon Gordon and he was depressed. He'd been drinking a lot—margaritas, which he had introduced to Miranda and which had become her drink. He had a hip flask with him on the boat, and unless Gregory was mistaken, it was already empty when Gordon decided to take a swim. That was why he hadn't had a life preserver on when the squall came up; he'd barely had time to swim back to the boat, and then it had taken their combined energies to keep it from capsizing—to try to keep it from capsizing.

Her father appeared to have gone under almost immediately. Gregory, wearing a life preserver, had been thrown clear of the sloop; by the time he'd swum around it there was no sign of Gordon.

Gregory himself had been in the water for most of the night, eventually losing consciousness. He'd been washed up on the shore, probably just around sunrise, at a point a few miles from the house, and had been found and brought, unconscious, to the hospital.

Meanwhile, the little boy next door had awakened, eaten his breakfast and gone down the road to see a friend. Walking back with his friend on the beach side an hour or two later, he'd noticed the absence of the Henley boat, then remembered about checking the baby. He told himself that Gordon must have come back and gone out again.

The boy fooled around on the beach for a while, but he couldn't quite dismiss the boat from his mind. He went inside to tell his mother what had happened and ask if he should go over to the Henleys'. The mother called Gordon's number but there was no answer. They walked over and found the house empty except for the baby in the crib. In a rather ghastly condition. Comatose. Hopelessly tangled up in her cotton blanket. Lying on her stomach, her face caked with mucous, vomit, even some excrement and what appeared to be dried blood.

The reason Gregory knew all these lovely details, he'd explained to Dawn, was that the boy's mother, full of vicarious guilt, not to speak of the universal indignation of womanhood, and having no one else upon whom she could vent her spleen, had chosen as her target the young Gregory Barnes, still in the hospital two days later, exhausted and depressed following the drowning of his lover and his own near-death.

Gregory had been awake for hours before he even remembered Dawn's existence, and God knows what would have become of her if the little brat next door hadn't finally remembered. Gregory didn't scruple to tell Dawn that she simply hadn't entered his mind; she hadn't had any importance to him except as a drag on his life. He wanted Dawn to be aware of this now because she'd seemed to be an absolutely lovely young woman. He'd received her thank-you note and was considering offering her a room in a place he owned just a few houses from his own on Commercial Street. But he wanted her, before accepting, to consider whether she had hard feelings about his indifference eighteen years earlier. Because if she did, she was to take them to a shrink, or EST, or anywhere else she chose, but he didn't want to know about them. He had not been put upon this earth to assuage the wrath of women.

"Hey, Gregory," Dawn had said to him, "you said *she* blamed you. *I* didn't."

So they were still friends. She had been offered the room on Commercial Street.

She had no conscious anger toward Gregory, either regarding the original accident and its aftermath or his current refusal to let her react as she might to this sad set of discoveries. When questioned on this point by Dr. Shinefeld, Dawn said she under stood perfectly how Gregory felt. He hadn't been responsible for her then and he wasn't now, and why should he take any shit at all from her?

Dawn had run into Lillian on the street a few days before and Dawn had had the feeling Lillian missed her. She herself was in need of a friend. Lillian had moved out of the dorm to live with her boyfriend. but that wasn't going well. She was restless. They were having dinner together that night, and if the friendship seemed revived, maybe Dawn would broach Provincetown. The more she thought about August in New York...It wasn't just Burger King—at the moment Burger King wasn't even on her mind. She was afraid that if she stayed in New York she was going to think about Tom Grace all the time.

"Tell me."

Dawn had had a dream the night before abou. being with Tom in China, and the idea of him was back with her now, stronger than ever. She was afraid of being haunted by him...or perhaps by Dr Seaver...Sometimes, in her dreams, they seemed to be the same person.

"Which dream was that?" the doctor asked.

"I don't remember, except it was in Vermont...1 don't even know if I was in it. Tom was. And Rob. I saw Rob just before I went to Provincetown. I guess it was right after school ended. He's really a sweet boy. He's growing up nicely. If he were only about ten years older, I could go for him." She giggled "He was with a friend who asked if I was his sister ... Actually, I wouldn't mind having a brother right now. To sort of pal around with. Maybe hitch cross-country and end up back in Provincetown. Or vice versa. No, that doesn't sound right. Anyway, I could only hitch with a boy. Or a man ... In the dream, Rob and Tom both had longer hair than they really have. I keep trying to remember what they were doing, but I don't know if they were doing anything ... Maybe they were just being there together ... Do people have to do something in a dream?"

"Only if you want them to," the doctor said when Dawn waited for a reply.

"I don't care if they do anything or not ... as long as they're there. It was really a very lovely dream."

9

IN THE MIDDLE of July there had been a message on Lulu's answering machine, a bolt out of the blue, Lulu had never thought of the machine as a weapon until then. Her heart skittered around like a rabbit

Hi, this is Sascha. Remember me?

Thus managing in a few words to communicate the strong sense that her mother had neglected her since her disappearance seven years earlier.

I'm coming to New York in a couple of weeks and I figured I'd stay in the apartment. I'll call you when I get there.

Coming to New York, my lovely daughter? Coming to New York from where? Will I know you? Are you still angry with me? How will I know you if you're not?

Seven years.

At first she'd thought she was seeing Sascha on the

street every time she left her own neighborhood, but invariably it had turned out to be some other young girl with dark, shiny hair.

The year Sascha left had been the year Lulu set up her practice. Lulu remembered standing at the door to Sascha's abandoned bedroom, thinking, If only you could fill up this space with an office. Make believe you never had a daughter. If Sascha came back, they could be friends instead of relations. She'd just completed a decent analysis so she'd been able to muster a small laugh at the fantasy. Nathan had found her a closet-like space in the back of someone else's professional suite which had been adequate for the first few years. By then she was earning enough to justify an office of her own as well as a housekeeper in the afternoons. That was the year the boys turned five and six and both were in school all day for the first time.

Lulu's mother had yet to remove herself from their midst with the aid of a decade's worth of leftover sleeping pills, but the signs were there. Lulu was already urging her father to get rid of all those half-filled bottles. What was the sense of having them there, lined up in the medicine cabinet, a perpetual invitation to a little rest, a lot of rest, eternal rest?

It was in 1974 that her mother had finally accepted the invitation, and her father, recuperating in Florida from the unpleasant nonsurprise, had hooked up with the widow of an old friend and asked Lulu to send his belongings down to the widow's condominium. Not the furniture. There was no room for that; Lulu could dispose of it as she wished. How fortunate that she had had pangs about throwing it all away. What she couldn't cram into their apartment she'd put in storage for an imagined country house and taken out when she and Nathan were dividing up their own possessions.

Sascha called Nathan once in a while but Nathan was still refusing to divulge her whereabouts. Nor was he willing to tell Sascha of her grandmother's suicide, although Lulu needed her to know. Nathan played Dr. Rational, arguing his daughter's right not to have her growing-up-and-distancing-herself process impeded by a mother seeking to restore symbiosis, and Lulu, too depressed to fight and too unsure to argue, hadn't pushed. Six months later Lulu had called Mrs. Samuelson to beg to know where Sascha was, but by that time Sascha was out of touch with the Samuelsons as well. Woody's wife was able to tell her that Sascha and a group of other women had left the radical commune in Berkeley where they'd been living in rage over the way they had been treated by the male radicals in the house.

Hi, this is Sascha. Remember me?

I remember everything, my love, but you're twenty-four years old now, and I don't feel the way I felt when you left, nor am I willing to feel that way again. The relief of not having to deal with you was inadequate compensation for the anguish of your disappearance. But eventually I got to be all right, and while I hope you're all right, too, we can't pretend that seven years haven't passed.

July ended and Sascha hadn't called. Lulu left a forwarding card at the post office and, with some qualms, she left the Long Island number on her answering machine tape. Bonnie had urged her to get one of the new answering machines with a remote-control device, but money was terribly tight and she was waiting.

She had to behave normally. She needed to remain steady, business as usual, whether Sascha showed up or not.

August 6th, 1977

Dear Dr. Shinefeld:

I decided to write instead of calling because when I looked at a map to see where you were in relation to me, there was only water between us, and I felt as though a letter would be more solid because it would go over land.

We're having a pretty good time, Lillian and I, as we used to before old What's-his-name came between us in her mind. Lillian took a waitress job at a place called Dock Malone's and she talked me into working there, though I don't know how long I'll stick it out. When I got here, I found Gregory just as cool as he'd been at the *beginning* of my first visit, and I told myself I'd better not count on being able to "hang out" around his place.

That was the smartest thing I could have done, because once he saw that I wasn't going to be a leech on his life, Gregory warmed up. Anyway, I like him the way he is, and I'm happy to say that I'm now allowed to be one of the people who comes and goes without notice at "the salon," which is what everyone calls his house. You never know who's going to be there, or even if Gregory will be. Half the time he goes upstairs to sleep or read. Upstairs isn't part of the salon.

I'm meeting lots of people at both places, but the ones at Gregory's are more interesting. In the daytime I often sleep on his stretch of the beach. The waitress work isn't very *compelling*, and I have a fantasy in which some friend of Gregory's with a research project hires me so I'm busy but not this tired. Of course, the job would be right here. So much for fantasies.

Love,
Dawn

August 12th, 1977

Dear Dr. Shinefeld:

I'm in Vermont. Left job. Mostly I'm writing so you'll know where I am. The weather got bad and I drove over to Boston for a couple of days, hoping I could find Caitlin MacLeod, but everything was a dead end, so I came here, thinking maybe I'd be able to dig up something from my father's effects. Vera's been wonderful. I love her as long as we don't talk about my father.

Love,
Dawn

"I used to have a dream," Sascha said, looking out toward the pine grove from the porch swing. "It was a barnyard, only it was on a stage, and you were the director. You were a cow, and Grandma and Grandpa were wise old turkeys, and I was this little soft thing, a rabbit, I guess, and you were always telling me to be something else. You were very nice about it except all the animals knew if I didn't do the right thing, you were going to eat me up."

"How old were you?" Lulu asked.

"I don't know," Sascha said. "I think it started when I was very little. Before Nathan. And then there were themes and variations on it over the years. But basically it was the same old dream."

"Hmm," Lulu said. "Interesting."

"Aren't you going to tell me what it means?"

Lulu smiled. "It's seven years later, Sascha. I've gotten a little smarter, too."

Her daughter had strolled onto the beach without notice the day before, already stripped down to a red bikini, her baggage left at the house. Lying on her side on the blanket, talking to Bonnie, squinting against the sun, Lulu had looked up to see a womanly form, at once lissome and powerful, standing closer to their blanket than a stranger would. The woman dropped to the sand near Bonnie. Lulu's head began to pound and breathing became difficult. It was and it was not the face of her seventeen-year-old daughter.

"Hi," Sascha had said offhandedly. "Nathan told me where you were. I couldn't get you on the phone."

Bonnie turned, saw Sascha, turned back to Lulu, gaping, said hello to Sascha, then jumped to her feet and ran into the water, at a loss for words for the first time since Lulu had known her.

"It's good to see you," Lulu said.

Sascha's eyes moved down the beach to the spot

where Teddy and Walden and Bonnie's boys were building an elaborate sand castle. Walden and Teddy were nine and ten now, still a self-contained unit. Sometimes they allowed other kids to join their charmed circle; if there were none around, they didn't seek them out, the exception being the Mayer boys, with whom there was often some ongoing project like a Lego city or a wireless radio. The boys had been two and three years old when Sascha left; Teddy had mentioned her occasionally during the first year; Walden, never.

Sascha's eyes lingered on the boys for a moment. Her expression was dreamy.

"Nathan didn't tell me about the divorce," Sascha said, her eyes coming back to her mother. "Or about Grandma. I never knew until a couple of months ago. I'm sorry about Grandma . . . and about the divorce."

Lulu nodded.

"Nathan can be a bit of a prick, you know," Sascha said.

Lulu looked toward the water.

"I don't know if you'll be any worse off, now that he's . . . He must've felt horribly guilty about leaving, or he would have let me know sooner."

Lulu was silent.

Sascha stood and walked over to the boys.

Bonnie came out of the water.

"Jesus," Bonnie said. "Are you all right?"

"Fine," Lulu said. "It was very aerobic."

Together they looked toward the group of children some fifteen or twenty yards down the beach.

For a while Lulu had made a point of referring to

Sascha, keeping pictures of her in the living room.
One of them was still there, in a group of family
snapshots on the bookcase, but there hadn't been
anything to talk about in a long time.

Sascha was speaking to the boys, who looked up,
chatted briefly, and then went back to their castle.
Sascha ran into the water.

Lulu thought of the crazed fourteen-year-old who
had stood over the crib of her new baby brother,
screaming: "What are you *talking* about? I don't have
any bad feelings about him! He's just a baby!"

In general, Sascha was much calmer. She *had* announced that she'd made a fortune as a coke dealer
in Aspen, but had finally confessed that for the past
two years she'd been going to the University of
Miami and earning her living as an Avon lady. "A
joke, two jokes, but easy." Now she was bored and
thinking of looking for a better school.

"So, what is there to do around here?" Sascha asked
the next morning as Lulu poured herself a second
cup of coffee. Lulu's daughter was sitting sidesaddle
on the porch swing.

"There's the beach, of course," Lulu said.

Sascha laughed. "I've been living in Miami for
four years."

"Yes. True. I guess I thought you'd want to go
down to meet people, not for the—"

"I didn't come here to meet people," Sascha said.
"I came here to be with you."

"That's lovely," Lulu said doubtfully, for the phrase
conjured up many moments in her children's history

when they'd wanted something from her that couldn't be named. "Well, there are plenty of things we might do together. Especially at night. Dinner, lots of movies, parties..."

"Have you learned to play tennis yet?" Sascha asked—as though everyone did, sooner or later.

"Uh-uh. But the Mayers' court is still in constant use, and I'm sure you can get a game up there."

"You're still all wrapped up in the Mayers," Sascha said.

"I'm not sure I'm wrapped up in them. We're good friends. This house still belongs to them."

"And she's still as icky as ever." Sascha and Bonnie had exchanged about ten words on the beach. "Never mind." Sascha jumped off the swing. "Maybe I'll go down to the beach after all."

"Okay."

"Wanna come?"

"I'll be down in a while. I like to do a few chores before I leave the house."

"Where're the boys? At the Mayers'?"

"Still sleeping, I think."

"You're kidding! Will I wake them if I go up to get my bathing suit?"

"It doesn't matter. They don't seem to hear anything in the morning."

"It's not healthy, you know," Sascha said darkly. "Kids need sunshine and fresh air. They're not meant to be night people."

Lulu smiled. "Please feel free to tell them anything about their habits that you want to tell them."

"*I'm* not their mother. *You* are."

"Well, I've already expressed my opinion on the

subject. But it seems..." Another wry smile. "It seems that the director of the barnyard only has a limited mandate."

"My God," Sascha exploded, "it's just like the old days! Anything I say, you turn against me!"

August 16th, 1977

Dear Dr. Shinefeld:

Seek and ye shall find—the trunk with all the business papers and the checks right on top. There were checks made out to a Mrs. Caitlin Hagerty until the end of May. Nothing regular to anyone after that. But before her, there was Mavis MacLeod. Vera thinks that was the nice one. There was no Mavis MacLeod listed in Boston so I called the woman who will be known hereafter as Mrs. Shitface, for reasons I'm about to explain. Namely, I told her whose daughter I was, and there was a complete, utter, absolute, total, DEAD silence.

Finally, I just began talking. I said I wanted to find out a few things about my father, about his last months. She said in this little pinched frozen voice she was sure she didn't remember a thing. It was too long ago. I could tell she was lying but there was no way to push it. So I asked if she knew where I could find Mavis, and the old beast said, "What do you want of *her*, now?" You know what makes me maddest? The first thing I had to do was deny there was something wrong with me. It worked, but I could kill myself now when I think about it. I said, "Look, Mrs.——, I don't know what difficulties you might have had with my father, but I'm not looking for any trouble. I'm just this normal orphan trying to find out who my parents were." Then there was another ice age. And finally she said in the same awful voice, "Mrs. Francis X. Hagerty." And the address. And then she hung up.

It *kills* me that I had to tell her I was normal. I feel as though I betrayed my father.

I'm staying at Gregory's apartment in Boston, doing some errands for him. A friend of his came by, also horrendously handsome, and we talked for a while, and he asked if I wanted to see a movie, but I had a funny feeling about him, that he was maybe homosexual trying to act straight, and I don't feel equipped to deal with that stuff right now.

> Yours for sanity,
> Dawn

August 18th, 1977

Dear Dr. Shinefeld:

Well, I've finally met Mavis MacLeod, who is Mrs. Francis X. Hagerty, and if I'm halfway sane, she's probably the reason, after my father.

At first I was disappointed because her voice on the phone was the most beautiful voice I'd ever heard in my life, with a delicious Scots brogue, more like a musical instrument than a voice. Or a lullaby, soft and sweet. I still get goosepimples when I hear her voice in my mind. I guess there's no way she could have looked the same as she sounded. She's somewhere in her forties now and just not that pretty, if she ever was. She looked a little coarse. Not fat, but sloppy. She'd gotten herself dressed up for me, but it wasn't in good taste.

Either she didn't know what to tell me because she didn't know what I already knew, or she may not know a lot herself. I think she was in love with my father. She left more than six months after my mother died and maybe she saw that nothing was going to happen and she couldn't stand it. She was terribly sweet and discreet and I have no idea of what she saw. That is, whether she understood about my father. She said that she'd known Hagerty for a while and he'd asked her to marry him before and this time she just said yes. She was never sure why. Then she found someone else reliable for my father, a cousin of Hagerty's. That was Mrs. Shitface.

At the end of the afternoon, when I felt very close to Mavis because of the way she talked about my father, I said something about how Mrs. Shitface sounded on the phone. She said that oh well, Mrs. Shitface was from the old country (I wish you could hear her say those words) and she was terribly strict and old-fashioned. But she had felt it was important for my father to have someone absolutely reliable, and Mrs. Shitface was that.

Mavis told me it was my father who took care of me from the day they brought me home from the hospital. She and my father. At first she thought my mother was worn out from childbirth. She hadn't known my parents before I was born. She was hired for when I came home.

Every time she mentioned my mother, Mavis would say the poor soul, or the poor, sweet creature. It would have gotten on my nerves except that she was so sincere.

She said that for the six months my mother was alive, she lay in the bed, sleeping, or crying. On a good day she'd leaf through a few pages of a magazine. My father waited on her hand and foot. Mavis did the cooking and cleaning, and she and my father both tended to me. My mother wouldn't take food from anyone but my father.

A lot of the time they would put me in the bed next to her, sort of up against her. I think they hoped she would show some reaction. But I don't think she ever did, although Mavis says you could tell my mother liked to have me there with her. Mavis is one of those people who's so good she can't really understand what most of the human race is about. She said the only thing that worried my mother was that she might roll over on me and smother me. Mavis kept telling me how much my mother really loved me. That she just didn't know what to do about it. But that seems to me to be just another example of her seeing only the sunshine. The truth is, how could anyone love her baby and then go kill herself when the baby was six months old?

Yours,
Dawn

One night Lulu and Sascha took the boys to the movies in Sag Harbor and Lulu became uneasy because there was someone in the audience, a male, guffawing loudly a few seconds *before* each gag was actually delivered, and she had the feeling it was someone she knew. After the premature laugher had disturbed everyone's responses a few times, people started telling him to shut up. He complied, but then gradually worked himself back into the old routine, and the cycle began anew.

After the movie, Lulu was torn between a nagging curiosity about who the laugher might be and a strong instinct to beat a retreat before she could find out. Fate, in the form of Walden's leaving behind the comics they'd bought just before the movie, intervened, and Lulu and Sascha were standing in front of the movie house, waiting for the two boys to come out again, when a large, handsome young man, whom Lulu knew to be the culprit before she actually realized who he was, emerged from the theater alone, spied their group and came toward them, grinning widely.

"Hi, Dr. Lulu. Am I having the pleasure of meeting young Dr. Lulu?"

"Go fuck yourself," Sascha said.

Mark Bluestein regarded Sascha with interest. "I apologize. I was just trying to get a rise out of your mother."

"She's not my mother," Sascha said no less unpleasantly. "She's my great-aunt."

The boys were coming out of the theater, thirty seconds too late to save this particular week in August for their mother.

"You never told me," Mark said to Lulu, "that you had a beautiful grand-niece."

"I'm sorry," Lulu said, playing for time to collect

herself... If she ran, Mark Bluestein would follow. "I know we've met, but I can't seem to..."

"She's lying, you know," Mark said to Sascha. "She had a very strong countertransference to me. Over the counter. Under the counter. You name it."

"You don't mean you were her patient!" Sascha's expression changed from incredulity to glee as she began to sense the possibilities of the situation.

"I was her most spectacular success," Mark assured Sascha. "When I entered treatment with your great-aunt, I was a fourteen-year-old sociopath. When I finished, I was an extraordinarily well adjusted seventeen-year-old tycoon."

"No shit," Sascha said. "How old are you now?"

"Twenty-two."

By Lulu's reckoning he would be edging up on nineteen.

"How old are *you?*" he asked Sascha.

"Twenty-four," she said.

"Terrific," Mark told her. "I was just getting ready for an older woman."

"I think you may be a real asshole," Sascha informed him.

"Finally, a woman who's smart enough for me," Mark said. "Let's have a glass of wine across the street. I'll get you home afterward."

It took Sascha a split second to glance at Lulu's face and realize that there would have to be more pleasure than pain in taking Mark up on his offer. Then the two of them walked across the street, Mark's arm around Sascha's shoulders. He hadn't acknowledged the presence of the little boys in the midst of their group.

"Who's that?" Walden asked.

"A friend of Sascha's," Lulu said.

Lulu dug farther under the sheet since the night was too warm for a blanket and she needed some kind of cover.

She could anticipate the worst. The situation was, as they said, overdetermined. It was essential—if nearly impossible—that she remain neutral about a friendship between Sascha and Mark. Anything negative she said about him would endear him to her daughter. As a matter of fact, she could easily envision Sascha's repeating some comment to Mark, who would proceed to make a scene over her ethics.

No paranoia, please, Dr. Lulu, she told herself, then shuddered at her own use of Mark's name for her.

It was important to remember that the smoldering young goddess who was her daughter had almost invariably, when she was younger, brought home boys who were acquiescent if not amiable, passive enough to enjoy her perpetual rage. If Sascha were left to her own reactions, there was a reasonable chance that sooner or later Mark's being a gigantic pain in the ass would outweigh his connection to her mother.

Mark Bluestein had been in some crucial sense Lulu's most spectacular failure, although his parents still sent her referrals and Chanukah presents with equal abandon and would have been astounded to learn that she was less than thrilled with her handiwork.

Brilliant, hyperactive, precocious at manipulation and psychologically sadistic in a way that would have been extraordinary even if he had been considerably older, Mark had been one of her first patients. A blessing, or so she'd initially thought. Five days a week at full rates, referred by an older colleague toward whom Lulu was never able to feel warm again. If Lulu had been a little more experienced, a little more sure of herself, and a little less eager to earn the money, it wouldn't have taken almost three years to kick him out of an analysis he'd never truly entered.

He'd already been expelled from four private schools. He was flatly refusing to hazard the public one in his neighborhood because he would get beaten up by the black kids. She had never known a New York Jewish kid who hated and feared blacks as Mark did, although he had a talent for drawing fire from all his schoolmates, not just the black ones. It had been arranged that Mark could stay out of school for a term if he entered treatment. He and his mother had been interviewing doctors for a few weeks before he settled on Lulu because, as he told her, she appeared to be just smart enough so that it would be fun to gull her. Also, he liked the way she dressed. A little sloppy, but colorful. In good taste. He hated women who didn't dress well and generally went with his mother to pick her clothes. He had been determined to have a female doctor, the problem being to find one who was "halfway intelligent."

His parents were wealthy. His father was a somewhat manic, supremely controlling television producer. (Mark hated all machinery, including television, to which he claimed to have a physical allergy.) His mother was a pretty, nervous former showgirl who, racked by guilt at having stolen Mark's father from his first wife and children, considered everything the boy did punishment for her sins. Mark had a sister three years younger whom he tortured in ways that were not apparent to his parents. He took great pleasure in detailing these abuses to Lulu, beginning with the days when the infant had been unable to lift her head and he would turn her over in her crib for a few seconds at a time so that her nose and mouth rested on the sheets and she was unable to breathe. There was no way for the doctor to ascertain whether this had actually occurred.

During the time between his accepting Dr. Shinefeld and actually coming into the office (his third scheduled appointment), he purchased *An Outline of Psychoanalysis* and *The Interpretation of Dreams*. He began their first session by challenging Lulu on the issue of countertransference. He didn't like the way old Sigar Freudenheim made it sound as though the patient went through this heavy shit while the doctor didn't. He'd been with her for a few weeks before she was confirmed in her suspicion that material he was bringing in consisted of simple alterations of basic dreams he'd found in the book. When she said that there was probably still meaning in his selection of dreams, he stopped telling them to her at all.

In the meantime, Mark's behavior at home began to improve dramatically, for all of his sadistic energies were redirected toward Lulu. He returned to school at the beginning of the new term. The kids still hated him, but he behaved well enough in his classes so that some of his teachers were able to appreciate his intellectual gifts.

During his sixteenth year, Mark became obsessed with the notion that his father stood between him and Dr. Lulu, and that to alter this situation, he had to pay for the treatment himself. In six months he had set up a going business under which he took and filled orders from the other kids in school, as well as from a couple of teachers, for rock albums and concert tickets that he picked up for them on the weekends. The problem, known to Lulu and the entire student body, was that the money was being paid him for dope.

After a couple of months of futile attempts to get Mark to treat this matter more seriously than he'd treated the rest of the analysis, Dr. Shinefeld had terminated his treatment.

At their last session, Mark had made various suggestions about the ways in which their yearnings for each other could be satisfied, now that he would no longer be a patient. She told him that while she could not prevent his contacting her, if he did so she would no longer consider information about his activities confidential.

And Lulu had not seen him again, because in his entire life he had never gone one step farther than reality would allow him to.

"Mark says you were very seductive with him. He says you were always sending him mixed signals. Do it, don't do it . . . You'd cross your legs so he could see halfway up your dress and then look at him as if you were daring him."

"Mmm."

Sascha, in the kitchen, squeezing oranges for juice, passed the glass, then the granola and milk, out through the window to the porch table, where Lulu sat lingering over her second cup of coffee. Sascha stuck her head through the window. "Are you listening?"

"Mmm."

"Don't you have anything to say?"

"You know I can't talk about my patients, Sascha."

Sascha appeared on the porch in her red bikini bottom and a white T-shirt. Her dark hair flowed becomingly down her back. Her hands were on her hips. Lulu had no idea when she'd come in the night before.

"What about *me*?" Sascha demanded.

Lulu looked up from her copy of *Better Homes and Gardens*. "I don't understand the question."

"I'm your daughter. Don't I have any rights? Is it only your patients who have rights?"

"Absolutely not," Lulu said. "You both have the right to privacy. I wouldn't talk about you to Mark, either."

"I don't think you're being funny."

Lulu was silent.

"What if he was an ax-murderer? Would you tell me?"

"Absolutely," Lulu assured her solemnly. "I'd do more than just tell you. I'd protect you in every way I could."

"Well, there are other kinds of danger, too. What if . . . What if you just thought he might hurt me? Emotionally, I mean."

"Wouldn't that be like playing God the Psychia-

258

trist?" Lulu asked. "Deciding who could hurt you and trying to steer you away from them?"

There was still in Sascha an adolescent girl who wanted Lulu to give her orders to fight.

Sascha sat down, drank her juice, prepared her granola.

"He's very bright, actually. Very interesting. I wouldn't blame you if you went for him. Although he was pretty young then."

Lulu studied carefully some muslin curtains being offered in the mail-order section at the back of *Better Homes and Gardens*.

Sascha giggled. "He's pretty young now," she said, her mouth full of granola. "But cute. And he's a great lay."

Lulu's coffee was gone.

"One of those crowd pleasers," Sascha said. "You know the type? Can't rest until everyone's exhausted and happy."

Lulu stood up in what she hoped was a casual manner, stretched, and said she was going to do some chores.

"Anything wrong?" Sascha asked.

"No," Lulu said.

"Are you mad at me?" Sascha asked.

"No," Lulu said.

"Mark's coming by to go to the beach. Do you mind if we go to ours? His folks' place is in Southampton, but he says he wants to try the sun here."

"Obviously," Lulu said, "you're free to go to whichever beach you choose."

"Mmm," Sascha said, finishing her granola and

picking up the bowl to drink the sweet milk. "Is it okay if we have lunch here, then?"

"No," Lulu said after a moment, "not really."

Sascha's eyebrows shot up in one of the world's more ludicrous imitations of surprise. "You're kidding! How come?"

Lulu struggled with herself for what seemed like minutes. She could hear birds in the woods and children shouting at the Mayers' pool.

Oh, fuck.

"Because I don't like him and I don't want him around."

"I thought you didn't talk about your patients," Sascha said triumphantly.

"I'm not talking about a patient," Lulu said. "I'm talking about myself."

Then she went to her bedroom, locked the door, and remained inside until Mark Bluestein's black Porsche had entered the driveway; Sascha had gone out to meet him; there had been an earnest conversation of which Lulu heard only Sascha saying, "Because I don't *feel* like hanging around here, I *feel* like going *someplace else*"; and the two of them had gotten into the Porsche and driven away.

August 20th, 1977

Dear Dr. Shinefeld:

I drove up to see the house at the shore. I took that boy who's been hanging around just to have someone with me. Often I think I'm better off being with people who don't understand me well. Then I have to hold myself together, whereas any kind of insanity that spills out of me is perfectly all right with you.

The house is on a cliff, which I didn't picture at all. There's a narrow highway, really a road. The houses on the right are behind a stone wall that goes on for what seems like miles, and here and there, you see a break in the wall for an entrance. Lots of trees, but then you realize there are no trees in the distance, and finally you figure out that must be the ocean. That was when I began to feel a little weird. As though my head were a giant seashell. When I had to move over on the road to let someone pass, I moved too far because I was clutching the wheel so tightly that the car swerved instead of edging over. I made Vernon, that's my new "friend," nervous.

In Provincetown, the ocean isn't scary, partly because it's the bay, but also because the activity on the street nearby makes it less awesome and overwhelming. The ocean, I mean.

The house. I was a little numbed out most of the time I was there. I don't think I "recognized it." The people who have it are grandparents now, but they bought it from my grandfather when their children were young. When I explained who I was, they let me look through it. Nothing looked familiar.

At the back of the house, the rooms are only ten or fifteen yards from the cliffs that slope down to the ocean. (Slope isn't exactly the right word. It's more like a straight drop down. Below, there are miles of sand and rocks to your right

and your left, and right in front of you is the
ocean, except that you feel surrounded by it
because it's so loud. You wouldn't play music in
those back rooms because it would be overwhelmed by the ocean. There was a stereo in
one of the rooms, so obviously everyone doesn't
feel the same way.)

Mrs. Reed, the owner, said the rooms hadn't
been changed much from when they bought the
house. Her children's rooms became her grand-
children's. In one of those little rooms facing the
ocean, I began to cry. I don't know why. I
definitely have no memory of it. Nothing in it
meant a *thing* to me. There was a crib in it. I
asked Mrs. Reed if there'd been a crib there
when they bought it and she said she couldn't
remember for sure.

Vernon and I went to the beach. By the time
we were halfway down the cliff (there are stairs)
I didn't want to go farther, but he said he had to
take a swim. I would no sooner have gone in
that water than—I can't think of a comparison. I
was terrified when Vernon went in, although I
tried not to show it. I just paced back and forth
on the sand making sure I didn't look at the
water, except I had to keep peeking to make
sure I could still see him. I couldn't wait to get
out of there, and when we left, I knew I wasn't
going back to Boston, or to the Cape, either,
although I didn't understand what I was actually
doing until later. I just knew I needed to get to
Marbury and Vera. I did something I probably
shouldn't have done, although I'll probably nev-

er know how much it bothered Vernon, which was to leave him at the outskirts of Boston and give him cab fare to get back to his house. He's young and doesn't even have a full-time job. Then I came here. I don't know if you noticed the postmark.

I realized later I was repeating what happened to me before, after my father died. I really drove here as though I were driving for my life. I had that seashell feeling again, empty but not empty at the same time, layers spiraling in on themselves into that strange, whispery, echoey sound. My head was ringing. When I got here, I ran into the house and hugged Vera. I don't know when I last did that. I think she's very self-conscious about being hugged by a female. I thought I was going to cry but I didn't. She gave me a cup of tea and she didn't make me talk, which was just what I needed. She got me through that first terror. (I don't like giving it that name. As though calling it that will give it more power.)

I need to talk to you but I don't want to leave here. I tried to call you this morning but there was no answer. I'll try again tonight but of course you won't know I tried until you get this letter—unless I actually reach you.

I mentioned casually to Vera that I'd love her to come to New York with me sometime, see some sights, be a tourist. I thought she'd laugh it off but instead she said she'd like to do it. Then I felt guilty because talking someone into going to New York City in August is really a dirty trick. But I want to see you and I can't seem to

face leaving here just now, so if I reach you, and
if you're still planning to be in New York, maybe
we'll do it. Vera doesn't care about the weather
that much one way or the other, and we'd stay in
some nice air-conditioned hotel.

Yours,
Dawn

Lulu asked Sascha if she'd picked up any calls. Sascha
said there had been a couple, but whoever it was had
hung up upon hearing her voice. She figured it was
just some creep. "Why?"

"I think one of my patients is trying to reach me."

"I'm sorry," Sascha said defensively. "All I said was
hello."

"Of course," Lulu said. "It's not your fault."

"No shit," Sascha said. "And speaking of shit..."

In spite of herself, Lulu laughed.

"It's not funny," Sascha said.

The doctor was silent but the mother couldn't
resist saying that the sequence had been neat.

"You don't even know what I want to say."

Lulu waited.

Sascha said that she wouldn't give a small, hard
turd about continuing to keep Mark away from the
house (glaring at Lulu to see if her mother dared
smile again) except that Mark, at a loss to understand why he was always being steered away from
Lulu's vicinity, was accusing Sascha of being jealous
of her mother, an idea so sick as to be intolerable.

"I really like him, you know," Sascha said, staring
intently at her mother as though she might thus find
out if what she herself was saying was true. "He's

very bright. I could have a real relationship with him, except that you've planted yourself in the middle of it in some strange way."

"Oh?"

"Definitely. You're more *there*, than you would ever be if you carried on normally and my friends could come and go like in any reasonable household."

Lulu closed her eyes. If only the phone would ring. Dawn, in desperate need of a consultation.

"Look, Sascha," she said after a moment. She must be careful. Try, as she groped her way across the board, not to press any of the buttons that would make Sascha's red lights flash. But the very issues were so loaded that this was nearly impossible. Maybe she should give in right now. Except that surrender would only advance the Implacable Opponent to the next plateau. "You're an adult now, and actually the household you're talking about, where friends come and go, consists of parents and children."

"You mean you're not my mother anymore?"

"What I mean is that when you were young, and now with the boys...I can put up with almost any *children*." She was being dishonest, generalizing about children and life in order to avoid the core fact, which, if voiced, would destroy any hope of peace. "Adults are different. Not to mention that you and I are two adults who are just getting accustomed to being with each other." And not to speak of Mark Bluestein, who is in a class by himself. "You may notice I haven't had the Mayers over. I just wouldn't think of asking them to be around when you're here, because you dislike them, and our time together is limited."

"It's fine with me if you have the Mayers here!" Sascha protested. "Have anyone you want. Is that why the house has been so dead? Because you think—"

"It hasn't been dead by my standards. There've been kids coming and going. We see people on the beach. I've been trying to write a paper for the first time since I went to school and I haven't been entertaining much."

"I'm not asking you to entertain Mark!" Sascha shouted. "I'm just asking you to let him be around!"

Lulu went to the kitchen to answer the phone. It was Dawn. She and Vera were coming to New York for a visit, but the jeep was at the garage and they wouldn't have it back until the next day or the day after. They had a reservation at the Plaza for the next night. Dawn made a tentative appointment for the afternoon of the day after the following one, with the understanding that she would get back to the doctor by the next evening if she wasn't able to make it. Lulu returned to the living room without the feeling of relief she would have expected to come from the knowledge that she had an excuse to drive into the city.

"Was that your precious patient? I hope It's going to get what It wants, even if I'm not. Actually, I know it's a She. It must be because a man would've asked who I was . . . Are you off on another planet entirely, Mother?"

Lulu shook her head. "I'm sorry. That was the patient I was asking about. I'm going to have to go in."

"Oh, brother," Sascha said bitterly. "How convenient."

"What do you want from me, Sascha?" Lulu asked wearily. "What do you mean by having him around? I'm not going until the day after tomorrow. If I say that Mark can come over—tomorrow evening, or for a while during the day—does that mean I'll have to see more of him? That I might find him here when I return? Because I couldn't tolerate that. I'm not particularly keen on having anyone around, but if you want to test my capacities, try me with someone who was never one of my patients."

"Are you saying that I can invite him to dinner tomorrow night?"

Lulu hesitated. "All right."

"And then I suppose you'll run right into your room afterward and lock the door."

"I don't know. It'll depend on how I feel. I might."

"Then it won't do any good. While you're running away, you're more important than I am."

"Why do you think that should be?"

"There's no *should*. It's just the way he is. He had a very difficult childhood. Neither of his parents wanted him."

"The way he is, Sascha, is that if I stay with you all evening and go into the city the next morning, he'll tell you that it was just a ruse having him in the first place."

"Paranoid," Sascha declared. "You know you're really paranoid? How'd you ever get a license to practice *anything*?"

Cooking was a trap. Either she'd fuck up because having to do it made her angry, or she'd do well and Mark would heap praise on her to ensure Sascha's jealousy and her own discomfort. In town she bought lobster salad, potato salad, cole slaw, tomatoes and a French bread. It was the middle of the day, when she could seldom be persuaded to go into town for any reason, but she'd been too anxious to relax until she knew that food for dinner was in the house. She drove home and found Mark's Porsche in the driveway. Trying to keep a grip on herself, she entered the house, which was empty. They'd already gone to the beach.

Lulu put away the food and got into her bathing suit, but she had no intention of going down to the beach. She would swim at Bonnie's. If Bonnie was there, it would be an opportunity to discuss her exaggerated (she didn't believe it) reaction to the presence of Mark Bluestein. If Bonnie wasn't there, the pool would still be a refuge. Maybe she'd even find Duke around; this was the kind of problem he was particularly good at—protective measures when pathology was driving daily life up against the wall. She took a book so she wouldn't need to go into the Mayer house for something to read if she were alone.

She walked up the slope toward the Mayers'. The children, including hers, were in the pool. Bonnie, just coming out, waved to her happily. There were a few other people sitting in chaises, their backs to her. Lulu wasn't sure who they were except she thought one was Duke. As she drew closer she could see that it was.

"We're all here," Bonnie called as Lulu approached. "Did they leave you a note?"

The other two people were Mark and Sascha.

Lulu jumped into the pool because Mark was terrified of the water. (He'd told Sascha he had a skin disease that kept him out of both salt and chlorinated water. Sascha, incomparably cynical in most circumstances, had believed him.)

Bonnie came back into the water and dog-paddled beside Lulu.

"I can't believe the change in Sascha," Bonnie said. "She's delightful. When I think of a few years ago..."

Lulu smiled painfully. She felt that they were being watched. "How'd they happen to be here?" she asked.

"They just came by," Bonnie said. "Sascha said she'd had a yen to see the old place. It was really very sweet."

"Did you have any reaction to the boy?"

"Well, he's very good-looking, of course. And pleasant. Bright. But, you know, these computer people... I really can't talk to them at all. I should say, *listen*. I was very good when he was explaining about his own company, but when he started describing everyone plugging into their home computers..."

Lulu broke away and began doing laps because she was flashing on a scenario in which she told Bonnie who Mark was, Bonnie betrayed her surprise in some way that was apparent to Mark, and Mark took steps toward suing her. For what? Malpractice?

Sascha was right. She was becoming paranoid.

Dawn looked wonderful—deeply tanned, wearing a striped tank top, white shorts, and sandals, her sun-streaked hair neatly upswept.

She sat down facing the doctor, then laughed. "I

guess I think I'm not supposed to lie down because this isn't exactly a session."

The doctor returned her smile.

"Who was that on the phone?" Dawn asked.

"Who do you think it was?" the doctor asked.

"No," Dawn said earnestly. "I'm willing to associate and all that, but first I *really have to know.*"

"Why?"

"Because she doesn't belong there," Dawn burst out. "No, wait a minute. That's not what I mean. I mean, I have a picture of you and your life and she's not in it. Where was that phone number I called, anyway? I know it's Long Island because it was five-one-six."

The doctor hesitated, then said it was in East Hampton.

"Oh, God," Dawn moaned. "So close."

"Close to what?"

"To where I could have been if I'd known."

"But here we are," the doctor pointed out. "Together in this room."

"Is she your daughter? Don't you see that I have to know? Don't you know that it's bad enough I have to share you with your other patients? That every time the door closes behind you and another patient, I think I'll never see you again?" She began to sob.

"No," the doctor said, "I didn't know that."

"Well, it's true. Especially if you're smiling, if it looks as though you're having a good time. I think, why would she ever come back to me when I'm such a miserable, whiny little drag? And then I have to remind myself of the times you've smiled at me. And if I can't think of any, I feel..."

"Tell me."

"No. You're trying to trick me."

"Trick you?"

"Distract me. Make me forget about your daughter. That's who she is, isn't she? You might as well tell me. I'm not going to be able to think of anything else until it's settled."

"But you *were* thinking of something else," the doctor pointed out gently. "You were thinking of seeing me with other patients and being sure I'd never come back to you."

"I need to be very important to you," Dawn said after a while. She was fighting tears. "The only way I can stand seeing you with other patients is to tell myself that they're only your patients but I'm almost like a daughter to you. Your *only* daughter. It never occurred to me you had a real one. I thought maybe you had a couple of little kids...you know, running around...like in the story about Dr. Seaver's brownstone...boys, I don't know, or no sex. I hear what that sounds like but I know what I mean. I didn't think about sex. It didn't matter as long as they were *little*. As long as they couldn't talk to you and understand things the way I can. But she's old, that girl. Maybe my age. She could know much more. She could be a housekeeper, I guess...But she didn't sound like a housekeeper. Oh, God, I don't know why I keep kidding myself, I know she's yours...In the drugstore I was looking at hair dyes again. I had this picture...I guess it was a dream...a big you and a little you. Not little. Just smaller enough so she could be your daughter . . . I don't know why the size is so important . . . How tall are you, anyway? You're taller than I am. I'm aware of it because I don't see that many women who are."

Silence.

"You mean you won't tell me?"

"I'd rather talk about your feelings about being big and little. And about feeling worried that you'll be left if there are two other big people."

"Well," Dawn said, "that's who did leave me, of course. Big people. My father and Gregory. The Bobbsey twins. Blond and handsome and . . . They probably laughed a lot. I can get a picture so easily, the two of them going off, laughing together. Maybe I thought they were laughing at me. No, that's not it. They were laughing at everything *but* me. I was the work. Gregory made that pretty clear."

"He made his own feelings clear. We have reason to believe your father's were quite different."

"Gordon must've been glad to find someone he could talk to," Dawn said sadly. "He must've been so lonely. Alone in the house in Boston with just this pukey little baby and old Mrs. Shitface . . . It must've been quiet all the time . . ." Her voice was sad, dreamy. "And then along came this beautiful boy, Gregory, terribly bright and funny and . . . They fell in love, and they were happy and they talked all the time, and I never understood a word they were saying, except maybe *No Dawn* . . . Oh, God, all that talk going on and that poor little baby, so out of it, not understanding anything . . ." A change of mood to the accusatory. "That's the way you're making me feel now, you know."

"Oh?"

"Not telling me anything. Not even if you're taller than I am. I know you are. I'm almost five-ten. You must be close to six feet."

The doctor, who was five feet eight inches tall without the low or medium heels she generally wore to the office, was silent.

"What's the big deal about not telling me? What does it mean that you're taller than I am?"

"Well," the doctor said, "it seems to mean that I'm a big person who might leave you."

Dawn burst into tears. "That wasn't fair," she said after a while.

"You mean answering your question?"

"That's not fair either. You're using what I said to prove you shouldn't answer my questions."

"It's certainly true that there are good reasons for an analyst not to talk too much."

"Just answering a question isn't talking too much."

"Unless it's something you're not ready to hear."

"Not ready to hear," Dawn said scornfully. "I knew already. All right, I know what you're going to say. I knew it but I wasn't ready to hear it. Well, maybe that's true. But I'm ready to hear if you have a daughter because I'm ... No, that's a lie. The truth is ... I'm ready to hear that you don't have a daughter. Not that you do."

But that night Dawn called the house in East Hampton and asked for Miss Shinefeld. Teddy asked if she wanted Sascha or his mother and Dawn hung up. Teddy reported this to his mother when she called from New York to say that she would be home the following afternoon.

* * *

Dawn did not immediately mention the call when she came in the next morning. She talked about taking Vera to the Statue of Liberty and of how Vera had talked about Tony without bitterness for the first time since the divorce. But suddenly she interrupted herself to ask if the doctor knew what she had done.

"What you did?"

"Calling your house?"

The doctor waited. Dawn explained. She said that she felt guilty but calm. Not as upset as she would have expected herself to be. Still, the doctor said nothing.

"Are you angry with me?"

"No."

"Then why do I feel this way?"

"How do you feel?"

"Awful!" Dawn burst into tears. "I feel as though I committed a crime, even though I know I didn't hurt anyone. I just couldn't let myself keep dreaming about something that wasn't possible."

"Why did you have to know it wasn't possible?"

"Because if I don't find out for myself, I'll find out anyway, sooner or later. You can't go along just thinking things are all right, and then... At least if you're prepared..."

"What is it you have to be prepared for?"

"For you to leave me."

"How does my having a grown daughter make it more likely that I'll leave you?"

"It's because," Dawn said after a while, "I'm not special anymore."

"Tell me what special means."

"It means... more than just liking me. Knowing

274

the difference between me and everyone else who comes in here for fifty minutes at a time is all very well. Essential, I suppose, if you're going to help people. But I'm talking about...being *important*. Having someone need you as much as you need them. Being so important that they can't leave you even if they want to."

"I see," the doctor said slowly. "And so...if I understand you correctly...there can only be one person you need that much. And if I have that type already, a grown daughter, say, then you can't be important to me."

"It sounds silly when you say it that way," Dawn said. "As though I've got it all down to some dumb little formula. All I can tell you...and I don't think I really want to talk about it anymore after this...is that I don't think it can be one way, this needing people."

The doctor said she thought this was important and that they would have to talk about it some more. But later that afternoon, Dawn called to say that she and Vera had gotten matinee tickets for the following day, and "since I don't want to impose on you to change my appointment," maybe they should just forget it. She would see the doctor at her regular appointment, after Labor Day.

Lulu returned to East Hampton, where Sascha had just gotten rid of Mark for reasons her daughter was unwilling to specify. Shortly thereafter, Sascha picked a fight with Lulu on grounds so specious that by the time her daughter had packed and asked for a lift to the station, Lulu couldn't remember what they had been.

"Sascha," Lulu said in the car, "even if it wasn't a perfect visit, it was wonderful to see you. And I hope you won't disappear again."

"Perfect. Hah."

"It wasn't really so awful. And there was no way it was going to be easy."

10

IN HER FIRST MONTHS with Dr Shinefeld that September, Dawn was cheerful, edgy, voluble and determined to "forge on with this analysis business." She would discuss with considerable freedom what it meant to have been an infant abandoned by the people who cared for her. She explored at length what it might have been like to be an eighteen-month-old alone in her crib for a period of nearly twenty-four hours.

"What it must have been like," she said the second or third time it came up. And finally "What it *was* like. I know it was like that even if I don't remember it."

Eventually she cried for that infant without choking and pronounced herself relieved at having gotten past "that vomiting business."

What she would not discuss, aside from the woman who had given birth to her and against whom she had lain on a mattress for much of the first six months of her life, was the matter of being special to Dr. Shinefeld. She assured the doctor that there was no need to discuss it. It was a natural need, everyone had it, and besides, she'd actually found a boyfriend to whom she *was* that special, and now she was happy.

Dawn had succeeded in splitting off the baby self she was discovering, and putting it under a microscope where she could weep over what the slide revealed without seriously endangering the feelings of the twenty-year-old who surrounded and rested upon that infant.

Dawn had spent the last week of vacation in Provincetown with Gregory Barnes and his friends. Bill Denton, her new boyfriend, had come by Gregory's with a girl he'd met on the beach, a former student of Gregory's, and while she and Gregory were immersed in conversation about the chemistry courses at Harvard, Bill and Dawn had begun to talk. They'd ended up spending the rest of the week together, though she hadn't slept with him, then. Now Bill was back at MIT and commuting to New York most weekends. Dawn went to Boston about one week in four.

Bill Denton was terribly straight (she had called him Mr. Straight Arrow for a while and he didn't even mind!), terribly smart in his field, apparently, and terribly decent. For the first time Dawn was able to find fault with Tom Grace by contrasting the way Tom had talked about the people he knew with the way Bill discussed his friends—always in terms of their best selves, their highest intentions. Then, of course, there was the difference in the way they felt about *her*, not to speak of about women in general. Bill Denton was falling in love with her. Unless she was mistaken, he had what you might call a real case. Whereas Tom Grace wasn't capable of more than an infatuation—not even an infatuation, really. It was more that he let out a little bit of the line. Tom Grace was a sort of ... technocrat of relations. He knew their mechanics, how to manipulate to get what he wanted, the problem being that when he got what he wanted, he ceased to be interested. Bill Denton was Old Faithful, and she supposed this was important to her.

"He had the same girlfriend from kindergarten through high school. He got into Harvard, but he went to the University of Chicago so he'd be closer to her. Their families are in Detroit. Then she went to work in an office when he went to college and she fell in love with her boss. He divorced his wife and married her. She never told Bill about him until it was settled."

The doctor was trying to decide if her boredom with Dawn's talk had to do with a certain phony brightness to the presentation; with the nature of Bill Denton; or with her own uneasy sense that a painful analysis, hovering at a point where it might or might not go forward, was endangered by this white knight her patient was fabricating to take her away from it all.

As time went on, she became convinced that this was a real and present danger.

_____

"You know who he is?" Dawn asked one day. "He's me before the divorce. Much more lovable than I am now, really. Because he's much more closed off. No, I shouldn't say before the divorce. Maybe I should say before I came here."

"I'd like to hear about that," the doctor said. "About your being attracted to someone who represents you before analysis."

"Well, he does and he doesn't," Dawn said quickly. "I mean, I _behaved_ like a good person, but I think he may really _be_ one. He's very solid. He feels like an anchor to me. Or even more... I've been wandering around in these dark corridors here, never sure of where I'm going or when I'm getting out. Or who I'll be when I do. I'm not in control of myself the way I was. Remember I told you I thought about food all the time but no one knew it because I controlled myself? And my metabolism, of course. Well, it's a much bigger struggle than it used to be. My wild horses are really loose... People go into therapy to be happier. Or better. But I'm not getting happy, or better, I'm just getting... wilder. More feelings and less control of them... It was different with Dr. Seaver. I was happy but calm. Not that he did anything special to keep me in control. I just... I wanted to do well at everything. I never had any trouble with school. Do you realize that three terms out of four I've practically flunked all my courses?"

"Really?"

"It's not that I've flunked a lot, but I've been close. I don't know what I'm going to be when I get out of school. I can't concentrate enough to care. I'm just sort of floating...Bill is one of those people who automatically do the right thing. Sometimes I think ...seeing all sides of an issue makes it harder to know what to do."

"Oh?"

"I'm not really talking about how he is or how you are. I'm talking about the effect you have on me. Also, I suppose, the effect I have on each of you. Bill can't wait to see me at the beginning of a weekend and he can't stand leaving at the end. It's even worse when I go there, because then he isn't doing something like driving, he's just *waiting*. I'm terribly important to him. He *needs* me. You might care about me some. I'm not saying you don't care. But in the long run...your life goes on the same way if you see me or not. I just don't *matter*."

"So you're more special to him than you could possibly be to me."

"That sounds unreasonable. I know this isn't real life. I'm just a patient. I don't expect you to be in love with me, or to go crazy when I'm out of your sight. You offer me something different, and that's fine."

"You're sure."

"You know what I mean. I mean that I understand."

"How would you feel if you didn't understand?"

A long pause, and then, frostily, "I don't think I care to get into that right now. I have more important things to discuss...Like whether I'm going to move to Boston."

She burst into tears and sobbed uncontrollably for some time.

"Oh, God, I didn't mean it to sound that way. It's not even that I'm planning to do it. We just talk about it. Bill's the one who thinks about it all the time ... Not that I blame him. He's the one who does most of the traveling. He's the one who ... You're not going to help me, are you."

"How can I help you?" the doctor asked.

"By telling me what to do."

"Even if I were sure of what you should do, how would that help you?"

"It would give me something to argue with. No. That's not what I mean."

"Maybe it is."

"You think I should stay here for the analysis, don't you."

"If I didn't think analysis would be helpful to you, I wouldn't be treating you."

"Do you think it would be a disaster for me to leave?"

"I think it would be a disaster for me to make any predictions."

"Why?"

"Because any prediction I make might have some force in what you make happen to you."

"Then if you care about me, why don't you predict that I'll live happily ever after?"

"Because people don't," the doctor said after a moment. "Anyway, we haven't talked about happiness as a goal. Only about being calm."

"I'm happy when I'm with Bill," Dawn said after a moment.

"Would you care to talk about what makes you happy?"

A long silence.

"No, not really. I'm afraid if I talk about it, it'll go away. It seems to me I should only talk about what makes me unhappy . . . I know what you're thinking. You're thinking I was happy with Tom Grace and I was happy with Dr. Seaver. But I'm happy in a different way with Bill. Calm. Just what you were saying I should be. No tension. He needs me so much that it makes me very calm. It's not sex; the sex is just sort of ordinary with him. And it's not anything he says. I just *like* him. I feel *needed*. That's the most important thing."

"The other qualities of your relationship might be important, too.

෨

But the doctor sensed that she was fighting a losing battle. If Dawn was aware of the feelings that were pulling her away from the analysis, she was unwilling to discuss the possibility that those feelings were the very reason for leaving. If she was aware of the wound she'd experienced in the discovery of Dr. Shinefeld's daughter, the pain was still too severe to be dealt with other than by a dressing—as in, "Of course. Everyone needs to be special." She sensed the possibility that she was making a mistake but was unwilling to approach the possibility through the route of her own unconscious. The doctor reminded Dawn of her earlier complaint that she ought not to have been permitted to leave analysis to work at

NBC. Dawn replied somewhat angrily that she and Bill had agreed that you could not make analysis a substitute for real life. She said she couldn't seriously consider the possibility that such a move would be a mistake unless the doctor gave her substantial reasons—i.e., threats about what might happen if she left. This, of course, the doctor was unwilling to do.

In November, Dawn told the doctor that she was applying for admission to both Harvard and Boston universities. She had barely a prayer of getting into Harvard with her recent record, but if they should by any freak chance accept her, she would leave New York in January. If she was going to be at B.U. she'd wait until June. Harvard didn't accept her and B.U. did but she decided to leave in January, regardless. She was eager for a fresh start. The knowledge that she would have one was salutary, and she found herself studying for her finals with better concentration than she'd been able to muster in ages.

As the weeks went on, her ambivalence surfaced more often. She needed to be reassured that if she chose to return the doctor would make every effort to find hours for her, and that she would be free to call or write as often as she wished.

↶

In Dawn's last couple of weeks with Dr. Shinefeld, enormous anxiety rose to the surface. She experienced difficulty in breathing and often couldn't take a deep breath unless she sat up on the couch. She remained in the chair for her last sessions. Her focus was vague and it was clear that she had a vested interest in keeping it that way.

"I know that it's not about Bill," she would say. "It's the same thing that happened with Tom, but it's not going to be the same."

Nor did it have to do with Dr. Shinefeld. Dr. Shinefeld was available when she was needed, after all. Or with returning to Boston, where Dawn had had an abnormally difficult infancy, only recently uncovered. Or with her new proximity to Tony, who wouldn't even have to know that Dawn was there. By a process of elimination, Dawn arrived at the change in schools as the source of her concern, and she spent her last sessions discussing what the change meant to her and how she would adapt to the new environment.

She cut short her last session because she had so much to do before leaving the city.

Standing up quite abruptly in the middle of a bland monologue about the difference in climate between Boston and New York, she went to the doctor's chair, leaned over to briskly kiss the top of her head, and pronounced herself grateful for all the doctor had done in enabling her to start a new life. Then, before the doctor had time to collect herself and make some appropriate reply and affectionate farewell, Dawn was out of the room, the door closed behind her.

That was in December 1977.

═══ 11 ═══

It was in January of 1978 that Charles Herman struck up a conversation with Lulu at a seminar they attended; took her out for a cup of coffee that turned into a few glasses of wine because it was too late for coffee; walked back with her to her apartment, which turned into her office because they were too deeply immersed in conversation to brook interruption if her children should still be awake; sat down with her in the waiting room chairs, which turned into the office couch because it was ridiculous not to be comfortable; and finally made love to her on the foam rubber mat in the playroom, because once the barriers to comfort had been eliminated, the barriers to pleasure were no longer adequate.

The trouble was that the theories were universal and encompassed everyone while touching no one, and the specifics were particularly compelling in this as in every affair.

The trouble was that they were two people whose brains had never achieved a respectable distance from their genitals, so that each had been able to function without sexual static only in periods when for one reason or another the lines were down.

The trouble was, there'd been no way to know in advance that a huge, freckle-faced leprechaun was going to be the first man to make her crazy since she was seventeen-eighteen years old and Woody Samuelson had entered-left her life.

If you really wanted to stay straight, she told Charles the third or tenth time, you always had to assume it could be that good and never risk it.

The trouble was that Lulu's father was dying in Miami and Dawn was gone. Dawn, the analytic daughter who, more than some, was to have redeemed Lulu for her human frailties. Who, with Lulu's help, was to have become happier. Because even if you were too smart to go for the happiness fantasy on your own behalf, that didn't mean you were exempt from wanting some for your patients. Something there was that could never buy the old saw about the purpose of analysis being to make them sadder but wiser.

Dawn might return, but Lulu's father would not. The father whose youthful nature she had uncovered only in her own recent analysis—going back through the layers of her own denial and her mother's scorn and his own alcohol-blurred self-hatred to find the charming and vital man to whom she had been in thrall during the early years of her life.

Now seventy years old, obscenely fat, his brain as active as the worm in a bottle of mescal, possessed of a practiced indifference to the rage and despair of the widow who'd snatched him upon his wife's death with the speed and skill of the old bargain shoppers at S. Klein on the Square, he kept hearing from the doctors who were the real and great welfare frauds that he could live another twenty years once this or that piece of his anatomy (last year it had been part of his colon; next week it was likely to be his rectum) was discarded.

Lulu was going to fly to Miami to be with him and was tempted to try to talk him out of the surgery but knew that she wouldn't. After all, who was she to tell someone else to die peacefully?

Now Lulu had been more than two years without Nathan, her insides had reconsolidated, and in those years no reasonable man had engaged her interest— or made a serious attempt to do so.

And here was Charles, who loved his cool but admirable wife; who adored and would never leave his children; who had a reasonable life that left him feeling needy.

Charles had always thought Lulu was sexy, he told her, had put her on his list of possibles (with a little bit of luck you could have a good analysis and still act out now and then) because of a combination of virtues that included her being divorced and probably needy, as well as seven years older than he and unlikely to threaten his marriage.

Thanks, she said. She would never have guessed that he was only thirty-five, she told him. He looked much older. Maybe, she said, it was that he'd already lost most of his hair.

Now here were Charles and Lulu, two people who needed a little pleasure in their lives and appeared to be uniquely equipped to give it to each other. Now that old party scene at the Mayers could be recast to encompass a clownish but generous-spirited person who made hilarious jokes to which his wife failed to respond. Now it was possible to sympathize with this man who had a greater capacity for pleasure than the bargain he'd made with life allowed him to fulfill. Now it was possible to believe that one could gratefully give and receive pleasure and gracefully pass on.

Had it been pointed out hundreds of times, or had she figured it out for herself—by the time you knew you were kidding yourself it was, by definition, too late.

Love may occasionally allow a reasonable view of its object, but the need to be in love is blinding.

Not that they weren't much too smart to talk about love.

They talked about transference.

Charles told Lulu that she'd divorced her husband because she couldn't bear turning forty, a midlife crisis like the ones men used to have; that he felt sorry for Nathan, "the poor schmuck" (whom he knew slightly from the Institute), who'd probably never known what the hell was bothering her when she left him; that he knew she was a difficult person in the real world and another much nicer one here with him in this little world they'd created while her real father was dying. A kitchen and a "playroom." Indeed.

Charles told Lulu that her face should be kept covered, it was private parts, too soft and responsive to be allowed out in the world unclothed; that he'd wanted to fuck her face, not a usual preoccupation of his, from the time that he'd watched her reacting to his jokes at that party—her eyes, her mouth; did she know that her mouth flickered the way other people's eyelids did?—every movement showing clearly what a prick she thought he was. Her face was like one of those Chinese characters that had seventy-two different meanings according to the slightest alteration in tone or line.

Lulu told Charles that he'd married a woman who was perfect for him, who wouldn't threaten his shaky young ego with warmth and abandon, and had spent the rest of his life holding it against her that she was precisely whom he'd married; that Anna was there with them in the room getting fucked; that she, Lulu, knew the extent of his rage toward this wife who was less than a perfect mother to him; that a mother was what he was looking for and all this other stuff about her not threatening his marriage was mostly bullshit; that he was full of shit in general; that it was important to analyze themselves out of this shit before someone's (his) life was disrupted.

He told her that he was aware of and deeply concerned with this risk; that he'd said from the beginning that he was totally tied to his family; that the moment he felt his family life to be endangered, he would make Lulu stop seeing him if she hadn't already dumped him because she'd recovered from her father's death or dying.

And then, in an orgy of understanding, of mutuality, of same-wavelengthedness, of one-could-finish-the-other's-sentence-ness, they made love on the mat in the playroom, doctor and patient, patient and doctor, father and daughter, mother and son.

He apologized that as he got older it got harder for him to come the second time.

She giggled.

They began to laugh uncontrollably. And the eleven-year-old boy who was such a large part of Charles was set off on a round of jokes of the When-I-was-young-I-had-a-repeater-rifle variety. And then suddenly, without preamble, without even bothering to tell Charles to cut out the dumb jokes, Lulu began, quietly, gravely, to talk to him. At first about Dawn, but then about Sascha, and then about the two of them. About how much easier it was to be the symbolic object of someone's hatred (love, too, Charles said) than the real object. About the terrible, hollow feeling she'd endured after Sascha's disappearance ... She only saw as she talked to him that the pain of Dawn's leaving had been sharpened by its echoes of Sascha's departure ... Of how her mother's death a couple of years after Sascha's disappearance, as dreadful as it had been, had had an anticlimactic quality. *After the first death there is no other*, she said. She told Charles about the Lonely Chair and about the terrible apple and Sascha's saying, the first time they met Nathan, *We don't have a husband*. Then, when she saw tears in Charles's eyes, she told him about Sascha and Mark Bluestein, and then they laughed together, and then they made love again.

Dawn called. Her voice was small and thin, as though she were frightened, but all she said was, "This is Dawn. I'm fine, but do you have my lithos?"

"Yes," the doctor said. "I'm sure they're in the back of the closet here." She checked to make sure. It had been a long time since she'd looked at them.

"Good," Dawn said. "I got scared. I thought I moved them with the rest of my stuff and then they weren't here."

"Shall I just continue to hold them?"

"Yes," Dawn said after a pause. "If you don't mind. I'm doing a print and... I don't really need them. I can remember..."

"I don't mind at all," the doctor said.

A long silence, then a sad little giggle.

"I guess I'm still leaving a little part of myself with you."

"I guess," the doctor said.

"Not such a little part," Dawn said. "The part that's a baby. The part I didn't want to bring with me to Boston." She hung up.

Lulu's father died of a stroke upon awakening from surgery to learn that having spent most of his life avoiding reality's random embarrassments by experiencing them through a bottle of booze, he would spend the rest of it watching television while shit dribbled down his leg through a tube.

Lulu had flown down to Miami thinking that she would be visiting him after surgery. While it had crossed her mind that this visit could be her last, it hadn't occurred to her that the surgery might kill him.

Sascha had been calling periodically but hadn't yet seen fit to give Lulu a number to call. On the plane, Lulu had considered going to the school to find her. But then, Sascha's grandfather wouldn't really want to see anyone—or, perhaps more accurately, wouldn't want anyone to see him—and he appeared to have forgotten Sascha's very existence in the years since she had left home. Sascha hadn't even met the woman he'd married...

...who had paced the hospital corridor with Lulu all day while her husband remained in Intensive Care, muttering a lengthy, often-interrupted monologue whose basic burden was that she would not nurse this man with whom life had been a series of ever-widening circles of disappointment and humiliation, now that he would be unable to control his body's most basic functions.

The Registrar's Office at the University of Miami had no record of a Sascha Shinefeld. Lulu wandered around the campus for a while, admiring the students— so tall, so tan, so unencumbered by books— returning at lunch hour to the office, where a different woman presided over the files and gave her the daily schedule of Sascha Samuelson.

Then she saw Sascha, coming from class with another girl and a boy, laughing and chattering, looking just like the secure and happy person the young mother Lulu had desperately wanted to raise.

Sascha stopped dead in her tracks, but it only took

a minute for her to figure it out and recover. "Hi. What is it? Your father?"

Lulu nodded and burst into the tears that had been denied her until now.

"He's dead, Satch," she cried. Where had the name come from? It had been Nathan's special name for Sascha during her childhood; no one had used it in years. "My father just died."

Lulu stood, head down, and waited for Sascha to take her someplace where she could keep on crying.

Sascha was wonderful. Motherly. Supportive. Attending the funeral to keep Lulu company. Being just polite enough to the suddenly grief-stricken widow, about whom she made just the right number of nasty jokes afterward. Insisting that Lulu postpone the flight back to New York to spend a day or two resting in the sun.

"You've been wonderful," Lulu said as Sascha parked her Volkswagen at the airport so she could help her mother to the plane with her one small suitcase. "I don't know what I would have done if you hadn't been here."

"Mmm," Sascha said. "It reminded me of when I was young."

"Oh? How do you mean?"

"Oh, you know. You were such a *waif* when I was little. So helpless.

"Helpless?" Lulu echoed.

"I remember, I used to have this awful sense that if I left you alone for a few minutes you would go to pieces. Just evaporate or something. I used to wait for Nathan to come home so I could walk into the next room without worrying about you. You were so depressed. So fragile."

"When was this?" asked Lulu.

"Oh, I was pretty young," Sascha said. "When Nathan first moved in with us. How old was I? Three? When did we move out of Grandpa's? I don't even remember having a real childhood, to tell you the truth. I think that's why I never played with dolls. I was too busy taking care of *you*."

"Mmm," Lulu said. "Very interesting."

She reached into the back seat to get her suitcase, but Sascha was already taking it from the other side.

"That's why I freaked when you turned into such a little Hitler later on," Sascha said amiably as they walked through the parking garage, out into the full daylight, toward the terminal. "I had absolutely no preparation for it. I was accustomed to pretty much doing my own thing. Taking care of myself."

"When did this change occur, in your view?"

"When I was around twelve, maybe. Thirteen. I don't remember exactly. It was gradual. You just got worse and worse...It was all before Teddy."

"Before he was born, you mean?"

"Before Teddy, period. Are you going to check your bag or do you want to take it on? Let's check it. No sense dragging it around the terminal for an hour."

Lulu agreed and Sascha took her mother's ticket, gave the bag to the porter, tipped him, and led Lulu into the terminal.

"You've been through a lot of dumb phases, Lulu, let's face it," Sascha said before kissing her mother goodbye and taking off. "But right now you're not such a bad kid."

Dawn called during the spring, the first time to say she thought moving to Boston was going to work, after all. She was headed for an A in every subject. In May she called to find out where the doctor would be all summer—in case she felt the need for a little chat. She said that she would like to come down for a few sessions, but Bill didn't want her to drive herself and he hadn't the time to accompany her. In June she asked that the doctor keep regular hours open for her in September. She was re-enrolled at Barnard and she was going to move into a nice apartment with Lillian and a couple of other girls. If it weren't for August, she'd probably come back right away. She and Bill... Well, it obviously hadn't worked out as she'd hoped, but she needed to keep that corked up in a bottle for now or she wouldn't be able to stick out her last months in Boston. She planned to spend part of August in Provincetown with Gregory and his friends. The problem was, it had turned out that Bill couldn't stand Gregory or any of his friends. She hadn't known that at the beginning. Bill didn't like to say bad things about people. It was really only after she was living with him that she had begun to acquire a sense of how different their tastes in people—in everything—were.

At the end of the first week of August, Lulu received a packet of mail from the post office in New York. One large envelope contained a watercolor from Dawn. The overall picture was of Dr. Shinefeld's office in its true colors, with the doctor sitting in her chair in a brilliant yellow dress and a girl with hair almost as bright lying on the couch. In the air over the patient was a balloon that filled about a third of the picture and contained a detailed picture of another room drawn in black ink and painted in sepia. The room was an old-fashioned parlor. There was a fireplace but no fire. In chairs on either side of the fireplace a man and woman sat stiffly. A large dog was at the side of the man's chair and one of the man's hands rested on its head. In front of the woman's chair was a small round table with several objects on it. Closely examined, these objects revealed themselves to be miniatures of those in Dawn's series—a tiny chair, a cluster of fruit that included a ravaged apple, and some marigolds, along with an elephant figurine and an Egyptian mummy.

Lulu wrote a note to thank Dawn for the painting and say that she looked forward to resuming their sessions in September, then she tacked the picture over the desk in her bedroom. That very desk where she had planned to put in two hours per day, five days a week, throughout August, writing a paper that would act as a lodestone for the thoughts and feelings that had been stirred up by her love affair with Charles. Unfortunately, Dawn's picture took on a meaning of its own in her mind, which was wrestling with the notion that Charles was spoiling her for her real world. Somewhere only a few miles away and in the same town, the Herman family was on vacation in full and glorious color (he had told her that vacations were the only periods when they had a good time together), swimming, sailing, fishing, playing ennis; and the once-satisfactory life of a mother, analyst on holiday, and honorary member of the Mayer clan had turned to sepia.

Charles had said he wasn't going to call during August. They were too close; it was dangerous. Maybe once a week from a pay phone, but if he wanted to see her, she should refuse, even at her cottage. He couldn't take the chance of being seen by Duke Mayer, an occasional antagonist at the Institute and someone he didn't trust. If Lulu had talked to Bonnie about him, Charles didn't want to know. It would make him nervous. Unless it was futile, Lulu was to instruct Bonnie not even to tell her husband. At the very least, that would give her friends some notion of just how careful Charles was being. Lulu had been irritated at the time by the notion that anything but his own actions would give them away; now she played with a hundred and one suggestions about how they could be together and not be seen. Her longing was worst at the beach, by nature a sexual place, but even quiet evenings with the Mayers were tainted by thoughts of how much more fun the conversation would be if Charles were there. Aside from the Mayers' annual party, there was only one she might have looked forward to, but the people were friends of the Hermans, and Charles had informed her that she wasn't to think of going. He couldn't handle it. She'd assured him that she couldn't either, but it still angered her. She met a reasonably interesting older man one night at the Mayers', a widower from Chicago. She had dinner with him a couple of times, but when he kissed her goodnight

the second time, she was as responsive as a pile
dry rags, and she didn't hear from him again.

Well, she would start with one hour a day. Sit
the desk. Refuse to leave the room until sixty mi
utes had passed. What she wanted to investigate w
the extent to which sexual appetite was determined-
or undermined—by custom. The paper might h
somewhat analytic in its viewpoint, but it would h
marvelous to somehow escape the analytic confine
In psychoanalysis as in art, God resided in the de
tails, the discovery of which required enormous pa
tience, unyielding seriousness, and the skill of a
acrobat— walking a tightrope over memory and spe
ulation, instinct and theory, feeling and denial. Treatir
patients all week often left Lulu with a desire
eschew the recognition of individuality; draw broa
generalizations; satirize; bemoan and caustical
condescend.

A launching point for a paper had presented itse
to her several weeks earlier, when she and Bonn
found themselves standing in a Broadway movie lin
with a woman named Charlotte Goldhammer, who
Lulu had known over a period of twenty-five year
Charlotte had been a well-intentioned but sexual
muted sociology major when Lulu met her at CCN
in 1958; a bread-baking, *Ladies' Home Journal* subscribe
when Lulu crossed her path in the middle of th
sixties; and the divorced mother of two childre
editing a feminist bulletin called *Against Invasio*
when Lulu encountered her on Upper Broadway :
the beginning of the seventies. Now she worked as
counselor in a hospital drug program and, as th
three of them stood in line on Broadway, had talke

of nothing but how one could get laid in a world where all the men who could be trusted not to give you venereal disease had just come out of the closet or entered it with an eighteen-year-old girl.

Thus, in the sixty or seventy years since Freud had documented women's sexual anxieties, those anxieties had metamorphosed into a set of lenses that did little more than refract the sexual anxieties of men.

Lulu made a glass of iced tea, closed the door to her room and sat down to work.

When I was in college, her notebook read, *the intellectual vanguard was also the sexual vanguard. Though I was already a mother and a less-than-full participant in campus life, it was easy to differentiate between the interesting and "bohemian" girls, liberal arts majors, who seldom graduated with their hymens intact, and the education and sociology majors, who seldom did not. Twenty-some-odd years later, almost everyone in both groups has been through EST, primal therapy, assertiveness training and/or various other measures designed to help them get what they want, and what most of them seem to want is—eureka!—to get laid.*

Unpublishable but not unrespectable. On the other hand, at this rate she would fill the notebook before reaching page two and waste a lot of time as well.

Lulu sighed. The once-precious month of August had turned into hours to be used up before she could see Charles again.

12

Dawn's first months back in treatment were spent largely on issues concerning Bill Denton. She and her friends were settled in a two-bedroom apartment on 116th Street near Broadway. Lillian shared her room with a girl named Sally Rothstein; Dawn with Polly Campbell, whom she herself had recommended as a fourth when she talked to Lillian in the spring. Everyone adored Polly, who was shy and quiet and served as a buffer between the others at tense times. Dawn thought that Polly by her example might make the others act nicer than they otherwise would have. The close quarters made it difficult to entertain men, but that was just fine with Dawn, who had no interest in boyfriends right now—although she had a couple of male pals, including one, Jack Stewart, who was becoming like a brother to her.

Judith Rossner

Dawn had gained weight during her stay in Boston but was losing it now, not through any particular effort but because she didn't have as much time to eat and wasn't as upset as she had been; besides, she and Jack were jogging on Riverside Drive a few mornings a week.

She called her experience with Bill Denton a nightmare and said that almost from the first, there had been no day when she didn't consider throwing away the money and the semester's credit and running "home" to New York. The reason she hadn't called the doctor more often was that she was afraid that the mere sound of the doctor's voice would weaken her determination.

She said that from the moment she had moved into Bill's apartment, he had become a different person. Not sexually, but there was no carryover from sexual feeling into their lives. It was as though there had been a piece of furniture missing from his apartment, he'd acquired it, and now he could go about his business. The night after she'd moved in, he had gone out bowling with his friends. Oh, yes, and there was his dog. How could she have forgotten for an instant? It was the dog in the picture. Spot. No kidding. No one in the world was as important to Bill, at least from the day Dawn moved in. When Bill was feeling affectionate, he fondled Spot. Nor did he ever get angry with the dog, no matter what, whereas he was always finding some reason to be angry with Dawn. Once he was furious because she'd burned her hand on a hot frying pan handle and yelled "Fuck!" in front of his

304

friends. Could the doctor believe that—in this day and age?

Dawn was dissatisfied when the doctor told her it was difficult to get a sense of Bill, relieved when she agreed that some particular bit of behavior sounded irrational or sadistic. The doctor pointed out that to the extent that Bill was to have served as a refuge, a substitute for the doctor-mother, and a final solution to the problem of dependence, the relationship had been heavily burdened from the beginning. Bill's behavior had been bad enough so that Dawn could evade this truth for some time. It was by remembering finally points at which Bill had tried to please her but she'd grown weepy and depressed that she was able to acknowledge that no matter how he had behaved, the relationship was probably doomed. She then drew a cartoon showing a stretched-out and fragile Bill Denton forming a bridge between two high cliffs, with herself walking him like a tightrope and, underneath, choppy water labeled Need.

In the office, looking at the cartoon with the doctor for the first time, Dawn realized that the cliffs and the water were related to her father, about whom she had been thinking a great deal.

She was considering transferring to Cooper Union for the following year. She was convinced that she wanted to be a working artist and she simply couldn't get the kind of studio courses she wanted at Barnard—or at Columbia, for that matter. Apparently she didn't need to worry about money. It was silly to be timorous about changing schools. On the other hand, she was too comfortable in her new apartment to imagine disrupting that arrangement; if she went to Cooper Union, she guessed she would have to "commute."

＠

Dawn spent Christmas with Vera and returned to New York in a state of excitement. She'd arranged to ship down a couple of pieces of furniture from the attic as well as a trunk full of what appeared to be letters and a group of her father's paintings. She'd come upon the trunk as she was preparing to leave Marbury and hadn't done more than check out a couple of sketches on the top, but she was excited by the prospect of going through it all. Perhaps the next time she had a day off. She was also anxious for Dr. Shinefeld to see some of her father's work so the doctor would know that she wasn't exaggerating his talent. That reminded her.

"Have I talked to you at all yet about the Eskimos?"

"Eskimos?"

She giggled.

"I guess I haven't... I've been reading about them."

Jack Stewart had lent her a book by Robert Coles and a photographer named Alex Harris about the Eskimos. She'd been enormously moved. Drawn to the Eskimos.

"I feel as though I want to be in their lives with them."

"Tell me."

"Which kind of a *tell-me* is that? A *How-did-you-get-so-crazy-tell-me*?"

"Definitely not. It's an *I'd-like-to-know-more-tell-me*."

"When I read stories about the Eskimos," Dawn said after a moment, "I feel as though I'm home. But I don't know what I mean when I say that...They have a very short summer, you know. Winter is what life is really about...I know what you're thinking but it's not just about my father. There's more to it than that."

At her next visit she brought the doctor a drawing she'd made of a sailboat that was intact but managed to convey the impression of being about to burst apart in the oceanic waves it tossed upon. Imposed over the waves was the dreamlike face of a long-haired girl. The caption on the drawing, Dawn told Dr. Shinefeld, was taken directly from the words of a woman in the Coles study. When her father died, the woman had told Dr. Coles, he had been weeping. She had touched his tears and put them to her mouth. Now she had her father with her forever.

⌒

In the following weeks, Dawn didn't mention her father's work but became absorbed in a series of drawings she was doing for her art class, finally bringing in her sketch pad to show Dr. Shinefeld. All the drawings were of Eskimo life, although they fell into two series, Indoors and Outdoors.

The outdoor series was simple: a flock of geese crossing the sky; a sled pulled by dogs; a parka-clad Eskimo fishing through a crack in the ice. The last had a caption from the Coles study:

When I fish in the winter, I can think, I can sing to myself, I can listen to my father—and my grandfather. I can remember the best times I've had in my life—when I got married, when my sister did, when the children were born, when my father called me to him and told me he was proud of me.

The first of the indoor drawings was a family scene. In a rocking chair to one side of a fire that would have melted an ice igloo in hours sat an ancient man; on the floor on the other side of the hearth a woman sat Indian-fashion. A little girl played on the floor near the man's rocking chair and his hand rested lightly on her head. On a slab bed in the background a woman lay sleeping under a fur rug, her straight, dark hair falling across the pillow and over the side of the bed.

"Do you get the joke?" Dawn asked. "It's a reverse of the picture of my Bill Denton life. Here it's supposed to be cold, but the feeling is warm. The people are together, even when they're apart."

What was common to the indoor drawings was that whoever was at their focal point, the woman lying on the bed was invariably there—sometimes awake, sometimes asleep, but always strangely still. Even the inanimate objects seemed to have more life than she did in all but one drawing. The last two pictures were called Darkness and Light. In both, she was the central figure. They were captioned with quotations from the Coles study and were done in an atypical style, the lying-down woman tending to flow into her surroundings. Darkness was full of airborne demons and vaguely ominous shapes that threatened to swallow her. The caption read:

> The end of winter is like the end of life; the Eskimo has become very tired, and the mind is playing tricks. My mind takes me into the corner of the room or into the cracks of the floor.

Lightness, drawn in yellow pencil, conveyed the effect of a terrible brightness. Sunlight streamed through a skylight, and the woman, awake for the first time, was propped up slightly on one elbow, looking terrified, trying to cover her face with the other arm:

> The light is everywhere during July. It hits you in the face! I'll be standing near the river, and there is the light above and the light coming at me from the water. I'll get drunk on the light! I'll throw myself at it—like a city Eskimo crawling, trying to find another can of beer. I'll try to stare at the sun—closer and closer to it, until I'm almost blind and have to look away. I can see the sun in the water, the windows, the flowers. The yellow flowers— small suns, making me blink. I want to stare but I want to be rid of the light. I want to go back to the winter...I want to wake up and see the dark, the welcome dark.

"Tell me about the woman on the bed," Dr. Shinefeld said when Dawn had stretched out on the couch.

"Nothing to tell," Dawn said cheerfully. "She's just another one of the family."

"Is she?"

"Sure...Well, not exactly. There must be something wrong with her, or why would she be lying on the bed all the time?" Suddenly Dawn sat up.

"What happened?" the doctor asked.

Dawn stood, paced the room, came to a halt at the chair facing the doctor's, and sat down. She was angry. "You know already so why are you asking me?"

The doctor was silent.

"What happened...was that when I said, *Why else would she be lying down?* I got scared, because I was lying down. Suddenly I felt as if I must be sick. If you think I don't want to talk about this," Dawn said, "you're right." She glared at the doctor for another moment or two. "She's everything I don't want to be. Sick. Fucked up...Not that I felt that way when I was drawing the pictures. I felt very loving. I loved all of them, but especially her. And I love Polly, even if she's...I've told you about Polly, haven't I?"

"Your roommate?"

"That's not all I've told you."

"I believe you said that she was very quiet and that she was a good influence on the rest of you."

"Mmm. Because she's so good herself. But she's also terribly sad....I always knew she was quiet, but until the past few weeks, I never realized how sad she was."

Polly had meant to be a dancer, but she was very bright and not ambitious, so while she took classes when she wasn't depressed, she'd decided to teach rather than go for the grueling life of professional dance. Polly had long, dark hair that she usually wore in a braid. You could tell when she was depressed because she left her hair loose all day so she could lie down on it comfortably for long stretches...If Dawn had one wish, it would be that she and Polly lived in the same apartment but in different rooms so that when Polly was low, Dawn didn't have to be in there with her. Polly was going home for spring vacation and Dawn hoped that would give her a lift.

"I really do love her. Sometimes I'm the only one who can make her laugh...Maybe that's silly, thinking it's a big deal to get a smile out of someone, but I feel wonderful when I can cheer her up. I just wish I could do it all the time...I really wish I could help her in some important way. She has a shrink and she adores him, but I don't see...She seems to be getting worse instead of better."

"Do you know how long she's been in treatment?"

Dawn shook her head. "I just know that it's a man. I've talked to her about female shrinks, about how it's different, but when I wanted to get more specific...I was afraid I'd upset her. I was going to ask you for the name of someone, then I realized I had the piece of paper with the names from Dr. Seaver tucked away in my wallet."

"Why is that?" the doctor asked.

"Oh, you know...just in case...When Lillian talked to me about the apartment, I thought of Polly right away. I wasn't sure if Polly had an arrangement for this year because I didn't know her that well. But I was sure she'd be easy. And she *is*. She's easy for us, just not for herself...I felt very drawn to her...It's not something that happens to me all that often. Especially with women. She has a beautiful...*mysterious* quality that made me . . . I think she makes me happy and anxious at the same time."

"How long do these depressed periods last?" the doctor asked.

"I don't know. Why?"

"Well," the doctor said slowly, "I guess before we go into the matter of what Polly's depressions mean to you, I'd like to get some idea of what they might mean to *her*. That is, of how serious they are."

"I told you she has a shrink, didn't I?"

"Yes. Do you know his name?"

"Uh-uh. Should I ask?"

"If you want to."

"If I told you that I was a little jealous, that I don't want you to care about her too much and I'm not sure I want to talk about her, would that be all right?"

"Yes," the doctor said, "but I'd want to analyze your jealousy."

"Okay, then. As long as I'm sharing you with her willingly . . . The reason I've been getting more worried is that the lying-down times are getting longer. It was beginning to happen before Christmas. Whole days when she didn't get out of bed. I know what you're thinking. I should've talked about her then. But I was afraid if I started to get involved, I'd screw up my exams. Also, I thought you'd tell me I should forget about her problems and think about my own."

"Not very easy to forget when she shares your room."

"I know!" Dawn burst into tears. "That's why I can't stand it anymore! Before Christmas, I thought she'd feel better after she spent some time with her family, but Christmas has come and gone and she isn't better at all! I'm scared! She's even stopped playing the flute. When she played the flute, sometimes I wanted to cry. But it's worse when she stops playing because then I know she's too sad even to play!"

Dawn cried a great deal during the remainder of the session, her tears interspersed with memories of Polly's composing a song for her as a Christmas present; once giving her a white rose for no reason at all; of various sad and wise comments Polly had made. Finally, she said that she didn't know what she would do if the analyst couldn't take care of Polly. If "anything happened" to her friend.

❧

"Dr. Harold Giddings," Dawn announced when she next walked into the room. She sat down. "That's Polly's analyst. Do you know him?"

It took a full minute or so for the doctor to collect herself sufficiently to respond, and then only weakly.

"Not really."

"There's something funny about the way you said that."

"Oh?"

"Uh-uh. This isn't about me, it's about the way you said it."

The doctor smiled. "There are pitfalls to discussing your friend's treatment with you."

"How come the pitfalls got worse after I told you his name?"

The truthful answer would be because Harold

Giddings, M.D., was one of the more extreme doctors whose name might have come up. Physically the very model, if not caricature, of an analyst—square, bearded, expressionless— Harold Giddings was a lunatic who thrived on crisis therapy, most particularly with potential suicides, and was worse than useless with neurotics trying to become halfway comfortable in their lives. He had managed to weather a crisis in which it became known that he was involved in a Krafft-Ebing-style affair with one of his patients The most bizarre story-within-the-story that Dr. Shinefeld recalled was that the two had been making trips to the graveyard where the patient's father was buried, digging up his grave and making love at the spot.

He had a close political alliance with the chairman of Psychiatry in the teaching hospital with which he was affiliated, and he hadn't been fired, although his referrals had dried up. However, in that remarkable way some of the undeserving have of landing on their feet in an improved position, he had become the chief psychopharmacologist at a large hospital outside Manhattan. Unfortunately, he had held on to the remnants of his private practice in the city.

"Let me try to find a couple of examples on both sides," the doctor said. "Say that I were to tell you that in my estimation Giddings was incompetent and couldn't help your friend. And you were to go back to Polly and—"

"I wouldn't do that. Not unless you told me to."

"But let's say your concern made you push harder than you would have. And that caused a rupture with Polly. You might be very angry with me in a way that would interfere with *your* treatment, which is my paramount concern."

"What's the other side?" Dawn asked after a moment.

"What if I tell you that as far as I know, Giddings is an excellent doctor and your friend is in good hands, and you take it for granted, and then later she had a really disastrous experience with him. Things went wrong that would've been all right under—"

"Why would I think that? If it was a mistake it could always be corrected later, couldn't it? There's something going on here that I don't understand. What's the big deal about being wrong? You don't think she's going to slit her wrists or something, do you?"

The doctor didn't reply immediately.

Dawn stared at her in horror. "My God! Is that what you think?"

"Not necessarily," the doctor said. "I can't tell what's going to happen to Polly. I only know what you're afraid will happen."

"What *I'm* afraid of!" Dawn rose from her chair. "It never occurred to me Polly would kill herself!" She walked to the room's farthest corner and stood with her back to the doctor.

"You brought it up," the doctor pointed out.

"Only to say she wouldn't do it. You put it in my head in some way."

"I don't think so," the doctor responded levelly. "You made the drawings before you mentioned Polly's depression."

"Which drawings?" Dawn shouted. "The lying-down woman? I didn't say she was Polly, I only ... thought of Polly because she's the one who's lying down right now. I don't even know if I thought of her then. Or if it was you all along... Besides, everyone who lies down doesn't commit suicide, do they?"

"Not at all. As a matter of fact, since the issue has been raised here, Dr. Giddings has worked with suicidal patients quite a bit and has a reputation for never having... lost one... as we say." Or cured one.

"Is that true?" Dawn demanded. "Or are you saying it to make me feel better?"

"I wouldn't say anything to make you feel better unless it was also true."

Slowly Dawn walked back across the room and sat down.

"Did I tell you that I was drawing Polly? Because I wasn't. She may have reminded me of Polly because of the lying down... Well, because she's so sad. Depressed. When you say someone's depressed you don't have to know how she feels. When you say she's sad, you can almost... Anyway, the woman in the picture is someone who doesn't exist outside my head."

"How do you think she got in there?"

"From the Eskimo book. Obviously. How come you haven't asked about any of the others?"

"Which of the others do you think I should ask you about?"

"Oh, God, now you sound like all the jokes about analysts! Maybe Polly should stick with her shrink; at least he's not a Freudian. And how come you like him if he's not a Freudian?"

"I didn't say I liked him. I said his patients were

thought not to commit suicide while they were seeing him."

"So he's good at that."

"Correct."

"Then, what's wrong with him?"

"I'll try to answer that," the doctor said, "but I'd like you to treat my answer as privileged information. It's not secret, but it might be harmful to one of his patients to hear something unfavorable about him."

"I promise," Dawn said. "It's not even a problem."

"Well, we'll see. In any event, he's been successful at treating some severely disturbed patients, especially those who do better with drugs than with any other form of treatment that's available now. But he's one of those people who's long since given up on the idea of analysis, and for that reason I think he can be helpful only in a certain way to a certain group of people."

"Polly isn't severely disturbed," Dawn said. "I mean, she's severely unhappy. But she's sane."

"Mmm," the doctor said. "Many severely depressed people are sane.

"I admit," Dawn said after a lengthy silence, "that if I hadn't happened to be rooming with Polly, I might not have had a lying-down woman in the pictures."

"And how did you happen to be rooming with Polly?"

"What do you mean? I asked her if she wanted to room with us. I told you that. I liked her."

"I think it was stronger than liking. I think you said you were drawn to her."

"So what?" Dawn was becoming confused and defensive. "Are you suggesting I have a lesbian attraction to her?"

"I wasn't thinking of sticking a label on it, and I wasn't thinking of a specifically sexual feeling."

"Then what *were* you thinking of?"

"Of your need to draw someone like Polly into your life."

"It wasn't someone *like* Polly. It was Polly."

"I think maybe it was both."

"I'm completely lost."

"Well, we know that Polly has certain qualities that you appreciate. She's kind, intelligent, talented, and so on. I'm suggesting that a lot of Barnard girls have those qualities, and that you were drawn to Polly for deeper reasons."

"Such as?"

"Well, describe her."

"She's nothing like *you*, if that's what you're thinking. You always look too healthy to be real. Once I drew a picture of you out in a pasture, calving. I mean, it was Elsie the cow, but with your face. I was going to show it to you, but then I thought maybe you wouldn't like it."

The doctor grinned.

"You always look as though you have enough health for two people," Dawn continued. "*Polly* is very *slender.* Frail. White skin, big dark eyes. Hair... Well, her hair's something like yours... or Tony's... It's not Tony you're thinking of, is it?"

The doctor waited.

"I need you to tell me. Tony hasn't been sick, you

know. She hasn't been lying down at all. She was fine when I saw her."

The doctor nodded.

"Tell me if this is about Tony," Dawn said, her voice growing shrill with anxiety. "My God! I don't even know what I mean when I say *it's about her*. *What's* about her? It can't be the picture, because I already admitted the picture's about Polly. At least partly. I know I didn't want to believe it at first. I didn't like the idea that it had to be someone real. But now it's out and there's something else...I'm beginning to feel crazy. I haven't felt that way in a while. Do I sound crazy?"

"No," the doctor said. "You sound as if you're battling with something you sort of know and don't know. Want to know and don't want to know."

"Well, if I don't want to, maybe I shouldn't."

"Maybe."

Dawn sighed. "All right. Let's get it over with."

"Get it over with?"

"I mean, if you don't think Tony's in the picture, maybe you'd better just tell me who you do think is there."

"How about your other mother?"

Dawn stared at her blankly. "My other mother? Who do you mean?...You don't mean my birth mother, do you?"

The doctor waited

"That *is* who you mean. I can't believe it...I can't believe that this conversation is really happening. I can't believe I've been sitting here, trying to get help with Polly, talking about matters that are important to me, and suddenly you've made an incredible flying leap right out of my life."

Still, the doctor didn't respond.

Dawn looked at her watch. It was close to the end of the hour. Slowly, quite calmly, she rose from the chair, gathered her belongings and walked to the door. When she turned to say goodbye to the doctor she was smiling as though at some irritating but unthreatening child.

"There's something you really don't seem to understand," she said, shaking her head sadly. "My mother is someone who doesn't exist for me."

13

CHARLES WAS HAVING what he advised Lulu were "peripheral but discomfiting fantasies of abandoning his family and coming to live with her. Short of the ghastly, tedious business of going back "once more yet again" into an analysis with some woman who was just enough like Lulu to "drain off some of the transference," the only solution he could think of was to try to spend just enough time with her to "work through" the feelings that were threatening his household.

At Christmas he had lain on the beach in St. Maarten, his eyes closed, thinking of her, pretending she was there with him, in a state of perpetual arousal that he constantly feared would draw notice. Eventually he'd had to turn over on his belly and pretend to be asleep. The activities he usually enjoyed with his family had held no joy for him. He was frightened. He wanted to spend a good chunk of time with Lulu and get her out of his system, or at least back to some minor part of it. It was a well-known fact that the intensity of feelings like this diminished with time, but they'd been together for a year now, and obviously they hadn't had enough time together for that to happen.

There was a report on one of his cases that Charles had been struggling to write up for months. He had told Anna that he was going to spend some long weekends by himself out at the house in East Hampton, just working. He had expected Anna to protest, but instead she'd agreed emphatically that the paper had to be done. That way, she had said, it wouldn't be hanging over his head when the house needed work at Easter.

"In other words," Charles said, his grin complicitous, as though they had an equal interest in this project, "we're going to fuck our brains out for a few days at a time for a few weekends. Not exactly out. Mine is just going to be so limp and exhausted that it'll be happy to go home and rest. Then we can resume some nice, civilized kind of affair. Couple of times a month."

"Maybe less would be more," Lulu grumbled, although she was thrilled by the idea of some weekends with Charles. "I can't just take whole days off from work, you know. I have just as many patients as you and I don't have a rich wife."

"Sweet," Charles said. "Maybe you don't want me to calm down. Maybe you were lying when you said you didn't want to break up my marriage."

Which made her feel just guilty enough to take

considerable pains to reorganize her schedule so that during February she could leave the office in the middle of the day on Friday and take Monday, as well, during the school holiday week. It turned out that Nathan's new girlfriend had a lodge at Sugarbush and Nathan *wanted* to spend some extra time up there with the boys. Nathan had never been a sportsman of any kind, certainly not a skier, but his girlfriend was going to teach them all.

"All the women have real estate," Lulu muttered, "except me."

But she faced their long weekends together with excitement— and only realized when they arrived at the house, a modest but attractive older home on Georgica Road, that she had carefully avoided thinking about what it might be like to spend time in the home of Charles's family. To sleep in the bed where Charles and Anna slept.

Of course Charles understood. It was what he loved about her, that beautiful, quivering sensibility that made it unthinkable for her to deny any of life's unpleasant details just for the sake of getting on with it.

"Getting on with life?" Lulu echoed, her eyes brimming with tears as she stared at the king-size bed with the brown down comforter and the Mexican serape on the wall behind it. (In general, Charles said, this house was more attractive than their city home, in line with Anna's unspoken philosophy that it wouldn't kill you to have fun once in a while on vacation.) "Getting on with life in Anna Herman's bed? Is that what you think my life's supposed to be about?"

And then she burst into tears because that *was* what her life was about, and she was a neurotic and a hypocrite if the symbol had greater power than the reality to deter her.

Lulu's cottage was shut down for the winter, with no heat or water, but Charles called his friend Moe Klebinoff, who had a small place down the road that he kept open all year to accommodate his own "endless affair." It was actually a series of affairs, Charles said, but it might as well have been the same one because Moe said the same thing about each at the beginning —"A wonderful woman, the woman I'd have married twenty years ago if I'd known what I was doing"—at the middle—"She's a great lay, but the pressure is getting to be too much for her"—and at the end— "She was a wonderful woman, but she was getting to be a bigger nag than Betsy. In kindness to both of us, I had to pack it in."

Lulu said there was a lesson in this for herself and Charles, but Charles said it wasn't a lesson he was interested in studying, particularly just then.

Moe had told him where to find the key. He could trust Moe, whose sole confidant he'd been for years and who had now become his. Until now, Charles confessed fondly, he'd never felt the need to talk about the extra woman in his life.

Lulu let it pass. Friday was shot by then, anyway.

From Moe Klebinoff's, Charles called Anna—a brilliant touch, he told Lulu—to say that the phone at the house was out of order (he'd taken out all the jacks) and that instead of dealing with a repairman, he was just staying at Moe's, where she could reach him if she needed him. Fewer distractions. He wouldn't have to look at all the things that needed to be fixed.

The phrase "if she needs me" fell harshly on Lulu's ears. Was she mistaken or was this a possibility that had never previously entered their conversation? As a matter of fact, hadn't Charles given her to understand that it was his wife's very failure to need him in any way, her ability to deal with any and all disasters on her own better than she could when he was around, her lack of even sexual needs to be filled, that left Charles so in need of a woman like Lulu who howled when he came, so to speak, bearing gifts?

Forget it, Lulu. You can think about it next week. In New York.

If it was important to act as though one's children were without unconscious motives, it was imperative that one's married lover be treated as a victim of nothing more serious than Growth and Change. In fact, nothing was more useful than the rhetoric of Growth and Change in filling in the pieces of the psychic puzzle that had fallen on the floor and gotten swept under the rug. As in: When he was young, Charles Herman would have felt threatened by a woman whose needs were as pressing as his own. Now, however, having experienced substantial Growth and Change, Charles needs and wants a sexually demanding woman, and stays in his used-up marriage for the sake of his children and a wife for whom he has a healthy respect and considerable fondness in spite of their failure to find a true meeting ground. Because that's the kind of fellow Charles is. He Really Likes Women.

But why now, Lulu? Why can't you just forget it for now and enjoy yourself?

Charles was stretched out on Moe Klebinoff's rickety old bed, his sweater, pants, and shoes still on because the house was freezing.

Because you are not supposed, to. That's why, dummy.

"Needs you for what?" Lulu asked Charles, tracing the flowers on the faded wallpaper.

"Whatever," Charles said. "The kids."

Lulu smiled. "Nathan thought we should stay together for the sake of the boys, but Nathan never gave a fuck for the boys until after I left him."

"What's with you, Lu?" Charles demanded. "I can't believe you expect me to be away for a week and not be in touch with my wife and my kids."

"No, of course not," Lulu said, looking at the photographs on the dresser of Betsy Klebinoff and the three ugly-adorable Klebinoff children, swimming, graduating, smiling at the camera, their enemy. Was it Lulu's imagination or was Betsy Klebinoff's smile never less than pained? "You're in touch with your wife and kids, and I'm in touch with the part of me that knows I shouldn't be here because you're in touch with your wife and kids."

"C'mere," Charles said. "I want to tell you something."

Reluctantly, she sat down on the edge of the bed. Charles, a master of timing, didn't touch her.

"It was taking you to the house," he said. "You were right and I was wrong. I wasn't just wrong, I was a real asshole. I should've been smart enough to ask Moe for this place to begin with."

Lulu searched his face.

"Oh, God," she said, "this is no good. You're too smart for me. I love you too much."

But she lay down beside him on the lumpy bed in the house Moe Klebinoff claimed to keep shabby so that none of his women would think for a minute that he could pay alimony and child support and have something left for her. And she pushed away the unpleasant realities that hadn't vanished of their own accord when she and Charles walked out of the Herman house. Because, after all, it would have been too crazy to do anything else.

But after the Washington's Birthday weekend Charles found the undertow stronger than ever, and in the ensuing weeks he was erratic, anxious, eager to quarrel, to find fault, to speculate on the various ways in which Lulu would disappoint him if he were to be so rash as to leave his lovely young (sic) wife and his darling children.

Lulu had never entertained the thought of breaking up Charles's marriage, and her initial reaction to Charles's view of her as a threat had been to assure him that she was no threat to anybody, had never meant to take him away from his wife and children, and furthermore had no illusions that if he did leave them he would end up with her.

Nevertheless, against her will, so to speak, the possibility began to gain a certain allure. If her intelligence and her conscience remained united in wanting to be innocent of a break-up, it was difficult not to imagine what it would be like on Wednesday nights if she didn't have to stay awake after they made love because Charles invariably fell asleep. If she was skeptical of the notion that she might enjoy a reasonable life with a frenetic, sporadically unfaithful man seven years her junior, she couldn t help but flirt with the notion of being able to abandon a life lived routinely around the attempt to Get Enough.

One week Charles called to say he wouldn't be over on Wednesday night; he was going to break with her cold turkey. That Saturday morning he called and wanted to visit, but both boys had the flu and she couldn't leave them for long enough to join him for a cup of coffee. It would have to be Monday night. He'd get someone to take over his class. He couldn't wait until Wednesday to see her.

The following week he was depressed. He had made a serious error with one of his patients, an error that undoubtedly stemmed from his anxiety over Lulu.

Louis Pomerantz had come to Charles as a CCNY freshman. Average height, skinny, hungry eyes and a metabolism that kept him thin, although he apparently never passed thirty consecutive minutes of any day without putting some kind of food into his mouth. Charles had seen in the eighteen-year-old freshman the eighteen-year-old Charles Herman and had agreed to treat him at vastly reduced rates. It had been irresistible to see if he couldn't do a better job with his young clone than his own analyst had done with him.

Louis's father had a small grocery store in the Bronx where he had been held up half a dozen times and hurt once (shot in the hand), the crisis that had precipitated Louis's breakdown, or near-break-down. There were four sons. The oldest one was on a full scholarship at Columbia Law School and intended to be the First Jewish President. The second was Louis, who said he also wanted to be the First Jewish President but didn't know what he would do with his life since his brother had already spoken for the job. Following Louis by two years was a severely disturbed boy, Max (for Maximilian), who couldn't learn and was unable to care for himself. For years, the father and the two oldest boys had been urging the mother to institutionalize Max, but she wouldn't part from him for long enough to see a movie. The youngest boy, according to Louis, was normal, but in a dim-witted sort of way, and spent a good portion of his free time watching television with Max.

Louis's dreams were full of water, most particularly a finite body he called the Gene Pool, in which swam every characteristic of intelligence, personality, and so on, possessed by any member of his family. Within that large pool also swam Louis and his relatives, in constant danger of inhaling, drowning in, or being attacked by the possibilities: stupidity, dullness, insanity, total dependence. More than anything, Louis feared (and was drawn to) the possibility of being like Max—crazy, helpless, and permanently tied to his mother. Food appeared to serve a variety of magical purposes in his life, including that of a solid barrier to block off the ingestion of mental illness and the other parasites in the gene pool.

It had taken almost two years for Louis to form a solid attachment to Charles, another year for the boy to get to a point where he could let go, for brief periods of time, of the notion that life was a constant battle with his demons. It was only this past fall that Louis had begun, quite unconsciously, to appear at some sessions without a bag of food cradled in one arm. Back and forth. One foodless session at a time. Then two. Three. All during a period when the boy was obsessed with other problems—his virginity, for example, which he was frantic to shed even while feeling a visceral dislike for those girls who showed signs of being willing to assist him.

And what had that stupid son-of-a-bitch Charles Herman done? Charles asked, pacing naked around Lulu's office, waving what remained of a baguette in the air as Lulu washed the two dishes and glasses in the Pullman kitchen. Just as the poor fucking kid was trying to climb out of the gene pool onto dry land, where his trusted analyst awaited him, Dr. Herman had casually referred to the day when Louis wouldn't be seeing him anymore. Worse, he'd compounded the felony in the following weeks, as Louis experienced a frightening regression to the state he'd been in when he arrived, by acting impatient with the kid; by withdrawing his empathy; by actually, at one point, giving Louis a little speech on the virtues of self-control!

Only then had Charles begun to understand that he needed Louis to exercise self-control because he himself was out of control. Only then had it struck Charles that he was trying forcibly to rid Louis of Louis's demons because he couldn't rid Charles of Charles's demons—most specifically, of Lulu Shinefeld.

"So," Lulu said after a while, "I'm threatening not only your family life but your practice."

"It's not you that's threatening them," Charles said after a moment. "It's me. But it doesn't matter."

Still naked, Charles stood looking down at the park through the window of the playroom. In one year's time, men's bodies that were not extremely white, large in the middle, and sprinkled with freckles over the upper back had come to look unappealing to her.

"If you want to stop seeing me, I understand," she said, with some difficulty.

"If I wanted to, I wouldn't be in this condition."

"I won't ever call you if that's what you want."

"What if I call you? Will you hang up?"

"I don't know, Charles. I suppose if you tell me to. I grew up surrounded by depressed people, you know. All you have to do is say I'm giving you more misery than pleasure."

Charles began to cry.

He had told her once, with a grin, that he was a crier, but she'd never seen him do it. It was a little frightening, and she was torn between the impulses to comfort and to hold back, the latter probably being what he would prefer.

She felt like crying, too, but they couldn't cry at the same time. It wasn't as though they were married.

14

DAWN WAS IN A WONDERFUL mood after Easter vacation. She arrived with a large brown cardboard portfolio, which she set on the couch and untied but did not open. She had run in Riverside Park every morning with Jack Stewart. Had she ever mentioned that Jack was from Boston? Not that it was important, but ... Anyway, she'd done a lot of reading and schoolwork but most important—a significant pause—she'd been through the contents of the trunk. The paintings. Not the letters. She felt they were too personal.

"Whose letters are those?" the doctor asked.

"My father's, mostly."

"Who were they written to?"

"Miranda, of course. Otherwise, how would they have ended up in the trunk?"

It was the paintings Dawn wanted to talk about.

They were extraordinary. Sometimes masterful, sometimes delicate, but always beautiful. He'd gone through various stages, all interesting, although she had to say that his best work had been done long before his death. Or perhaps she should say, before his marriage. The doctor would have to see the contents of the portfolio before she could appreciate their range. There were watercolors as well as a couple of small oils. The only drawings were dated 1955, the last year in which he had produced anything.

On the floor of the office Dawn spread out the work in chronological sequence, according to the dates marked in the corners—'46, '47, '49, '50, '51, another gap, this time three years, then '54, '55...and silence. Dawn had been born in 1957.

It was an impressive display. In style and spirit the paintings varied so greatly as to make it difficult to believe they had been done by one person, particularly in a span of only nine years. Beginning with the delicate Japanese brushwork and calligraphic design of the early period, ranging through abstract oils in bold strokes and brilliant colors, they moved on to some pleasant watercolors and then to a set of landscape drawings that were technically breathtaking but less rich in effect. Perhaps, Dr. Shinefeld first thought, it was simply that she'd responded to the brilliant colors of the oils and the delicacy of the Oriental work.

Having looked at each painting for a considerable length of time, the doctor returned to the first set. Two were virtual pastiches of Japanese watercolors, while the next two seemed to be attempts to integrate what the artist had absorbed of the Japanese techniques with an American perspective. One was of fireworks over what was probably a park, the other of a gate and a garden.

"Forty-six and forty-seven," the doctor murmured. "How old was your father then?"

"I don't know. Wait a minute, he must've been...My God! He was only twenty in nineteen forty-seven. Isn't that incredible?"

"Mmm."

"What are you doing? You look as if it's a diamond and you're searching for flaws."

"Actually," the doctor said, "I was looking at the signature."

"What about it?" Dawn asked. "It's so small and scrawly that you can hardly see it."

"Well, on some there are initials, GH, and they're large enough, but on these...I'm not sure. Does it look like Henley to you?"

"What do you mean?" Dawn snatched the piece of paper from the doctor's hand. "Sure it does. What do you mean? Is this some kind of joke?"

"Of course not," the doctor said almost sharply. "I never joke about anything important."

"All right, then." Dawn was less shrill but no calmer. "If it's not a joke, will you please tell me what you're seeing?"

"Well, I'm not absolutely certain," the doctor said. "It's quite a scrawl, as you say. And small. But the first letter doesn't look like an *H* to me. It looks more like an *M*. And if I had to take a guess at the whole name, I'd say it was Miranda. Or Mirandy."

Dawn stood up, walked to the window with the painting and scanned it in the bright light for a long time. When she looked up, there were tears in her eyes, although nothing in her expression suggested that she was crying.

"It's not true of all the pictures," the doctor said softly. "The drawings seem to be your father's. And some of the earlier watercolors. We know that he was a talented artist, if only from the wonderful oil that he did while Gregory was with him. Both your parents appear to have been talented artists."

Dawn returned the picture to its place, then picked up each of the others in turn, spending the longest time on the brilliant oil abstractions of the middle period, which were Miranda's. When she had finished, she took a tissue from the box on the doctor's table, wiped her eyes, and returned to the chair where she'd been sitting since the day she had equated being sick with lying down.

"I don't know what to talk about. It's as though all my thoughts were based on something that isn't there anymore, and now there's no place to start thinking from." She returned the pictures to the portfolio, sat down again. "It's not that I'm upset. I don't even feel confused. I just . . . I'm empty. There's nothing there . . . Ever since I began to find out about my father, I've thought of myself as my father's daughter, and now . . . It's not that I'm not his daughter anymore, it's just . . . Actually . . . I've probably been too hung up on that whole business. Having a father who's an artist isn't enough of a reason to do it for an *occupation*. There has to be a more sensible way to decide how to spend your life . . . I know what you're going to say now. That I was interested in art before I knew about my father. It's true, but I never thought of doing it for the rest of my life. Of course, I didn't think about the rest of my life at all. Now . . . time is passing. I've spent too much time in school already. I'm almost twenty-two years old. I have to prepare to do something. I can always paint if I want to, but that business about Cooper Union, throwing myself into the artist's life . . . Lately, I've been thinking . . . when Jack talks about computers . . . He makes that stuff more interesting than most people do. Maybe it's that he's so smart. Or maybe I'm getting more interested in . . . After all, in the twentieth century, machines are what evolution's about . . . I guess I haven't talked about Jack much . . . It wasn't as important as . . . But something's been happening there . . . I mean, over the holiday, we didn't just go running. I slept with him. It was all unplanned. Well, when I said that, he said I should speak for myself, but what I mean is, we really have been like a brother and sister until now. I wanted it to stay that way. At least, I don't want it to turn into one of those crazy, fucked-up affairs that blows up in your face . . . But . . . well, Jack isn't someone I'd ever fall madly in love with . . . Maybe it'll be all right . . . Do I sound as though I'm absolutely out of my mind?"

The doctor shook her head.

Dawn nodded with satisfaction.

"That's what I thought. I don't *feel* crazy. Although I can't honestly say I feel wonderful. More as though

I drank a lot of wine last night . . . and now suddenly it's morning."

&

"How come you're so quiet?" Dawn asked halfway through her next session. "Are you mad about something?"

"What would I be mad about?" the doctor asked.

"Well . . ." Dawn's manner was almost arch. "Maybe because I don't want to talk about Miranda's paintings."

"Why would that make me mad?"

"I don't mean mad, exactly. But you've wanted me to talk about her for ages. You think I can't tell? If you think she's that important to me, naturally you want me to talk about her."

The doctor was silent.

"So I will." Very chipper.

"Maybe instead you should talk about feeling coerced to talk about her."

Dawn smiled. "No, that's all right. I don't feel coerced. I know you want me to get better, and if you think that's the way it's going to happen, well, you're the doctor. I don't mind."

The doctor was silent.

"Do you believe me?"

"No."

"Oh, dear." Dawn sighed comically. "I don't know if there's much I can do about that. Would it help if I lay down?"

"Help what?"

"I'm trying to cooperate in this treatment," Dawn said, "but you're making it very difficult."

"You sound as though we're having a consultation about a third party," the doctor pointed out.

"In a sense we are. We're talking about Miranda Henley. This woman I used...No. You see, I was going to say *I used to know*. I was being a wise guy. But the truth is, I *didn't* know her. You seem to think I should have, and so I'm willing to see if I càn come up with something. You've always said the couch was better, why not now?"

"I'm not arguing against your lying down on the couch," Dr. Shinefeld said. "I'm arguing against your doing it to please me and then not wanting to talk about how it feels to have to please me."

"Well," Dawn said, utterly reasonable as she moved to the couch and stretched out on it, "let's say I'm doing it to give whatever is there a chance to come up."

"All right," the doctor said. She was afraid of losing the girl at this difficult time by pushing too hard.

"Miranda Henley was a talented painter and a very disturbed woman," said Dawn in a voice reminiscent of a junior high school lecturer. "Not an unusual combination in the history of art. Van Gogh immediately comes to mind. This isn't to suggest that Henley's talent was genius. On the other hand, it was considerable. She might have gone far if she had lived to a reasonable age."

"Do you know how old she was when she died?" the doctor asked.

"No. I imagine she was a little younger than my father."

"That would have put her in her middle teens when she did the Japanese paintings."

"Mmm. True. Well, maybe they were the same age. I guess I could find out if it ever seemed interesting . . . I mean, it *is* interesting. I'll ask Vera the next time I talk to her. I suppose the most important thing about those pictures . . . if I'm going to be honest about this . . . I have to be honest, don't I . . . It wasn't just that Miranda did most of them. It was that hers were the ones I liked . . . Technically, maybe Gordon was better. But the ones that aroused feelings in me like the ones the artist must've had—those turned out to be hers. Even between their abstractions I felt that difference . . . It's fascinating, really . . . I suppose I've never given much thought to the differences between men's art and women's. To whether there are real differences. Now I'm getting curious about it . . . Maybe I'll do my term paper on that. I don't mean about Gordon and Miranda. Maybe I could find a way to use them, but . . . Oh, God, it's a dumb idea, really . . . I couldn't do it without getting much too personal."

∽

Dawn became absorbed in issues of art and feminism and might have been able to hold Miranda at bay for longer if Polly Campbell had not begun to deteriorate again. Dawn had talked to Polly about seeing a woman analyst, and Polly had smiled sadly and begun to cry. *I know it would probably be good for me*, Polly had said, but *I just can't bring myself to do it.*

"I think she's in love with that idiot Giddings,"
Dawn said. "Oh, God, I wish I could help her!"

The doctor stifled a *tell me*.

"I wanted to hang up some pictures of Miranda's
but now I'm afraid. I'm afraid Polly would see them
and pick up something terrible. Feel suicidal because
of some message she got from the pictures. Do you
know what I mean?"

"Not precisely."

"Well, I guess I don't, either... What if she asked
who'd done them? What would I tell her? This
woman who committed suicide who happens to have
the same last name I do?"

<u>"What would you like to tell her?"</u>

"That's easy. I'd like to tell her the paintings were
done by a beautiful, wonderful woman. She was my
mother. She might've been a wonderful painter if
she'd lived a little longer, but... she didn't... She
died... suddenly. I was very little... Not childbirth
... She just... It was a terrible accident... I mean,
terrible for everyone else because one day she
just... disappeared. But she didn't feel any pain.
She... Oh, shit! This is stupid... One day this perfectly wonderful woman just happened to vacate her
life... Who do I think I'm kidding? Perfectly wonderful people don't go around killing themselves."

"How about imperfectly wonderful? Talented, interesting, much loved by others."

"I don't believe that. I don't believe people who
have enough love go around killing themselves...
Unless... they have it and they don't feel as though
they have it... The truth is, we all love Polly to death,
and somehow it doesn't matter... I don't know what

341

her real family is like. I know she's crazy about her father. I think she's got sisters. Maybe brothers, too. She never mentions her mother."

"Why do you think that is?"

"I don't know. Maybe her mother's a monster. Or there's something terrible between them. Or maybe Polly feels guilty... Maybe she was the only one her father showed affection... Or it could be just that her mother's some pathetic creature and Polly's frightened of being like her mother if she talks about her, or even thinks about her. Maybe she just can't afford to think about her mother at all."

A weighty silence.

"It's not the same thing at all, you know. Polly grew up with her mother. I'm sure she would have told me if her mother had died... Why'd you start talking about Polly's mother anyway?"

"We were talking about why Polly never mentioned her."

"Mmm. Very tricky."

"Tricky?"

"Sure. Trying to make me see what I'm doing with... Miranda... by getting me to talk about Polly and her mother."

"What's tricky about that?"

"Oh, I don't know." Dawn stood up and stretched. "I guess it's only tricky if it isn't true. If it's true, then you're just trying to make me see something...." She looked at the clock, wandered to the window, looked down at the park. "Not just see what's there. Make me *be* there. Turn me into a baby again."

"How about, shed some light on the baby who's there so the adult can see her?"

342

"Shed some light," Dawn echoed. Her voice was muffled because her face was pressed against the window. Finally she turned around. "We shed more and more light on my baby until finally . . . she's like an overexposed photograph. You can't even see the places that're supposed to be dark anymore."

"How would you feel about lying down on the couch and talking about that?"

"It's happened to my father already," Dawn said, returning to the chair as though it were what the doctor had suggested. "We shed so much light on my father . . . he turned out to be my mother."

"I think that's true in more than one way," the doctor said.

"Ohhh . . ." Dawn was exasperated as well as heartsick. "What's the use of all this? I don't want to talk about losing things anymore. I want to talk about . . . I'm very *hungry*. That's what I really want. Some food. When I leave here I'm going to eat myself sick."

"Oh?"

"Mmm. Now say *tell me*. All right, I'll tell you. First, I'm going to find a Sabrett's stand and have a couple of hot dogs. Mustard and sauerkraut. No, that's only if I go downtown, that's what I used to do on the run between here and NBC. God, I've known you a long time. Almost four years. At some point do you become my real family instead of them? Do I become your real daughter instead of your adopted one? I should say, do you become my real mother? I'm going to need one if we shed any more light on Miranda Henley. And don't tell me I have Tony. If I'm going to get a new mother, she's got to be healthy." Abruptly Dawn stood up and began pacing around the office again.

"The thing about someone like Miranda is that it wouldn't take much light to make her vanish. There wasn't much there to begin with."

"I don't know about that," the doctor said. "It seems to me that the light that's been shed on Miranda has turned her into a more substantial person than she was before. A person of considerable talent. Someone it would have been worthwhile to know."

Dawn stopped. Considered.

"I don't understand," she finally said, "how you can talk about getting to know someone who does nothing but lie on a bed all day and finally... All right. I hear myself. We've gone right back to Polly."

&

At her next session, Dawn announced that she'd had a dream about the playroom.

"In the dream it was a bedroom. I don't even know why I think it was that room, except the brown carpet and yellow chairs were there... Before I went to sleep last night I was rearranging our apartment in my mind. Did I tell you Sally's leaving? Who shares Lillian's room? We're thinking of dividing the apartment three ways. I'd move into the living room. In other words, I wouldn't be sharing a room with Polly. Not that I gave that as a reason. I'd rather stay than have her think I mind. Once or twice I've thought about getting out altogether rather than..."

"Maybe it's something to consider."

"Oh no. I couldn't do that. This'll be fine. And once I'm in my own room Jack'll be around more. The other girls like him. Lillian says he's sexy but in this nice, lazy way ... I never even noticed. Lillian used to tease me, but ... Anyway, I don't want to talk about it."

"Why?"

"I don't know. Sometimes I feel awkward when I talk about boys. I'm afraid I'm going to make you feel lonely."

"Tell me."

Dawn laughed nervously. "I don't think I will. I can tell by the way you said that that I'm being fucked up."

"Would you like to tell me about the dream?"

"I can't believe I forgot it. I was so full of it when I came in ... Last night ... Polly was in bed but I knew she wasn't asleep. I wanted to go into the living room. But I didn't want her to know it was because of her. Finally I went and stretched out on the couch with a boring book, and I thought I'd fall asleep, and it would look as though I hadn't meant to. But then something awful happened. I guess I fell asleep for a few minutes. Maybe it was the dream, actually. It was as though the wall had disappeared and I wasn't on the other side anymore. Do you know what I mean?"

"I'd like to hear more about it from you."

"I don't know how to describe it. It was as though Polly and I were on opposite sides of the same skin instead of the wall. Not really separated. I can't ... I want to cry or scream when I think about it. There are no words. I'm not even sure there are pictures. If I tried to draw ... Have you ever noticed that I don't do abstractions? The only abstract art I like at all is very strong stuff, like Miranda's, but I've never had the slightest urge to draw abstract art myself. I like to draw what I can identify."

Dawn twisted around to point to the sculpture on the table, the egg, with a less distinct, flat object curling around it.

"I can see mother and child in it, so I can love it. But if it were just a little more blobby, if you couldn't tell where one ended and the other began ... I guess that's the feeling I had last night. I was in the next room but I was feeling Polly's feelings instead of my own."

"It might be useful," the doctor said, "to remember that you were feeling both. The fear was yours, and the will to fight."

"Yes, but what if I stopped fighting?"

"Well, I suppose I think the place for you to stop fighting is here, when we can talk about it."

"I'm only here for little bits of time."

"We can get a lot of work done in that time."

"But then I have to go out into the world."

"You can always go back to fighting if you need to."

"How do I know it would work?"

"It's worked for most of your life."

"What do you mean?"

"What do you think I mean?"

"I have no idea. Most of my life! What's most of my life about? I've only known Polly for ... We're not talking about my mother again, are we? Are *you*?"

"I think we're talking about both."

"*I* wasn't."

"You brought up the mother and child," said the doctor.

"That was because talking about Polly reminded me..." Dawn stopped, reconnoitered, sighed. "Oh, God, that's what all this is about, isn't it. What reminds you of whom... What I don't understand is, I love Polly. You say I'm fighting off my mother. At least I think that's what you're saying. Well, of course I'm fighting her off. I don't want to be like her. But if Polly is like her... why did I want to be with her?"

"Why don't *you* try to tell *me*?"

"The sadness is part of it," Dawn began with some difficulty. "I have to admit that. Softness. No hostility. A lot of girls are hostile to me just on sight... Do you believe that?"

"Yes. But I also think it's a cover for feelings you have toward them."

"I don't have any feelings toward most of them. I just want them to leave me alone."

"That's a feeling."

Silence.

"With Polly... I came toward her... It was almost as if she were someone in a dream, a beautiful dream I had, and there she was out of the dream in my real life... this lovely woman... I think part of it is her speech. She has a beautiful speaking voice, and her speech... It's not an accent, exactly. Maybe there's a bit of a—her parents, her father is—oh my God, it's just a little bit of a Scots lilt! Or Irish. It doesn't matter, really... I don't know why I didn't see it before. It's not about my mother, it's about Mavis... Although... I don't associate Mavis with sadness... Do you think I loved my mother?"

"Do you?"

"Love. That was practically the first thing you and I ever talked about. Thinking you're in love. Of course, a little baby doesn't think it's in love . . . But it must feel . . . Of course it feels, that's a dumb thing to say . . . But what does it feel? What's love, anyway? I don't know if I could even tell the difference between my mother and Mavis . . . The one who was supposed to be feeding me but didn't want to and the one who was doing it."

"How about, wasn't able to?"

"Didn't *want* to . . . All right. I know that's not fair. Polly wants to be up and around, and she can't . . . You see? I *can* tell the difference between them . . . Maybe . . . I was just being a wise guy again. Your memory can do all kinds of funny tricks. If I felt like it, I could close my eyes and see Polly lying down in a room someplace else entirely. Like in Boston." She shuddered, then grew calm.

"*I am a part of all that I have met* . . . Do you know that poem? *Ulysses?* I loved it very dearly, more than anything else, any other poem I read in high school. *It little profits that an idle king . . . By this still hearth, among these barren crags . . . Matched with an aged wife I mete and dole unequal justice unto a race that sleeps and eats and knows not me* . . . I'm missing a lot . . . *I am a part of all that I have met. Yet all experience is an arch where through gleams that untravelled world whose*—something . . . *margins?* —*fade fore'er as I move* . . .

"I'm a part of all that I've met, but I don't want to be part of the person I was really a part of . . . The Eskimos have that idea, you know . . . Did you think I'd forgotten the Eskimos just because I haven't talked about them for a while? I'll tell you why I stopped. I took a sociology class last term where they used another book of the same guy's. And there are pictures done by some of the Eskimos he visited. Not *of* them, like in the first book. *By* them. The photos that were done by a white man . . . I could see what he saw. But the paintings made me realize I could never be like the Eskimos, and that made me feel very lonely. My pictures are full of *things*. Maybe it's just that I grew up surrounded by things. When I did the outside pictures, they were simple, but not as simple as the real Eskimo paintings. Most of their pictures are . . . almost all whiteness. Two seagulls. A bird. I like my pictures to be full of things like my dreams are full of people. So I won't get lonely. I'll tell you something funny . . . When I go to sleep at night . . . I feel very sexual toward things. My pillow. I can look at it, and my face is close to it, not touching, and it doesn't have a name, or a sex, the way it does in a fantasy. It has no identity other than what it really is . . . a pillow . . . a wall . . . And I'll feel the same as though it were a lover or a mother or . . . Did you hear what I just said? Funny . . . Well, I always knew I had a mother . . . I just thought her name was Tony."

An extended silence.

"All right. You did it. You got me back there. Now what happens when I'm still there and you go off on vacation?"

"It's only May."

"The whole year is like a cycle," Dawn said, "with its own seasons. A cycle of birth and death. Every September I come here and get born . . . laid . . ." (giggle giggle) ". . . like an egg. And I slowly evolve into a little fish, making it through the choppy waters. And if there aren't too many short vacations, I slowly start to feel bigger and stronger, more able to cope with life, and I begin to think I'm going to make it to the shore instead of just breaking up in the water ... And I get closer and closer ... and then August comes, and you pick me up and toss me back into the middle of the ocean."

◠

At her first session the following week, Dawn handed the doctor some letters from Gordon Henley, at his Beacon Street address, to Miranda Lewis, in Roxbury, Massachusetts.

"I'd rather you talked to me about them first."

"I can't."

They sat down. The doctor opened the first letter, which had been written in July of 1953, when Gordon Henley was, if she remembered correctly, twenty-five or twenty-six years old. The handwriting was beautiful; it might have been on an ancient scroll.

My darling Miranda,

I doubt that even if you were here beside me I could make you believe the degree of desolation I feel in your absence. Upon sight of you, I would be all right again, and then you would tell me that I'd been all right all along. Not so. Without the sun the earth might continue to move in its orbit but the journey would have neither warmth nor meaning.

I have been doing the drawing exercises you assigned to me. The book is indeed marvelous but it's not fair that you ask it to be my companion in your place. I lack the will to do what you are certain I can do unless you are with me, your soft voice urging me to do better, your beautiful brown eyes reproaching me when I do not. (Please don't tell me again that all these signs happen only in my own imagination.)

Why won't you tell me where you are? I promise not to come after you. I can tolerate the humiliation of having Nell forward my letters, but not the delay, and the sense that I am out of touch with you.

Please come back to me, my love, and failing that, tell me where you are so that I may know where I am living.

Yours,
Gordon

Dr. Shinefeld looked up. Dawn was watching her intently. Neither spoke. The doctor turned to the second letter, dated a few weeks later.

My dearest,

I hope you are having the rest you so badly needed and that in general you are being treated well. It is true, as Nell said, that I cannot really picture how you are when you are like this, and so I am writing to you as though you were the Miranda I know and who is my life. If you are still not yourself, perhaps Nell or some wise soul at the clinic will hold my letters until you are my Miranda again.

Our last conversation left me thinking very seriously and finding, too late, dozens of things I wanted to say to you. If I had known then that I wouldn't see you for a long time, I would have tried harder to phrase my thoughts.

You say that you adore me and you call me your beautiful boy, all the while telling me you do not wish to marry me or anyone, that we were not meant to be. Could this really be about our ages? Do you really believe that five miserable years make some crucial difference? What if they were reversed—would your being five years younger than I be a problem? Those years represent a simple coincidence of fate; surely they were not meant to prevent the bond between us.

You are the perfect complement to me, the magic element needed to complete my life. Dark where I am light, airy where I am leaden, talented where I am a craftsman, plodding but sincere. You are a woman and I am a man; I'm not sure I understood, until I knew you, why I'd been made a man.

All this being true, you may ask why on earth you should marry me. Leaving aside the delightful possibility that you feel—though you go to great lengths not to use the word—something resembling love for me, I have the *will* to care for you, the *will* to make a good life for us, the *will* to make you happy, and, though I never thought I would say this to anyone as long as I lived, certainly not in the interest of bribery, I have the money required to give you a comfortable life. *What difference does my age make?* There is little question of my being at an age where it is acceptable for me to marry. Perhaps I should ask, rather, what difference *your* age makes? You tell me that you do not wish to take care of a man, but it isn't someone who will care for me that I seek. Rather, it's someone to care for, someone around whom I can organize the energies I have and cannot use—a magnet, if you will, to attract the bits and pieces of myself and turn them into a coherent mass.

I want to give to you, not take away. I want to be allowed to love you, whether or not you return my love. I ask only that you give me a chance. You say that if we are going to live together, we might as well marry and restrain your mother's wrath. This is what I most urgently desire without consideration of your mother. So be it, then. Let us marry. I promise to let you leave me if I make you unhappy.

Send me a message when you are yourself and can bear to see me.

As ever,
G

Once again, Dr. Shinefeld looked up.

"You have to read them all," Dawn said. "I picked each one for a different reason. Well, the first just because it was the first. But the others tell you something important."

October 2, 1956

My darling wife,
I am desolate that you have found it necessary

to hide yourself from me at this difficult time. I will stay here until you are willing to see me, of course. But I want you to know that as far as I'm concerned, whichever course you choose is right and good. If you decide to have this baby, I will love you and I will love the baby. If you decide that you cannot go through with it, I will understand and help you to do what needs to be done. What I don't understand in your note is the statement about not having a choice. I have talked to all of your doctors—Slivkin, Parsons, and Marks—and each says, independent of the others, that he thinks it best for you to have an abortion if you really do not want the child.

I'm assured that these matters are not what they used to be. We can fly together to various places in the United States—or out of it, if you prefer, to someplace like Cuba where it would be legal. Or Parsons intimated that he could make arrangements with someone right here in Boston if you should decide that you are less concerned with the likelihood of anyone here finding out.

Please, my love, don't continue to hide from me. I cannot understand your meaning when you say you are ashamed to face me, so far is it from my understanding of our situation. But without facing you, how can I make you believe there is no cause for shame?

Your husband always,
G

"They make me ache for him," Dawn said. "So beautiful. He wrote so beautifully. It made me feel

better about her being a better painter. At least...He
was wonderful in other ways...So loving. The big-
gest shock of those letters was how much he loved
her. It made me feel weird. I guess I always
thought...The world was him and me and my mother just lying on a bed someplace...Out of it...I
called Vera to ask if she knew who Nell was. She said
it was Miranda's sister. There were a few sisters.
They lived in Roxbury. That was the postmark. Vera
was never there. She only saw Miranda in Boston...I
called Gregory Barnes, too. I wanted to know if my
father ever talked about her. I can see now it was a
dumb thing to do. He was awful. Although I don't
know if I had any way of knowing in advance that
he'd...It crossed my mind that I should talk to you
first, then I just couldn't wait, I had to do it. He was
cold as ice. If Miranda's name had ever come up, he
said, it didn't make enough of an impression for him
to remember. Something ridiculous like that. Could
he have been jealous of her, d'you think?"

"It's certainly a possibility."

Silence.

"Oh, God!" Dawn was crying now. "That poor
woman! She never even wanted to have me...Not
me...It wasn't that she knew I was going to be
Dawn....She knew she wasn't meant to get married
and have children. She knew she didn't want to be a
mother. Maybe she knew what would happen to
her...My God, when I think of what she went
through...Do you realize that if I hadn't been born,
Miranda might still be alive?" Dawn stopped crying.
"How come you're not reassuring me? How come

you're not telling me if I hadn't killed her something else would have?"

"Killed her?"

"You know what I mean."

"No I don't."

"I don't know, either...I must feel responsible. Well, not responsible, but if she hadn't had me, she might've been all right. Don't you think that's possible?"

"Anything's possible. Particularly if you give a broad enough definition to the words *all right*. There's reason to believe from those letters that she was less than all right for years before you were born."

"Tell me what you see in the letters."

The doctor hesitated.

"Please. I need to get a feeling for what someone else sees. I'm scared. I'm in a whole new place."

The doctor picked up the letters again. "Well, the first one might be the letter of almost any suitor who's hopelessly in love and having a difficult time. When he talks about her saying the signs he sees on her face are in his own mind, I wondered if that might not be true. Especially since she's chosen to go away without telling him where. But later it's clear that she's having some serious difficulties. Perhaps a breakdown."

"You think?"

"Something along those lines. It doesn't sound like a physical illness."

"She was all fucked up," Dawn said, shaking her head sadly. "I wonder what...I think I'm going to try to find her sister...Nell...over the summer. I need to know more about what she was like when she was younger...I don't feel quite the way I felt about finding my father, to tell the truth, but I think I need to do it anyway... You know what I kept remembering when I read the last letter? I kept remembering how I said... I mean, it was true when I said it. In a way it's still true... that she doesn't exist for me. And now I find out that she never *wanted* to exist for me! She never wanted me to be born!"

15

That spring Charles Herman's wife left him for a convict from a class in criminal law that she taught one afternoon a week at a prison in upstate New York.

Actually, she asked Charles to leave. It made sense, she pointed out, if only because of the children. (Her father was their landlord.)

Charles took a six-month lease on a furnished apartment on West Sixty-sixth Street that was large enough so he could have his children stay over and far enough from Lulu's building so that he wouldn't be bumping into her all the time.

Actually, for the first two weeks after it happened, Charles didn't tell Lulu. He didn't call her at all, so that she was quite frantic, knowing something was up but determined not to phone his office. Was it possible he'd finally decided to go cold turkey without so much as a brief note to warn her?

When she finally learned—from someone else—about Anna, she understood all too well. It even occurred to her that she might not hear from him again. (Charles dismissed this possibility as having nothing whatever to do with him.)

For almost two years they had inhabited that charmed atmosphere peculiar to domestic arrangements of one or two evenings a week. Now reality had thrust them out of their magical place into a world where they might be together without subterfuge for weeks at a time. If Charles had been less frightened, she would have been more so.

Anna Herman, a member of Their Crowd, as Charles called it, had been born to wealth, and, too prudent to renounce it, had settled for rejecting comfort. For almost two years Charles had reveled in the red wools and kilim designs of Dr. Shinefeld's office, then returned to the brownstone near P.S. 6 that his wife was inclined not to furnish beautifully because the children would mess everything up. For almost two years, on most of the evenings she saw him, Lulu, who in this period seldom cooked for anyone else, had made some superb little stew that she reheated in the Pullman kitchen for Charles, whose wife had a housekeeper who was nice to the children as opposed to one who could cook, and whose kitchen pantry was full of tuna fish and Rice-a-Roni. Anna Herman didn't care, as Lulu did, that Charles had a palate that discerned every subtle seasoning in each dish, not to speak of the difference between a four-dollar Beaujolais and a five-dollar

Chaize. For several years Charles had had a bad back, which disappeared with miraculous regularity during his evenings at Dr. Shinefeld's office. Although occasionally when they had finished dinner and returned languorously to the sleeping bag some accommodation to his spine had to be made.

No problem.

Nothing had seemed like a problem except that they had so little time.

Now there was a bigger problem; now they had all the time in the world.

When he finally called, when she heard his voice on the other end of the phone, she was so relieved that she almost cried. She asked him to hold, put down the receiver, and walked around the room for a couple of minutes. Returning to the phone, she took a deep breath, sat down and picked up the receiver again.

"Let me guess," she said. "Your back is out and you've used up every eighteen-year-old in Manhattan who knows how to fuck around a bad back."

She'd never worried about eighteen-year-olds before.

"Don't be dumb, Lulu," he said. "Fucking's the last thing in the world on my mind. I'm walking around like a whipped dog."

She was silent.

"Do you know everything?" he asked.

"Only one or two things," she said.

"He's a psychopath. He should've been in Rockland State. He's out in her custody. She couldn't stand not being able to fuck him! This woman who always thought sex was just another form of overeating.

Who I had to get down on my knees, literally, for Christ's sake, to—" He broke off with a groan.

"Maybe she just doesn't like you."

"Lulu, what the hell are you doing? I need you."

She reconnoitered the territory. She had vowed to be tough when (if) he finally called. When he was married, such vows invariably had come to nothing. There was no time. Now there was world enough and time, and the question was whether she was willing to risk driving him away. The answer was no.

"You couldn't have expected me not to be angry," she said.

"All right. But I also expected you to understand."

Fuck understanding, said a small voice within her that had been hyperactive during the last part of her marriage but silent, hitherto, when she was dealing with Charles.

"Yes," she said. "Well, I do understand. Against my will, so to speak. But Mrs. Sallie's leaving early tonight and I have to get home." Her voice was softening without being told to.

"Can I come over?"

What was he talking about? Did he really believe the old arrangement could—

"I told you, I'm leaving."

"I meant to the apartment. Hey, Lu! I don't have to hide anymore!"

A certain forced heartiness, said the voice. *Anyway, maybe there'll be nothing to hide.*

"How about nine, nine-thirty?" she asked. "Then I can get the kids into their rooms."

"If you're not going to make me dinner," he said,

just a trifle sullen, "you may as well come to my place."

If she told him she was tired he would say that his back was out.

"I'll give you dinner," she said, "but I need a little time. Please, Charles. I can't help it if you couldn't bring yourself to call until you were desperate."

But...

If the married Charles had dined on beef bourguignon and blanquette de veau reheated in Dr. Shinefeld's kitchen, single Charles's first meal in the kitchen of Lulu Shinefeld, working mother, would be Dinty Moore's Beef Stew, a favorite of her children. True, Lulu could have dragged herself over to Columbus Avenue and shopped for a little something to avoid this rude shock to his taste buds. But it was just as true that his phone call had already caused her to be ten minutes later than she'd told Mrs. Sallie she would be. And even truer, perhaps, that her understanding of his problems was twisting her anger around her brain instead of crushing it. In any event, Lulu made a Caesar salad in case she wasn't being fair—and even though she wasn't certain that she wanted to be fair.

As a matter of fact, there were moments during that first evening when it seemed that her resentment at the inequality of her position in the affair, at his inconsiderateness, at the visible way he walked a tightrope between the women in his life—that all those feelings that had always seemed to disperse in the air when he walked into the office had actually accumulated and were boiling away on the surface of her brain, waiting to find a way out of her mouth.

He'd had to be checked out by the doorman.

Now they stood facing each other at the door, not eager, as they'd always been, to touch, to grab, to kiss, to run to bed. They stood there awkwardly, Charles's availability, their Anna-lessness, a thick wall between them.

"Listen," Charles finally announced, "we both know what we're going through. We're both nervous as hell."

"You look awful. As though you haven't slept in—"

"I haven't. If I'd been able to sleep I might've waited even longer to get my bearings before I called you."

"Gee," she said, "I really appreciate your being so Open and Honest with me."

"Look," he said, "do you think I wanted to arrive here like something out of the Hundred Neediest Cases?"

"You could've brought dinner," she pointed out.

She'd never had the impulse to say anything like that to him. After all, before tonight her time with him had always been stolen from someone else.

"Oh, shit," he said. "Maybe I'd just better get a cab and go home."

Charles *never* took cabs. He ran every place, bad back or no bad back.

"All right," she said, "I'm sorry. I am nervous. I'm something much worse than nervous."

"And I'm starved. What have you got to eat?"

Finally he entered the apartment and she closed

the door behind him. He walked through the kitchen, stood at the entrance to the living room.

Charles had only been in the apartment a few times—a couple of hours on random weekend afternoons when the boys were with Nathan—and he'd seemed oblivious to his surroundings. What was he seeing now? Aside from her own bedroom retreat, she had never taken the pains here that she had with her office. The living room contained primarily furniture from her father's old apartment; only the Chinese rug and the prints on the walls were hers, and they weren't new. Even if she'd had the money, it wouldn't have made sense to her any more than it did to Anna Herman to spend a lot of money on decor with two small boys running around, jumping on the upholstery.

Then, too, what did Charles see when he looked at *her*? He'd once said she was going to be a wonderful-looking old lady. Was he noticing that she was somewhat farther along toward that end than he'd thought of her as being? She'd put on more makeup than usual and only remembered when the doorbell rang that he didn't care for makeup. On the other hand, she couldn't honestly say that he looked very appealing to her. He'd described himself as a whipped dog, and something of that quality came through as she opened the door. There was something less lovable about his very features. Maybe it was that he'd lost weight and was haggard. She wondered, for the first time, if his patients ever noticed the extraordinary sloppiness of his attire.

He sat down at the kitchen table, took one mouthful of the beef stew after inspecting it sniffily, set aside the plate without comment, ate the Caesar salad, drank a beer, then asked if she had any ice cream, thus making it clear that he suspected there was nothing else in this house that might be fit for him to eat. He devoured three Good Humors—two toasted almond and one chocolate—then sat back, tilting his chair so far that it seemed he would tumble over backward, a lifelong habit of his with which she was unfamiliar since in their previous life there had been no dining chairs and he'd always been tilted toward her. Maybe he would tumble over backward and finish his back and they would live together forever after, she pushing him around in a wheelchair.

"There is an ex-convict living in my apartment," Charles said now. "With my wife. Being a role model for my sons. Planning, in all probability, to molest my daughter."

Really taking up where Papa left off.

"Why did you let him move in?"

"Because if I'd refused, she would have moved out and taken the children with her. And that, obviously, would have been even worse. For them. Either way it would have been worse. If I let her do it or if I took her to court. Aside from the horror of custody cases, with which you are possibly familiar, she happens to be an excellent mother, a fact with which you are definitely familiar."

And that he had always taken pains to keep before her. The first of a long list of reasons, all legitimate, that he would never divorce Anna.

"What does the judge say?"

Anna Herman's father was a powerful and much-hated judge who for many years had been a powerful and much-hated lawyer and politician.

"She just left Kid Psycho out of the story. You know how the old man feels about me. All she had to do this time was complain about me to the judge. Daddy, I never told you but—lousy father—doesn't play football with the boys—fucks around."

"How does she know that?"

"She doesn't. Just filling in whatever she thought would work. And, just for the record, there hasn't exactly been an unending chain of—"

"Of Lulus," she finished for him, smiling sweetly.

"Fine, if that's the way you like it."

"How do you know what she told the judge?"

"What do you mean, how do I know? I know the way I know most things. And I know from her that she didn't mention Kid Psycho because she threatened me with all hell if I told. Not seeing the kids. Stuff like that."

"What's his name?" Lulu asked.

"He doesn't have a name," Charles grumbled. "Kid Psycho. I told you. *Why do you say that he's crazy, Charles? Why don't you just say that he's poor?*" He was mimicking Anna. "*He's never been convicted of assault, Charles, only of robbery.* But he's been tried for assault three times! He's twelve years younger than she is. No jokes, please. I can wait a few weeks for jokes. I have no sense of humor at all yet." He let his chair come forward with a thump.

Lulu smiled. For the first time that evening she felt something other than hostility toward him. He was still Anna's victim, the questionable fact that had provided the rationale for giving him aid and comfort all along. Briefly she wondered how Anna would behave toward Charles if he were to become Lulu's victim.

Charles stood up and yawned. "Where are your kids?"

"In bed."

"Asleep?"

"Don't know."

"Let's go into your room."

"I want to clean up in here."

"Will they see me if I walk across the living room?"

"Unlikely."

Lulu's bedroom was on one side of the living room; the boys' were off a hallway on the other, next to Sascha's room, a.k.a. Storage.

"Just be careful," she said. "Don't call out to me."

Taking his jacket but leaving his tie on the table, Charles left the kitchen. Slowly and deliberately, Lulu picked up the dishes, put away the uneaten food, washed the dishes (which she often left for Mrs. Sallie to do the following afternoon), and straightened up. Then she sat down at the table with a magazine she would not later be able to identify.

She would serve as a kind of halfway house for him. She would be there, helping him to stave off depression, feeding him, comforting him, getting accustomed to having him around more and more. Perhaps, if it were possible, she would fall even more deeply in love with him. Need more from him because there was the possibility of having more. Love, as she'd suggested to Dawn not so long before, turned people into babies for a while, and if, as babies, they'd felt their needs to be endless and seldom satisfied, they were likely to turn back into that sort of baby again. Only a few years of life together could provide an antidote for the dreaded baby disease.

While Charles was growing stronger, she would become weaker. *Not exactly your classic analytic mode of thought, Lulu.* But she was helpless to stop herself. And then one day, as his divorce was becoming final and he'd become his old self again, it would occur to Charles, who, after all, had always gone for cool, slender women with no visible needs to support, that if he was going to have a big baby on his hands, she might as well not be forty-four years old and a trifle flabby.

Eighteen-year-olds weren't his speed; he'd been right to say that was about her. But New York appeared to be full of extremely attractive—thirty-year-olds, say—who had no children to bother a man, who made excellent salaries at interesting work, and who would generally be more appropriate wives than she for a frenetic thirty-seven-year-old divorced father of three.

In fact, there was reason to believe that here and there someone was emerging who might legitimately be called the New Woman. Just like the traditional male, this terrific female contained her feelings so well that it couldn't be proved that they found symbolic outlet in the business world. Off to work she went each day in perfect makeup, a well-tailored suit that did full justice to her slim but curvaceous figure, and high heels. At work she held her own in conversations with the men, apparently free of the emotional freight borne by generations of women. And she had or didn't have a boyfriend to whom she could say—and, unlike Lulu's generation, *mean*—that she wasn't ready for marriage and wasn't certain she ever wanted children.

Never mind the crucial denial at the bottom of it all; denial was easier to live with than assertion. Never mind if she wasn't given to joyous abandon. Never mind who was sexier; nine tenths of sexy was in the mind of the beholder, and if *she* was who you wanted, then *she* was who excited you, and your mind could provide the warm, moist climate for the love culture to thrive in—at least for long enough to marry her. Maybe even to start a new family when she changed her mind about babies.

The thought of Charles's making a baby in some young woman caused Lulu to stand up so abruptly that her magazine flew across the table and fell to the floor.

She was looking into his eyes.

He was standing at the kitchen entrance and had apparently been there for a while. His shoes were off, his glasses were off, his shirt was unbuttoned, his hair was more messed up than usual. He'd been lying down.

He said, "You're being paranoid."

She shrugged. "It may be called for."

When he had been married and read her mind, she had hugged him and kissed him and told him that no one had ever understood her in the visceral way that he did, not even her analysts. Now it was frightening that he already owned so much of her that he would take with him if (when) he left.

"Maybe understandable," he said. "Not called for. Paranoia by definition is never called for."

"In fact," she said, "reality, as we all know, has marched more than halfway toward meeting everyone's paranoia since the term came into general use."

"Very cute," Charles said, "but wherever it marches, it begins with a delusion."

Her eyes filled with tears.

"What is it?" he asked softly. "Eighteen-year-olds?"

She shook her head. "Twenty-five-year-olds. And thirty-year-olds. Thirty-five, for that matter. Some adorable thing whose brain you can mold, even as you delight in her youthful body and her dope-induced sexuality...Someone with money, especially."

He laughed. "Money turns me on, huh? Yours, especially."

"You didn't need it before. Now you're going to need it. Anna'll make you pay child support. She's probably convinced herself the divorce has nothing to do with Kid Psycho. Not just convinced her father. She's probably certain your faults drove her to this. You need to have a stronger sense of responsibility toward your kids. She'll settle for the symbol of support if she can't have the reality of your concern."

He rolled his eyes in his head but couldn't resist a smile. "You hit the nail on the head that time, kiddo."

She was silent.

He came around to her side of the table, sat next to her, turning their chairs so they faced, smoothed the hair back from her forehead.

He would see the gray coming in. See it in a

different way than he had before. It would become the reality principle.

He kissed her forehead. "Where does I love you come into all this?" he asked.

She looked into his eyes, straining to see if it was real or if he was conning her. She saw both. She closed her eyes.

He lifted her from the chair by her elbows, embraced her, kissed her eyes.

"Nobody's ever been into me as deep as you are," he whispered.

She opened her eyes. She smiled, but she was still fighting tears.

"That's as good a reason to leave me as any," she said.

"Come into the bedroom." He took her hand. "Come on. You just need to get laid. Three weeks is too long for you, Lu. Unless you're getting it elsewhere. Maybe *that's* what this is all about. Maybe I'm just dealing with a classic case of projection."

"And I'm dealing with a classic case of manipulation."

The cleverest kind. Using what *could have been* the truth to deny what *was* the truth.

But she let him lead her into the bedroom, tiptoeing across the living room just in case the kids were awake.

He closed the door behind them and kissed her, pressing her against the wall.

Suddenly a bloodcurdling yell erupted from the other side and a hard object banged against the door.

She pushed Charles back and threw it open.

Teddy stood in his pajamas, holding his baseball

372

at, sobbing. Walden stood a couple of feet behind him.

"Teddy!" She bent over to hug him, but he moved back. "What is it?"

"I saw a man drag you in here."

Walden eyed her anxiously.

"Oh my goodness, no," she said, forcing a little laugh. "He wasn't dragging me, love."

The baseball bat remained poised for use.

Charles had had a telephone identity—a false identity and a name, Phil, that went with it—but they'd never seen his face. Supposedly he lived in California her friend Phil, which was why the boys hadn't met him before.

"It's my friend," she said. "Phil."

It had to be someone they'd heard of; her position was too compromising. And they might recognize his gravelly voice.

"I want to see him."

"All right."

She turned on the overhead light and stood aside so the boys could enter the room. She avoided looking at Charles for fear that one or both of them would laugh. Or cry. The boys had never seen a man other than Nathan in her bedroom.

Teddy marched into the room, followed by his brother. Charles stood in the space where he'd been trying to hide; now he was aiming for nonchalance. The boys regarded him somberly

"He's not wearing any shoes," Teddy announced.

"Maybe his feet hurt," Walden offered.

"Did he move?" Teddy asked after a moment,

addressing his questions to Lulu without taking his eyes off Charles.

"Why don't you ask him?"

But Teddy wasn't prepared to address the bushy-haired intruder. "Or is he just visiting from California? Where was he supposed to live, anyhow? You never told me the city."

As though the very fact of Charles's being here now were proof that he'd never lived in California.

"He moved," Charles said.

Oh, God. There was going to be so much explaining to do later on. If there was a later on.

"He lives in New York," Charles continued. "On Sixty-sixth Street. It's an ugly apartment, but he hopes you'll come to visit him sometime."

Teddy was not amused. "Tell him to go into the living room."

The baseball bat remained up and poised. Charles raised his arms as though there were a gun trained on him.

"I'll go quietly," he said, easing himself around the door and out through the small hallway to the living room.

"Permission to be seated requested," Charles said to no one in particular.

"I think it's time to stop this nonsense," Lulu said. "If you want to talk to Charles—his real name is Charles, in case I never mentioned it—Phil's a nickname... Anyway, if you'd like to talk to Charles for a moment before you go back to bed, you can. But then go Both of you."

Teddy slowly lowered the bat. Walden moved clos

er to him. Charles sat down. The curfew tolled the knell of parting day.

"Look," said Charles, who was unaccustomed to dealing with young boys other than his own and refused to take anyone less than seventeen in his practice, "I know how you feel, having me bust in here like this. A stranger. With my shoes off, yet."

Outrage battled anguish on Teddy's face and both won. The stranger had not only dragged his mother into the bedroom but was now invading Teddy's mind!

"Have you ever considered," Teddy finally managed to get out, his lip curling even as it trembled, "getting on a slow rocket to the moon?" Then, pulling himself up to a height at least three inches greater than his normal one, he marched out of the living room, Walden two inches behind. The door slammed behind them.

Lulu grinned.

"Jesus Christ," Charles said. He was grinning but he was also not grinning. "I knew I should've taken the place on the East Side. I kept thinking this one was a perfect walk to my office, right through the park. Just long enough. And from here, too. Through the park at Seventy-second."

There was a pause.

"Why did you say it was ugly?" Lulu asked.

"Because it is. Furnished. Two bedrooms. All of it ugly. The lobby's one of those Mafia hybrids—crystal chandeliers and modern carpets and doormen out of some parking garage— and whoever furnished the apartment thought the lobby was real class."

"Why'd you take it?"

"Because it was available right away. Six-month lease. It was easy. I'm not up to furnishing a place now. I don't know where I'll be in a year. I don't know where I'll want to be. Where *you'll* want me to be. You know I couldn't have just moved in here, don't you?"

She nodded. She knew, but she would have liked him to ask so she could explain what a bad idea it was. The nature of their times together had always been that she wanted more than he could give.

He laughed shortly. "I knew I couldn't do that even before I knew about The Enforcer in there. The Juggernaut. Teddy-Walden Juggernaut. You know, Kid Psycho isn't getting as hard a time as I am. I think my kids are scared of him. I mean it. *I* am. Why the hell shouldn't *they* be? Of course, I know more about him than they do, but enough's filtered through. They heard Annie and me fighting. She could never tell them who he really is. If she did, she might have to let herself know."

Annie. Lulu was sure she'd never heard him use that affectionate nickname before.

She stood up. "I'm tired."

He rose to follow her into the bedroom.

"I don't think you should be here in the morning," she said.

"Once I fall asleep," he said, "I'll be finished. I haven't slept through the night in two weeks."

"You'll have to be careful," she told him. "You'll have to stay in the room—I mean, really hide in it—until they leave. It shouldn't be too difficult. They never come in here in the morning."

"They're going to have to get used to me."

"This week? You mean this week Annie kicked you out of the house so this week they have to get used to you?"

"Maybe," Charles said grimly, "I should go home right now."

Maybe he should.

She sat down on the edge of the bed. her eyes downcast, her insides tied into some new and complicated knot.

They'd had fights before without ever really being angry. They'd been playing house. Pretending to have a real relationship in which matters had to be straight between them, difficulties worked out. Now there was real anger but there would be no fight. She was frightened at the thought of his leaving even if she wasn't sanguine about his staying.

Their lovemaking had been a perpetual astonishment to both of them; normally spectacular, it had never been less than lovely. What if that, too, were to change? What if they were to lose what they'd always had by mingling it with the new and less good?

What's all this magical-chemical thinking you're suddenly into?

Charles sat down beside her, put an arm around her.

"It's bound to be difficult at first."

"I don't want it to be difficult."

First it would be difficult and second he would be gone. She was afraid of sounding petulant, so she let the tears come instead of fighting them.

"I want it to be easy."

"Easy, huh? Well, then we'll have to start by getting rid of your kids."

"That's not funny, Charles! They had a real father who didn't give a shit about them. They survived because they had each other, but I can't stand... They're wonderful kids! I don't have any trouble with them! They just go along—sometimes it's miraculous to me the way they make their way through life. They need to know that I'm there, but they... Teddy leading and Walden following, they just... It seems to me that if you really loved me, you'd love my kids, too."

"This week?" Charles asked after a moment. "Anna threw me out of the house this week so this week I have to love your kids?"

"Oh, Charles!" She threw herself into his arms, blubbering. "It's no good, I love you too much, I mean it! You know what to say to me even when you're full of shit! I can't stand it! I don't want to love you this way, not more than one night a week! I don't trust it! Nothing good will come of it, I know it, I know it!"

He allowed her to continue mining this rich vein for a while, moving only once—to close the door so that they were really alone in the dark room. Finally she wound down and sat huddled against him. He moved around her to turn on the bedside light.

"No light," she said dully.

"Oh? I won't love you in the light, right? Red eyes. How could anyone love a woman with red eyes. And she's senile, for Christ's sake!"

She began hitting his chest and he began to laugh, and then they were fighting and tumbling together, and soon they were making love, and it was fine, if not one of the great times, then certainly well above the poverty line. The only difference between this time and numerous others was that while Charles fell asleep as he always did, Lulu didn't have to struggle to stay awake. She didn't seem to have any choice in the matter.

16

"**I**'VE BEEN THROUGH my prior life this summer," Dawn said with a grin. Tanned and trim, she wore white pants and a T-shirt that said TRURO. She sat down in the chair facing the doctor.

"Boston, Vermont, Truro...Truro is where my Aunt Nell goes in August. My mother's sister. Their maiden name was Lewis."

"Tell me." The doctor smiled.

"I love it. Practically the first thing after hello. It makes me know I'm home again." Dawn shifted in her chair. "God, I love you. Let me just look at you for a minute. You have the deepest tan I've ever seen. You get much darker than I do, don't you, but I'm pretty dark for a blond. Right?"

"Indeed."

"Don't be impatient. I'll tell you pretty soon. There's

plenty, and I won't have any trouble with it. It's all too interesting."

But she stood, walked to the window, looked into the playroom and returned to the window before settling down in the chair.

"My mother was Jewish. So my father copied Vera, whatever, down to that last detail. I was crazy about Nell. This adorable little lady with curly white hair. Married to a doctor. She's in her fifties, maybe sixty. He's older but they're both very lively. They jog on the beach and play tennis and all that. He was a widower, his kids grown, when she met him. She married late. He didn't want to have more kids and she never cared to have any... There were four sisters. In my mother's family, I mean. Nell said she'd show me pictures when I go to Boston. She lives a few blocks from the house where I was born. She knows the people who own it now. She's going to take me there. That feels delicious and scary at the same time."

"Can you talk about it?"

"Not yet. Wait a minute. There was something I wanted to say and you made me lose it." Silence. "Anyway, there were four sisters. My mother was the oldest. Nell's a year and a half younger. I don't remember the next one but she's successful in business. A broker, maybe. She never married but she has a lot of boyfriends, even now. She's the one Nell's not close to. It wasn't that hard to find Nell, you know. The people who bought the house in Roxbury from her and her sisters still live there. I didn't go, I called them. Nell's very close to the youngest sister. She lives in L.A., but they talk on the phone every week. Rosalie was a Rockette when she was younger. Do you know what that is?"

"Yes."

"Rosalie's been married six times. Nell says she's bright but scatterbrained, never developed herself. My father had Nell and her mother to visit after my mother died, and brought me to their house. But then Vera...Nell thought it was obvious that Vera didn't want to have anything to do with them, and they were scattered all over the country by that time anyway...I wanted to sit here so I could see your reactions. But you're hardly having any."

The doctor smiled. "Well, then, maybe you'd like to lie down."

"Oh, very tricky...It's no big deal lying down, actually. I mean, I don't have any resistance to the idea, I just"—she gave a little laugh—"I just don't want to do it, yet...Jack is staying with me until Polly gets back. He couldn't come to the Cape with me because of his job. I missed being able to talk about what was going on. I asked Lillian if she'd mind if he sort of moved in for a while. She wasn't all that keen on the idea. I don't know, it seems to me if I had a record of who had the most men around last year...Anyway, she said okay until Polly gets back and real life begins." Dawn yawned. "If I lie down now, I'll fall asleep."

"I don't mind."

"You don't?"

"It seems to me you often take a nap when you've been away and come back."

"Hmm. Maybe it's that when I was younger, I'd be so relieved that I had made it in one piece that I'd just collapse. Maybe I'm more grown up and it's not so frightening to me when you're away. Doesn't that make sense?"

"Maybe," the doctor said.

"But what?" Dawn asked.

"Well, how would you've felt today if I hadn't been here?"

"Are you kidding? I'd have felt terrible. I have a lot to tell you."

"Well then, wouldn't it have made sense for you to have flopped down on the couch and relaxed?"

"No, because I was too full of what I needed to tell you. I had a sense of urgency about it."

"Which part?"

"Come on, Dr. Shining Field, give me a chance. I haven't even told you half of it yet."

"What I'm suggesting is that you not only want to tell me what you've learned but control the flow of it. Keep it relatively free of your own associations."

"But I just got here!" Dawn protested. "I'm not ready to plunge into the moat!" Dawn whistled. "I can't believe I said that. I haven't thought of the moat in ages. I haven't even been having those dreams. I'm not having any dreams at all. The moat... The moat must be my own unconscious. I don't want to know what's in there right now." An uneasy laugh. "When I said that, I thought, now I can go lie down. But I didn't... You know, I think I feel possessive of all this stuff about my family. They are mine, after all. I know I never would've known them if it weren't for you, but that doesn't mean... Oh, God, I'm such an ingrate. You led me by the hand till I found them, and now all I can think of is that you look as though you belong to them more than I do. You're taller, but you all have that look I love. That dark Jewish look. If I put you and them and Tony in one room..."

"Yes?"

Dawn burst into tears. "Oh, God, I can't believe this. I can't believe I'm such an idiot. I hate myself. I really do." But she stopped crying fairly soon. "Do you believe me?"

"I think that there's a lot going on," the doctor said. "I certainly believe that you're jealous of this new group your mind has created—Tony, Nell, the other Lewises, and me."

"The Conspiracy," Dawn said with a giggle. "You're all part of a dark conspiracy."

"And a moat."

"Doesn't sound as if I should be jealous at all. Right now I don't even feel as though I am."

"Oh?"

Silence.

"Are you trying to trick me?"

"Into what?"

"I don't know."

"Into becoming part of the conspiracy?"

"What is the conspiracy, though?"

"*You* tell *me*."

"Oh, God, I don't know. I told you. It's a conspiracy of dark-haired women."

Silence.

"My mind's a blank."

"Try lying down."

After a visible struggle with herself, Dawn moved to the couch.

"All right. Now what? How come you're pushing me so hard, anyway? You don't usually do that."

"I guess I think it's time."

"Time for what?"

"Time to push you."

"Push me where? Into the moat? Thanks a lot. That's just what I need while I'm finding my mother's family...to be shoved into this...dark slimy place. Full of shit and crocodiles."

"What else?"

"Oh, I don't know...Fishes, I guess...Did you hear what I said? Fishes, instead of fish...like a little girl...Some frogs, maybe. Dead birds. Yuk. That's something I never thought of before."

"Tell me about them."

"I can't. It's too awful. They're dead. Crushed. Bloody. Feathers sticking out all over them. Filthy...No wonder I'm not having dreams. This is awful. I don't think I can stay lying down."

"Try."

"All right, but then I'll have to—I think I'm sick."

"Can you talk about that?"

"I'll gag."

"What do you find so sickening?"

"The crushed bird. Oh, God, I think I'm going to throw up!"

"Have you eaten in the past hour or two?"

"No. Around eleven."

It was three-thirty.

"I doubt that you'll throw up. Why don't you take a chance?"

Dawn sat up. She was angry. "You think I'm just concerned with the rug? Do you know how it feels to throw up? Anyway, it must be almost time for me to go."

"We have more than fifteen minutes left."

"I can't believe you're all that eager to have me be sick."

"I was thinking," the doctor said, ignoring this last. "You began with your fear that you were out of the conspiracy and moved to your fear of being pushed into it. Into the moat, at any rate, and we know they're linked."

"Mmm. But they're not the same thing."

"How are they different?"

"I don't know. I guess the conspiracy is about the conscious part. Being one of a group of women, looking like each other. Being left out is lonely because you're shut off from the people in the world who could really understand you. They think you're different so they won't let you in. The moat is the unconscious part, all the dark, terrible stuff that can swamp you. The stuff that made my mother kill herself. Do you realize that I haven't even begun to tell you about my mother?"

But first there was something else important. Polly hadn't returned. Two days earlier, Lillian had telephoned Polly and reached her mother, who had been polite but not overly communicative. Polly wasn't at home now, her mother had said, but she had a plane ticket for the following day that she might use. Lillian felt that they shouldn't call again, but if Polly didn't arrive by the weekend, Dawn was going to try. Although she spent most of the next session talking about her mother and her mother's family, much of what she said led her back to her anxiety about her friend.

As a young girl, Miranda Lewis had been high-strung and difficult, at war with her mother and sisters—most particularly with Nell, who followed her in line. Miranda had hated their mother with a vengeance, giving love and obedience only to their father. If it was their mother who pushed all four girls toward some form of achievement, it was their father whose favorite Miranda believed herself to be and whom she wanted to please. It was her father who felt that her talent was serious and encouraged her to study in New York...at Cooper Union...Could the doctor believe that Dawn had nearly transferred to her mother's school without even knowing it? Miranda had written to her father every day while she was at school in New York.

Nell had referred to their mother as "a tough old bird," marvelous in her way, if you could take her way, but hard. Each of the girls had been told that she was an unwanted baby and at some point treated to stories of her mother's attempts at self-abortion. It was in fact their father, a tailor, who provided the warmth and steadiness in the girls' lives.

But during Miranda's second year at Cooper Union, their father died suddenly of a burst appendix.

Miranda had her first breakdown the following year, and although she didn't have another for a long time, she was never again the spirited young woman she'd been.

In the period after Miranda was released from the hospital, when she wasn't yet capable of much activity, she and Nell grew close. In this period, Miranda literally couldn't bear the sight of their mother, whom she blamed for the death of their father as well as for crimes actually committed. Yet financial circumstances dictated that Miranda remain at home. Home was a good-size frame house in Roxbury with a back staircase that led directly to the second story and a separate apartment. Nell was able to persuade their mother to live downstairs with Rosalie (Alice had already moved to Chicago) while she and Miranda lived upstairs.

Miranda never returned to Cooper Union. When she was sufficiently recovered, she took a sales job at Filene's, where she remained for some years to the chagrin of their ambitious mother. At Filene's, Miranda met and fell madly in love with a man named Frank Barnwell, an executive of the company and a married man with two children. Their affair lasted for many years, although there were interruptions. Nell had never met Frank Barnwell, but her impression was that the relationship had a somewhat sadomasochistic nature. Nell had no evidence. It was just a feeling. There would be conflicting statements about Frank's availability from week to week; insinuations about leaving his wife followed by reports of yet another second honeymoon.

There Nell had stopped herself and switched to Gordon.

It was during a period when Miranda appeared to be teetering at the edge of another breakdown that Gordon Henley entered an art class she was attending and was smitten with her and her work.

Miranda hadn't mentioned Gordon, so when she

told Nell she was going to a movie with someone from class, Nell assumed it was a pal. When Gordon showed up, she still assumed that. Nell remembered clearly the moment when Gordon walked into the house, an incarnation of golden youth. Terribly young, perhaps twenty-two at the time, but with the beauty of a Greek statue.

"I have never seen such a beautiful boy in my whole life," Nell had told Miranda the next morning.

She never forgot those words because they—or something else to which she hadn't a clue—altered again the relation between herself and her sister. If Miranda was jealous, that jealousy was doubly strange. Not only did Nell have no designs on Gordon nor Gordon any interest in her (other than the support she might give Miranda), but there was no sign that Miranda cared about Gordon. During Nell's remaining time in the house (the following year she would meet Dr. Litsky and move to St. Louis, where they would remain for more than ten years), she was not allowed to lay eyes on Gordon. Nor did Miranda speak of him except to say things like, "He's a sweet boy, but the last thing in the world I'd do would be to marry him." When Miranda finally went to live with Gordon in the brownstone he'd bought "for her," it was because Frank Barnwell had gotten himself another mistress; she'd had another breakdown and was unable to work; and she couldn't face the alternative, returning to her mother's home from the hospital.

Nell didn't see her sister again, although they were in touch by phone when Miranda, pregnant and distraught, was deciding whether to have an abortion.

"Once in a while I get the creeps," Dawn said after

a pause. "At places where I did something she did. The abortion...Cooper Union's not such a big deal, it's a natural place to go if you want to be an artist, but...The way she was about her father sounds like me with Gordon. Not wanting to have anything to do with her mother. Not that we both didn't have good reasons. Her mother sounds like a monster, and my mother...well, in a sense she really *didn't* exist for me...At least, not the way a mother's supposed to exist...*for her baby*...I must've been angry with her, that was why I didn't want her to exist in my mind. I didn't want her to be important after what she did. But at least...it didn't have anything to do with me. It wasn't that I was some kind of rotten baby. She knew she shouldn't have a baby. Women have to want babies to...I never really had a lot of women friends, girlfriends, whatever...I had them, but not close. Some would've been more friendly if I'd encouraged them...You know, I really like Lillian, and I was upset when she got all jealous, but the truth is, What's-his-name, he really did flirt with me and ask me out later on, so I guess she was right to be jealous. It wasn't insane, like Miranda's jealousy about Gordon, if that's what it was. I suppose we can be friends as long as we're not in competition for the same guy...Maybe that's one reason to get married. You've got your guy and your friend's got her guy and you can relax and have a good time. At least until the end of the world ...or boredom...sets in...Nell told me my mother never had a single girlfriend. First she had her father, then she had Frank Barnwell, and Gordon...and then..."

"Yes?"

An unhappy little laugh. "And then she was dead...I think I was relieved when I saw that she was sick all along. Not that I thought she got sick from being married, but..."

"But?"

"I don't know. Maybe I thought giving birth to me did her some damage. I mean, it *did*, because she never painted another picture from the day she became pregnant with me. I've checked now. I've been through every one of the pictures..." Dawn began to cry. "She never did another painting or drawing. That was the end of her life." She wept. "When I think of the woman who made those paintings, lying there like a...like a lump of wet clay...not even wet...dry...but soft...I don't know...Mavis said my mother never cried. She just lay there on the bed all day...like Polly."

Abruptly, Dawn sat up.

"What is it?" the doctor asked.

"I just had an *immediate* sense—About the possibility—I don't want to say it—I don't know what I would do if Polly killed herself. If suddenly she wasn't there...I think it would destroy me. I'm very frightened."

"Tell me."

"I feel the way I felt when Tom Grace left me. Not after. As awful as that was, it wasn't as bad as the dread. The dread and then the emptiness...I suppose a parting is a kind of death. Once you know what it means to have someone disappear...I don't know what I felt when my mother disappeared...I don't know if I could feel that she was the one I came out of, out of all the people in the room. But I

must've known something... I must've felt her there
... large, warm, gentle... I didn't know she was depressed, I probably just felt her, soft and gentle...
That's it, isn't it... I didn't know, but I *felt*. I felt her
with me and then I didn't. There isn't a word for not
being able to feel someone anymore the way there is
for not being able to see them... disappear.... I felt
her disappear... This warm, soft, sort of living pillow that I was attached... Oh, God!" A silence, then:
"My mother, my father, Mavis, Tom Grace, Polly... It's
all the same isn't it... After the first death there is no
other..."

*

Dawn said at her next session that it was the first
time she'd ever said those words without seeing them
in the italic print she'd used at the bottom of the
lithographs.

*

In the ensuing weeks, Dawn was composed but
depressed—or sad, as she and the doctor preferred
to call it. They agreed that this sadness was what
she'd spent a good deal of her life warding off, and
Dawn said she could endure the feeling if it didn't
grow worse and if she could keep up with her work.

Polly returned to school two weeks late with special
permission to begin classes. Dawn was relieved, although Polly wasn't certain she would complete the
year. It was difficult for Polly to think of giving up
her life in New York. On the other hand, she seemed

to feel better back home. She had a suitor there, a businessman she knew because he was the accountant for her father's business. He was thirty-six years old, divorced, no children. Polly said she was comfortable with this man in a way that she didn't remember being since she was a little girl. He had limitations, of course. That was what he *was*, a nice, stable *businessman* with no interest in art or ideas. But what did that matter, compared to feeling all right when she was with him?

That was the way Polly had put the question to Dawn, who was dubious about the lasting quality of the bargain Polly was making. On the other hand, she could now see the extent to which her own anticipation of disaster, not only with Polly but with Tom Grace, had been based on her first terrible losses, and the weight of her friend's depression on her own life had lessened considerably.

Dawn began to get acquainted with girls in school who'd been around but who she'd assumed didn't want to know her. She grew restless. She found herself withdrawing from Jack. Not that he wasn't interesting on his own subjects, but when she tried to talk about what was on her mind—her mother, Polly, the analysis—he became dumb. The most casual conversation with girls she knew brought forth better responses on personal matters.

Jack's inability to identify with her in any way had somehow made her self-conscious with him. Not just about her conversation, but about her body. She found herself feeling vulnerable in front of him when she was naked. Wanting to hide. His failure of understanding had made him a stranger to her. She felt nothing but relief that he had to spend more time at his own apartment now that Polly had returned.

ᕲ

Dawn grew close to a girl named Jessica Rubinstein who lived on West End Avenue and walked to school most days. Jessica was an art history major, a year younger than Dawn but "she seems much older and smarter, the way New York people do." Partly because of her need to get away from Jack, Dawn often slept at Jessica's when they'd been talking till all hours.

Dr. Shinefeld made some attempts to get Dawn to talk about that need to get away from Jack, but Dawn felt it wasn't important.

"It's just that when I talk to women, they understand right away what I'm saying. Sometimes even before I say it."

"It seems to me," the doctor said, "that the first time you talked about being irritated with him, or bored, was after you discovered your mother's family. And the female conspiracy."

"Why does this have to be about male-female? Why couldn't it just be, this is a person with whom I have a lot less to talk about right now than that person? Jessica was just saying, of all the reasons we divide people into sexes, only a tiny percentage are directly related to sex. Don't you agree?"

"As you've put it, there's nothing to disagree with."

"Then why do you sound all hedgy and funny?"

"It's hard to say right now. If you keep talking, I'll let you know if something specific comes up."

"What was I talking about?"

"Boy-girl activities."

"Jessica has a brother who's two years older. When he reached the age of two, they gave him matchbox cars, and when she was two, they gave her a doll and a carriage. If they'd reversed it, she'd probably be able to put together a car engine and he might want to cook and take care of babies. Not that she wants to do either of those."

"Perhaps. But you've just reminded me of a young man I knew years ago in a small town in New England where I vacationed. He'd been raised by his mother, a shy, lonely woman who wanted a companion and confidant rather than a boy who would turn into a man and leave her, and by his grandparents. The boy was heterosexual but his sense of himself as a male was fragile and he needed perpetual reinforcement. He spent some time at our house and got into the habit of talking to me, perhaps because he'd heard somewhere that I was a doctor who listened. In any event, he said once that his only clear memory of childhood was of his third birthday, when his grandfather gave him a toy truck. *That was the first time I knew who I was,* were his words to me."

"Oh, God. Sounds just like anatomy is destiny. The old saw."

"Possibly," the doctor said. "Though when Freud said that he wasn't thinking of male and female. He was talking about the physical closeness of our sexual organs to the ones we urinate and move our bowels with. So that those functions are inevitably linked in our minds with sex from earliest childhood."

"Hey! That's pretty wild. I'll have to tell Jessica."

But she became restless, stood and stretched, walked to the door of the playroom.

"The first time I looked in here I didn't even see the cars and trucks. Of course that could be...except I wasn't indoctrinated, was I. Vera fiddled with cars. I chose to be like Tony...Or I didn't choose. I just was. Like I just was blond...You and Tony have dark hair but I'm a blond. People attach all kinds of meanings to it but when you just are one, because you were born that way..."

"Tell me."

"Well, it certainly doesn't mean the same thing to me as it does to other people. Men especially. Men think it means being some kind of sweet little dope. A baby, really. I guess babies are blonder than other people, generally. Blond and innocent. They call you babe sooner than if you're a brunette. Lillian and I compared notes on that once...I don't know...Blond means being like my father to me...Having something from him...Nell told me that when I first got out of the car in Truro she thought to herself, *My, what a beautiful girl*. Then she realized those were the exact words that got her into trouble with my mother years ago, and she didn't say it."

"So," the doctor said slowly, "to the men who like blonds, being a blond means being a baby, not a mama. But to you, it means—"

"Being a papa, not a mama," Dawn finished promptly... "Oh, God, sometimes I can't believe how simple things are."

"Do you think it's simple?"

"What could be simpler? I have a healthy father and a sick mother... I must've thought she was sick, anyway. After all, she was always just lying there... inert... some kind of inert gas... I don't mean that the way it sounds, I don't think ... What I mean is, not solid. I like solid things. That sounds dumb, but I know what I mean. Do you think children know the difference between liquid and solid? I guess they must have some sense... They can feel, after all, someone's there, not there... You touch something and it's nothing... a cloud of gas, a puddle of water— or it's solid. You can touch it. Hold onto it. It's a person. Or a thing. Sometimes I feel as though that's what I've been looking for my whole life. Just something solid to hold on to."

She began to weep and wept for some time.

"I didn't know I was saying something momentous until it was out. Now I can see my whole life flashing in front of my eyes as though that's all it's been about. This little blond baby trying to walk, teetering, like Susan's baby, always thinking she's going to fall, frantic to reach a solid place... And then the ocean... trying to reach some kind of shore... and then there's this crazy teenager cracking into a car. It sounds like a contradiction—wanting to be solid, wanting to break up—but it isn't really. There's no surer way to know you're solid than by breaking ... Liquid doesn't break, or gas... Losing Tony... I must've felt that I lost Vera, too. Vera was still in the house but the Vera was gone out of her. I think it must've been very frightening. She lost her spine, sort of, became a blob... She seemed like a different person entirely... You know, I'm not even sure when

I realized that Vera was a girl...A girl, that's funny. But that's what I'm talking about, girls and boys. Having a penis or not having one. I don't know when I found out that Vera didn't have one. Or what difference it made in my view of her. Maybe I never thought about it until Tony left her. No, that's not possible. Anyway, another picture's coming through while I'm saying I don't know."

"What's in the picture?"

"I don't want to tell you...Not that it's anything so awful. It just makes me uneasy because...it's so dark and I can't tell exactly what I'm looking at."

"Oh?"

"Mmm."

"Is it dark because it's nighttime?"

"Must be."

Silence.

"It's two figures. Grappling on the bed. Not making love. I don't know what they're doing...wrestling...This is making me very uncomfortable...I don't know...I think I'm making it up. Like the pictures I draw. Except when I draw, I feel as though I'm seeing something outside of me. This makes me uneasy because without a pencil in my hand...It's so amorphous. I feel as though if I let go with it, it could just take me over."

"It won't, though."

"I suppose they're both women. I can see the legs of the one on top, and they're all lean and muscular, like a man's, but that's what Vera's legs are like. A man's."

"How do you know it isn't a man?"

"Because I can see between her legs and there's

nothing there!" Dawn burst into tears. "This couldn't be real. It's not possible that something like that could've ... I think the whole scene's my imagination. Don't you think it's possible I imagined the whole thing?" She had stopped crying.

"Yes," Dr. Shinefeld said, "it's possible. Either now, or then. Or both."

"But even if I imagined it, it happened. In my mind. I saw it, or I thought I saw it ... I don't know if they were making love. I mean, they were, but you couldn't exactly call it ... I don't think it looked like it to me ... Vera was over Tony, but I don't know what she was doing, maybe sucking her—Oh, God, I don't think I can stand much more of this."

"Sure you can."

"I don't want to know what they were doing. I don't want to know about Vera."

"What don't you want to know about her?"

"That she hasn't got one either ... Oh, God!" Dawn sat up and turned to the doctor. "Sometimes I don't believe what goes on in this place."

The doctor smiled.

Dawn lay down again.

"I think I saw hers ... I mean, saw that she didn't have one ... after I saw Patrick's. I'm pretty sure his was the first one I ever saw, and I must've still thought Vera had one because I went home from school and Tony explained to me about males and females, and breasts and vaginas, and so on. I remember that she did that ... Is it possible that I still didn't know Vera was a female when I was six years old?"

"I think so."

"I think so, too. After all, that's when I was having all the trouble about who was what at school. And she wasn't exactly a female, anyway. So what would they have told me, except....mmm...There are lots of funny things coming in here at the same time."

"Such as?"

"No. The first is too incredible. Anyway, I'm tired. Really tired. I don't think I can handle any more of this nonsense."

Silence.

"I was thinking about Patrick. We used to call him Paddy, not Patrick. His second name was Mason. Paddy Mason. It suddenly occurred to me...my town, the town in my dreams...Patterson...Oh, God, this is too...I don't believe how tired I am...I think the name changed a few times. Patrickson. Paddyson. Patterson. I'm not sure, but I think it kept changing, and then maybe I heard somewhere...Is there a poem about a town called Patterson? Or is it mentioned in a poem? I don't know when I started having those dreams, but the name of the town...It was always about Patrick...I don't believe this...What time is it? I'm exhausted. I feel as though I've been here forever."

17

THE LEASE on Charles's apartment would expire in November but was renewable on a monthly basis at nearly double what he'd been paying. Charles was articulate to the point of elegance in describing his sentiments about living full time in territory occupied by T. W. Juggernaut, slower to discuss the possibility that if they were going to stay together, they should look for a place that would be Theirs. Another step on the commitment gangplank. Lulu wanted Charles to want to take that step, but often thought he would be out of his mind if he did.

For where was the Lulu they had both known and loved? The powerful anchor of their lovely affair? Whose passion in bed had been matched only by the placidity of her person and the generosity of her perceptions? That Lulu often appeared to have retired to Girlfriend Heaven, leaving her body to some alien female whose anxieties were ignited by all those hyper mannerisms of her lover's that had once been welcome evidence of his life force; who was irritated by a sense of humor dominated by those same fecal materials that preoccupied her young sons (dirty jokes were their only meeting ground with Charles); who found in Charles's finickiness a declaration of her own inadequacies instead of a perpetual challenge to new heights; who couldn't believe, as she often told Charles, that she'd known him for two years without having an inkling that he went through apartments straightening up after the people he lived with, or that it was possible for him to spend three precious Saturday afternoons settling on the pattern of the sheets he must buy to supplement the supply in his sublet. His sloppiness of person had suggested to her mistress's senses a certain spiritual largesse; now that largesse appeared to extend to himself and his standards for the rest of the world to be more rigorous. This didn't prevent her from loving him as intensely as ever but she liked him, and herself, somewhat less.

After all, it was she who'd put on the rose-colored glasses to view him.

After all, she was the one who had changed.

In the context of a real life, her view of him was more critical; her devotion to his needs less than wholehearted; her patience with his antics finite.

Furthermore, she'd always suspected it was no accident she'd had a first husband who'd abandoned her body and a second who'd never inhabited her mind. Even in retrospect, both seemed less threatening than the energy mass that was Charles Herman, who

fter a day at the office was usually ready to screw,
lay tennis, take a long walk, or, failing to arouse
nterest in any of these, lead a tour of the inside of
is loved one's head. If Lulu's tolerance for humans
vith a vitality comparable to her own had increased
vith analysis and the passage of time, it was still true
hat her formative years had been spent largely
mong shadows, and she'd had a considerable dis-
ance to travel in this regard. There were times when
he felt certain she'd never make it to a point where
Charles was a suitable companion for her; other
imes when she was convinced her very fears were a
rick she played to deny herself the pleasure of
aving him.

His own patience with her was considerable, but
hat, too, she used against him. If he could stand the
vay she was behaving now (certainly *she* couldn't),
hen it was because he needed to live with a harri-
lan. As soon as she calmed down he would leave
er. If she didn't calm down, she would turn into the
arridan waiting at home while he spent evenings
vith some loving new mistress.

Moreover, *why was he letting her be this way?*
He could stop her if he wanted to.
Couldn't he?
Or was this the way it was going to be?
"It's too soon, Charles," she said. "We need more
ime to get used to each other. At least it's an escape
atch when things are impossible here."

Charles now became certain that it was absurd to
pend $2000 a month instead of $1000 for an apart-
nent that had been worth $500 to begin with.

"Let's not turn this into a big deal by expecting to be one," he said.

But when she suggested that they try emptyin out the storage room and turning it into an office retreat for him, he pointed out that the room adjoine Teddy's. What kind of retreat did she expect him t make in the middle of the Gaza Strip? And indeed on the Sunday night when the boys returned from Nathan's to find the storage room full to the ceilin with cartons and the hallway narrower by half wit the same, Teddy marched into the living room in fury and asked Charles in a shaking voice where h got off doing this to their apartment, it wasn't a though he was their father.

"I know I'm not your father!" Charles shoute back. "I don't want to be your fucking father! I jus want you to treat me like a human being!"

Teddy was civil for two days after that.

But most of the time Charles refused to engag Teddy at all, saying that he dealt with infantile neu rosis all day and wasn't prepared to handle it a night. This hurt Lulu, who could not view her ow children merely as two prime examples of infantil neurosis. It evoked memories of their own father' rejection of them and made her wonder whether i was unreasonable to hope that a man who lived wit her sons might have good feelings for them. Was i possible that she could continue to love a man wh did not love her children?

Anna and Kid Psycho were going to Anna's father' ski lodge in Aspen for Christmas. Charles's eyes stil grew moist when subjects like skiing in Aspen o

surfing in Hawaii arose. Anna's parents would be on
a cruise at that time and Anna asked Charles if he
would take the children. Of course he consented. He
pointed out that it was time that his children met
Lulu, anyway, and she pointed out that it was *he* who
had kept *her* a secret until now. Charles assured Lulu
that any woman who'd lived with T. W. Juggernaut
for all these years would undoubtedly find his children easy to be around. The boys would be easy on
her because she was a woman, and Victoria—well,
Victoria was a sugar plum.

Perhaps. But the only example Lulu had been able
to find among her friends, her friends' friends and
acquaintances of a little girl's succumbing rapidly to
Daddy's girlfriend's charms had been one in which
the real mother was so abusive as to make any other
woman seem like a fairy godmother to the child.

It would all work out.

But here? In this apartment? All those extra children for ten straight days?

How come only his children were extra? Charles
wanted to know.

Lulu paced around the bedroom, to which they
now retired at nine o'clock when Charles was there
since Charles had been unable to convince Teddy
and Walden that it would be suitable for them to
retire to theirs. Panic was spreading within her, a
stony mass that threatened the stomach and lungs,
settling in the latter to impede her breathing even as
it cloned itself in her head to produce an ache so
severe that it would blind her if she opened her eyes
so she could see where she was walking.

"C'mere and lie down," Charles said.

She sat down on top of a pile of clothes on one of the two chairs in the room, the other being full of Charles's papers.

"What'll we do if the weather is awful? Snow would be all right, preferably the first snow of the year. Then they could spend all day in the park."

And the house would be full of wet parkas, wet boots, wet...

Lulu opened her eyes; she'd never lived with a man who didn't think she was impervious to wet boots. She *was*. She *had* been.

"The Mayers offered us their place in East Hampton," Charles reminded her.

"Please," Lulu said. "I can just picture the seven of us stuck together in that house."

"A marvelous image."

"At least in New York we can make some plans. We have resources... I can always jump out of a window ...or push you out of it."

"Meanwhile, come on over here and lie down."

"I don't *feel* like lying down. I don't feel like fucking and I don't feel like being analyzed."

It had been shouted in anger but suddenly the anger imploded and she was crying.

Dr. Herman waited.

"Mommy? Are you all right?"

Teddy was on the other side of the door. If she asked Teddy a question when he was two feet away, he didn't hear her. But an argument with Charles through a closed door at the other end of the apartment brought him in a flash.

No. I'm not all right. Charles is beating me with whips and chains.

"Of course I'm all right," she snapped. "Go back to bed."

"Why are you crying?"

"It's none of your business, damn it!"

She put her hands over her mouth as though she could push back the words. There was silence on the other side of the door. Charles was grinning. She would have yelled at him, too, if she'd been certain that Teddy was gone. Instead she threw herself onto the bed and curled up on her side like a fetus someone was trying to abort. When Charles made a move toward her she shrugged him off.

"You don't understand *anything*," she said to the man whose understanding had bound her to him more tightly than blood or sex could have.

"All right," Charles said, "then let's just fuck."

"I don't want to," she said. "I don't want you inside my body."

And I don't want your fucking kids inside my apartment.

"I suppose," Charles said, "I can get my body out of here altogether. If you really want me to."

"I don't really want you to," she said after a while, her voice muffled by blankets and tears.

"All right," he said. "Then let's think of a way out."

"Maybe," she said, "we could talk about work. Not about mine. Let's talk about yours. Tell me something stupid you've done recently. Or at least something I might be able to make a useful comment about and stop feeling like an infant and an incompetent... Tell me what's going on with Louis Pomerantz."

"Oh, Christ," Charles said. "Lulu does it again."

Louis Pomerantz... Well, Louis was getting into

older women (Louis's phrase) and maybe it was good that the kid was getting laid, although the idea of the analysis, of course, had been to get him to put some psychic distance between himself and a mother who had dominated her sons by unfailing kindness. He and Louis had gotten back onto some sort of even keel, but the trust wasn't there and in some crucial sense, the analysis was over. It had occurred to Charles more than once that it might be appropriate to bare himself to Louis to the extent of explaining that events in his own life had caused him to make that decisive error. And then—Charles was embarrassed, defensive—he simply couldn't do it. The risk seemed too great. Maybe if it had been a female. He simply couldn't leave himself "open" in that way to "another male animal." (Charles had confessed once that it was impossible for him to be in a room for any length of time with another male without speculating on their relative sexual prowess.)

Lulu suggested that Charles might be able to bring up the mistake in the time-honored context: Analysts are human, too, not the omniscient characters of the patients' imaginations. For a while they explored this and other possibilities. Then something reminded Lulu of her patient Rosalind Fox, whose dominant symptom was bulimia, which the girl persisted in calling anorexia nervosa—a so much more romantic-sounding name—though the weight Rosalind maintained through a combination of perpetual eating and self-induced vomiting hovered around the 300-pound mark. Far from thinking she was obese, Rosalind saw herself as a sort of Camille figure, felt that she was wasting away on the rare occasion when the scale went down a notch below 290 pounds, and couldn't be convinced that her life (not to speak of her relationship with her skinny boyfriend) would not be endangered by further loss. This reminded Charles that he had briefly treated a sixteen-year-old anorectic homosexual boy whose stated ambition it was to play Camille. And so on...

The emotions raked up in a passionate affair make pale events in the world beyond the lovers' room, and until now, Charles and Lulu had remained their own favorite subject. Now it was time to move on. If that seductive interior world in which they plied their trade would remain more compelling than the one the newspapers claimed was out there, it was essential that they bring the force of their respective intelligences and energies to bear on that world.

Lulu told Charles about her plan to write a paper on changing sexual mores that would in itself be a sort of antidote for the seriousness of analytic work. Charles immediately picked up on the idea and pointed out that some of those experiences with anorectics could tie into such a survey, for food appeared to have become, for the sexually liberated young woman of the late twentieth century, what sex had once been to the sexually constricted young woman of the Victorian era.

"Marvelous," Lulu said, her eyes lighting up. "If her weight doesn't dictate that she starve herself entirely, the possibilities for eating are still..."

"Severely circumscribed," Charles filled in, and they went on like that, adding to and qualifying each other's ideas.

The guilt that had once attached itself in its mos
extreme form to masturbation now rested at th
bland door of the carbohydrates, most particularl
upon chocolate and the richer desserts. Where onc
it was feared that the indulgent would suffer from
the withering and dropping off of vital organs, swell
ing and protrusions were now the betraying symp
toms of the greedy. Oh, yes, and something called
cellulite, which always sounded as though it had
been isolated during cancer research.

The anorectic disorders were the twentieth centu
ry's abortion on demand for a large number o
young women to whom sex (or abortion) was no
more optional than three meals a day had once been
but whose time between fucking was dominated b
anxiety over what they'd last eaten, fear about which
craving would next overtake them, and concern ove
how they would avoid gaining weight when they had
(inevitably) binged on it.

Lulu and Charles were reminded of how wonder
ful life was when their brains worked in concert. The
paper became their modus operandi for dealing with
situations in which one of the resident paranoia
threatened to destroy an evening or leave a residue
too bitter to be absorbed.

"I still don't see," Lulu might say, "how five chil
dren and a hundred and seventeen cartons can find
happiness in this apartment in what might be terri
ble weather for a period of ten straight days."

"Did I ever tell you," Charles might reply, "abou
the partner in Anna's firm who eats at the Four
Seasons every day and never orders anything but the
veal paillard?"

"Oh, Charles," Lulu would say, twirling a particularly inviting lock of his remaining hair around her pinky, "I'm too frightened. I'm frightened of how you'll be with me if the whole thing's a disaster."

"Given the way your mind works," Charles would reply, "that's perfectly reasonable. After all, you love me so much it scares you. And you trust me so little it scares *me*."

18

DAWN WAS BORED with Jack Stewart. She had to admit she was treating him rather badly. If she hadn't had her female friends, she might spend a lot of time with him and never know what she was missing, but as it was... Well she was just somewhat "turned off."

"Who turned you off?"

"Not exactly turned off, but not *on*. I don't feel close to him. I don't want to undress in front of him, or turn him on... There's a lot of stuff roiling around inside me and I can only let it out here..."

"What's the stuff that's roiling around?"

"I don't know. That dead bird has been haunting me... When I was in grade school one of the first pictures I ever drew was a bird. Not a pigeon; that's a city bird. A robin redbreast, perched on a tree branch, singing. Tony hung up the picture in the kitchen. I haven't thought of it in years. Now he turns up, a dead pigeon in a moat. I suppose he got killed someplace else and then dropped into the moat... I did another picture of Tony in a beautiful red velvet dress that she framed and put in her bedroom. I've been avoiding Tony since the summer. I guess you know that. I don't know why I'm talking about her now. Oh, yes, the dress. The red dress and the robin redbreast... Oh, God. Tony's breast! I don't think I can stand this... Tony used to say to me, *Do you want to ruffle through my feathers and finery, dear?* On a rainy day, or if I was sad, she'd ask if I wanted to go through her fathers—I mean, her feathers and finery. In the workroom where she did her sewing there were two chests. One with six big drawers, full of fabric. Cottons for curtains and summer dresses. Those French provincial cottons you see all over now. Woolens. One year she made Vera a tweed jacket with leather elbow patches. She had two machines, a regular old Singer and a heavy professional job she got from a factory in Brooklyn that was going out of business. She made our winter coats on it. The other chest had lots of small drawers with different collections. Buttons—mother-of-pearl, glass octagons with flowers trapped in them, leather, brass, fabric-covered ones from dresses. Another drawer had collars. Lace and piqué. Then zippers, ribbons, little balls of wool left over from knitting and crocheting, rolled-up fabric belts, patches, woven initials and insignias, everything from the Girl Scouts to the Four-F Club—I mean, the Four-H Club—to a couple of military ones. I don't know where she got those."

"Four-F and four-H," the doctor murmured.

"Four-H was something to do with the Clean Plate Club. It was during the Second World War. Tony told me. The stuff in the top drawers was the best. I couldn't reach it when I was little. Pins, brooches, hat pins, costumey stuff. The other was the most precious of all. A couple of rolls of strung sequins, gold and silver, handwoven French ribbons with pictures. One had lords and ladies dancing around, like on a frieze. Old lace. Ropes and tassels. Peacock feathers. Silk flowers. When I graduated from grade school she wove the stem of a yellow silk rose into my ponytail and somehow it got lost. It was one of the tragedies of my childhood... Do you realize I haven't seen Tony since last Christmas? When I get close to her I get scared and I move back again. She doesn't even know Jack. Not that there's much to know right now... Maybe it's something about Boston. Maybe the combination of Tony and Jack makes me feel as though a web is closing around me... They have nothing to do with each other except that they care about me. I guess it's Boston... You know, ever since I started talking about Tony I've been thinking, all the pleasures of my childhood came from this woman I've been avoiding like the plague."

"What kind of plague do you think you're avoiding?"

"Oh, God, I don't know... the plague of women! It's not a conspiracy, it's a plague. I enjoy women more than I ever did but I'll tell you something, if that's what being a woman is, you can have it!"

"If *what's* what being a woman is?"

"Being sick and messed up! Being operated on! I know I've been through this before but... Men don't get sick. Vera was never—All right, Vera isn't a man, but she's like a man. And look at my mother and father. When someone's sick it's a woman. At least men don't talk about what they have, and it's nothing to do with being a man. They hurt themselves at work or they break a leg or they have a heart attack. Something connected to being human ... Why aren't you arguing with me? Does what I'm saying make sense?"

"It seems to make sense to you."

"But is it true?"

"Is what true?"

"That women are sicker than men?"

"I don't believe so."

"Then why do we *think* we are? It's not just about physical ailments. It's about shrinks, too. Every girl I know has been to some kind of shrink or thinks she ought to be going. Jessica has a feminist therapist. She sounds very pleasant, actually. Soothing. Like a warm bath. Much better than what goes on here. I came here four years ago thinking I was okay if I'd stop trying to crack myself up, and here I am feeling like a dead bird ... God, I feel angry right now. Backed into a corner. All fucked up ... Why is it only women who go to therapists? If Jack's in a bad mood and you ask him what's wrong he'll say he wanted to play racquetball and the weather's rotten or he's worried that Reagan's going to get the Republican nomination next year. If you ask Jessica or me, we'll say our heads are messed up, we don't know why. Men are always looking on the outside to solve problems and women are always looking into our own ... our own heads. I was going to say ... You're not going to try to tell me that it's all about having a vagina!"

Silence.

"Are you trying to reduce my whole life to whether I have a vagina?"

"I've barely spoken. You've been talking."

"But we were talking about a lot of different things, weren't we? About Jack? About going through Tony's drawers?...Oh, God, I can't stand this...Do you remember the time I said something was only in my mind and you asked how I thought it got there? I think about that often...You know, when I'm away from here I split myself into You and Me, and if I think I'm doing something fishy, the You person questions the Me person. The difference is, the You-Me doesn't know as much as you, so she's not so likely to say things I don't want to deal with."

"What have I said that you're not ready to deal with?"

"Nothing, really," Dawn said after a while. "It's what came out of my own mouth that I'm not ready to deal with. But it only came out because you were questioning me because I was doing something fishy with Jack."

"Something fishy?"

"Mmm." Dawn laughed. "Squirming around like a fish on a hook. All wriggly and uncomfortable, not wanting him to see what's inside me...The problem is *inside* me, you know. It's not that I don't have a penis...It's more that people think I'm something I'm not...It's as though when I take off my clothes my insides are exposed. I feel horribly vulnerable. And Jack...if Jack understood what it was like to be a woman, the way I think I understand a little what it's like to be a man, then I could be a naked woman in front of him without feeling uncomfortable. I'd feel safe. If he understood he would be careful. Not that he isn't careful, but he doesn't even know that care is *required*, he just happens to be . . . Oh, God, I feel very stupid right now. I feel as though I've been angry with him for all these things he hasn't even done. All these feelings about being a woman came up and I . . . I can't tell you how badly I've been treating him. I've been sitting around wishing Lillian would steal him away from me so I wouldn't have to get rid of him myself!"

⟳

That was on Friday afternoon. On Monday morning as the doctor walked toward her office, an agitated, disheveled Dawn Henley scrambled out of a car that had been double-parked near the building entrance.

"I have to talk to you," she said, her voice trembling.

"Has something happened?"

"Yes."

The doctor paused to consider. Dawn's appointment was for three, but the girl was too upset to be driving around until then.

"When is your first class?"

'I'm not going to school.'

"Let's get into the car and talk for a moment. Then we'll see. You can park and do whatever you might find tolerable until your regular session."

"It's Jack," Dawn said when they were seated inside. "When I got home Friday...I was going to make a nice dinner. I bought wine. I was going to apologize, ask him if he wanted to come to Tony's for Thanksgiving. I got home around six. I knew something was wrong as soon as I walked in. Polly was in the kitchen and she looked funny when she saw me, but I thought it was about the way she was feeling. I tried to call Jack for the second time but there was still no answer so I went to Lillian's room. I could hear talking, laughing...I knocked on the door and Lillian called to come in and I opened the door...and he was in there with her!" Dawn wept, her head against the back of the car seat.

"Were they in bed?"

"No. Yes. I mean, they were on the bed but not in it. It didn't matter. I could tell just from the way she acted."

"She might be defensive even if they—"

"Please. He admitted it without blinking his eyes. I guess he wanted me to know...God, I hate men. How're you supposed to know what to do when they're mad if they don't even tell you they're mad?" This brought a fresh outburst, which eventually subsided.

"I have to go up," the doctor said. "You can sit here for as long as you need to, until you feel comfortable. Then...is this a rental car?"

Dawn nodded.

"Well, you can return the car. And I'll see you at three."

"I don't think I can live without him," Dawn said.

"I think you can," the doctor told her. "But I don't think you should assume that you'll have to."

∽

"I guess I don't have to tell you how utterly I've taken him for granted," Dawn said when she returned, somewhat subdued but still miserable. "I know you tried to get me to talk about what I was doing, but I assumed it didn't really matter. I was going through some rites of my own and when I was finished he'd just be there, waiting...I thought no one ever would leave me unless I needed him too much...I must be in love with Jack. Not In Love, maybe, but I surely...My life has gotten all wrapped up with his. Even when I'm running away from him he's in my life in some way. It's like the straws in a basket. You can't just pull out the straws that go one way and have something reasonable left...It certainly never crossed my mind that I loved him when I was being so awful."

She'd packed a small bag, determined to rent a car and go to Marbury. Before leaving, she'd met Jack in the hallway and just stared at him, unable to speak because she was determined not to cry. That was when he'd sort of shrugged and said he was surprised she was upset. He'd thought she wouldn't even know the difference.

"Did you tell him that wasn't so?"

Dawn shook her head. "What's the point? He's through with me."

"I'm not sure that when someone's through with

you, he moves one door down the hall. He was certainly very angry."

"He was right to be!" Dawn wailed. "I was awful! More awful than I let you know!" She cried bitterly. "I went to Vera's. I thought of Tony but I wanted to be where there weren't any men. It's as though...the more I admit to loving him, the more I hate men in general. I hate it when I even *say* I love him, whether or not it's true."

"You didn't like the idea much before, either."

"No wonder! Look what happened!"

"From loving him or from acting as if you didn't?"

"I just remembered a dream I had over the weekend," Dawn said after a while. "Vera has a new friend. I don't think it has anything to do with sex. She has her own house in Marbury. Her husband retired and they moved to Marbury and he died last year. She's all right, I guess. Dull...I think Tony and Vera are the love of each other's lives and they don't even *want* something like that to happen again...I'm glad Vera's found a friend, but I was sort of upset to find someone...extra...in the house when I got there Friday night...In the dream, I was in the bathtub. Or I *was* the bathtub. If I was in it, I was sitting the opposite of the usual way. With my back against where the faucets are supposed to be. It was one of those old-fashioned tubs with claw feet and a rolled edge. Tony has one in Boston but Vera had all modern plumbing installed in Marbury. Cavorting around the edge of the tub were these two tiny, beautiful, golden-haired twins...both boys...Beautiful...You know, I don't think I ever saw another little kid in my first few years of life...You know

how you see a movie on TV that you'd thought was
wonderful and you realize its original power came
from the size of the people on the screen? Bigger
than life? This was the opposite. I could focus everything on them because they were tiny. I was watching
them run along the edge, naked, doing somersaults,
then suddenly... they began to fly away somewhere
where I couldn't see them... At the same time as I
was trying to get them back, I began to drain. *I* was
emptying out instead of the tub. It was terrifying. I
was losing my own insides. I wish you could tell me
what that was about. I'm frightened of having the
dream again, but I couldn't bear never to see the
twins. I can't associate about draining. That's the end
of something, not a step along the way."

"Would you care to talk about the twins?"

"It made me so happy just to watch them. You
know who else had a bathtub like that? Gregory
Barnes. In Provincetown. It's funny, I haven't thought
about Gregory in a long time. That's who the twins
must be, of course. Gregory and my father. The two
beautiful blond boys. Complete unto themselves. Not
sexual but very beautiful. There was no sexual feeling in the dream."

"Oh?"

"Maybe they were just too little. The only part that
was sexual in a way, a bad way actually, is when I talk
about the drain... When the women's movement first
got to me... I was at Sidley already... and I heard
this business of getting a speculum and looking into
your own vagina, my first reaction was, No way. But
the truth is, it doesn't look all that bad once you get
used to the idea. It just looks... vulnerable. Terribly

soft. As though it could get hurt easily. Or it *was* hurt. Not that it hurts at all when you touch it. As a matter of fact, I was surprised...I don't know if I ever told you this...It was Tom Grace who taught me about my—Oh my God! How much time do I have? I can't believe I've forgotten about Jack!" She wept. "I feel as though the world's coming to an end. The real world and my inside world. The real world is Jack's. Politics. Computers. Law school. How was I supposed to tell he even noticed how I was being? ...My whole life's totally messed up and I don't know what to do about any of it!"

"Well," Dr. Shinefeld said, "you might begin by telling Jack how you feel."

"Are you kidding? What would I tell him? That I love him? I don't know if I love him or not. I only know I don't want to live without him. Is that love? I never feel about him the way I felt about Tom Grace. *Crazy* in love. But what I never had with Tom was this simple sense of contentment...I could never say that. Especially now. I'm much too angry."

"You could tell him you're angry first."

"How can I when I know he had good reason? I just think he went too far to get back at me."

"You could tell him that, too."

"I guess. But it isn't very appealing. I mean, where do we go from there?"

"That would depend partly on him."

"What if he tells me to—shove off?"

"Then I imagine you'll be unhappy."

"Unhappy! You make it sound like something reasonable."

"Tolerable. It certainly won't have the effect that it

would have if you were a baby and he abandoned you. Probably not nearly as much as when Tom Grace left."

"...On the other hand, what if he asks me...for some kind of commitment."

"What about that?"

Dawn arrived at the conclusion that she really wanted Jack to be committed to her but that she was less than willing to commit herself to him. What she couldn't bear was to surrender the hope of falling madly in love with some incredible man she hadn't even met yet. Someone with all of Jack's virtues and none of his drawbacks. A man with whom she could enter that extraordinary state she'd been in during those first months with Tom. It would be doing that condition an injustice to describe it as happiness. It was so much more intense than mere happiness. You might call it a state of grace. Of Grace. Why hadn't she thought of that before? In any event, how could Dawn, at the tender age of twenty-two, close off the possibility of being in that state again?

⌒

"I went straight to his apartment. I marched into his room and began yelling and crying. I told him he'd hurt me terribly and he asked what about the way I was acting? I tried to explain that it had to do with the analysis and he said if I wanted to spend time and money on all that crap that was my privilege but he didn't want to hear about it...What is it with men, anyway?"

For a while Dawn discoursed upon the question of

whether it was worth bothering with men when women were so much better. Then that train of thought was interrupted.

"When I called Lillian his revenge he said it was only seventy or eighty percent revenge, the rest was fun. That nearly made me crazy but I tried to be cool. I said if I were going to look around for someone else in that apartment, I'd pick Polly."

"Not my type," Jack had replied.

Dawn had told him it was humiliating to have to be someone's type, and Jack had informed her that she wasn't actually his type either, that her type tended to be a little turned off for his taste, although they were good to take on camping trips because they were game. Then she'd gotten upset at not being his type and he'd laughed and said maybe she was his type to look at, and then it had turned out she was human, although recently he'd begun to wonder. And then she had thrown a pillow at him and they'd had a pillow fight and then they had made love. She had slept at his place and planned to do the same tonight, going home to get clothes and books when Lillian wasn't around. Their lovemaking had been more intense than usual. Still not the way it had been with Tom. On the other hand, pretty good for the real world. As opposed to...

"To?"

"Oh, I don't know. It seems to me that for most of my life nothing that happens in the outside world has been as intense as what happens at home. Marbury. Dr. Seaver's office. Here. Tom Grace was the exception, but he also wasn't because...he was about you...Tom Grace...Maybe nothing like that will ever happen to me again...Even his name was special."

"Oh?"

"Sure. Grace is a very special kind of name, you know that. Aside from being a woman's name it means...Grace is what you say at the beginning of a meal..." (giggle giggle) "...if you happen to come from that kind of family. I didn't, of course, but in my family there was plenty of the other kind of grace...You know, something funny happened when I said that. I was talking about grace in the sense of elegance. But I wasn't thinking about Tony. Vera's the one with the extraordinary grace. Even now. Tony is lovely. Not ungraceful. But elegance...That's Vera's...I'm confused right now...Something's coming in here that's foreign to me...I don't know what to do with it...It's Vera. But it's a very sexual picture. Not male, not female...or I should say both. Extremely both. I don't think I can bear this."

"What is it you think you can't bear?"

"I'm very uncomfortable. Like being excited only...I think I'd better just go to the bathroom."

"Could you try to talk about it instead?"

"You know how tall she is, don't you? Close to six feet? Actually, in the picture I was seeing before she was even bigger. Her hair is loose. This...noble ...head with long blond hair but not in a braid—It's loose...over her shoulders...She's wearing a black silk kimono, or pajamas. With embroidery. Red and green fire-breathing dragons. It's not all closed in the front. I mean, it's not open but it's not closed either. I can see she has breasts. Usually, the way she dresses...Oh, God...I'm squirming...I'm looking up at her. It's too much. I feel excited in an awful way. I feel as though I want to make myself come but I can't do anything like that because I'm here. I feel like running out of here and finding Tom Grace. No, Jack. No, it's Tom I mean. I told you, physically Tom could have been a member of my family... Sometimes if you have to go to the bathroom you feel as if you're excited but you're not really. Or at least it goes away if you urinate. That's why I want to go. I don't like feeling this way... What I don't understand... I went through all this stuff with Dr. Seaver, about wishing Tony was out of the way so I could have Vera, and so on, but nothing like this ever happened to me there. It wasn't that I was holding it in. It wasn't there. It was more like when I was looking at the *Winged Victory*. My brain was full of feeling but it had nothing to do with the rest of my body... It's good I don't have to look at you and say things like that... Sometimes I need to see you, take you in, but now...

"Yes?"

"Maybe I think you'll get disgusted. You'll make that face and order me out of here. *Buzz off, Dawn, you're not supposed to be a lesbian. That's not what I'm treating you for*... That's not your face I was thinking of, that disgusted look. It's Vera's... God, I'm in some peculiar state where... Jack makes love to me and I come here and dream Vera's over me and I want... I don't know what I wanted her to do... Vera never even wanted me to be a lesbian. She wanted me to be straight. Get along in the world. She wanted to be a man, but she didn't want to be a lesbian because it was a sign of something...I'm exhausted. What time is it?"

They'd gone past the hour, though the next patient hadn't rung the bell.

Dawn stood up wearily and picked up her satchel. "What'm I supposed to do now?"

"What do you mean?" the doctor asked.

"Nothing," Dawn said. "I'll probably just go home and go to sleep."

℮

On Friday Dawn was frightened. She had gone from Dr. Shinefeld's to Jack's apartment, where she'd let herself in, then fallen into a deep, dreamless sleep from which he'd awakened her two or three hours later. Well, sort of awakened her. She'd been half-awake and in an extraordinarily aroused state and had ravished him. Or did she mean ravaged? Both, she guessed. She had never been so wild and uninhibited, even with Tom Grace. Well, the difference was, this time with Jack, she'd been the leader. It had been her imagination that inflamed both of them. They were all over the room and they would have been all over the apartment if the other men hadn't been there. At one point the guy in the next room had knocked on the wall and told them to have mercy. She'd almost gotten dressed and run out of the apartment, but by a minute later, they were making love as though nothing had happened. She couldn't go back to Jack's and face that guy but she also couldn't go home and face Lillian. She feared that what had happened in the doctor's office had left her without protection from her impulses, and indeed, there were impulses she hadn't suspected were there. Maybe she should stay close to home for a while. Away from men. But also she wondered if she wasn't copping out because she was worried about being a lesbian. On the other hand...

"If I push my imagination to what would turn me on with a woman, there's nothing I can think of that compares to having a man really over me and in me. That's much closer to the feeling about Vera than anything with a woman could be. What happened Wednesday night...It could've been sex with any man. That was the scariest part. Whoever was with me had less reality than what was happening in my head...I came and I came and I came and then I fell asleep again. I think I had a dream...I don't remember it, except there was a sunset. The colors were more beautiful than any real sunset. You could *feel* that the sun was on fire, it wasn't just something you happened to know was true...The water turned gold. Or they came closer to each other in color until they were the same. Then they grew pale. All my images of sunsets have water in them, but there was no water in Marbury. I mean I didn't live near it. It was just a pond where we swam in the summer... Water is about my father...When I said that, I was thinking of the ocean. But when I heard it, I heard...peeing is about my father. Making water." She laughed. "Boys make water. Girls just lose it."

"Tell me."

"Actually, it wasn't just peeing that came into my mind. Two different things came in at the same time. The other was Patterson. I don't know why. The moat certainly wasn't full of pee...although...it had everything else smelly and yukky in it...Maybe that's what it really was full of...I want to ask you something. I was just thinking of how I always said—I *believed*— that I never saw a penis until Paddy Mason's. Maybe that isn't true. Do you think it's possible that I saw my father naked? Or Gregory?

"I think it's even likely."

"You don't think they danced around naked, do you? That wouldn't be very responsible."

"Not necessarily. Little girls usually find a way to see their fathers naked during the second years of their lives. Of course, we're not sure how much navigation you were actually managing on your own."

Dawn laughed. "I love the way you said find a way. Do you mean that they do it on purpose?"

"What do you think?"

"I don't know. It's hard to see what would make you...You'd have to be curious. You'd have to have some vague sense of what you were looking for. Like that scientist who found the jumping gene. If she hadn't been looking for it under the microscope she'd never have found it...You'd have to suspect something...Maybe one day I said to myself, Hmmm, what's that funny bulge in Daddy's diaper?" (giggle giggle) "I don't have a bulge like that in my diaper ...bathing suit...whatever."

She considered for a while.

"Unless we're just talking about some kind of blind instinct. Like the lemmings going down to the sea. Little baby girls looking for whatever might fit into that space they...When do little girls find their vaginas? Do they play with themselves at that age?

Because if they do...if we do...it begins to make sense. Mmm, this little finger feels pretty good, but let's see if I can find something better...Some nice round peg that fits into this nice round hole. Now, let's see, what's behind that door? Daddy's always coming out of there zipping his pants. Aha! That one's a little too...Maybe I'd better try the next door." She became giddy. Every sentence was punctuated by giggles, hums, and ho-hos as she turned the saga of the little girl into a sort of Goldilocks and the three bears. Suddenly, however, she ran out of the manic energy she'd been investing in the tale. "I'm depressed. I don't know why. I expected you to— How come you let that business about the lemmings go by?"

"I'm not sure that I let it go by, precisely."

"The lemmings are about blind self-destruction. They're driven to destroy themselves in the most matter-of-fact way. That isn't what I wanted to talk about. I wanted to talk about...When I mentioned the lemmings...I don't even know what they look like. Like rats, maybe. With longer tails. And when they jump into the water...off a cliff into the ocean...I want to ask you something. Do you think my father committed suicide?"

"Do *you?*"

"Well, he certainly wasn't being careful with his life. Or with mine. He actually tried to take better care of me than he did of himself...I don't think he threw away his life knowing that that was what he was doing. If he'd known, he would have made arrangements for someone to take care of me...I think he didn't have the strength to keep his life

from drifting out of his own hands. My mother was
drifting, too, but he didn't see her that way . . . Have I
said anything that sounds wrong to you?"

"No."

"I think it's time for you to tell me something."

"I was interested in your moving from the question of whether your father could hurt you to the
question of whether he hurt himself."

"Hurt me? You mean by leaving me alone?"

"No."

"I don't understand. What was I talking about
before? The lemmings? How'd I get to the lemmings, anyway?"

"By way of their long tails, I believe."

"I don't even know if lemmings have long tails. Do
you?"

"You seemed to think they do, which is what
matters."

"Why? What was I talking about before lemmings
and their tails? . . . Oh, I remember . . . Daddies and
their . . . tails. Except when you say *tail* it doesn't
sound so . . ."

"So?"

"Hard. Threatening, I guess. Talking about pegs,
like in those little hammer sets . . . That makes me a
little nervous, I think. But not in a way that I connect
to Gordon. I can't associate him with anything dangerous at all. I wish you could see those photos of
him. Sometimes I suffer from not being able to—I
want you to see him with my eyes. That sounds silly
when I don't even remember seeing him myself. But
I have a very strong sense of him, and I need you to
have it too."

"What kind of sense would you like me to have?"

"Of how lovely and gentle he was. How it's impossible to associate him with anything coarse or ugly. As a matter of fact, that might have been his problem. He was too much that way to become a man. Although it probably had a lot to do with the way he was raised. I remember Vera said their mother wanted him to be the way he was."

"Why, do you think?"

"Well, first of all, she wanted a companion. Her husband was away a lot, and they kept moving, and even when he was around he wasn't the sort of person you confide in. But also she must've wanted someone who was different from the admiral. The admiral doesn't sound like someone you'd want to get close to. I'm talking about a metaphorical closeness, of course."

"Are you?"

Dawn groaned. "Of course! I was talking about the reasons Gordon's mother raised him the way she did. I mean, he might have been that way in any case. Maybe just having a father like that made him the way he was. The admiral sounds very threatening. Maybe it's natural for a boy to respond to a father like that by turning inward, not outward, like a man. He's protecting himself. Like a woman. Maybe that's even what some fathers want. Men like that think they want a rugged son like themselves, but a rugged son would be competition, and they don't really want competition. That's probably what they're so ferocious about in the first place. To scare off competition. Does that make sense to you?"

"Yes."

"Well then, what's the argument about?"

"Which argument is that?"

Dawn sighed. "I don't know. Honestly. What were we talking about?"

"About why some people don't want boys to be boys. Or to become men."

"Mmm. Right . . . I guess some kind of fear's always at the root of it."

19

In October Charles had advised his children that he had a lady friend, and at the beginning of November he had informed them that he was, in fact, preparing to move into an apartment with his lady friend and her children. At the beginning of December Charles brought his two sons for a week-end visit and was surprised and delighted to find that their very presence kept the Shinefeld boys off his back. Victoria, Charles had informed Lulu with a wise grin, would be unable to attend in the light of a "subsequent engagement."

Donald Herman, a chubby, anxious twelve-year-old, looked like Charles and acted very much as the twelve-year-old Charles would have acted had he had the restraints of an upper-class childhood. Donald, Charles said, was the child who, like many first children, gave the lie to the myth that he and Anna had a simple, happy marriage. Adam Herman, at eight, was slender and dark-haired like his mother, quiet and reserved in personality.

Teddy, now twelve and a half, quickly became the leader of the group.

On the second weekend that the boys spent together, Victoria, who was almost eleven, had another sleepover.

Yes, Charles said, of course the child had some complicated feelings about meeting her father's new girlfriend. Did Lulu think her own children had a monopoly on jealousy? Not that Victoria at her worst was capable of inflicting half the indignities to which Teddy at his best subjected Charles. On the other hand, Charles said, even for people whose brains didn't run to the layered look, it could be a more difficult time than he'd anticipated.

So Lulu was prepared. But she was insufficiently prepared.

She'd expected to meet a hostile ten-year-old girl, but how could she have been prepared for this particular ten-year-old girl, who had an aplomb a real princess might have envied, an arrogance only the king, her father, should have achieved, and a beauty whose components were her father's coloring (minus the freckles but including extraordinary, waist-length, wavy, reddish-gold hair) and her mother's face?

Good God! No one had ever told Lulu she was going to spend Christmas with Anna Herman's face!

With the face of the woman with whom Charles wanted to be skiing in Aspen! With the face of the woman with whom Charles had shared hundreds of (reported) miseries and (unreported) pleasures and at least enough of her body to create this incredible, free-standing unit: one who looked like him; one who looked like her; and one who looked like both of them, an indissoluble mixture of Charles and Anna Herman, now twain.

How could she have been prepared for the moment when unknown to her, Charles and his daughter had entered the apartment and she would look up from the brownie batter to see beaming father and beautiful child with Anna Herman's face, the latter staring at her with the condescension of a missionary who, having been sent to teach the natives, has first been constrained to sit through a performance of the old, messy way?

Or the murderous rage that swept through her when Victoria thwarted her most carefully planned day by convincing the boys that the movie Lulu wanted to take them to was terrible and there was something else (inappropriate) they'd all enjoy more?

Or the tears to which she'd surrendered in her bedroom when, having inadvertently interrupted a ghost story Victoria was telling the boys to advise that lunch was ready, she'd been told by the young lady that "I know it's hard for you, being ignored like this. But you really should know better than to barge in on us in the middle."

She might have known, of course, that when she tried to talk about her feelings to Charles (who, with her consent, was maintaining a nearly full work schedule that Christmas week), he would sit there grinning. Wasn't it Lulu who had calmly suggested that Charles cease to react to Teddy's childish capers as though her son were a fully trained Green Beret instead of a distraught little boy who was afraid of losing his mother? Wasn't it Lulu who...?

Astonishingly, for Charles was in a marvelous mood at the beginning—well, maybe not so astonishingly, for she was distraught and he was finding revenge too sweet—it began to turn into the worst fight they'd ever had. They pulled back simultaneously because each saw that there would be no reasonable resolution, only feelings so bad that it might be impossible to live with them. These arguments should never have had to happen, they said. Probably no one should ever have to live with anyone else's children. That, Lulu said, was the truth she hadn't seen when it was only Charles being difficult about her sons. Few people ever admitted it, or the divorce merry-go-round would have had to change its tune to a funeral march, but that was the truth. She saw it more clearly with every moment that Victoria was in her home. (It had just become hers again, instead of theirs.) The heritage of divorce was a complex bitterness that mixed with the difficulties of adjustment to new situations to provide a poisonous brew... All the violent, competitive feelings of the child toward its own parents...undiluted by blood, unmixed with love, unbounded by custom.

If a natural parent was not untouched by jealousy of his/her children, there was the enormous balancing factor of those children's being part of oneself. The child was also, of course, part of someone else...So in a sense, in adoring his daughter, Charles was still loving his wife. She said it sadly, feeling old and wise. Charles said if that were the case, she must still love Nathan, and then she said that when he put it that way, she realized that these feelings that were being tampered with were deeper than love.

"I remember how I felt when I left Nathan," she said. "It was as though he'd been removed from me surgically, and the Nathan was gone but the patient was worse. It's much more frightening to think of being tied into someone if you can't cover it up with a word like *love*. When you come up against its primordial quality. Nothing at all to do with the brain. It's not even symbiosis I'm talking about. I think it's synthesis, not symbiosis. Does that make any sense to you?"

Charles grew restless. The crisis had passed, they were both calm, and he could do without talk of either symbiosis *or* synthesis. He wanted to fuck it all away. Lulu wasn't averse to the idea of fucking but synthesis stuck in her mind, and when she was half-undressed and already quite aroused, she reached around for the paperback dictionary on her night table and found *synthesis*, reading aloud the first definition: *The combining of separate parts or elements to form a complex whole.*

"You see? That's what I was talking about. A new complex whole gets formed. Just because the elements were put together in the same place."

"Mmm," Charles murmured, playing with one of her nipples, sucking the other, insinuating himself past the clothing she hadn't yet taken off.

Lulu let fall the paperback dictionary, ready to make love in the service of synthesis even as Charles wanted to make love to get rid of the thought. She had helped him to remove her remaining clothing and was welcoming him into her body when there was a knock at the door.

"Daddy," Victoria Herman's voice called, "I think there's someone trying to get in the front door!"

"No, sweetheart," Charles called to Victoria, who'd insisted on sleeping in the living room instead of in Walden's room with her brothers because there was a fire escape in Walden's room and she'd heard that there were thousands of burglars on the West Side. Even if they couldn't get through the window gate, she didn't want them standing out there, looking in at her. "It sounds that way when the people next door come home."

But he remained poised in and above Lulu, knowing this wasn't the end of it, trying not to smile but not angry either because it was his own Sugar Plum rather than T. W. Juggernaut who was interrupting his pleasure.

"I'm scared, Daddy," said Sugar Plum in a voice considerably smaller and younger than anything she'd adopted during the day and which Lulu tried to force herself to think of as a symptom of anxiety rather than a sign of calculation.

Charles played with Lulu's nipple as though it were a worry stone.

"Why don't you tell her you're fucking?" Lulu whispered. "That's what you always tell me to say to Teddy."

"Listen, baby," Charles called through the door. "Go into the bedroom with the boys for a while. If a burglar's trying to get in the front door, he can't be on the fire escape, too."

Silence.

They couldn't tell if Victoria was still at the door.

Carefully, almost absent-mindedly, Charles began moving in and out of Lulu, listening, listening for Victoria, Lulu becoming increasingly irritated by his abstraction as she became increasingly excited.

"Maybe we should just forget about this," she finally suggested. "Sugar Plum'll only be here for another five days."

Charles looked down at her, grinned, thrust himself into her once very hard, then stopped moving. Holding himself almost entirely outside her. Teasing. Knowing he was in full control.

"The foot's on the other shoe now, isn't it, my love?" Charles whispered before proceeding to give her the thousand percent of his attention that was all she'd ever wanted.

Sascha called to say that she was in New York and would like to come visit the following day.

For the first year after her grandfather's death, Sascha had called her mother with some regularity and talked about taking her senior year of college in New York. This year, some time after Charles's separation but when he was still encamped on Sixty-sixth Street, Sascha had called one night and Charles had picked up the phone.

"Who's this?" Sascha had asked.

"No. Who's *this*?" Charles had responded jocularly.

"Who's that creep answering your phone?" Sascha had demanded when Lulu picked up the receiver.

"That was no creep, that was my boyfriend," Lulu had responded.

A moment of silence.

Lulu herself was remarkably uneasy—with the word *boyfriend*, with the situation, with the knowledge that she'd passed up opportunities to mention Charles's existence to her daughter.

"Boyfriend," Sascha said. "Jesus."

"And what's happening with you, Satch?"

"Nothing . . . I was going to . . . You living with that guy?"

"His name's Charles Herman."

"Herman. What is he, one of your patients?"

Lulu tried to laugh again but this time the sound wasn't strong enough to make its way through the receiver. "He's an analyst."

Sascha groaned.

"And he's got his own apartment, to answer your question, but he spends a lot of time with us."

"Well, listen, uh, Lulu . . . I'll be talking to you . . . I'm not sure if I'm coming to New York. It looks as if it's going to be too expensive. I can't pay tuition and rent, too."

"Mmm," Lulu said. "Well, let me know, okay, Satch?"

In the spring, Sascha had decided to stay for her last year at the University of Miami, which had spoiled her for a real school, anyway. Maybe she'd get an M.A. in New York.

Since that time, Sascha had called infrequently. Now she was in New York and was to be added to this— what was the opposite of a synthesis? This pot of unmelting ingredients. The possibilities were end-less, and none was very appealing.

Lulu dreamed about Sascha and Victoria—or was it Sascha and Dawn Henley?

You see?" Sascha was saying with a sad smile, "this is the way she really is. You think of her as some sort of wise old guru, some kind of decent human being. But the monster you see in front of you, that's who she really is."

Lulu woke up trying to see the face of the girl Sascha was talking to, and once awake, was thirsty. With extreme caution she opened the door to the bedroom, peeking out to make sure that the living room was quiet, then tiptoeing to the bathroom.

Victoria slept soundly, undisturbed by any of the thousands of criminals on the Upper West Side.

Back in bed, Lulu tried fitting herself around Charles, but he became restless in his sleep and moved to his stomach, then, soon after, onto his other side, facing her. She maneuvered herself into the curve of his body, reached back and brought his arm around her, then went back to sleep, this time dreaming that Sascha was protecting her from the accusations of a child with reddish-blond curls.

"She's an orphan herself," Sascha was explaining to the judgmental child. "She does the best she can, but don't you see how hard it is? She really doesn't know how to be!"

As it turned out, Sascha did defend her mother to Victoria, though not precisely on the grounds Lulu had envisioned. As a matter of fact, Sascha salvaged the Christmas vacation. She arrived the following morning with her new boyfriend, Walter Crawford, who was an accountant in Miami and with whom she was staying at the Plaza. Walter Crawford was a handsome, amiable young man who clearly adored Sascha, who hung on her every word, who was looking for a job in New York in the event that Sascha should decide to go to New York University for her M.A., and who was more than willing to join Sascha in comforting Victoria Herman.

"She's not so bad now," Sascha said to Victoria at one point. "You should've seen her in her Hitler years."

"Let's face it, Victoria," Lulu overheard Sascha saying to the child on another day, when Walter had gone sledding with the boys in Riverside Park. "Who could your father've moved in with who you'd be able to stand?"

"Natalia Makarova," Victoria answered without a moment's hesitation.

"Hey, you know, you're a pretty far-out kid?" Sascha responded. "I think I like you."

The feeling, clearly, was mutual. Victoria now followed Sascha and Walter around the apartment and ignored the boys, who went back to playing the games that interested them instead of the ones Victoria wanted to play. One night Victoria took a sleeping bag down to the Plaza and slept on the floor of their room. The mood in the apartment lightened. Charles was charmed. He was of the opinion that whatever problems might have visited the Shinefeld household in Sascha's adolescence, Lulu's daughter had grown into a charming and well-balanced young woman of whose pathology, in the time-honored fashion of mothers, Lulu was excessively aware, and whose sanity Lulu had a mother's neurotic need to disparage.

"Let her grow up," Charles advised Lulu before taking his children home to their Aspen-tanned mother and her boyfriend. (Now *that* was a boyfriend.) "You can always find someone else who needs you." Grin. "Like me."

"I hope you know what you're doing, Mother," said Sascha, when they had lunch together on her last day in New York, Walter Crawford being occupied with an interview. "Your pal is a real creep. A child molester. He was getting set to make a pass at me."

Lulu smiled cardboard. "You're not a child."

"Oh, come on, you know what I mean. I mean he would've if I'd . . . Did you see the way he looks *at his own daughter*?"

Lulu regarded Sascha in what she hoped was a speculative manner, trying to remain calm without becoming analytic, reminding herself that all the worst times with Sascha had been related to fathers and stepfathers, to the man who was, or was presumed to be, the object of Lulu's affections.

"Being an Avon lady is very instructive, you know. You see guys like that sniffing the pants on the clothesline."

Lulu's brain wasn't functioning in any useful way, but fortunately Sascha was too carried away by her own rhetoric to perceive that she was at any advantage, and continued pressing on to what turned out to be safer ground for her mother.

"I mean, here I am trying to get up the courage to

come back to New York and be a part of your life, and you're telling me that that's what I'm going to have for a stepfather?"

"I haven't said a word about marriage," Lulu pointed out. "Or stepfathers. But it doesn't really seem sensible to worry that much, Sascha. We haven't lived as a family for years now."

Sensible. A word that, when it came up in her practice, was used by a patient who was then assured that the word *sensible* had little to do with human emotions.

"The fact that I stay away from you doesn't mean that you're not my family," Sascha said. Then added, with all due deliberation, "Or that you're not very important to me."

A long significant pause, full of lies and truths, promises and potential betrayals, dangers already experienced and possibilities less real than either of them would have liked to believe. Over the steaming onion soup which the waiter placed in front of each of them, Lulu smiled her best Dr. Shinefeld smile and told Sascha that those words were pleasant to hear, but that even if they'd been the closest of mothers and daughters, her daughter obviously couldn't dictate to her the choice of a lover or husband.

"After all, Sascha, you wouldn't allow me to dictate which man you should love simply because *I* love *you*."

"If you'd ever loved me enough," said Sascha, who consistently refused to notice when she'd hit rock bottom, "I would've."

"But you'd be wrong. Aside from the question of whether and how much I love you, it's you who knows if you want to be with him, if you want to go to bed with him, whether you can find comfort in each other."

"Comfort," Sascha said darkly. "Some comfort you'll find in that jerk and his pukey daughter."

Lulu laughed and then laughed again to realize that her pleasure in learning that Sascha had been putting on an act with Victoria far outweighed her dismay at her daughter's comments about Charles.

For a while, they occupied themselves with the runny cheese, the soggy toast, and the hot soup.

"Tell me how your father is," Lulu suggested after a while.

Sascha shrugged. "He's all right, I guess. But he's really gotten awfully old and stodgy."

"Mmm. Well, he's not exactly a kid anymore." Woody was sixty years old, by now.

"It's not only that. I mean, he's got this head of beautiful white hair, but he's just like a kid in a lot of ways. That woman's got him completely under her thumb. He wanted to come down to Miami to see Walter and me for Christmas and he couldn't because he had to visit her aged fucking mother in South Dakota, for Christ's sake. He never does anything just because he feels like it. Did I say thumb? Her hoof is more like it. It's disgusting."

Lulu sat lost in admiration for the woman who had managed to control Woody with her thumb or any other part of her anatomy.

"Was Woody the first man you ever loved?" Sascha asked.

"Yes."

"Do you still love him?"

Lulu smiled. "I haven't seen him in twenty-seven years."

"So?"

"What's true..." *Very slowly, now...* "Someone who leaves you when your love is very intense keeps a kind of edge in your imagination that someone you've emotionally finished with loses. It takes a long time for your mind to stop running over the possibilities."

"I'd love to see you and Woody together," Sascha said.

Lulu smiled. It had been impulsive, genuine. Perhaps the first of Sascha's words to be both. In her years of practice Lulu had not spoken to a child of divorced parents who didn't harbor at some level the fantasy of bringing the parents together. Even the most uncompromisingly Oedipal children needed this; divorce hampered their fantasies, depriving them of the framework in which they needed to be woven. Still, this was a first; for many years Sascha had accused her mother of breaking up the family that would have allowed her to grow up happy. At the age of twenty-six, Sascha was gaining on her own adolescence.

"Sascha," she said, "there's something you need to know. Your father's still a romantic figure to me, but I'm totally tied into Charles. I wasn't just using a phrase. I'm in love with him, whatever the difficulties."

Sascha put down her soup spoon, leaned back in her chair. "What about Nathan?"

"What about him?"

"Did you love him?"

"No. I was fond of him. I wanted a father for you, not to speak of for myself." She smiled painfully.

"Nathan is sort of a schmuck but he's a very good person," said Sascha, who, not having been married to one, was still under the illusion of the holiness of the sort-of-a-schmuck-who-was-a-very-good-person.

"Perhaps. He was certainly very good to you. He loved you a lot."

"I told him yesterday . . . I guess I was feeling sort of . . . I don't think this new bimbo is good to him. Anyway, I told him I was sorry about all that shit I laid on him once upon a time."

"Mmm. That was a nice thing to do. I'm sure it made him feel good."

"It turned him into a soggy mass, if you want to know the truth. He *cried*."

"You're kidding."

"I'll tell you something else. I don't like having that kind of power over people. You get a lot of power just from being sure of what you want. But what I want is *not* to have it. I don't want someone to feel like killing himself because he's in love with me and I have no use for him. If I want to act like a crazed adolescent and attack this man who's been madly in love with me since I was two years old, I want to be able to do it and not have him be destroyed by it. I liked it when you told me to fuck off about What's-his-name. You hardly ever did that when I was a kid. I never learned right from wrong because you were always understanding what I wanted so well you could never just tell me it was bad. Cut it the fuck out, kid."

Lulu smiled sadly at this version of their lives, which was much closer to her own memory than Sascha's earlier stories had been.

"I know. I was such a novice in psychology and so thoroughly immersed in it. I just... When I saw what I was doing, it was too late. By then you were angry with me all the time."

"Anyway," Sascha said, "you're wrong about What's-his-name and he's going to make you miserable, but you're right that it's none of my business. I like it when you're tough. Now that I'm old enough to stand it, anyhow."

Lulu's eyes misted over in spite of her brain's knowledge that this was not what was called for.

"Oh, shit," Sascha said. "What did I do now?"

20

"**S**OMTIMES I GET very frightened because I don't know where I'm going. Like Susie's baby. Or one of the little kids you see in Riverside Park, just learning to walk. They're not really walking yet. It's more like—*careening*—tilted, happy. The only trouble is, they can't stop when they need to. I saw one of them nearly get killed. Her mother was sitting on a bench talking to someone and she was heading for the street. A car was coming down the drive and if a man hadn't grabbed her, she'd have been hit. Even if she'd seen it, she couldn't have stopped in time..."

Dawn had spent Christmas in Boston with Jack, primarily with his family but they'd also slept over one night at the Silversteins'. She referred to the experience as "schizophrenic." Jack's family was "the other end of the world" from Tony's in their way of being in the real world. At the Stewart home the talk had been of little but the Iranian hostages and the coming presidential primaries, while Tony and Len's real world consisted of families, friends and the problems encountered by each. Jack's family, including his mother and sister, was political, athletic, averse to discussion of personal matters. While you were with them it was hard to believe there was such a thing as the unconscious. People were discussed as though they were sometimes unintelligent but seldom irrational. Dawn thought that while Vera and Gordon were examples of the clash between deep drives and a system designed to thwart them, the Stewarts were a glowing symbol of how that system could work to protect people from themselves.

"Do you think maybe," she asked, "there are people who live in the real world and hold down their feelings and are better off than they'd be if they dug them all up?"

"Yes," the doctor said.

"Oh, God," Dawn said with a laugh. "Sometimes I love you so much I feel as though it's impossible that I could ever leave here!"

She was beginning to suspect, however, that she was in the process of doing just that, which was why she was frightened. Soon Jack would begin writing for job interviews to law firms in Boston and Washington. He had begun to talk as though he wanted her to go with him but he was also making it clear that he would go where he had the best offer, and that he had no desire to stay in New York. That meant that come graduation, she would have to give up Jack or Dr. Shinefeld— prematurely, she felt, in either case. Giving up Jack seemed increasingly out of the question, and that in itself was upsetting, for there were times when she felt she barely knew him. At the Stewarts' she had seen "a red-faced, angry side" to her boyfriend that hadn't been visible before.

Jack had a sister, Liz, who was in her last year at Radcliffe and hoped to enter Harvard Law School in September. The three of them had been discussing the question of the woman's (Dawn's) having to move to wherever the man (Jack) took a job. She supposed in a way she and Liz had ganged up on him, with Liz trying to explain to her brother about women and choice and Jack finally exploding in both their faces.

It was pure bullshit, Jack had shouted at the top of his lungs, to say that men had choices. This house-husband stuff was bullshit. It was all very well for John Lennon to be a househusband, but the average guy not only had a living to earn but had his pride and his place in the world to maintain. Let anyone who wanted a househusband go find some vegetarian acidhead who wanted to be one. True, the average man could choose to spend more or less time with his children. But the average mother ended up having at least as much leeway, since she didn't have that eight-to-twelve-hour work chunk out of her day to begin with. Unless she *chose* to go to work. When Liz finished law school she could practice for a while if she liked and then get married and have children or she could do both at the same time. Or neither. Could they please show him where he had choices comparable to that? When men could have children he'd be willing to talk about choices.

After that argument, Dawn had called up Nell Litsky, who had taken her to the house on Beacon Street where she had been born. A disappointing experience.

"She could've taken me to any house in Boston and it wouldn't have made any difference. Sometimes I think if I could feel connected to the beginning of my life instead of just inventing it here, I would feel more sure of myself. My self...Once I asked you what my self was but you never really answered me. I've almost asked you again dozens of times but then every time I think, what if there's no real answer?"

Later she and Nell had looked at photographs of her mother's family. Physically they weren't so different from herself as she'd once thought, and yet...

"The truth is, Vera and Tony are my family because they're my history. Those women I never knew. Vera and Tony and you and Dr. Seaver...You're the most important one. Right now, anyway. Not just now. You're the person who turned my life into a life. I don't know what I mean by that, but it's true. If I have a self who's a stranger to me...as opposed to not having one at all...this is where I got her...Pretty weird. A self...a mother...you get on some kind of installment plan. Not exactly Bob Cratchit and his merry brood. Of course, they may not have been all that merry, either. Not if they were hungry all the time. Maybe Cratchit and his family were to Dickens the way Patterson was to me. This lovely, warm fantasy to deny what life is really about...Tony says she's fine but she looks awful. Gray and thin...She used to put on makeup in the morning whether or not she was going out. No more. Most of the time she was wearing a brown sweater and pants. I couldn't believe it. Tony meant color to me. Now she's forty-three years old and she looks as old as Vera and she watches soap operas in the daytime...Maybe she would've been better off staying with Vera. I mean, I can understand how she felt. She was bored. She wanted to be with a man. For most of her life she only wanted a woman. Not that Vera's exactly your typical woman...Maybe" (giggle giggle) "she just wanted a man without a penis...Maybe once she saw what Len was like she wished she'd stuck with Vera...Maybe she'd have been better off if she had."

"Who do you think you're talking about?" the doctor asked.

Dawn sighed.

"I know, I know, but...I want to ask you something. Do you have the feeling that Jack's someone who's all right for me?"

"I really can't tell," the doctor said. "I don't have a strong sense of him yet."

"How is that possible? I've hardly talked about anyone else for the last...You know that he's very big, don't you?"

"The only thing I remember your saying is that he wasn't a Henley type, as Tom Grace was."

"Right. He's not slender and elegant. He's more ...He's huge, maybe six-four. Brown hair...Aside from Dr. Seaver, I don't think I've ever had much to do with a man that tall...It makes me feel funny when you say you don't have a sense of him. The two most important people in my life and you're strangers to each other... Weird...Although sometimes I feel...You know, Jack's face changes when he makes love to me. Not just that he takes off his glasses. Although that makes him look less...civilized...to begin with. But when we're making love, his face actually...gets all loose in a funny kind of way. I don't know where he *is*. You have this idea that when you're making love you're closer than any other time and it's almost the opposite of the truth. In a way, I'm closer to you when we're talking than I am to Jack when he's making love to me."

A lengthy silence.

"Jack's parents had a party on New Year's Eve. It was nice...Their friends, Jack and Liz's friends...but I had a weird experience...I went into the library because there's a bathroom in there and the other one downstairs was in use. I opened the door and it was like that scene in *Star Wars*, the nightclub, with the smoke, and the wookies and Chewbacca, only worse because it didn't feel so friendly...This bunch of men that looked ordinary an hour earlier, with big fat cigars coming out of their mouths, and the smoke filling the room, smelling awful...hurting my eyes... making me feel as though I'd choke to death...I just closed the door and ran upstairs and went to that bathroom, but it left me...I think I was scared. It wasn't that they were really hostile but they looked..."

"Looked?" the doctor prompted.

"Ohhhh...Foreign, I guess...I couldn't tell who they were or what they might do. Not that they were doing anything but because they were...creatures from another planet. And the thing is, Jack was in there with them..." She began to cry. "Smoking one of those things. Grinning at me. I felt as though he was telling me, This is who I am. Or who I'm going to be in twenty years. Later he told me he doesn't even like most of those men, that if he had to sit around with them and talk one at a time, he'd probably go crazy. But he still likes . . . being a part of that . . . man thing . . . Yuuccchhh . . ."

The doctor waited.

"When you come upon something like that, there's a sense of hidden violence. Not hidden. Possible. You don't know what could happen because they're so strange to you. That's what makes homosexuals so easy to deal with. They're not as different from you . . . I imagine some people would feel sorry for me, hearing about my family, my father, and so on. But it seems to me that it must have been much easier . . . less scary . . . having someone like that take care of me, than it would have been if he were some rough, loud . . . I mean, can you picture my father smoking a cigar? Everything I know about him . . . Not that he and Gregory didn't do a certain amount of . . . carrying on . . . But . . . Actually, when you read about homosexuals, there seems to be more violence in their lives than . . . No. Those're just the ones the media pick up on. They do the same thing with straight people . . . On the other hand, Gregory isn't a particularly gentle soul. Though he was younger then . . . The gentle-homosexual thing is sort of a cliché, when you come right down to it. But my father . . . All you have to do is read his letters to know that he would never hurt my mother . . . Of course he did hurt her, eventually, by getting her pregnant when she shouldn't have had children . . . He needed to do that and it happened to hurt her . . . I really have no way of knowing how I saw my father when he was a year and a half . . . Oh, God, did you hear what I said? When *he* was? I was making him the little one. I was big and he was little . . . I did that with Jack, you know. I didn't realize for a long time how big he is. I tend to see myself as bigger than I am in relation to other people . . . I need them to be little, if they're not going to be gentle . . . gentle if they're genital . . . That's what the golden twins are about, isn't it. They're small enough so I don't have to worry if they get a little crazy. The kind of carrying on they were doing at the edge of the tub, if they were ten times as big as me it would've been . . . They were, too. Weren't they." She began to cry. "When I said that, I saw them as though they were up on a pedestal . . . like the *Winged Victory* . . . Bigger, even. Huge. Hard. *Alive,* the way she is, almost *electric. Charged* with life. Much scarier than she is because they've got these huge—*rods*—sticking out in front of them. These huge, hard . . . lightning rods! My God! What's a tiny baby supposed to make of something like that?" She sobbed violently. "Do you realize . . . It's possible that when I was that age I didn't even know which one was my father or who was supposed to do what? Do you realize . . . when I was a year and a half . . . if one of those men had an erection . . . their penises were maybe as big as my head?"

"How do you think that made you feel?" the doctor asked when Dawn fell silent.

"Terrified," Dawn said. "At least that's the way it makes me feel now."

∽

At her next session Dawn said that she had been unable to put out of her mind the image that had troubled her. What had happened, and it was awful, was that the whole world had become alive in a sexual way, so that walking along Broadway, for example, she'd been unable to look at a baby in a carriage without wondering if the baby had seen its parents naked, and so on. Once home, trying to do schoolwork, she'd been continually disturbed by unbidden thoughts—often about Susan and her baby, whom she hadn't seen during this last trip to Boston. Since she couldn't work anyway, she'd jogged for a while, then at night she'd gone to the movies. Jack was writing letters for job interviews. Finally all that stuff had seemed to leave her mind, but then she'd had a dream.

"I was in Tony's room. Marbury, not Boston. The one in Boston is hideous. When she moved she put everything from the drawers into plastic bags and she's never unpacked it. This room was very bright and beautiful. I was playing with someone, or something, in one of the boxes...drawers. I don't remember what it was but it was very beautiful. I was enormously happy. Then something awful happened. I don't know what it was. Maybe someone came in and I wasn't supposed to be there. Or...Oh, God, I just...I don't think I can talk about this...Whoever came in...After that I realized...I was sitting in my own...you know...shit...It was everyplace. Inside of me. In my vagina. I didn't know what to do. I was so ashamed. *Mortified*...But you see, until then, everything was fine. Beautiful. I was very happy. And now it was terrible. Maybe someone was beating me. Or I was beating myself to show that I knew I was bad. I was terribly ashamed, but...This is very hard for me to say, harder even than the rest...The excitement didn't go away. My whole body was frozen stiff. I was so humiliated. But I was just as excited as before. Maybe more so ... Oh, God, I can't bear this!"

"What is it you think you can't bear?"

"I don't know. Maybe that it's about shit, which is supposed to be disgusting. I mean, it *is* disgusting. But it felt ... wonderful. Not disgusting. When I woke up I was like an overwound clock. I couldn't lie still. I wanted to masturbate but I was afraid. Jack was right next to me on the bed and I was terrified of waking him up but I was also afraid if I walked around someone would hear me and come out to see what was going on, and one look at my face and they'd know. So I stayed there. I put my pillow between my legs and I made believe I was tied down and couldn't move. Not that it's the first time I ever did that but ... The reason I'm talking isn't that I want to, it's that I'm too wound up to stop. I'm very embarrassed. Worse than embarrassed ... I was sucking a penis ... cock ... Oh, God, that isn't even the worst of it. I had all those before. It was hard enough with Dr. Seaver, but the part I never had ... It's good I didn't because I would've shot myself before I told him ... It was like in the dream. With shit, I mean. Except it wasn't my own ... Someone else was doing it to me. And it was hard. Well, harder than it really is, so it could go up into me. I was lying on my stomach and he was sitting on me and ... That's what was happening ... And when I came it was so intense I could hardly stand it, and it spread all through me. Not just the way it usually is when you masturbate. All in one place. It started that way and spread out, the way it does when someone's really in you... I really can't stand this. I feel as though you must be very disgusted with me. I'm seeing Vera's face when she came to get me at school and I messed my pants and she was so disgusted. That I had that stuff in me made me disgusting. I'm making her sound like a monster. She isn't. It's not fair."

"You're talking about your own feelings, actually."

"My feelings. I'll tell you what my feelings are right now... When I graduated from Sidley the caption on my picture was "Golden Girl." Dr. Seaver was amused that it bothered me, but I'll tell you how I feel now. As though that's what the Inside Dawn has always been about. Shit. On the outside I was the Golden Girl. But inside I was... am... just a piece of shit..."

"One of the things this session has been about is the time when the two—gold and shit—weren't opposites in your mind. When you were still more than satisfied with your own excrement. It gave you sexual pleasure. And the time when you learned to be disgusted by it without abandoning the memory of that pleasure."

"Are you saying," Dawn, who had been crying, stopped abruptly, "that I—babies—like their own shit?"

"I'm saying that disgust at body functions is learned from the outside."

"But which body functions were you talking about?"

"Which were *you* talking about?"

"Both, I guess. But I don't see how a baby can tell the difference. It's all in the same place... Almost... Actually, you told me something about that once. That Freud said."

"Anatomy is destiny."

"Meaning...everything's all mixed up with everything else."

"Not in reality, but in our baby minds. So that shame and disgust learned toward one attach themselves to the other."

"I don't think I ever had that feeling with Tony," Dawn said after a while. "That she was disgusted with me. I always felt I made Tony happy. When I was little she used to say to me, *You're not just my Dawn, you're my whole Sunshine.* I called myself *Shunshine* at first because I couldn't pronounce it properly. I could be cheerful for her, even when I wasn't feeling good for myself. I'd come down as soon as she left the room. With Vera...Vera never smiled much. Once in a while, maybe, at something Tony made...or said...Tony was the one who could make Vera smile. I guess I was jealous of that...Tony was the one who fussed over pictures I brought home from school. She really looked at them and saw what was in them, do you know what I mean? I think I wanted Vera to really look at them, too...I heard myself as though I were saying that about Dr. Seaver. And the lithographs. I needed him to—my paintings are about what's inside me. Analysis is about what's inside me but the paintings were different. I didn't have words yet for what was inside those paintings. I had to use someone else's words...Vera always tried to be terribly rational. If she refused to do something and you thought of a way to make it sound unreasonable not to do it, she'd change her mind. But there was no way in the world for me to explain why I needed her to love my paintings...or laugh and clap when I practiced my part in the school play...I needed to show off for Dr. Seaver, too. Make him smile. I needed him to enjoy me. I get frightened when I feel like a drag on someone's life...I guess I needed Dr. Seaver to be different from Vera. To make up for what she didn't do. When he laughed it took away the tension I felt a lot of the time I was there...At the beginning it was very bad. When I went for my consultation, he looked so forbidding. I thought I could never be easy with him. But then he said some wonderful things, and I looked around...The greenhouse was there. It was a home. I could hear children running around upstairs and there were no names on the door but Seaver, so I knew they must be his, even if he wouldn't admit it or even say he was married. Well, maybe he did say that...He wanted me to talk about my fantasies and of course I did, though they weren't like the ones I have here ...If they were, I don't know what I'd have done with them...."

"Could you talk about that?" the doctor asked.

"No, I don't think so," Dawn said. "I don't like to think of that stuff at the same time as I think about Dr. Seaver...I mean, I know I had fantasies about him but they weren't sexual, at least not the same way as these are...I wanted him to hold me and cuddle me, not to...I don't know what word to use. If I say *fuck me*, it sounds as though I'm talking about that sort of thing. Well, that's right. That's what I didn't want him to do. But if I say *make love*, it's really not clear any more because making love can be so many different things."

"Such as?"

"No. I feel as though you're trying to trap me."

"Oh?"

"Trap me into talking about Dr. Seaver when he's not who's important in all this. We've been talking about when I was a baby. I know he came up but that's only because of Vera. Dr. Seaver was just an analyst. Vera was *my father*."

"Was?"

"All right," Dawn said angrily. "*Is* . . . I feel as though you're doing something. Being here in this analysis has helped me to put Dr. Seaver into perspective, and I like it that way. Before he was like a god to me. If he made a mistake with me it was like being struck by lightning. Now it's more that this mortal person wasn't careful enough . . . Not that I like that, either."

"Are you willing to talk about that?"

"No. I don't think so. I feel as though you're taking me off to someplace wrong. I feel as though . . . You wouldn't strike me with lightning but you're . . . Is there a female Poseidon? I'm this little fish swimming in the ocean and you scoop me up in your net, and the harder I struggle the more I get tangled up in it. That makes me angry, but I can't sound angry because then it's proof. And what you think is proof scares me, because everything you think is very powerful to me."

"So now I'm the god instead of Dr. Seaver?"

"You know what I mean."

The doctor was silent.

"Anyway, the hour must be over. I feel as though it's just as well. I've about had it for now. Maybe I should skip one or two appointments. End of term. Lots of work. I'll call you tomorrow morning and let you know if I'm coming on Friday. If I do, I don't want to talk about Dr. Seaver . . . Unless I bring him up...Dr. Seaver's my person, anyway, not yours...I know I sound like some awful little baby. But I'm not really a baby. I'm growing up now. I want to take charge of my own analysis. And I think for now we'd better concentrate on the past."

"The past is interesting," the doctor said as Dawn picked up her satchel and headed for the door. "Unfortunately it can't be useful until its place in the present is found."

===================== **21** =====================

CHARLES AND ANNA signed their separation papers upon Anna's return from Aspen and Charles began to talk to Lulu about moving to a larger apartment, or at least one with a better layout. They began to look, but the few places they saw in their price range had some fatal flaw (like the eight rooms whose every window faced an airshaft or a brick wall) or some flaw that seemed fatal to Charles (like smokestacks across the way that would make it impossible to keep surfaces clean). Lulu required that the boys not have to take more than one bus to school. Aside from that, Charles's needs were so numerous and complex as to make it unwise for her to add others to their list.

In theory, they were willing to buy a cooperative. In practice, the prices were insane, and unless they should stumble upon a spectacular bargain, they wouldn't be able to buy. There were even fewer rentals than co-ops, but Charles had inveigled the newsstand dealer in his neighborhood (his kids' neighborhood, as he was trying to become accustomed to calling it) into giving him the Sunday real estate section on Friday, so they could have a head start on the meager pickings.

One Saturday morning there was a phone call from Charles's sister (who, Charles only now told Lulu, had never been crazy about Anna). Some friends of hers were going to sell their apartment as soon as the building had gone co-op. Right on West End Avenue in the eighties, a block from the boys' bus stop, it was huge and light, with two of its nine rooms overlooking the back buildings to achieve views of the Hudson River, and it would cost a fraction of what the same apartment would cost on Central Park West. Charles and Lulu were free to look at it any time during the weekend as long as they called first to tell the Seldens they were coming.

Charles wasn't crazy about West End Avenue. He found a greater-than-tolerable difference between that "cold gray canyon and the cozy block" near the Metropolitan Museum and P.S. 6 where his family lived because Anna was committed to the public schools. Charles thought they should continue to inspect apartments whose faults they didn't know in advance. The Selden place wasn't going to disappear over the weekend.

None of the apartments with unknown faults turned out to have any virtues to get acquainted with, so Charles insisted upon checking with the three agencies where they were registered just in case something had turned up. He didn't call the Seldens until nine-thirty Sunday night. There was no one home.

On Monday, Charles called from his office to say that he'd talked to the Seldens but didn't have time to come over to the West Side during the day and they would be out for the next couple of nights. Would Lulu look at it and tell him about it?

Lulu looked. She thought it was a spectacular apartment and an excellent bargain (the Seldens had grown wealthy in recent years and weren't eager for a real estate killing) but she presented it coolly to Charles, knowing that any pressure would make him pull back further.

It was Thursday before he found the time to take a look at the apartment—alone. He said he could tell she was crazy about it even if she was too smart to say so, and he didn't want to feel coerced by her enthusiasm. He wanted to make A Sane Judgment.

There were no obvious problems with the Selden apartment, Charles said when he came home that night. And surely at some point they would have to consider West End Avenue. But he didn't feel ready to make that big a compromise. He paced the apartment as though it were a cell, finally taking a walk and returning to confess that he felt uneasy about buying a place with Lulu before he was actually divorced. Lulu should please not try to deal with this on the level of common sense—not that it was their favorite level—but he didn't want to pretend he was being sensible. What he had to do was work it all out in his head. Which he fully intended to do.

On Friday morning Lulu was irritable and abstracted and found it difficult to concentrate on her patients. She felt as though someone had tied her up in a bundle and handed her to Charles, saying, 'Take this if you happen to have some use for it." Except that it was she, not someone else, who was presenting him with the package. Charles's ambivalence about committing himself to her was so clear, his attempts to conceal it (for whatever good reasons, including his assumption that he couldn't) so feeble, that his doubts filled any room the two of them were in and left none for her own. Which at first had been so much greater than his.

Her mind, as she walked home in the evening, would be full of dialogue in which she broached to Charles the possibility of his taking a place close to hers until all of their children were living away from home. At that point, if the attachment held in spite of her age, which would be more than fifty, they could consider . . . Well, yes, of course it would be more expensive, but emotionally . . . After all, Charles, isn't it true that our best times, our only simple, pleasant times, really, are when none of the children is with us? And you're the one who has the worst of it. I may be convinced that Ms. Sugar Plum's preadolescent bitchery is more insidious than the boys' full frontal attack, but the fact is, I only have Victoria every other weekend and you're living with my sons almost all the time! Furthermore, Charles, I'm not all that crazy to share an apartment with someone whose mouth turns down at the edges as though he were about to cry when he enters a sloppy living room at the end of the day. Also, I *love* Hellman's mayonnaise. I always thought it was one of the few good reasons for jars to have been invented. Like tuna fish and cans. There are times when I actually prefer that taste to the stuff I make with good olive oil just to see your face light up! Not only that, but I'm gaining weight from cooking almost every night! I don't want to live this way, Charles—fat and defensive all the time!

And then she would arrive home to find Charles sitting in front of the seven o'clock news, stewing over some new indignity Teddy had perpetrated, and she would immediately move to the defensive position. How could you turn away from someone you were always defending against because he needed an excuse to retreat from you?

She wanted to talk to Bonnie. Too long a time had passed since their last heart-to-heart. It was one o'clock. She left a message with Bonnie's service, turned off the lights, closed the window, and lay down on the couch.

A few men, in passing briefly through her life, had spent time with her and the Mayers, but to say that was to describe the situation; it had been the three of them with an extra man. At the beginning of her real-life relationship with Charles, both women had been led by wishful thinking to believe that there would now be a better bond between the men, although both men knew better, largely because it was they who would determine that this would not be the case. Charles's rambling, chaotic style had little to do with Duke's taste in analysts, and Charles had made it a point to tell Lulu, after their first stiff evening together, that he'd always suspected that the other man was a bit tight around the asshole, if she knew what he meant. She said she didn't.

Bonnie and Lulu still had an occasional lunch, but

their precious evening walks had slipped away, now that there were arrangements to be made on both ends before either could get out. The difficulties had been more acute in East Hampton, where, this past summer, Lulu knew, there'd been times when she and Charles hadn't been invited to the Mayers' for small dinners at which the single Lulu would automatically have been a guest.

Just now she was missing Bonnie terribly. The phone rang. Bonnie. Lulu picked up the receiver.

"I know I'm being an asshole," Charles's voice said. "Maybe you're having second thoughts about putting up with me."

"Every day," she replied.

"I don't blame you," he said, and hung up.

"I need to talk to you," Lulu said when Bonnie called a few minutes later.

"Anything wrong?" Bonnie asked.

"Not exactly. I just need to talk. Like in the old days." When Charles was in a pigeonhole and life could be easily— if not exactly contentedly—run around him.

"Duke has a meeting tonight," Bonnie said. "Do you want to have dinner?"

Lulu hesitated. It was Friday and the boys were going directly to Nathan's after school. She and Charles could be alone. On the other hand, since the apartment turmoil had begun, their times alone had been almost as difficult as the times with the boys. Anyway, how long was it—could it be she'd never done it? Simply told Charles that she was otherwise occupied? She should be able to take off an evening even if he weren't being an oppressive son-of-a-bitch.

"Good idea," Lulu said, feeling like an adolescent about to break curfew for the first time.

They arranged to meet at Lenge at seven. That settled, Lulu hung up the phone and burst into tears.

By the time dinner came, however, she felt like talking about anything *but* Charles. So that after dinner, she didn't want to go home because she hadn't gotten any of her problems off her chest. She went up to the Mayers' for a nightcap. Duke had come in early, and they sat around talking about various people and places of the past, gently nostalgic— all of them, perhaps— for the days before the intruder had come to snatch Lulu from the home of her spiritual parents. Her Freudmother and Freudfather, as she'd once called them.

It was close to midnight when she entered the apartment, drunk and very tired, and found a note from Charles:

Gone to the movies.

C.

P.S. I get it.

Oh, fuck you, she thought wearily.

She took a couple of aspirin and stretched out on the bed, thinking she would awaken when he came in. Instead she woke up in the morning with her clothes on.

There was no one next to her and for one horrible moment Lulu thought Charles hadn't been there during the night. But the pillow and quilt were rumpled, and a moment later he appeared in the room, fully dressed, grinning widely and bearing two cups of *cafe con leche*.

He closed the door with his foot, set down the coffee, kissed her hugely, and told her that he'd just called Nick Selden to inform him that they wanted the apartment.

"We do?"

"You don't sound very happy about it." He couldn't stop grinning.

He handed her one cup and held on to the other, walking around the bedroom, chopping the air with his free hand.

"I asked myself what the hell I was doing, screwing around like that. I mean, I understood what I was doing..."

All too well.

"...all too well. That's the problem. When you see what you're doing that clearly, you have to cut it out even if you're not ready to cut it out. Then...when you didn't come home last night...It worked, kid. It really scared the hell out of me. I asked myself, was I just trying to fuck it up with you? I knew you weren't going to put up with that shit much longer."

That, unfortunately, would have remained to be seen.

She suspected that she might have. On the other hand, now that it was ending, she would begin to feel free to react.

"Did I really feel," Charles continued, retracing the steps in his recent conversion, by which he was clearly enthralled, "like going into swinging singles drag for an indefinite period and then beginning to hunt for someone again? Not that it doesn't have its temptations..."

Who asked you?

"And then the answer came back loud and clear— *Time to stop being an asshole,* Herman!"

"Are you sure you can stop just because you think you're ready?"

"She's who you want, Herman. And that little bonbon is a sample of why. Where're you gonna find a thirty-year-old in all of New York who can call you on your own dazzling shit?"

"Just how I always wanted to end up," Lulu muttered. "Toilet-training a thirty-eight-year-old."

They had breakfast and then Charles wanted to make love but Lulu wanted to do the grocery shopping early and get it over with.

If she was alone for a couple of hours, maybe she'd be able to sort out the tangled skein of feelings that was suddenly making her trip over invisible rugs and turn off faucets that weren't actually dripping. Relief at this commitment from the man she loved; resentment toward that man, who had put her through an ordeal from which she was now released to feel her resentment; the doubts naturally accruing to a forty-four-year-old woman about to mate financially and residentially if not legally with a man seven years her junior in the last quarter of the twentieth century; fear of her own boys' frantic rage and dread of Victoria Herman's icy anger; misgivings over the move itself, which was certain to be a ghastly ordeal— all had combined to put her on Emotional Overload. Why hadn't she pushed harder for finding a way to redivide this apartment? Surely they could have come up with some kind of cubicle for Charles right in the large master bedroom!

If she'd been protective of Charles and reluctant to divulge their difficulties to Bonnie the night before, now she would love to ask her friend some hard questions. What did Bonnie really think of Charles, anyway? Bonnie would be too smart to answer that but she might address the question of Lulu's chances of having a reasonable life with someone *like* Charles. At least Lulu might be able to get some sense, by seeing where her friend evaded straight answers, of Bonnie's opinion of the possibilities.

Charles wasn't in the apartment when Lulu returned, but about an hour later he came in with two full shopping bags from Zabar's. High as a kite, he informed her that he'd been back to the Seldens' to check a few details and draw a layout; that the Seldens had said it would be fine if he and Lulu brought the kids to see the apartment the following weekend; that he'd run into a couple of friends in Zabar's and decided that he and Lulu were giving a little party that night. He hugged her and kissed her and said that through the Milners, the couple he'd run into, he'd invited a few other couples as well. Needless to say, she could invite some of her friends if she really wanted to. But since he already knew a lot of them and she hadn't met any of his...

"I don't feel like a party."

"Why not?" Charles asked, refusing to believe her for a moment. "It won't be any work. I bought all the food already. Hey! How come you're not more excited? Our lives are finally coming together the way they're supposed to! We're settling in!"

She managed a wry smile, although she felt like crying.

"*You're* settling in. I've been settled for a while... Anyway, it's just an apartment."

"What do you mean, just an apartment?" Mock indignation. "It's more important than marriage! It's about money!"

Indeed, it was about money. She was going to have to borrow against her life insurance policy to come up with her half of the down payment, and at the moment she felt more as though it were her life she was borrowing against.

But by evening she was feeling a little better.

She actually looked forward to meeting Charles's friends...

...and was astonished at how little she cared for any of them.

Charles had referred to one or another of them in the past. That afternoon he'd given her thumbnail sketches as they prepared the house for the party. The Milners, the Landaus, the Lombardis, the Tranes... It wasn't that there was anything wrong with them; it was just that she wouldn't have recognized them from his descriptions.

Charles had grown up with one, gone to school with another, lived through numerous crises with the third. Why should he have noticed that they weren't interesting? How could he have understood that the energy and wit he'd invested in them had made them more than they were? The real articles...

Here was Jules Trane, who was in the diamond business (none of Charles's close friends was an analyst) and who'd been married six times and had numerous wives and mistresses as well as nonsexual adventures on three continents. Jules turned out to be a slight and almost morbidly quiet man who wore a toupee and had an accent that cried out from the last stop on the Canarsie line...And Sue Landau..."a wonderful woman"...It was an article of Charles's faith, of course, that women were wonderful...Anna had adored Sue Landau, thought of her as a role model in the way she managed a *real* career and *real* motherhood and enjoyed both, whereas Anna sometimes felt that she went through all the motions without enjoying either...What Sue Landau didn't have was the need to hold a real conversation with the woman who was stepping into Anna Herman's place. Anna and Kid Psycho weren't socializing with the Herman pals, but Sue Landau was far too noble to make a small conversational sacrifice of Anna in the interest of getting to know Charles's new (they all seemed to think) girlfriend.

And they were so young! Jules Trane, for all his women and adventures, couldn't have been much more than Lulu's age, and the others looked younger than Charles. Not just looked, for Christ's sake. They were five, maybe ten, fifteen years younger than she, and if the women's movement had expanded the conversational repertory of young mothers, the way they earnestly dissected their *au pair* girls' problems with female authority and their bosses' problems with women in general was markedly reminiscent of the earnestness with which the park bench mothers of the previous decade had discoursed upon the contents of their babies' diapers and the more important chapters of Dr. Spock.

When they finally left, Charles was high and expansive, eager, as Lulu collapsed on the sofa and he began to clear the debris, to have her (favorable) reactions to the fascinating human beings who were his friends. And Lulu lay on the sofa, thinking of how much she loved Bonnie and Duke, of her deep and easy companionship with them. Aside from his antagonism to Duke, well, Charles had supposed Bonnie was a wonderful woman, but he preferred any of the women Lulu happened to spend time with because their schedules coincided. How much time would Lulu have to spend with Charles's friends that she would otherwise have been able to spend with people she enjoyed?

Not to worry, Lulu.

After all, with Nathan she'd needed to seek pleasure and vitality in outside sources; with Charles she had more than enough of both at home. Friends would be less important... unless he insisted upon seeing them a lot.

Take it as it comes, Lulu. You can't spend your whole life on Red Alert.

But what about...?

Sssh. It's all being taken care of.

All Lulu's Charles problems would shortly evaporate because that week Anna Herman, having already discovered that living with a psychopath was less invigorating than occasionally fucking one, and now hearing from her old friends that Charles was about to buy an apartment with Lulu Shinefeld, pulled up the line and reeled her husband back in.

Charles managed the presentation carefully so that recognition would dawn slowly and not destroy her.

First he acted impatient and irritable and stalked out of the room when she asked him what was going on.

Then he had dinner out and was evasive about the composition of the group he'd been in.

The second time he had dinner out he returned close to midnight and said he was prepared to be grilled.

In a rage, she told him that she wasn't about to cash in her life insurance to buy an apartment with someone who was acting the way he was.

Silence.

"Oh," she said quietly, her breath caught somewhere in her chest where it was useless to her. "So that's what you were after. I wondered."

She'd wondered the first time, too, but then he'd come home and made love to her so passionately that her fears had been quelled.

Now it was Friday morning, only two days later. The boys had left for school. She and Charles were sitting in the kitchen over their second cups of coffee. He'd calculated that, too. You told people about a death in the morning, not at night when they would have to go to bed. She'd have one workday to absorb the initial shock, then a weekend without the boys to collapse.

Charles stood up and walked away from her, toward the window.

"All right, what's up, Charles?"

When he didn't reply, she knew how bad it was.

"Who'd you have dinner with last night?"

"Anna."

Lulu set down her cup.

Her head was a drum. Taut and empty.

In their early months she'd often had the sense that part of him was still home with Anna; recently she'd lost it and begun to feel that all of him was with her in the room.

Charles turned to see how badly she was taking it—on a scale of a hundred to a thousand. Fortunately, or unfortunately, she'd gone off the scale and wasn't registering. In fact, she had switched over to automatic pilot since her normal resources were inadequate to deal with this emergency.

Anyway, someone else's husband shouldn't be privy to one's strong emotions. Certainly not to the rage that she would eventually be able to feel.

"I've been trying to find the right way to tell you," Charles said. "But there is no right way."

So sensitive. We—you and I—really appreciate your sensitivity, Charles.

"You know that this isn't about love," he said. "I don't even know how I feel about her. I love you."

You know what you can do with it, Charles, Lulu might have said to the man she lived with.

"This is about retrieving my life, Lu. About living

with my own kids instead of yours. My kids. My home. Her. My *past*."

"When are you moving out?"

"I don't know. Whenever you want me to."

"Now."

After all, he was already gone.

"Later," Charles said. "I'm not just going to disappear from your life, you know."

"Oh yes you are."

"No."

"Yes."

"We have to talk."

"I'm not going to talk," she said, "and I'm not going to cry while you're here, and I'm not going to—Don't try to make me understand. I don't want to understand any more than I do."

She would assault him if he tried to keep her from feeling only for herself. Once she could feel.

"I'll go out and come back," he told her after a while. "I canceled my appointments for today."

So he could condole with her over the loss of Charles.

At the door she insisted that he give her the keys. She said that she, too, was going to cancel her appointments, and that she would spend the day neatly packing his possessions and putting them in one place where he could make arrangements to pick them up at a specific time. If he didn't give her the keys, she would throw his possessions into the hallway or out of the window.

"This is ridiculous," he said. "You think I'm just

going to disappear forever? You think suddenly we're not in love anymore?"

"I have no doubt," she told him, "that someday I'll be able to laugh at your having said that just now."

She tried to close the door but his foot was in it.

He said, "I'll call you later."

She said, "No, don't call me. I'll hang up."

He tried to meet her eyes but she looked at a spot due south of his chin. After a moment, he withdrew his foot from the door.

22

JACK WAS SCHEDULING job interviews in Washington for Easter vacation week. Dawn had some doubts about accompanying him because her reactions weren't going to affect his plans in the least.

Lillian had found a terrific new girl, Sandy, for Polly's old room. Sandy and Dawn were already fast friends. With Sandy around, Dawn and Lillian had begun speaking to each other, and gradually they'd even gotten to the point where they could talk about what had happened. Lillian had said she had no idea of how important Jack was to Dawn, and Dawn said she guessed she could understand that, since she hadn't until then, either. After this talk, the two girls had become close again, although Dawn suspected that neither would ever like the other as much as each liked Sandy, who was terribly bright and funny and turned all her experiences into little stories that kept them in stitches.

One night the three girls had sat around talking about men and about the extent to which one should be willing to be controlled and/or give up personal ambition in the interest of having a man. As they talked, Dawn had begun sketching a new character, whom she now brought in for the doctor's inspection. Kinga, Queen of the Jungle, was a supremely androgynous deity with long hair, a form at once sensuous and muscular, large round breasts and a huge, erect penis that was fondled by one set of its hands. On its head was a massive yet delicately wrought crown. Flowers were woven into its points and small birds fluttered around them. A second set of hands held the crown in its place; the arms connected to those hands were laden with bracelets. Snakes wound around the other set of arms. Large wings sprouted from Kinga's back.

"Her advantages are obvious," Dawn said. "She doesn't have to bother with men or shrinks because she's got her own penis. She's got breasts so she can . . . We still have to figure out some way for her to have a baby. I suppose it'd have to be through her rear end because it's hard to picture a baby squeezing through that thing, as big as it is. I made it humungous on purpose. I wanted her to be very powerful. No problem too large or too small . . . Living in the jungle she has certain advantages, anyway. No boyfriend to tell her he's got a job in another jungle and she can go along or forget about him. She goes after her own food. Shelter. Nobody comes along and says, *Here's a lifetime supply of mangoes, bananas and Cutter's lotion so you can just sit and rot in the jungle* . . . You know, I never cared much about the money but it gets important when I think about leaving here. In a bad way. I think I resent the freedom it supposedly gives me. Sometimes I assume I'm going to follow Jack wherever he goes, but it's not because I want to. It's that I have to do it because I don't want to lose him and you're my only excuse for staying and he won't buy it."

The other girls had been so crazy about Kinga that their chat had turned into an all-night talkathon, complete with midnight trip to the convenience store for banana split makings, cheese doodles, and God only knows what else. When they'd eaten until they were nearly ill, they had begun to talk about their families.

"I hardly ever do that. I always know more about my friends than they know about me...I showed them Gregory and Miranda's paintings, and then I began to describe the First Death series and what happened here. I went to get the portfolio, and then I realized I'd never brought it home...I guess it was somewhere in the back of my mind, but suddenly it seemed wild that I'd left it here all these years. You have it, don't you?"

"In the closet."

"Do you mind if I take it home?"

"Not if that's what you want to do."

_ᐟᐟ_

When she next came to the office, Dawn was very angry. "You let me just do it. I couldn't sleep all night. I knew what it was about. I kept remembering the story about the little girl...*I'm leaving a piece of*

Judith Rossner

myself with you. So this is the first time I haven't left a
piece of myself with you in five years. It scared
the—shit—out of me. You should've known that would
happen. Why didn't you ask me questions? Why
didn't you tell me it might have a bad effect?"

"Prediction is a dangerous business."

"You could've found a way. You could've told me to
talk about what it meant to me that I was taking
them home."

"You might do that now."

"I *told* you what it meant. I feel scared out of my
wits. I came in here after all that business with Dr.
Seaver... and you really looked at them, you let me
leave them here, and they turned out to be very
important. My earliest life. The pukey little baby Dr.
Seaver didn't want to know. You took her in... and
now I feel as though you're throwing her out."

"Oh?"

"All right. Not exactly throwing her out... But I
want to bring her... them... back. Are you going to
let me?"

"I'd like to discuss it with you."

"That means you're not going to let me. Talking
about it is instead of doing it... You know how I
feel? As though you're punishing me for growing
up."

"And why would I punish you?"

"I don't know! It's not that I don't love you, or I
feel disloyal. I love you as much as ever! That's part
of the problem. It's time for me to grow up and I'm
still your baby! Last night I dreamed you were wearing your red dress. You wore it once last year. You
must have been going out at night and you didn't

have time to change your clothes. I remember I felt jealous that you were wearing that dress for someone else... You see? That's exactly what I'm talking about. Here I am, a jealous little baby who's being confronted with choices only an adult should have to make."

"Tell me about the choices."

"Are you kidding? I'm graduating from college in *four months*. I'm confronted with the end of childhood and the end of analysis at the same time."

"Who's confronting you with the end of analysis?"

"I'm confronting myself."

"As long as you know you're the one who's doing it."

"I'm confronting *reality*."

"Which reality is that?"

"The reality that Jack is going to leave New York in June and I'm going to have to decide whether to go with him."

"June is four months away. Is a lot of preparation required?"

"It's not preparation. I'm too anxious and confused to think about anything else. One minute I'm convinced I have to stay and finish, and the next minute I think of what happened with Lillian and I get terrified."

"Didn't that happen because of the way you were behaving?"

"Maybe. But he's very desirable, in case I haven't mentioned it. All kinds of women'll try to steal him from me. I don't think I could forgive you if you got me to stay and then I lost him."

"Got you to stay?"

Dawn sighed. "If I stayed because I wasn't finished and then I lost him."

"People don't get finished," the doctor said. "They're not books or statues."

Dawn sat up and turned around. "You did that on purpose," she said with an uncertain laugh. "You remember I said that once."

"It also happens to be the truth. The important work of an analysis can be more or less finished, but even that has to be continued by you when you leave. Life isn't a problem that gets solved. In the best analysis every question isn't answered, every difficulty doesn't disappear."

"Then how will I know when to leave? I can't imagine going unless I'm pulled away. Aside from Jack . . . it seems I could keep on forever . . . But then, when I say that, I think, no. Sooner or later something will happen."

"Oh?"

"I just had a picture . . . Coming here one day . . . opening the door to this room . . . and all the colors are gone and you've disappeared." She began to cry. "It's the same place except the life has gone out of it because you're gone." She sobbed uncontrollably. "I understand it's about my mother and father, but it feels as though it's about you. I don't know what can happen to you, is the truth. Because I don't even know who you really are. I have fantasies but they change. Sometimes I think you're married. Other times I'm sure you're not. Most of the time I know you have a daughter, but once in a while I start thinking of other explanations for that girl. Like she's your husband's daughter by a previous mar-

riage. Except I don't like that because I see you and
your husband as childhood sweethearts. You stay
with people forever. Utterly loyal ... I don't even
know how old you are. You seem healthy but I can't
trust what I see. Sometimes I feel you're as big as the
Winged Victory—on her pedestal. Other times you
seem like a normal-size person. Maybe a little taller
than I am. Tall, but normal ... I don't think you
realize ... When I leave here I won't even have anything to prove you exist. If you were my real mother
I'd have photographs. Memories. The house. There'd
be things I could take with me. A chair. A trunk ... If
you were my real mother, then when I was gone
from here I'd still be sure you existed because you
would have given birth to me ... Of course you *have*
given birth to me in a way. It's because of you that I
am who I am. Whoever that is ... With Dr. Seaver for
a while I felt like a different person ... but it was like
wearing Tony's high heels and feeling like a grownup."

"If I'm your mother in some real sense, who would
you say is your father in that same sense?

"It was immaculate conception," Dawn replied with
a little laugh. "I know you mean Dr. Seaver. I remember the old fantasy. The mommy analyst and
the daddy analyst. But I haven't had that in a long
time ... I'm pretty sure now ... I guess I could call
him and ask if I weren't. Maybe he'd give me a
straight answer since he's not my analyst anymore ...
The only time I ever think about you and Dr. Seaver
now is—when I saw you wearing that red dress, for
example, and I thought maybe you were going to
some party for analysts and he would see you and
fall in love with you if he wasn't already ... because

you were so beautiful...This is making me very anxious. You're doing what you were doing the other day...sending me back in time, but to the wrong place. Once upon a time the whole world was full of Dr. Seaver. I don't want it to be that way again. I told you that."

"Why, do you think?"

A long silence.

"I think I was very angry with Dr. Seaver. And... angry at myself for still loving him when I was so angry...I don't think I ever solved that...feeling both ways. That's why I can't stand to think about him too much. That's why it was a relief to talk about my father. My father is dead and that makes him safer than Dr. Seaver...If I get up and run out of here I could be at Dr. Seaver's office in fifteen minutes and that's much too scary. Not just because I'm angry with him but because...he could do anything to me that he wanted to. It doesn't matter that I'm angry. He could make me stop being angry in a minute. Anything he really wanted...When I said I could run out of here, I almost said fly...But then when I thought of flying I saw the dead bird...all mangled and crushed and bloody. Dead. Caught in the currents. The crosswinds. And it doesn't know what to do...in the place where love turns to hate...Finally it has to break itself up against something...or impale itself on a steeple. Chew its hands...This morning I woke up early. I had a bad dream. I don't remember what it was but I couldn't go back to sleep and I couldn't wake everyone up so I was sitting in the chair in my room, chewing on my hands. Some of the marks are still there...Crack up a car. Do something to hurt itself. To stop being blown around in the storm. The terrible storm... Because when love turns to hate...the love doesn't go away..."

☙

"I remembered the dream," Dawn declared at her next session. "I talked to Jessica last night for the first time in a couple of weeks and I remembered how I once told her when she was talking about forced motherhood, all that stuff, I said it might be fun to have a little baby that looked like Jack or Liz, and she was absolutely *disgusted* with me...In the dream...I was with Jack on Long Island. Or maybe it was Cape Cod. I was terrified that I was pregnant. I was trying to reach you but someone would keep hanging up your phone whenever they heard my voice. The panic got worse and worse and finally I figured I'd better try Dr. Seaver. He picked up the phone right away and I felt enormously relieved...But then I couldn't understand a word he was saying! His speech was all garbled, as though it was being put through a synthesizer. I couldn't stand it and I hung up, but when I tried to explain to Jack, he didn't understand, and I got so angry that I ran out of the house. But I didn't know where to go because I couldn't tell where I was...When I woke up I was crying...sweaty...cold. I was very angry with Jack. I couldn't let him near me even though it was my fault he was up because I'd been screaming in my sleep. I wanted to go running by myself but he said it was too late. Finally he said if I had to go he'd come with me. We ran for a while but I had to pretend to myself that he wasn't there. When we got home I was so exhausted I just flopped into bed and fell asleep but then I woke up at five o'clock and that was when I was going crazy, biting my hands...except I couldn't remember the dream...In real life when I need to talk to you it's no big deal. Half the time I don't even need you by the time you get back to me. Because I knew all along you'd call. I had hope. In the dream there was no hope. Everything was gone. It was the end of the world...like the phone conversation with Dr. Seaver."

"Which one is that?"

"You know. The first one. Before the abortion. I was frightened but I was trying to numb out. Go through it quietly. You realize, I barely understood what an abortion *was* in the sense of how it was done. I'd always avoided knowing things like that. The night before...I felt as though it was my own life I was about to lose. Not a baby's. I wanted to find out what was going to happen but I didn't want to call my doctor. I hated him. I guess I hated him because he was going to take away my baby. I figured if I could reach Dr. Seaver...Of *course* I wanted to talk to Dr. Seaver. In my mind it was his baby, not Alan's. It was Thursday night at the beginning of July. I was so crazed I didn't know what I'd do if I couldn't reach him, and when he called me back I was so relieved that everything just poured out of me... uncontrolled...crazy...He probably couldn't even understand what I was saying. It was like some insane babble. And after a while he said...I don't know if I'm going to be able to repeat it...Oh,

God . . . He said . . . *'Hold it, hold it, I feel as though I'm drowning!'* "

Seaver's words hung in the air.

In five years Dawn had referred once, obliquely, to that conversation.

"When I hung up I called Alan and Bevvy and told them the abortion had been changed to the afternoon. I was home, finished, when they came to get me. I couldn't talk to them. To anyone. I needed to keep a very tight rein on myself. The feelings were coming up and I had to be very rigid to keep them out."

"If you'd felt anything, what would it have been?"

"If I'd felt anything I would have run out and killed him instead of the baby!"

Dawn burst into tears.

"That's what I was talking about yesterday. That's why I can't stand to think of him. I'm still very angry but I still love him so much and he's afraid of me! It's very painful to love someone who's afraid of you. I guess I really think that's why he forgot about me . . . about the lithographs . . . that he pushed me out of his mind because I frightened him . . . the way I'm doing with him . . . He couldn't bear to know how much I wanted from him. What power he had over me. Maybe I didn't really drown him, or do anything terrible, but he could feel what I wanted from him . . . My God, I just realized I didn't even know about my father then . . . Well, I knew he'd been in a sailing accident . . . I guess I knew . . . I wanted Dr. Seaver to be everything to me the way my father was . . . At night I would imagine that he was my pillow, and I would rest my head on him . . . and I'd get sleepy. It was like when he was in back of me and I was on the couch, except the couch and the chair, his chair, were all part of the same piece of furniture, so that he was sitting, and I was lying down...and my head was between his legs...like a little baby except...it was a penis instead of a breast...I didn't just want him to be my father, I wanted him to be my mother as well, so that I'd never need anyone else...Maybe that's what he was scared of...The thing about a mother is, she doesn't turn into something else...something hard that can hurt you...I hear what that sounds like because I saw myself lying in this soft place...my face against his penis, like a pillow...and suddenly...I feel a little bit ill...Maybe I'd better talk about something else...I really feel as though I'm going to throw up...At Sidley there was a girl who threw up a lot and got very skinny and finally they made her leave. None of us had ever heard of anorexia. My first couple of years there it wasn't all that fashionable. Then, when we knew what was happening to her, there was a whole round of throwing up. You know, when everyone ate too much they'd just automatically go to the john and stick their fingers down their throat...Throwing up was too awful to me. I couldn't understand how they did it. But later...it was when Dr. Seaver started tying the end of my analysis to graduation. Until then I'd always assumed I would graduate and go to college in New York and continue with him. We argued about that, and finally one day I asked him why I had to finish before the summer. He said the first week in June was a good time because he was going on a trip for a few weeks, anyway...I went back to Sidley ... Even on my way to Grand Central Station, I ate every kind of junk food I saw on the streets. Hot dogs, pretzels, cake from the bakery at Grand Central. More hot dogs. I got so sick I threw up while I was still at the station. That was when I discovered that if you do it soon enough after you eat it doesn't taste like real vomit. I began doing it regularly for a while. It was like an orgy. Not just the eating part, the throwing up, too. An orgy of rage. Love and hate. Eating and throwing up. I don't remember when I stopped doing it. I guess when I went to Europe I just sort of forgot about it ... I guess I was pregnant already. I guess I had him in me in that way ... When I say that it sounds more as though I want to be his mother, hold him inside of me, than have him be mine." Dawn laughed softly. "Well, that would've been all right ... The truth is, I never knew what I wanted. Or I did know, and it was everything ... I always thought that was why he was afraid of me ... But maybe he just didn't know ..."

*

At Easter time Jack was interviewed for several jobs in Washington and before coming home accepted a position in the firm that had most interested him from the beginning.

At first Dawn swung wildly between the desire to run off with him immediately after graduation—never mind about August or anything else—and that of not going with him at all. Some days she was convinced she would be comfortable, if bored, in what was essentially "a man's world, an external, WASPy kind of place where problems can be solved because they're only on the surface anyway," other days when she was convinced she must remain in the "woman's world" that consisted of New York, Dr. Shinefeld, feelings and friends.

"After all," she said, "now that I understand that I was looking for a mother in Dr. Seaver and even in Jack, I know better what my real needs are, and that they're not going to be met in Washington." The doctor suggested that whatever else was true, the notion of a simple split in two worlds was rather simplistic, that far from being absent, complex emotions informed every aspect of political life and often created problems impervious to solution. Finally acknowledging that "even politicians must have an unconscious," and that there were likely to be women with feelings in any major city, Dawn became concerned with the moral issues attendant upon political life. The big hitch to Jack's new job, for example, was that his firm did a great deal of work for Democratic officeholders and the job's permanence depended upon Carter's reelection. If Carter should by any freak chance be swept out in November, Jack's job and many others would end soon after. Yet Jack could not attend the Democratic convention in August, which he sorely wanted to do, because the firm had to avoid the appearance of interest. Was Dawn supposed to spend her life among people this dishonest? Upon reaching the conclusion that there were politicians and conflicts of interest in New York, and remembering that she had always managed to avoid dealing with people she didn't like, Dawn felt briefly "at sea."

"After all," she said, "if people are the same or almost the same everyplace, then I just have to sail along and be sure of my own ... How do I know the same thing won't happen to me as before? After the divorce? And after Dr. Seaver?"

"Why should it?" the doctor asked.

Dawn laughed appreciatively but then fell silent for a while.

"I've constructed a life here," she then said. "When I came to you I didn't know about my parents ... I've made a life and now I have memories of it. When those things happened I didn't have the words to remember them ... and so I couldn't remember. Now I have the words and the memories but they're all connected to you in some way. Not just Gregory and Nell, who I'd never have found without you ... Even Tony and Vera. New York. New York is you ... and Dr. Seaver ... Sometimes I think since Dr. Seaver turns out to be just a human ... a hu*man* ... I should write him a letter and tell him what happened ... Someone should tell him what happened to me ... Except I'm not always sure that I know myself ... I think what I'm asking you is how I know my life will come with me if I go to Washington. That sounds like a new version of Inside Dawn and Outside Dawn. The Outside goes off to Washington and leaves the Inside. Funny, I started to say it was bad, to go to Washington without my insides. Then I remembered how that was the part I always wanted to leave with you. The fucked-up baby. Hold on to this baby for me so Tom Grace will think I'm a grownup. Remember? Now I think I have to take her with me ... Maybe that's part of being an adult, actually. Not being too scared to let the child come with you . . . knowing she's there . . . so you can handle her. You have to be able to do that because she's you. If she's telling you she's been left on the doorstep in this dumb city where you don't know a soul you can . . . what? Pat her on the head and tell her she's all right. Find something for her . . . you . . . to do . . . I'll tell you something . . . There are times when I feel quite certain that what I want to do is commute to Washington for weekends until the end of July, then move there. Jack's firm is going to find him a furnished sublet until the election is settled. And then there are other times when I know that there's no way in the world I'm going to walk out of this office forever and into August . . ."

23

EARLY ON THE HOT brilliant Friday just before Memorial Day weekend, Lulu and the boys rode out to East Hampton with the Mayers in their station wagon because the gas shortage had become serious and it didn't make sense to use two cars. At Bonnie's suggestion, the Shinefelds stayed in the big house with the Mayers for their first country weekend of the year.

While this was a thoughtful notion, Lulu did not become peaceful. From her bedroom she could see across the great lawn to the cottage that was now pervaded by memories of Charles. By craning her neck she could see the porch chair that had become his favorite and the swing he'd wanted to get rid of because swings made him nervous. (On the rare occasion that he'd been persuaded to try one as a child, he'd expected at each forward motion to fly

503

into the air and lose his brains on the pavement.) Hanging from a hook over the kitchen window would be the food mill she'd bought because he found lumps in the cold soup when it had only been through the Cuisinart.

"Is it possible for you to believe," she had asked Charles during the only phone call with which he'd succeeded in reaching her, "that I never want to see you again?"

"It's possible for me to believe that you believe it," he'd replied.

And she'd hung up because even that wasn't true.

Often Lulu remembered Dawn Henley's concern that the vessel Captain Ego was sailing would turn out to be sinking or empty. In this period of Lulu's life it was what she experienced as a problem that her own captain and vessel were sturdy to a point where they might sail indefinitely through black waters with gray skies above them.

The children had been wonderful. Sascha had flown to New York for a brief visit, assured her mother that she was "much better off without that creepy son-of-a-bitch," discussed her plans to move to New York in June, and appeared undaunted by the difficulty of locating an apartment she could afford. If Sascha had previously been showing signs of trying to find some reason for her mother's continued existence, it was clear that Teddy and Walden were motivated solely by the desire to make up to their mother for what had been done to her by the Outsider, the Invader, the Rogue Male. Lulu felt that she had to be careful and spent more time than she otherwise might have with Bonnie and Duke; the boys had to know that she didn't need them to take care of her. Still, Teddy continued to behave like a cross between an angel and a cavalier, and Walden, as usual, followed his example.

"I might find myself another boyfriend, you know," she warned them one Sunday morning when they surprised her with breakfast in bed.

But in truth she didn't feel that this would happen. She was weary and she was terribly cynical. Traditionally she had found it easy to turn off the concerns of her own life in dealing with her patients. Now she had to monitor herself regularly to ensure that the despair she was feeling about life and love didn't lead her to make unnecessary comments or draw inappropriate conclusions. The thoughts that flowed through her nonprofessional mind, however, were considerably more difficult to monitor.

She was forty-five years old. She had no interest in meeting another man but knew that sooner or later she would, and that she would not necessarily be the better off for it. Bonnie and other friends kept inviting her to meetings and parties, but they were mostly places where she could run into Charles, or places that were associated with him in her mind, and it was inconceivable that she might find herself absorbing a lecture, or being flirtatious, or even just enjoying herself in such a context. She would feel disloyal—not to him, but to herself. It would be about Charles. She would only be kidding herself. Everything about men was about him. Unfortunately, to envision a time when this would not be so was to see herself as a potential member of that vast army of anxious single women whom the changing times had mobilized along the landscape in the years since the Second World War and its spectacular finale. There appeared to be females who were comfortable in their single lives, but they were more often widows than divorcees, more often in their mid-fifties than Lulu's age. Had anyone written about the difference between being divorced and being widowed insofar as it affected the desire for another man? This reminded her of the paper she'd once intended to write on Charlotte Goldhammer and that expanding legion of women who appeared to have become increasingly driven by sex as it became increasingly easy to drive all night without getting anyplace.

It struck Lulu now that she had been ignoring the most obvious therapy she might find for her free hours. Between the boys, the Mayers, and a practice that was becoming almost too full for comfort, she hadn't made any attempt to speed along her recovery. What she needed to do was to mobilize her energies toward writing that paper.

On Saturday morning Lulu asked how Bonnie would feel about keeping the boys for the remainder of the weekend while she returned to New York and made an attempt to begin writing. Bonnie thought this was a terrific idea if it was what she really wanted to do. Lulu caught the first possible train to New York and six hours later she was home, brewing a pot of coffee.

She sat down at her desk and spread out her pad, ballpoint pen, and a box of tissues.

She got up to check the coffee. It was ready but there was no milk. She would leave the coffee machine on and run out to pick up milk and a couple of other necessities. Then she would hole up until the boys' return. She got her bag, opened the front door, and there was Charles, his finger raised to press the buzzer.

"I throw myself on your mercy," Charles said. "I can't stay with them unless I have you. I can't live without pleasure. Be my pleasure."

Lulu began to cry.

Charles closed and locked the door, took her hand, and led her through the apartment, glancing toward the boys' rooms but asking no questions, continuing on to her bedroom, which was cool and dark, its shades down. He closed the door, gathered her into his arms, kissed her, licked the tears from her cheeks, kissed her wet eyes, kissed her lips again, made her suck his tongue. She was a rag doll; she sagged when he let go of her to guide her to the bed. At first he tried to hold her up but then he sank to the floor with her instead. Letting her lie on the rug, he opened her brassiere, pulled up her T-shirt, pulled down her jeans and slid into her...How had he managed to get off his own jeans? Or maybe he was still partly wearing them...And there they were, like the embodiment of some overriding law of physics...or was it chemistry? What has been lost must be restored and its place must have been waiting...

"Oh my God, Charles, oh my God...Where have you been? Oh my God..."

She only stopped crying as she was coming; each time she finished coming she began crying again, and even after Charles had come with her, and they were lying inert on the rug, Charles still on top of her, still in her, the tears didn't stop entirely but continued to dribble from her eyes. She fell asleep and awakened because Charles was withdrawing from her.

He took off his clothes, then returned. Kneeling, he took off her sneakers, then her jeans. Lying between her legs, leaning over her so she wouldn't get cold, interrupting his undressing chores to kiss her thighs, her bush, her belly, he got one arm and then the other out of the sleeves of her T-shirt, lifted her torso to pull it over her head, got the brassiere, fondled her breasts, sucked her nipples, kissed her neck...touched her, fondled her, touched her. No one had touched her in so long and she hadn't even... At this moment it was difficult to understand how she had lived all these weeks without being touched, caressed, without the feeling of another warm skin next to hers. When was it that she'd last endured such deprivation? For so many years there had been children around to touch even when there weren't men. Now the boys were at an age when you had to leave them alone; it was threatening to them to be fondled all the time.

There were no tears left.

When Charles moved away, she began to shiver, but he was only helping her up to the bed, pulling back the blanket, slipping a pillow under her head. Covering her.

"Let me look at you," he murmured. "I need to see what you look like. I haven't *seen* you in...You look like hell, Lu. It hasn't been good for you, not having me around."

She laughed and then she began to cry again. "Asshole," she blubbered.

"Why'd you hold out for so long?" he asked. "I know you had to do it for a while, but—"

"My brain is still holding out," she said. "You just can't tell from my body."

"It'll be better than it used to be, Lu," he said. "I'm not going to be paranoid. I'm going to make more time for you, not play any of the old . . . I'll be careful but not like before. If she finds out, she'll find out. If she doesn't like it, I'll give her the choice. Both of you or just you."

Uh-oh. He was out for revenge.

"Don't be dumb," she said. "I'd stop in a minute if Anna found out. I hope I'll stop anyway." But slowly this time.

"What are you worried about? You think Anna gives a shit about how you felt when I went back?"

She would be Anna all the time again. Never Annie or any of the other softnesses that had grown in the space between the two of them when they were separated.

"She doesn't *have* to give a shit for me, Charles. For all I know, she suspected that we were . . . Anyway, if this is mostly revenge you're into here, please try to be a little more subtle about it."

"I love you," he said. "You are the love of my life."

"I'm starting work on a paper," she said. "On the penis as the lost breast. As the symbol of everything one doesn't have but needs to be happy."

"Where're the boys?"

"At the Mayers'."

"I'm supposed to be at the office. Also working on a paper."

"But I'm really doing it, Charles. And it's important to me. It's an important subject. Women thinking we need men much more than we do."

"Thinking, thinking, thinking," Charles murmured. "Is that what your pussy was doing? Thinking?"

"When I finish the paper," Lulu said as he began to make love to her again, "maybe I'll be finished with you, too."

But she didn't feel moved to work on the paper because she was all right again. If her brain kept a distance from Charles that it hadn't previously maintained, if she argued with him as she had when they lived together instead of reverting to that condition in which negative feelings couldn't be indulged because one eye was always on the clock, if she had to guard against Charles's desire to turn her into a visible weapon in his marital wars, she was still all right. Resentment at the fact didn't keep her from being so.

Now she was the paranoid one, refusing to go out to dinner lest they be seen, and Charles was the one who was willing to take risks.

Now she was the one who complained of interference with her work. Charles had much less trouble getting away than he'd once had. He even got into the habit of spending Saturday afternoons with her when the boys were with Nathan.

It was on a Saturday afternoon, when they had made love and then Lulu had vacated her side of the bed to do some work, that the half-asleep Charles rolled over onto her side to pick up the phone before remembering where he was. He said hello and the person at the other end hung up. Lulu thought it must have been Anna, but Charles said Anna was at someone's house in Sag Harbor with the children.

A few days later Sascha called to express her rage and disappointment. Just as she'd finally thought her mother was turning into a reasonable adult, Sascha was pained beyond description to find Lulu tied back into a relationship right out of the Marquis de Sade.

"Nothing human is alien to me," Lulu murmured.

"What?" Sascha shouted.

"Nothing," Lulu said. "Anyway, remember about being your own person? About not feeling endangered by my weaknesses?"

"Some fucking role model you are, Lulu!"

Lulu sighed. It was easier to deal with Sascha when her daughter was utterly insane than when Sascha was a mixture of insanity and perception so that it became necessary to pick one's way between them.

"I'm not sure we can do too well with this over the phone, Satch," Lulu said. "Weren't you supposed to be in New York by now, anyway?

"The apartment situation is impossible," Sascha said, "and I can't afford to spend the whole summer in East Hampton. I think I'm going to California. Maybe in the fall. Anyway, I don't want to be in New York while you're hanging out with that middle-aged creep."

24

By the beginning of May Dawn had committed herself to the plan of moving to Washington at the end of July to live with Jack but commuting until then. The decision brought up a new set of anxieties.

"I'm thinking of what happened to Tony and Vera right after I left...I spent so much time talking about the divorce with Dr. Seaver, and I understand a lot of my feelings about it, but still...I really *was* the glue that stuck them together and they really came apart when I left. Maybe they'd have come apart anyway, but I don't know that. Not deeply. If I try to look at our lives, what I come up with is, if I'd stayed for another five or ten years maybe Tony and Vera would have been together that much longer."

"And if so?"

"Well then...I guess I should have stayed. But I don't know if I could have stood Marbury for that long. Even when I was a teenager, there wasn't that much there for me...It was beautiful and cozy but...I mean, I always said they'd sent me to boarding school against my will, and it wasn't a lie in the sense that I really was scared. But it also was a lie because I'd have gone crazy if I had to go to high school in Marbury. I was bored by seventh grade. I used to wonder what was in the world past Vermont and Boston...without exactly wanting to go and find out. But I never could've admitted that to Tony and Vera. It would have sounded disloyal...What did you ask me before? I know. What if I did cause them to break up by leaving. When you ask me that I hear, maybe I had to do it anyway. But that certainly never occurred to me before. That's a new idea to me, that they weren't my responsibility...Not that it doesn't make sense...I was *their* baby, after all...They weren't mine...But it feels weird even to say it aloud...that it was time for me to go no matter what happened behind me...Weird, but not uncomfortable...Actually, there's a knot that gets untied just from thinking of it that way. That it was all right to go no matter what. I wasn't responsible...Marbury is a very small town, you know. I really couldn't...I didn't *want* to stay there forever."

Dawn cried softly.

"What about here?" the doctor asked, almost as softly.

"Well, this room is even smaller than Marbury, of course...But it's also the whole world...Once I dreamed that I brought Tony and Vera here to meet you and we all sat around together, talking, hugging ...but really they're in this room with me all the time. It's the only place I can still be with both of them ... Everyone is here ... On the other hand, you have to go to new places and meet new people. From the world of the present ... Not that it's such a terrific world ... You fixed me up so I could go out into it but it's a pretty rotten place ... I don't suppose you'd want to go to Washington with me and start fixing up Congress ... I had an idea for a cartoon, after what you said about politics being full of emotion ... It was the inside of the Senate, with tiers of seats. All the members were sitting in their places, thinking, orating, whatever, and under their seats were their little demons, carrying on, screaming, fighting over who gets what ... Washington ... I guess if I weren't afraid of being too much on my own ... and if I didn't feel guilty about leaving ... I might like to be in Washington for a while ..."

Just before Memorial Day weekend, Dawn and Jack had flown to Washington to look at the sublets Jack's firm had lined up for them. They had had a terrible fight because of the two serious possibilities, Dawn had been drawn to the top floor of an attached house in Georgetown, while Jack had been uncompromisingly in favor of a super-modern place close to his office and the Capitol. Dawn came into Dr. Shinefeld's office after the weekend in a state of rage. She was infuriated by the idea that she'd ever even considered moving to a strange city to be with "that rotten pig. Maybe Jessica is right after all and men aren't just different, they're pigs."

515

After their argument and while Jack was in the bathroom, Dawn had packed her overnight bag, taken a cab to the airport and caught the first plane to La Guardia. Saturday morning of Memorial Day weekend. She hadn't known where to go from La Guardia except that she was determined not to return to the apartment or anyplace where Jack could find her. She'd tried to get a rental car, thinking maybe she would drive to Boston, or Vermont. She had tried Vera from both airports but gotten no response. She'd called the doctor's summer number and been told it wasn't connected yet. As she was standing at the Hertz counter, trying to figure out what to do next, one of two businessmen standing in line next to her had asked if there was anything wrong. A pick-up but a nice one. The men were driving out to Long Island. To Southampton. Could they be of service.

"Of course I thought of Tom Grace right away. I'd thought of him before I even got on the plane. I was trying to figure out how to find you and then I thought if I couldn't ... I was so angry with Jack and it seemed as though I had to do something to get back at him. I didn't know what I'd do if Tom wasn't there, or if he was with someone. Yes I did. One of the guys was the other's guest and he wasn't married, or at least his wife wasn't with him. They made it clear they'd be delighted to have my company. Germans, you know, with that perfect English. Or maybe once I was out there I'd be able to get a car and just drive around. As soon as I thought about going into Manhattan I thought about the old Burger King sidewalk and that old disgust came over me. Besides,

I didn't want to see Jack before I talked to you. I didn't know—don't know—how I'll deal with him. We said everything there was to say. Tom drove me in this morning. I feel very guilty about Tom. Maybe because he was a substitute for you, in a way. Like the first time. I felt as though I was fucking up and you'd disapprove. Then just now when you were looking at me, sort of serious, sympathetic, I had to admit that I was the one who disapproved. I don't even like him that much. I just had no choice. Not that it was an awful weekend. Loads of people around the house and you couldn't tell who was attached to whom. Tom was perfectly charming. He bought my whole grownup act. I'm calling it an act because that's what I felt as though it was this weekend. I told him the truth about how I got there except what I didn't show was how much I cared. I mean about Jack. So I didn't really tell the truth. Not that anything I do with Tom Grace matters. This weekend he thought maybe I was the woman he was really ready to settle down with, but just let a little time pass. Let him see some signs that I can love someone... It infuriates me that I love Jack because then I feel as though I have no choices and I can't stand to feel that way... I want to ask you something. Do you think I'm wrong about the apartment?"

"What do *you* think?"

"I can't tell. I feel as though I'm going such a long way to please him and—"

"Just to please *him?*"

"Well, I guess... All right. I want to be with him. I just can't stand for it to be a hundred percent on his terms. It's not that the city apartment is so awful. I could stand it. I can buy a car. I can drive to Georgetown. But I like Georgetown as a home. Washington doesn't have the same feeling. And more than that, I want him to give way to me on something. He acts as though he can take me or leave me even when he says he wants to get married. It's as though he has no stake in whether I go or not. Jack's never had to compromise with women, you know. If I was giving him a hard time there was always a Lillian waiting around to help him feel better. If his sister thinks I should have choices he can always go out and find some little . . . cocksucker . . . Oh, God, I don't think I ever used that word before . . . someone to tell him she wants him to make all the decisions. But that's not me! I'm not going with him unless he takes the apartment in Georgetown!"

Dawn's diatribe came to an end but her body didn't relax. She sat expectantly, facing the doctor, her body tensed as though for an argument. "Does that sound crazy to you?" she finally demanded.

"How about to you?"

"It sounds perfectly sane to me."

"Well, it sounds perfectly sane to me, too."

Dawn burst into tears and cried for some time. "I'm relieved in a way but I feel terrible. I don't have any idea of what he'll do, and I'm going to miss him in the worst way if . . . I can't even stand to think about it . . . . At least I could be in analysis a bit longer. Maybe until December. Or January. I'll be all right once the autumn comes . . . I guess I can spend some time with Tom in Southampton. I have no illusions about him as a Jack substitute but he can be fun. I can take Tom for who he is . . . Not that I'm all that crazy about who he is. He's really worse than he used to be...I think he's had a hair transplant and that really turned me off. I remember I was...Oh my God!" She stared at the doctor in horror. "I left my diaphragm in Washington! I can't believe this. Saturday morning, I thought we were going to be in the hotel for another night, and I put it in the night table drawer. When I left I never thought about it, and I haven't thought about it since...This is awful. I can't believe I did the same thing I did with Dr. Seaver!"

"I was thinking as you talked about Tom Grace, that the way you discussed having to master your feelings with him reminded me of times when you talked about having to do that with Dr. Seaver."

"How can I think when I'm worried sick about being pregnant?" Dawn wailed.

"All right. Talk about being worried sick that you're pregnant."

"You make it sound as though it's some kind of fantasy."

"When is your period due?" the doctor asked, glancing at the clock. The hour was over. Her next patient was waiting.

"I don't know exactly. This week. Couple of days. I can feel I'm pretty swollen. Sandy was pregnant for three months once. She said it was just like right before your period except the feeling doesn't go away...I don't remember how my body felt last time. I don't think I was aware of how it felt."

"Our time is up," the doctor said. "But, I'll tell you...If you failed to use your diaphragm for a few days there may be some reason for concern."

"Concern! Are you kidding? Do you realize it's not even Jack I'm pregnant by? If it were Jack I'd have to go to Washington however I felt! But it's idiot Tom Grace! Who if I never see him again it won't be a minute too soon!"

"On the other hand," the doctor continued, rising from her chair although Dawn was frantically gripping the arms of hers, "I don't see any automatic cause for panic. Your period isn't even due yet. It's possible that you're pregnant. But it's also possible that you've just been frightened by your own wishes."

ℭ

On Wednesday afternoon Dawn came into the office without meeting the doctor's eyes, sat down in the chair, stood up, went to the couch, and lay down.

"Jack signed the lease for Georgetown. He was trying to find me all weekend to tell me. He signed it and came home the next day. He didn't even ask where I was. He just said he was wrong. He'd been a real shit. He didn't realize until then what it would mean to lose me. He'd taken me for granted and he wouldn't do that anymore... You know who feels like a real shit now, don't you? I don't know what I'll do if I'm pregnant. I guess even if he has to know about the abortion there's no reason he has to know it's... Oh, God, I couldn't go through it pretending it was his. I wouldn't even want an abortion if it were his... I mean, there could be worse things than going off to a strange city with a little baby to keep you company." Dawn laughed uneasily. "I think I'm waiting for you to tell me that's fucked up. I don't like not being able

to see your face but I didn't want you to see mine.
That's why I lay down. I feel like such an idiot. I
feel... Why didn't I go back to Vera's this weekend?
That's what I was thinking about doing. Tony or
Vera's. If I'd waited around at the airport for long
enough I'd have gotten on a plane. I think in my
mind that's what I was doing... going back... Tom
Grace is about you, after all... and about Vera. But
it's also true... just like with Alan Gartner, it was Dr.
Seaver who was on my mind... This weekend it was
Jack who was on my mind... If I had a baby—it
would be the baby of my anger at Jack... Actually, I
feel as if I'm getting my period. I have that dull ache
in my lower back. Just a few hours before it comes I
get that...Now I don't know what to say...or feel...if
I'm not pregnant, I mean. All my energies have been
centered around that for the past day. No, the truth
is I forgot about it entirely when I was with Jack. I
was so happy but I also felt odd...It's odd that I
love him so much, I really do love him, and I was
prepared to lose him...if I had to. Right now it
doesn't seem as though I could stand to lose him, but
that's partly because of the things he said that he
never said before."

"Why do you think you worry about being pregnant when you're here but not when you were with
Jack?"

"I don't know. It's tempting to say, well, I always
knew I was going to go with Jack and if I went with
him...well then, the baby is a present for you. It's
the part of myself that I'm leaving with you...But I
didn't know, or at least I don't think I did...I love
you very much, you know...I feel as though you

love me...Not in the same way that you love your own children, but it's real anyway...I remember the time I threw up in the middle of your office and you said you didn't care. At first I didn't believe you, but it was very important. I needed you to love every part of me...my vilest wishes...I needed you to be able to bear everything I wanted...You can't give up something until you know that it's all right for you to want it. I think I can feel that I have my period..."

25

CHARLES WAS FREER than he'd once been to make time for Lulu; his lovemaking was as great a joy as ever, his appreciation less hedged than before.

The trouble was, Lulu's brain wasn't allowing her to enjoy her good fortune.

The trouble was, Lulu hadn't been able to recover that mistress's sense of Charles as someone whose faults were lovable and did not affect herself.

"Every time she looks at me," Charles had once said of Anna, "she sees the dopey little butterball she married who stood on tables and recited *Gunga Din* when he was drunk and told dirty jokes at her grandmother's funeral."

The trouble was, while Lulu had once been able to enjoy the boy's manic energy and high spirits even as she luxuriated in the physical and mental prowess of the man, the boy now felt like a threat to her as well

523

as to Anna. The boy wanted too much from both of them and the man had so little motive to control the boy.

Certainly Charles hadn't been lying—as far as she knew he never told her outright lies—when he claimed that Anna was cool, unpsychological (the cardinal sin), devoid of visceral need. Why, then, couldn't Lulu regain the sense of Charles as Anna's victim that had furnished the original rationale for providing aid and comfort? Particularly when Anna had discarded him in such a humiliating manner only to pull him back as he began to adjust?

The trouble was, she was identifying with Anna instead of with Charles.

Charles told Lulu that while he loved more than ever that quivering sensibility and wide-angled vision that wouldn't permit her to shut out one part of the world in the interest of enjoying another, Anna didn't need or want her sympathy. If Lulu was looking for someone's wife to worry about, she might give some thought to the wives of the Iranian hostages. There was that terrific-looking one in Brooklyn who he thought could use some comfort, not that he was certain Lulu was the one who should give it to her. Better yet, let Lulu start thinking about the Pentagon's taking over the country if Reagan got the nomination and then was elected in November. Charles's own theory was that the army had fucked up the helicopter raid to make sure Carter didn't get any reflected glory. In the meantime, Charles would like to suggest, in all due modesty, that Lulu count her blessings—particularly one he'd been saving as a surprise: Anna was involved in an important case in Washington, D.C., that would come to trial at some point during the summer. Because Anna's schedule was uncertain, the boys were being sent to camp for the first time and Victoria would spend the summer with her grandparents. In other words, Charles would be free, *free,* FREE for a good portion of that time of the year when he and Lulu had the greatest leisure to enjoy each other. If Lulu should happen to be able to find it within herself to enjoy him as she once had. If not, maybe he'd have to divorce Anna, marry Lulu, and go find himself some nice, dumb, happy-go-lucky—

"THAT'S NOT FUNNY!" Lulu screamed.

Lulu told Bonnie that from now on she wanted to go to all the parties and meet men and feel trapped because she liked Charles better than any of them instead of feeling trapped because there weren't any. But by the time summer rolled around Lulu had attended too many parties and suspected that she was doing with her evenings what Dawn Henley had once done with her dreams—stocking them with crowds of busy, brightly dressed people to avoid feelings—of what, in her own case?

Guilt. And the anxiety that stemmed from the sense that one was due for punishment.

Anna had spent much of July in Washington. Lulu's boys and the Mayer children had remained in East Hampton with the Mayer housekeeper while their parents commuted. Lulu left her car at the cottage and rode back and forth with the Mayers. While the gas shortage made it desirable to use only one car, she was less than comfortable with Duke these days and usually tried to go to sleep on the seat in the rear. Duke was acting cool because he was irritated by the resumption of an affair he found undesirable on several grounds. Beginning with his dislike of Charles and ending with that complex brew that masqueraded as professional disapproval and pervaded the Institute when one of its members broke rank.

Sascha had returned to New York after all; with nearly perfect grades from the University of Miami and excellent recommendations from people there and at the New York Psychoanalytic, she had been admitted to New York University to study for a master's in social work. Through an ad in the *Village Voice* she'd arranged to take a room with a divorced woman on the NYU faculty who had two small children. She would babysit a set number of evenings per week in exchange for her rent. In the meantime, she was working as a waitress at a restaurant in Montauk, "edging up on New York," as she put it. Walter Crawford awaited only a signal from Sascha to begin looking for a job in New York, but at the moment Sascha felt like "keeping open my options."

In the last weeks of her analysis Dawn was commuting to Washington most weekends but spending an occasional weekend with the Silversteins in Boston or a few days with Vera in Vermont. Dawn was on what she referred to as "my emotional merry-go-round, visiting the feelings of the past, straining to see the ones in the future." Her mood was volatile. Following some happy adventure in her new city she would become morose over the loss of her New York life, or angry with the doctor for letting her go too easily.

"I guess you don't love me enough to make me stay, is how I feel. Not *make* me stay. You couldn't do that. But urge me to...Well, not urge, because then I'd be scared that you thought I couldn't manage on my own, or that you needed me...I don't want you to need me exactly. But I need you to care about what happens to me. I couldn't bear it if I thought you would forget me."

"Do you believe that it's possible that I might?"

Dawn cried softly. "No, not really...Even if I don't think about you all the time...That's not the same as forgetting you."

Dawn was scheduled to spend July Fourth weekend with Vera. On the morning after that weekend the doctor's phone rang and she picked it up, noticing that the machine was still on and she'd forgotten to listen to her messages. The caller was Dawn, who asked in a trembling voice if the doctor had gotten her message.

"Not yet," the doctor said. "I just walked into the office."

"Vera's had a heart attack."

"I'm sorry. How is she now?"

"I don't know," Dawn said, her voice barely audible. "She's in the hospital and she doesn't want to see anyone yet. I went up there not knowing. With Sandy. The house was empty so we just...I don't suppose you have a free hour."

"I'm sorry. I'm looking at my book but there's no time at all...How soon is Vera expected out of the hospital?"

"I don't know," Dawn said. "About a week."

"That sounds encouraging. A heart attack isn't the end of the world anymore, you know. People live after them for many years."

"You don't understand," Dawn said. "Vera is Wonder Woman. The first time I saw the comic strip I asked why they made her hair black instead of blond. I thought her bracelets were the same as Vera's big gold watch only she had two of them."

"I think we'll have a lot to talk about tomorrow," the doctor said. "In the meantime, you might want to think about the possibility that as you've been seeing Dr. Seaver and me more realistically, you've been reinvesting that need for a god in Vera."

∽

"I hadn't told her about Washington. I think I still felt a little guilty. I just said I might be coming up July Fourth but then I decided to surprise her. Lillian's gone home already but I picked up Sandy in Westport and she came with me...Nobody was home when we got there. The jeep was in the garage, which was peculiar, because that's the car she always uses, but I figured something was wrong with it. I have a key but the house isn't locked in the daytime ...It seems to me now that it felt a little strange but maybe I'm just remembering...I took Sandy through the downstairs and the second story, then when there was still nobody home we went up to the attic. Wait. I remember when I became uneasy. It was the greenhouse. I looked in it and I saw that a lot of stuff that would normally have been transplanted to the garden already was still there. And the orchids looked neglected. I remember it occurred to me that maybe Francine was sick and Vera was spending too much time at her home to take care of the plants. That was when I remembered Francine..."

"How long has Vera had a greenhouse?" the doctor asked.

"Always," Dawn said. "Haven't I mentioned it before?"

"I don't believe so."

"That's funny... I told you about Dr. Seaver's greenhouse, didn't I?"

"Yes."

"Well, that was one of the reasons I felt at home when I got there. Not that his is comparable... Anyway, when Vera still didn't come home, I took Sandy up to the attic. She got all excited about the trunks. She started doing a number— Sandy Drew and the Secret of the Old Trunks. We were looking at the old clothes and stuff. I wasn't worried about not asking because I thought everything belonged to my parents. But one of the trunks turned out to be Vera's. Her name was on the inside of the lid but I didn't see it at first... Well, maybe I saw but it didn't register. Maybe I didn't want it to. The trunk was full of photos— Trophies. Yearbooks. There were a lot of big pictures of my father and his father. I could see what they looked like much better than in the snapshots. I smuggled one out and brought it home. I didn't want to ask Vera because I didn't know how she'd feel about our having seen all of them. In the one I brought home, he's smoking a cigarette and he has a white silk ascot around his neck. He looks as though he just came from the theater. He was very beautiful and very young. Before he met my mother. At least there are no pictures of her in the trunk. It's a shame. There're lots of snapshots of other people ... girls at school, school plays. Traveling. Sometimes Vera's in them but mostly I think she was the photographer ... I never thought of Vera as having woman friends. Maybe after Tony she didn't bother .... There was also stuff of Gordon's in the trunk ... this is the wildest part ... yearbooks, school compositions. At first I thought it was an accident that they were in there, but then ... There were hundreds of letters and postcards between the two of them. Mostly from Vera to my father. They were very carefully wrapped, as though they were precious. And they went back to when my father was, I think eight, maybe ten. Vera had graduated from Smith and she was traveling in Europe and she wrote to him almost every day, dozens of cards and letters, telling him about her adventures and promising that she would come back to Europe and bring him with her when he was old enough ... I was astounded, after the way she talked about him ... I figured maybe she adored him when he was little and turned on him later. But they continue. She wrote when he was in college and sounded very loving. His answers sounded more like a kid who's got to write to his parents. My mind was blown by the whole collection. I wanted to talk to Vera but I hadn't a clue what I'd say ... It was as though she loved him but she was ashamed of loving him. But maybe if he hadn't been...No...She was angry with her mother for making him who he was but she loved him that way, too...When I came downstairs I was feeling so loving toward Vera. In the past few years, the way she spoke of my father put a warp in my attitude toward her. I wanted to tell her I loved her more because she cared for him...She still wasn't home, so I picked up the phone to call Francine's house but then the sheriff's car pulled into the driveway. I was puzzled because he'll come by if he sees a strange car in the driveway and no one home...But Vera's jeep was in the garage..." Her voice grew tearful. "I went out to talk to him. I've known him forever. I told him it was my car and asked if he knew where Vera was. I could tell something was wrong from the way he looked at me. He said not to be alarmed, she was going to be all right, but Vera was in the hospital in Rutland. Francine came home a little while later...Oh my God, did you hear what I said? I said she came *home*...You know what I'm upset about, don't you? That I called it her home and it's not. But it's going to be. She's selling her house and moving in with Vera. I have a feeling she wanted to do it before and Vera wouldn't let her, but now...At the moment I said it was her home, it felt like a mistake. That's because I want it to be. I can't stand to think of her living there." Dawn began to cry. "That house is Vera's and Tony's and mine and the thought of that fat, dopey little woman moving in is enough to drive me crazy. But then as soon as I hear my own words I hate myself! This woman who may have saved Vera's life, who drove her to the hospital and visits her every day and is going to care for her, and I can't stand—I can't even stand that she's the one who's doing all that! *I* want to take care of Vera. I know it's crazy but it's the way I feel. If Vera wanted me to, I'd drop everything and spend a few months in Vermont... Well, not everything. But I'm sure I could take care of her just as well as that idiot Francine. Then I hear myself again and I can't tell you how disgusted I am. After nine years of analysts' couches I'm lying here being jealous of someone who's caring for the person I love most in the whole world. That's disgusting. It would be disgusting even if Vera hadn't had a heart attack. I still would hate myself for having feelings like that at this stage of my life."

"Which stage is that?"

"The stage where I'm supposed to be nearly grown up."

"Grownups don't have feelings?"

"Yes, but not those awful, miserable, babyish... Well, I suppose feelings are feelings. Grownups... I guess somewhere you assume you're bringing up those feelings to get rid of them. The bad ones, at least. But how can I get rid of feelings about Vera when she's one of the most important people in my life? It's not even as though she was just herself. After all, she was also my real father in my mind... I think I always wanted to be everything to her... So when I was little I was jealous of Tony... And now I'm jealous of Francine... You know, however crazy it sounds, I think... in some crucial sense... I never knew that Vera was going to die. Tony got sick. Vera went on and on. The only person in my life who's always been there... Well, first she was my father, then she was herself, then...She was there...in Tom Grace...in...Maybe Jack looks more like Dr. Seaver but his personality is more like Vera's...Do you realize, if it weren't for Vera I never would have found Dr. Seaver...and without Dr. Seaver, I wouldn't have you?"

For some time Dawn spoke of her love for Vera and her fear of not being able to endure Vera's death. Eventually the doctor asked Dawn when she thought Vera would die.

"How'm I supposed to know?" Dawn asked.

"That's the point."

"But what am I supposed to do in the meantime? How am I supposed to be? I don't want her to die but I don't want her to be old and sick, either. I just don't know how to be. Nothing like this has ever happened to me before!"

"Well, I suppose the first thing to say is that you aren't going to affect the course of Vera's recovery, which will proceed along its own lines. The second is that something like this *has* happened to you, and you dealt with it in the same way. You were ready to write off Tony as soon as she became ill, rather than endure the uncertainty. You're not just concerned about Vera, you're so frightened of losing her that you want to get the mourning over with."

"All at once," Dawn said slowly. "I'm saying good-bye to you...to her...to everyone...Then I'll really have to start a new life...There won't be any choice."

26

THE FIRST OF AUGUST fell on a Friday, but the week's big party was being thrown on Wednesday night in Manhattan by an analyst named Ben Hirschfield and his wife, Patsy Mayweather Hirschfield, who was active in Amnesty International and in the Carter campaign.

It was a cool evening. After some deliberation Lulu decided to wear the beautiful red silk dress that Charles had given her the year before for her birthday. She swept up her hair on one side only and clipped a fresh iris into the barrette, where its deep, brilliant blue was set off by the almost black and almost white streaks of hair against which it rested. Lulu was becoming almost fond of those hairs, perhaps because they seemed to know their place at her temples and were not progressing at the rate she'd once feared they would.

"Now there's a fine, healthy-looking woman," Duke said when Lulu met the Mayers in the lobby.

Lulu smiled. Perhaps Bonnie had asked him to be nice; they were his kindest words to her in a while.

A fine, healthy-looking woman. Bonnie and Duke knew as her other friends did not that it had taken a second analysis for Lulu to be able to accept any tribute to her health or strength, which had always been an embarrassment to her, her father having reacted to both as though the responsible genes should have known better than to come out of the closet in a quiet Manhattan apartment where there was no conceivable use for them.

Because it was not only cool but dry and clear, Lulu and the Mayers decided to walk through Central Park and up to the restaurant near the Hirschfields' where they had dinner reservations. She was in a nostalgic mood and parks tended to be evocative for Lulu, a child of Riverside Park, only a block from the apartment house where she'd been raised. In Riverside there was the eagle statue onto which little Lulu had climbed to terrify a succession of nurses who'd screamed at her in foreign languages from half a block away, where they'd been talking to someone else's keeper. Here in Central Park there were the various nesting places of adolescence, safe from her parents' friends because they were more than five long blocks from home. In another world. And the lake where in a safer era, on high school prom night, Lulu and her gang had stripped and jumped into the icy water. When she was little it had been her father's chore to take Lulu to the playground on weekend afternoons so her mother could have some time to herself; years later he would want to know why there were grass stains on the back of her clothes when it was only the beginning of April. A fine, healthy-looking woman. Perhaps as a child she had wondered how he could be so distressed by signs of her life, he who kept a book of dirty limericks in his underwear drawer and drunkenly pinched his wife's backside when he thought no one was looking.

More than a pleasure, Charles had been an enormous relief to Lulu. Here, finally, was a human who stood in relation to the world as she'd felt herself to have stood in the world of her parents—large, a trifle grotesque, and endlessly needy.

Lulu and the Mayers walked in silence. Gradually Lulu relaxed. First she forgot about Charles. Then they left the park and she forgot about her father. By the time she'd had dinner and a few glasses of wine, she was mellow and didn't mind when Duke couldn't see the point of the Charlotte Goldhammer paper. Duke was unremittingly analytic and didn't know why anyone would bother with sociology, once the psyche was well in hand. Lulu smiled benignly at Duke, who told her she'd better not continue drinking when they got to the party.

Lulu knew, however, even before she saw the hundreds of bodies waving like wheat stalks in the Hirschfields' high-rise, that she was going to disregard his injunction.

They had passed through the welcoming committee: Ben Hirschfield, tall, white-haired, bearded, and profoundly melancholy; his second wife, Patsy, slender and attractive, poised in that special way that only the rich from birth are poised, but pleasant nonetheless, wearing a white silk safari suit and telling them all how pleased she was that they could come; Patsy's brother, Lloyd Mayweather, tall and handsome, in a white suit with black pinstripes, a lavender shirt and a purple tie, his arm around an extremely fat woman in gypsy regalia whom he was introducing to each arrival as the love of his life.

They had managed to get some wine and Lulu had edged her way through the crowd toward the long balcony outside the glass-walled living room. On the balcony, which was lighted by Japanese lanterns that whipped madly in the wind, Lulu found Miles Tepler, an attractive younger man with whom she'd been in the postdoctoral program at Columbia. Still married to Nathan and the mother of two very young boys, Lulu had carried on with Miles one of those pleasant flirtations in which she was always offering some young girl in the program for his consideration and he was always complaining that the girl wasn't enough like Lulu. Miles was with a ravishingly beautiful young woman named Diana. He approached, introduced the women, and told Lulu that she was looking ravishingly beautiful. Diana smiled tolerantly and Miles began to recall their Columbia days. A dark-haired man edged up to Diana and began to chat with her; Miles didn't appear to notice. He was beginning a funny story about Lloyd Mayweather. Lulu noticed that Patsy Hirschfield was coming in their direction and warned Miles, which was fortunate because Patsy was speaking to a group that opened to include Miles, Lulu, Diana, and the dark-haired man. Patsy said she hoped she'd be forgiven, she always thought it should be possible to discuss issues, even in a group this size, and how was everyone feeling about Carter these days? Miles said he wasn't actually feeling too terrific about Carter and was thinking of starting a Peanuts for President movement, or was that the same thing? Someone laughed, two people facing Lulu moved away, and time stopped.

On the other side of the glass wall, Charles and Anna Herman stood chatting with another couple.

Lulu wrapped her arms around herself for warmth and only then realized that she was holding a glass of wine and the wine had splashed against the bosom of her dress. She held on to the glass but dropped her purse, Miles picked up the purse, looked at her, and took the glass from her hand.

"You okay?" he asked.

Charles and the other man were laughing-arguing.

Anna and the other woman were listening-interrupting.

Anna, small and slender, neatly contained in a simple gray seersucker suit, all in all a perfect complement to the overflowing spirit beside her, looked up at Charles as he spoke.

"Lulu?" Miles asked. "Do you want to get out of here?"

Anna's expression as she looked at Charles was in turns absorbed, amused, irritated, adoring, impatient, disgusted, absorbed again.

Lulu nodded without looking at Miles.

Anna's attention faltered. She looked around and through the glass wall and saw Lulu. She squinted slightly to make sure she was seeing correctly, clutching her husband's arm as she did so. She was stricken. Her eyes filled with tears. She knew.

Her husband looked through the glass, saw Lulu, then turned toward his wife, his body moving to shield the women from each other's sight.

"Is something wrong?" Patsy Hirschfield asked Lulu.

"No," Lulu said, "I think I just need some air."

On the seventeenth-floor balcony, the wind gusting through her hair, Patsy laughed.

Miles took Lulu's elbow, and with a word to Diana began the job of steering Lulu off the balcony, through the large living room, and out of the apartment. A few minutes later they were on the street. Miles hailed a cab, but Lulu said she'd rather walk through the park. Or around the park. The sky was nearly black. Miles said he would come with her.

"What about Diana?" Lulu asked as they walked toward the park.

"Diana can take care of herself," Miles said.

"What does that mean?" Lulu demanded.

Miles chucked her under the chin. "Dr. Shinefeld is worried about my friend Diana."

"She is your friend, isn't she?" Lulu asked, trying not to sound like a schoolmarm. *Anyway, it's not Diana I'm worried about.*

"I'll tell you about Diana," Miles said with his endearing, lazy grin. "Just because I don't want you to have her on your conscience. Diana's in love with her boss, who wants to get a divorce, except he doesn't know what his wife'll do or what'll happen to his children. Diana can stand it. She's a stockbroker. Handles my account. She's unstoppable. Beats the shit out of the other young brokers in the office because she's so gorgeous that all the idiots, like yours truly, want to deal only with her. If I don't get back to the party Diana'll leave with some other guy who'll turn over his account to her, or introduce her to a guy who makes commercials, or offer to leave his wife for her."

"Oh, Christ," Lulu said miserably. "Everyone only wants who they shouldn't have."

"Now," Miles said, "are you going to tell me what happened up there?"

"No," Lulu said. "Let's go to my place and have a drink and talk about politics."

"Politics," Miles said. "My life is too fucked up for politics. I have to go back to Chicago to get a home-cooked meal."

The boys were watching a movie. In the voice of a person who would brook no nonsense, Lulu introduced them to Miles and ordered them into the storage room to watch the rest of the movie on the old black and white set. Then she brought cognac and a couple of glasses into the living room, where she and Miles toasted each other with an earnestness both mock and real, and she filled their glasses again. It had been a long day and she was very tired.

"I saw a man I had an affair with," Lulu said when she'd finished her second drink. She filled the glass again, although the first two shots were already doing their work. "And his wife. From the way she looked at me, I realized she knew."

"Did she care?"

Lulu smiled wearily.

"Everyone cares."

"I'm not sure. At least they care in different ways. Sometimes they're relieved not to have full responsibility for someone else's life."

"I'll tell you something, Miles. Once I had a husband and I didn't like him or want him, but I didn't want anyone else to have him, either."

"Not nice," Miles murmured flirtatiously. He moved closer to Lulu on the sofa. Lulu was still drinking, but Miles was measuring himself now. He took the small glass from her hand and put it on the coffee table. "I was considering you for one of my Nice Lady medals, but now I'm not sure you're going to make it."

Miles put his arm around her shoulders, gently drew her back with him to rest against the pillows. Lulu rested her head on his shoulder.

"Have you ever been married?" Lulu asked, though her head was cloudy and she was terribly, awfully tired, and she didn't know why she was asking.

"Uh-uh. Lived with a woman for six years."

"When you broke up, was it okay because you weren't married?"

"No."

"Have you noticed," asked Lulu, who was no longer able to keep her eyes open for a minute at a time, "that nobody likes dogs anymore? Everybody wants a cat. People only like an animal that can take care of itself."

She was sure there was some connection between what she was saying and what she—or he—had been saying a moment before, but before she could figure out what it was, she had drifted into sleep.

* * *

When she awakened, Miles was gone, the living room was dark, and someone had covered her with an afghan, but she was cold. She undressed and got into bed, then realized that she was wide awake and very thirsty. She got out of bed, put on a nightgown, took a couple of aspirin, and drank as much water as she could bear to swallow, then got back into bed with a stack of professional magazines in which she thought she would find something to lull her back to sleep. What was it she'd been dreaming?

Lulu opened the magazine on top of the stack and remembered that she had been dreaming about the little girl who gave Nathan the clap. What had been her name, anyway? Rosamonde? Juliet? Something improbable pushed to the absurd by the girl herself, a chubby creature with curly hair, dimpled cheeks, and doleful eyes that begged the camera to love her as she was. She'd wanted Nathan to carry a picture of her and he'd been too touched to refuse to keep it in his wallet, where Lulu had been searching for change of a ten.

Lulu got out of bed, wishing desperately that there was a pack of cigarettes in the house, although it was at least five years since she'd smoked.

In the dream, Rosamonde-Juliet had been walking down West End Avenue, looking for Nathan and Lulu, wanting to explain that she hadn't meant to do any harm, it was only that she loved Nathan so much.

So the name of the little girl in the dream was Lulu.

It was just past midnight. Columbus Avenue would still be lively, and on the block between Columbus

543

and the park there would be enough people for
safety. In any event, she needed to move. She put on
a T-shirt, cotton pants, and sneakers and let herself
out, leaving a note for the boys where it would likely
be seen if one of them should awaken. She bought a
pack of Kools from a restaurant vending machine on
Columbus Avenue, then began walking home—except
that she became aware as she walked that she was
heading toward West End Avenue, the home of her
childhood. She lit a cigarette and continued walking
across Seventy-second Street. There was the delicatessen where Rosamonde-Juliet and her Romeo had
met, the beauty parlor across the street where Lulu's
mother had had her hair cut for thirty years, the
bank from which Lulu and Woody had withdrawn
her savings before leaving for Atlanta. At West End
she crossed Seventy-second Street and walked the
two remaining blocks to the house where she had
lived, aside from her brief period with Woody, from
the time she was an infant until finally Nathan had
come to give her another true home. She leaned
against a car and stood staring into the renovated
lobby, waiting to be overwhelmed by childhood memories; instead, the relatively recent past gnawed at
her brain.

   The past isn't useful until its place in the present is found.
   How quickly and how thoroughly she had dismissed
the array of violent feelings that had overwhelmed
her when she discovered Nathan's infidelity! How
inappropriate, that a man she held in disdain should
have caused her such grief! How unbecoming to
have wanted to strangle a miserable, lonesome fifteen-
year-old who didn't like to go home after school

because her father had left years before and her mother was at work! The disease had been a symbol and a diversion, a way of not attending to the meaning of his act—as though it would have been quite another matter if only the girl hadn't had gonorrhea. Lulu had lived with Nathan for eighteen years and been fond of him for much of that time. He had become a father to her adored girl child and, inevitably, a father to her. And he'd slept in their bed with a grubby child he'd picked up in a delicatessen when Lulu went to a conference and left him alone with the children for two days.

She was crying.

She moved from the well-lighted spot where she'd been resting to a darker place on the block. But then, instead of leaning against another car, she continued to walk uptown, and to cry. When she reached the last block of West End Avenue, she had stopped crying. She walked over to Broadway, hailed a cab, went home, took some more aspirin, lay down on her bed, and fell asleep.

On Thursday morning, July 31st, Lulu was awakened by a phone call from Charles.

"Are you okay?" he asked.

"No," Lulu said.

"Oh, Christ," Charles murmured, "what a disaster. When did we stop telling each other which parties we were going to?"

It was, of course, when Anna had left him. And they hadn't gotten back into the habit when they resumed their affair.

"Charles," Lulu said, "Anna knows, doesn't she."

A pause.

"What difference does it make?"

She didn't reply. They both knew he was only playing for time.

"I'm coming over," he said. "And don't tell me not to and don't tell me you're going to the office because I'll come over there and make a commotion."

"I only have two appointments today," she said, "and the first one is at eleven. I think it's an excellent idea for you to come over here."

He came in shouting, angry or feigning anger, striding into the living room as though he still lived there, not waiting for her to close the door to begin chopping at the air with his hands.

"I told her when I went back to her, that's when! I told her I wasn't going to give you up! I told her I loved you and I couldn't turn you on and off like a faucet!"

What a sweet revenge he had enjoyed.

"I told her that I wasn't going to break your heart!"

She stared at him. The context was so unsavory, the notion of his discussing with his wife the breaking of his mistress's heart so appalling, that Lulu was tempted to close off this particular avenue to her long-delayed rendezvous with the truth.

"I don't like the way you're looking at me," Charles said. "There's something peculiar about this whole conversation anyhow. *She's* the one who left *me*. Remember Kid Psycho?"

"She had reasons, too. Maybe she knew before. She must've needed to prove something. You were always the one who needed more than anyone, who was sexier than anyone, who had affairs be——"

"I had a couple of affairs, goddamn it!" Charles shouted. "But she *left!*"

So there it was. Anna hadn't followed the ground rules.

He began moving toward her but then saw her expression and stood still.

"Listen to me, Lulu. I don't have much time and I'm not going to waste what I have on bullshit. I'm terribly, horribly, overwhelmingly sorry that you're hurt. I want to make it better but I don't know how and I don't have time to figure it out now. I have a ten o'clock appointment. I can't think under these circumstances."

She nodded.

"Are you driving out tonight?" he asked.

"Yes," she said.

"We'll have dinner tomorrow. We'll drive up to Nepeague."

She shook her head.

"Why not?"

"Because I have to be finished with you, and that's very hard for me to do. And I can't do it by having dinner, and drinking a little wine, and then the next thing I know——"

"Why?" he shouted. "Why do you have to be finished, goddamn it?" He circled wildly around the room, scratching his head, chopping the air, tugging at his shirt. "Never mind the fucking ten o'clock patient! Just explain it to me! Is it that you're angry I told Anna? I had to tell her if I wasn't going to be running around like a maniac, rationing my time, driving us both crazy. I didn't want to give you up. I *couldn't* give you up. And I knew how you'd feel about her knowing. That's what you're angry about, isn't it."

"Oh, God, Charles," she said, feeling her throat constrict and tears well in her eyes. "I'm not even angry anymore. It's true that you lied to me, but it's just as true that I lied to myself. The picture I had of your life was a lie and I told it to myself, so I'm just as much to blame as you are. I had to be saving you from an ice maiden, I couldn't be doing it just because I needed to get laid! I wouldn't believe that Anna was all wrapped up in you and getting hurt because that would mean I was doing something hurtful and what did that make *me*?"

Charles sat down heavily on the sofa. "I don't think I can believe this," he finally said. "You think Anna and I have this rich, full life that I'm lying about? That we have a good time in bed? Or we can talk about people, about anything that interests me, the way I talk with you?"

Lulu shook her head. She was fighting the tears.

"Then what?"

She took a deep breath, as though that might help her to keep the tears from spilling over.

"I'm telling you it can't matter to me anymore what the truth is. The truth is very complicated. I saw the expression—expressions—on Anna's face when you were talking. When she agreed with you and when she thought you were being a jerk. I saw the way you were standing together. Your bodies comfortable. And your brains... her brain curving around yours in some places, jutting into it in others... like the pieces of a jigsaw puzzle. I felt like an intruder. An invader. I'd never felt that way before and I can't live with it. Aside from the question of your using me to keep her in line."

Lulu began to cry freely, turning her back on Charles because that was a way of saying that she didn't expect him to do anything about the tears.

"You're making me angry for the first time," Charles said. She could hear him rising from the sofa. "*Use* you? The love of my life? Who I've turned myself inside out to keep seeing while I hold together my family? And suddenly you're some innocent victim I'm using to—"

She whirled on him furiously. "I never said anything about innocence or victim! I said that I thought I was making your life better without doing any harm and last night I saw that it wasn't true!"

"Bullshit! It *is* true! Most of the time she doesn't give a fuck about me! She cares more when I'm— Most of the time she doesn't even want me around! And if I have to listen to all this pious crap about having my life made better, let's hear a little about your life. You draw this wonderful picture of yourself as Florence Nightingale, kiddo!"

She smiled, although she was still crying. "I know," she said. "You're right. What I should have said was, I was taking what I wanted and telling myself it didn't matter . . . I'm not lying to myself about needing you, Charles. I'm not pretending I don't love you. It's not that I think I'm going to be fine."

A long silence. Charles stared at her, waiting for her to meet his eyes, but she looked at the rug on the living room floor.

"Well, I'm glad," he finally said, "because in a week you're going to be begging me to come back. In twenty-four hours you'll be getting your pal Bonnie to tie your hands behind your back so you can't call me."

"Possibly," she said. "But if that happens... I don't know..." She let her eyes meet his. "If it gets really bad..." She smiled again, but not without an effort. "Maybe I'll buy myself a puppy."

"Charming," Charles said after a moment. "Have you figured out yet which breed'll be a good replacement for me? Are we talking about fucking, by the way, or just conversation?"

She was silent. She wasn't certain when or how the idea of acquiring a dog had entered her mind. Somehow it had gained currency in the course of the morning. She was crying again. She looked down at the floor so he wouldn't see her face.

Charles stood up, walked quickly across the living room without looking at her, opened the door, and walked out, letting it slam behind him.

Lulu sat down in the place on the sofa where he had been sitting a moment earlier.

I REMEMBER WHAT you said about how important it is for me to know that you're human...to
know deeply...that Dr. Seaver is human...That
you might have made mistakes that we don't know
about yet...and maybe we'll find out...If I know
that you're human it'll be easier for me to accept that
you make mistakes...At this moment it's very hard
for me to think of you as human ...You are so
beautiful to me...It's hard to believe that I'm going
to get up and walk out of here at the end of the
hour...knowing.." Dawn smiled. "Say, tell me."

27

"I REMEMBER WHAT you said about how important it is for me to know that you're human...to
know deeply...that Dr. Seaver is human...That
you might have made mistakes that we don't know
about yet...and maybe we'll find out...If I know
that you're human it'll be easier for me to accept that
you make mistakes...At this moment it's very hard
for me to think of you as human ...You are so
beautiful to me...It's hard to believe that I'm going
to get up and walk out of here at the end of the
hour...knowing.." Dawn smiled. "Say, tell me."

Dr. Shinefeld smiled.

The room was bright. Dawn wore a blue cotton
sundress and didn't seem to notice that the air
conditioning was on at full speed. She stood up,
stretched, walked around the room as though to
memorize any feature that might have eluded her

until now. For a moment she stood at the window and looked down over the park.

"Joggers. We have joggers in Washington but they're not quite so colorful." She turned back to the doctor. "When I saw what you were wearing today...not that there's anything wrong with tan cotton...but I thought to myself, she's not wearing one of her beautiful dresses because she doesn't want me to do it any more than I'm going to do it anyway. If she wore the red silk dress maybe it would be harder for me to go...Is that right or is it just...you know..."

"It doesn't matter," the doctor said. "You're doing fine."

Dawn's eyes went to the brown paper parcel she had set against one leg of her chair.

"I brought you a present. I guess you figured out that's what it was. I think I want you to open it after I leave. Is that all right?"

The doctor nodded.

Dawn returned to the chair, sat down, regarded the doctor with gravity.

"What are you going to do when I leave here?" she asked. "I mean, right after."

"Well," the doctor said slowly, "I think that probably I'll come back to my chair and just sit by myself for a while...and think about you. Perhaps I'll open my picture then. At least I imagine that it's a picture."

Dawn nodded.

"And perhaps I'll cry a little..."

"You will?" Dawn asked in a whisper.

"Perhaps. At least I'll feel what someone referred to once as a sweet sadness...pleasure in the work we've done...regret that I won't be seeing you."

Tears brimmed in Dawn's eyes and rolled down her cheeks.

"And then after a while I'll close up the office... you're my last appointment today... this analytic year... and go home... and finish packing whatever I need to go to East Hampton tonight."

"East Hampton," Dawn said with a little smile. "What do analysts talk about in the summer?"

"The weather," the doctor said. "Baseball. Real estate."

"Do you remember my dream?" Dawn asked. "I know you do."

For weeks after making the decision to move to Washington Dawn had dreamed that she was wandering the streets of what appeared to be another planet. The inhabitants were not unkind but didn't have her language or even gestures that corresponded to earth people's. In the last version of this dream, the inhabitants still couldn't understand earth language but Dawn had begun to learn theirs. Dawn thought the dream was sort of amusing because the more people she got to know in Washington, the more she found they spoke what she'd thought of as being the language of this room. It was only that a great deal of the time they didn't seem to know what they were talking about.

"It's just another place," Dawn said now. "When I'm happy, I'm happy in Washington. When I'm miserable, I'm miserable. It's not boring because it's new... Maybe in a few years I'll be bored..."

They sat together in silence and then it was time for Dawn to go. The women stood up together. Hesitantly, Dawn approached the doctor and hugged

her. Then she stepped back and searched the doctor's face.

"How tall are you, anyway?" she asked.

"Just under five-eight," the doctor said with a
slight smile.

"Oh my God," Dawn said, shaking her head slowly.
"That's the most remarkable thing I've ever heard."

Lulu heard the outside door close behind Dawn,
then realized there was still someone moving around
in the waiting room. Her heart skipped a beat; she
had no appointment for this hour.

"Hello?" she called.

"Hi," a familiar voice said, "it's me. The prodigal
daughter. I had a lift in from Montauk and I'm
going back with you and the Mayers."

Lulu walked out to the waiting room as Sascha was
coming in.

"Let me pack up my things and turn off the air
conditioner," Lulu said.

"That girl who just left," Sascha asked, "she wasn't
a patient, was she?"

Lulu smiled.

"I know she's not a patient," Sascha said with a
snort. "I've never seen anyone look more satisfied
with herself."

Lulu turned off the waiting room air conditioner
and lights.

'I'll just be a minute, Sascha. I have to collect my
stuff from the other room."

"Not that she's wrong," Sascha said grudgingly. "If
I looked like that I'd be happy, too."

"Do you think you're not as pretty as she is?" Lulu asked.

"Think nothing. I know it. If Walter saw her I'd be in the garbage can in a minute."

"Doubtful."

"Mmm. He wants to get married, actually."

"Oh? Are congratulations in order?"

"I don't know. Why're you making such a big deal over whether she's a patient? Anyone who wants to find out just has to hang around the office for a few hours. When I was a kid—well, not such a kid, actually, in my teens—I used to do that once in a while. Hang out in the lobby after school and guess who was coming from your office."

"You're kidding."

"Uh-uh. Anyway, I saw her coming out of here, so I know she's a patient."

"Okay."

"Yours?" Sascha asked incredulously, as though until that moment she'd expected some more reasonable explanation for the fact that someone who looked like Dawn was leaving her mother's office.

"She must've looked that way when she started," Sascha announced after a moment's thought.

"Quite right. She looked very much the same, except for her age."

"How old is she?"

A dare.

"Early twenties," Lulu replied after a moment's hesitation.

"How old was she when she started?"

"No. That's definitely over the border."

"Let me guess," Sascha said as her mother turned

off the lights and gave one last look around the waiting room. "I have it! She was left on your doorstep as an infant and you've raised her as one of your own. Except you did everything *right* with her. She was a sort of control."

Lulu laughed. She opened the front door. "Come on. Let's go and get some lunch."

"Wait a minute. I have a better one. She was really my identical twin, only we were separated at birth, and she was raised by someone else secretly, only she was all fucked up, just like me, and when she was fourteen years old someone brought her to the great Dr. Shinefeld for help, and you've seen her every day since then, and finally"—a dramatic pause—"she came out looking like that!"

Laughing helplessly, Lulu moved toward Sascha in the dark room. Still laughing, they put their arms around each other. Then Lulu began to cry.

"Oh, Sascha," Lulu burbled, "do you still not know that you're beautiful?"

"The only time I ever think I'm beautiful," said Sascha, who was also crying now, "is when some man is staring into my face in broad daylight and telling me I'm beautiful. And then as soon as he turns away for a minute I think he changed his mind. And if he doesn't turn away or change his mind, I start thinking he's one of those idiots with no taste."

Together they cried for a moment longer over Sascha's insanity. Then the tears subsided.

"The girl who left," Lulu said, "used to think that if people knew what she was like they wouldn't think she was beautiful anymore."

"Fat chance," Sascha said. "Anyway, thanks for telling me."

"Let's go someplace special for lunch," Lulu said after a moment. "And have a nice cold alcoholic drink. It's not as though either of us has to drive."

Sascha went into the powder room and Lulu returned to the office, combing her hair, getting together her belongings. After a slight hesitation she cut the string on Dawn's package and drew the picture from the brown paper.

"You haven't mentioned the Creep in a long time," Sascha called to her from the waiting room. "Is he still around?"

"No, he isn't around," Lulu called back, and realized that she was smiling. "Anyway, he isn't a creep."

She turned on her desk light to look at the framed oil painting that Dawn had left with her. Done in a more primitive style than the one Dawn usually employed, it showed a young woman emerging from what might have been a subway kiosk in a city whose buildings resembled Washington's. The woman had blond hair and wore a dress in a brilliant print of purple, red and blue. Painted inside that large woman, so that she constituted a good portion of but not the entire body's interior, was another considerably smaller woman whose small head reached the place where the large one's heart might have been, whose tiny arms fitted into the other's large ones, and so on. The small woman wore a brilliant red dress and had dark hair close to the color of Dr. Shinefeld's.

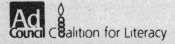